L'Art de la Guerre

Ancient and Medieval Wargaming rules

2014 Edition

Hervé Caille

ONYX Editions

Acknowledgements

The author wishes to thank the members of Central London Wargames Club and all those who helped to translate and correct this book: Stéphane Barry, Julien Bonnard, Philippe Borreil, Hervé Dubois, Andy Finkel, Simon Finney, Sebastien Gimeno, Patrick Lefebvre, Jean Marie Maries, Clive Mc Leod, Nenad Nicolic, Tim Porter, George Reis, Grant Thomas and Cédric Roudil.

The author also wishes to express special thanks to Paul Elvidge.

And finally, Cyrille Barillot's beautiful figurines used in our pictures deserve a mention.

Edited by ONYX Editions
46, chemin du bois
69530 Brignais - FRANCE
Editor's number: 2-952-7922

Pictures and Miniatures : Marc Adda, Marc Bardet, Cyrille Barillot, Christophe Caillaud-Coquet, Pascal Donjon, Philippe Duthil, Olivier Fischer, Bertand Jacquemart, Stéphane Langlois, Eudes Lefevre, John Manné, Bertrand Mangez, Xavier Morlec, Laurent Meziani, Jean-Baptiste Pégourié and Stéphane Thion.

First published in September 2014 by PURE IMPRESSON - France
ISBN : 978-2-952-7922-57

Cover : The battle of Hastings – Tom Lovell - Copyright Bridgeman Images

INDEX

Advance 28
Adjust positions 43
Allied corps 78
Allies 25, 73
Ambush 63, 70
Army lists 75, 76, 77, 79
Arc of fire 47
Area of play 75, 76
Armour 16
Armour (heavy) 16
Army 10
Artillery 14
Attach a commander 24
Attack on flank/rear 54, 56
Basing 7
Battle plan 69
Big battles 76
Budget /points cost 74
Burst through 42
Camels 16
Camp 8, 69
Camp attack 59
Cavalry 14
Cavalry (Light) 14
Charge (furious) 58
Charge (illegal) 37
Charge (uncontrolled) 40, 41
Charge (spontaneous) 22
Charge 9, 36, 50
Coastal zone 64, 67
Cohesion points 12
Command points 22, 24
Command range 23
Command value 21
Command 21
Commander 7, 21, 23, 24, 25, 57, 73, 77
Conforming 52, 53, 54, 55
Continuing a charge 36
Contact (flank) 51
Contact (front) 51
Contact (illegal) 52
Contact (rear) 51
Contact 52
Contraction 31
Cover 63
Crossbow 48
Demoralisation 76
Deployment 71, 75
Deployment zone 71
Difficult manoeuvre 32
Difficult terrain 63
Disengage 44
Dismounted troops 19, 72
Disorder 56
Disordered 9
Displacing units 53
Distance 6, 27, 28
Elephant rampage 61
Elephants 15, 17
Equipment 7
Evade move 37, 38
Expendables 18
Extension 30
Fields 64
Firearms 48
Flank march 72, 73
Flee 73
Fortifications 60, 69
Free command point 24
Good order 9
Groups 10
Gully 65
Half-turn 29
Heavy infantry 13
Height advantage 57
Hill 64
Impact 17
Impassable terrain 63
Impetuous troops 17
Initiative 22, 66, 75
Interpenetration 43
Javelin 17
Knights 15
Leaving the table 40
Light infantry 13, 52
Light troops 33, 48
Line of sight 47
Longbow 48
Lost commander 23
Main unit 50
Manoeuvrability 32
Marsh 65
Measurement 6
Medium infantry 13
Melee 26, 50, 55
Missile support 8, 18
Missile weapons 16
Mixed units 8, 19, 49
Modifiers 48, 55, 56, 57
Movement 26, 28, 34, 36
Multiple opponents 59
Nearest unit 9
Open terrain 63
Orchard, etc 64
Orders 22
Orientation 9
Pavise 18
Pikemen 8
Protection 12, 48
Pursuit 26, 61, 62
Quality 12, 55
Quarter-turn 29
Rallying 45
Rampage 61
Receiving a charge 9
Region 63
River 64, 67
Road 65, 68
Rough terrain 63
Rout 26, 61, 62, 75, 76
Routed 9
Sand dunes 65
Scales 6
Scrub 64
Scythed chariots 15
Sequence of play 26
Setting up 66
Shooting limitations 46
Shooting overhead 49
Shooting range 46
Shooting results 48
Shooting support 48
Shooting 26, 46, 47
Sliding 28
Small battles 75
Stakes 18
Strategist 22
Support modifier 50, 56
Target priority 46
Target 46, 47
Terrain adjustment 68
Terrain and deployment 76
Terrain 57, 63, 64, 65, 66, 75
Time 6
Troop category 12
Two-handed weapon 16
Types of contact 51
Types of troops 12, 13, 20, 77
Units in front 9
Unit status 9
Unmanoeuvrable 32
Unreliable 25, 73
Victory 26
Village 65, 68
Visibility 63
War wagons 14, 60
Wheeling 29
Woods 64
Zone of control 9, 33, 34, 35, 53

CONTENTS

OVERVIEW ... 5

INTRODUCTION ... 6

Scales ... 6
Equipment ... 7
Figures ... 7
How units are represented ... 8
Unit status ... 9
Definitions ... 9
Groups of units ... 10
Army composition ... 10
Game etiquette ... 10
Rules organisation ... 11

TROOPS ... 12

Troop attributes ... 12
Troop description ... 13
Special abilities ... 16
Dismounted troops ... 19
Unit characteristics tables ... 20

COMMAND ... 21

Commanders ... 21
Army Initiative ... 22
Orders ... 22
Movement of commanders ... 24
Commander in melee ... 24
Commander included in a unit ... 25
Allied and unreliable commanders ... 25

SEQUENCE OF PLAY ... 26

Movement ... 26
Shooting ... 26
Melee ... 26
Rout and pursuit ... 26
Victory ... 26

MOVEMENT ... 27

General rules ... 27
Movement distances ... 27
How to measure distance ... 28
Types of movement ... 28
Second and third movement ... 32
Manoeuvrability ... 32
Light troops ... 33
Zone of control ... 33

SPECIAL MOVEMENTS ... 36

Charge ... 36
Evade move ... 37
Uncontrolled Charge ... 40
Interpenetration ... 43
Disengage ... 44

RALLYING ... 45

Procedure ... 45
Rally test ... 45
Particular cases ... 45

SHOOTING ... 46

Overview ... 46
Shooting limitations ... 46
Shooting ranges ... 46
Target selection ... 46
Shooting resolution ... 47
Specific cases ... 49

MELEE ... 50

General Principles ... 50
Types of contact ... 51
Contact restrictions ... 52
Conforming ... 52
Melee resolution ... 55
Melee modifiers ... 55
Furious charge ... 58
Multiple opponents ... 59
Attacking a camp ... 59
Fortifications ... 60
War wagons ... 60

ROUT AND PURSUIT 61

Routed units 61
Elephant rampage 61
Pursuit 62
Demoralisation 62

TERRAIN....................................63

Terrain size and shape....................................63
Types of terrain 63
Visibility & ambush....................................63
Cover from shooting....................................63
Terrain description 64
Terrain table....................................65

SETTING UP 66

Game preparation....................................66
Set up 66
Initiative 66
Regions 66
Camps & fortifications 69
Battle plan 69
Ambush....................................70
Deploying army corps....................................71
Flank marches....................................72
Allied or unreliable commanders 73

BUDGET....................................74

Army budget 74

OPTIONAL RULES....................................75

Reduced format 75
Big battles 76
Rerolls 76
Average dice 76
Demoralisation rules....................................76

ARMY LISTS....................................77

List description 77
Commanders....................................77
Types of troops 77
Allied corps 78
Lists classification....................................79
List Index....................................80

ANCIENT PERIOD....................................83

CLASSICAL PERIOD....................................99

ROMAN PERIOD 125

DARK AGES 148

FEUDAL AGES....................................173

LATE MIDDLE AGES....................................199

AMERICA....................................227

DESIGNER'S NOTES 234

OVERVIEW

The supreme art of war is to subdue the enemy without fighting. Sun Tzu

This new edition of *l'Art de la Guerre* incorporates changes resulting from clarifications, as well as from suggestions discussed on the internet forum. The many games of *l'Art de la Guerre* played at tournaments and conventions have allowed the system of play to be improved while retaining the original simplicity. At the end of the rulebook you will find a summary of the main changes so that players familiar with the previous edition will quickly be able to identify the new features.

L'Art de la Guerre is a set of rules for miniatures that allows you to fight battles ranging from early Antiquity (3000 BC) to the end of the Middle-ages (1500 AD). *L'Art de la Guerre* is a simple rule set that focuses on ease and speed of play. A game can be played in less than two hours and requires about half the miniatures used in most other rules.

A two-sided reference sheet summarises the rules and can be used as a reminder while playing. The rules allow a wide variety of armies to be used, but we recommend limiting battles to those between armies of a similar historical period. You will find army lists grouped by historical period and geographical area in the second part of this rulebook. These lists were also revised for this edition and offer even more opportunities to enjoy the game.

L'Art de la guerre is played with bases comprising from one to four figures or a single model. A unit is the basic element for manoeuvre and combat. Units are represented by a single base for mounted and light troops or a combination of two or three bases for other foot units.

An army will generally consist of from twenty to thirty units divided into three corps, each led by a commander. Adjacent units from the same corps can move together as a group. Each commander can issue orders to his units (or groups of units) every game-turn.

The more capable the commander, the more different or complex orders he can give to his troops. Some army lists include one or more Strategists that represent particularly brilliant historical generals, like Alexander the Great, Hannibal or Julius Caesar.

The main objective of L'*Art de la Guerre* is to allow a historical and enjoyable representation of ancient and medieval battles. Therefore the rules focus on the key factors that influenced the course of a battle and leave aside details, such as the particular training of this or that army.

Each troop type is defined by the armament and tactics it most commonly used on the battlefield. Thus a cavalry unit armed with bows and spears, which did not usually engage in close combat, is classified as cavalry with bow. It does not benefit from the impact ability just because it possessed spears. This method ensures consistency and balance between the different armies.

A battle was won by breaking the enemy's morale, i.e. by making the enemy lose cohesion and by disrupting its formation. When the cohesion of a unit was destroyed, it fled the battlefield and this is when its opponent inflicted most losses.

In *l'Art de la Guerre*, each unit has a number of cohesion points. Heavier troops in close formation start with more cohesion points than lighter ones. The losses from shooting and close combat gradually reduce a unit's cohesion and when it reaches zero the unit is routed and removed from play.

The Internet web site **www.artdelaguerre.fr** contains playing aids, advice and a forum to contact other players.

The author would especially like to thank all players who contributed directly or indirectly to the development of the rules and the play testing. This second edition of *l'Art de la Guerre* has been improved by the opinions and ideas of all participants. We hope you enjoy it!

INTRODUCTION

Control of a large force uses the same principles as control of a few men:
It is merely a question of dividing up their numbers. Sun Tzu

SCALES

The issue of scale is always a bit of a problem in miniatures games. There is always a distortion between the simulated time scale, movement distances, ranges and the size of the figures and scenery. But whatever the chosen scale, the game will always be about measuring distances on the tabletop, counting the game-turns and rolling dice. It is therefore not necessary in game terms to be precise about scales. That being said, here is a summary of the measurements and scales in the game:

Figures

A unit of heavy infantry represents between 500 and 1000 men, with half as many for light infantry. For mounted units, the size may vary between 125 and 250 men, i.e. about one-quarter of a foot unit. Levies may represent hordes of many thousands of low-quality troops while elephants, war wagons and artillery represent between 10 and 20 animals, vehicles or artillery pieces.

Distance

The measurement of distance is based on the range of a typical infantry bow which was about 250 metres. For 15 mm figures the range of a bow in the game is 16 cm which gives a scale of 1 cm on the table for about 15 metres.

Time

A game-turn represents about 30 minutes of real time, i.e. the time necessary for a unit to move, shoot and fight in close combat. When a unit moves, it does so much slower than an individual and its movement is punctuated by halts and pauses.

Measurements

In the rules all measurements are expressed in units of distance (referred to as UD). The value of each UD varies depending on the scale of the figures used and corresponds to the width of a base:

- 6mm – 15mm figure scale UD = 4 cm
- 20mm - 25mm figure scale UD = 6 cm
- 28mm - 32mm figure scale UD = 8 cm

This variable measurement method takes into account the different figure scales and avoids the problem of distortion of distances when figures of a larger size are used.

The Duke of Burgundy and his proud knights

EQUIPMENT

To play *L'Art de la guerre* you will need some figures, an opponent and a flat playing area, usually a table. The size of the table required varies according to the scale of figures used (for example 120 x 80 cm for 6-15 mm figures). You also need some scenery to represent different elements of terrain such as hills, woods or scrub. You can buy pre-made terrain pieces or create them yourself.

A ruler marked in UD (depending on the chosen figure scale) is useful to measure movement, as are markers to indicate the cohesion status of the units. These markers can be made out of cardboard, but it is possible to use coloured tokens or even figures. You can find files to download on our Internet site with markers than can be cut out and glued to cardboard.

You will also need a few six-sided dice. Throughout the rules, wherever it says you need a 4+ for success, it means that you must roll 4, 5 or 6 on a die.

FIGURES

L'Art de la guerre can be played with any figures, whatever their basing and size. You can play with figures between 6 and 32 mm and even with 1/72 scale plastic soldiers. The only constraint is that the width of each base must be the same for all troop types in both armies. The base depth can vary because it does not matter much in the game.

Each unit is represented by a single base (or stand) for mounted and light troops or by two or three bases for other foot units. Essentially this is to permit the easy identification of different types of units, as well as to allow for a more pleasing visual effect.

Each base must have a width equal to the UD corresponding to the scale of figures used, namely 4 cm for 6 - 15 mm figures, 6 cm for 20 - 25 mm ones and 8 cm for 28-32 mm. By mutual agreement the players can decide to adopt a different basing system more compatible with their figures.

Basing

The number of figures per base and the depth of the base allow different types of troops to be recognised easily. The table below gives the base depths and the number of figures for each category of unit. These values are compatible with most common basing systems, but can be adapted by the players to be compatible with the existing basing of their figures.

It is not necessary to rebase figures if the depth of the base does not match what is indicated here. You are only required to inform your opponent of the type of troops represented. If you use single-based figures, just regroup them on larger bases of the appropriate size. If the depth of a unit comprising several bases is more than one UD (or 2 UD for war wagons) the player is allowed to temporarily remove the rear base if it impedes the movement of the unit.

Commanders

An army includes a commander for each of its corps. Commanders can be based separately or they can be modelled as part of unit, on a base of the standard size for the troop-type of the commander's bodyguard. To easily distinguish a separate commander it is possible to use a square base, each side measuring a maximum of one UD or to use a circular base of up to one UD in diameter.

Troop categories/types	Number of figures		Base dimensions		
	6-10 mm	15-32 mm	6-15 mm	20-25 mm	28-32 mm
Light infantry	2 or 3	2	40 x 20 mm	60 x 30 mm	80 x 40 mm
Medium infantry	6 to 8	3 or 4	40 x 20 mm	60 x 30 mm	80 x 40 mm
Heavy infantry	8 to 12	4	40 x 15 mm	60 x 20 mm	80 x 30 mm
Light cavalry	2 or 3	2	40 x 30 mm	60 x 40 mm	80 x 60 mm
Cavalry and knights	4	3	40 x 30 mm	60 x 40 mm	80 x 60 mm
Cataphracts	4 to 6	3 or 4	40 x 30 mm	60 x 40 mm	80 x 60 mm
Levy	10 +	4 +	40 x 30 mm	60 x 40 mm	80 x 60 mm
Light and heavy chariots	1 or 2	1	40 x 40 mm	60 x 60 mm	80 x 80 mm
Elephants and artillery	1 or 2	1	40 x 40 mm	60 x 60 mm	80 x 80 mm
War wagons	1 or 2	1	40 x 80 mm	60 x 120 mm	80 x 160 mm
Camp	Variable	Variable	40 x 80 mm	60 x 120 mm	80 x 160 mm

Note: For 6mm, the number of figures per base may be increased.

How units are represented

The diagram below shows how different types of units are represented both on the tabletop and in the various diagrams throughout the rules. When a unit is composed of several bases they can never be separated (except see Basing, above) and must always be placed in edge contact, one behind the other, aligned corner to corner and facing in the same direction as shown in the diagram.

Using several bases for one unit allows the use of figures based for other sets of rules. It also makes it easy to represent mixed units. It is quite acceptable to base all the ranks of an infantry unit together on a single stand or base of either the appropriate depth or one UD deep.

Pikemen

Pikemen fought in very deep formations and they are represented by at least three ranks of figures. In order to remain compatible with existing basing, it is possible to use 3 or 4 ranks. The 3rd and 4th ranks form an integral part of the base of the unit, but may be removed temporarily if they impede the movement of the unit. An alternative is to place 3 ranks of figures on a single base one UD deep (4 x 4 cm in 15 mm).

Units with missile support

Foot units sometimes receive *missile support* from an additional rank of light infantry armed with bows or crossbows in order to better withstand the charges of mounted or impetuous enemies. This missile support can be represented by a base of light infantry (4 x 2 cm for 15 mm) adjoining the rear of the unit. This base is then treated as an integral part of the base of the unit, but can be temporarily removed if it impedes the movement of the unit. Alternatively, a player can simply point out to his opponent that those specific units benefit from missile support.

Mixed units

Mixed units combine troops with different weapons, for example spearmen and bowmen. In such a case the shooters are always placed in the second rank.

Camp

Each army has a mandatory camp, fortified or not, often represented by a small diorama. The camp represents the civilians, baggage and supplies that accompany an army. Since its loss would be demoralising for the army, it must be defended. The size given in the preceding chart is the minimum required. It is possible to have a camp of larger size (maximum 2 UD x 3 UD) to give players enough room for making a beautiful diorama.

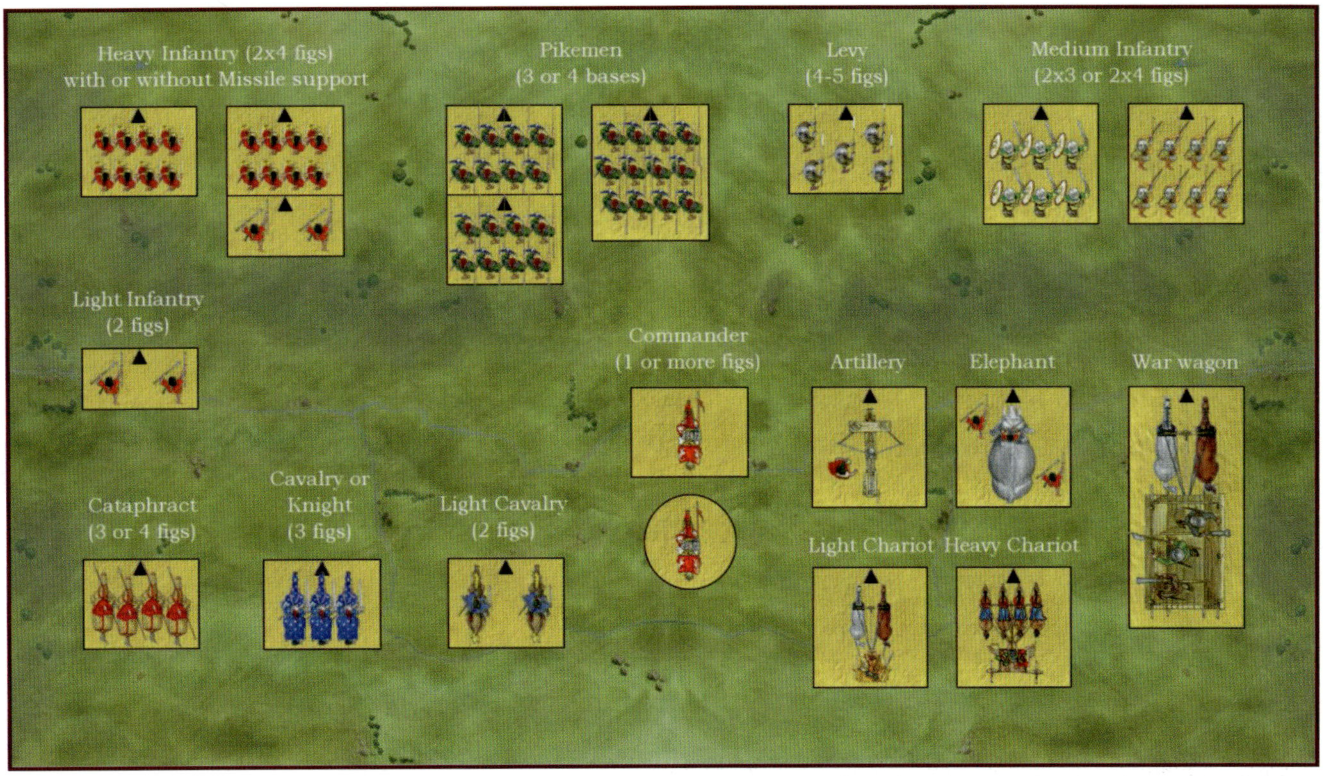

UNIT STATUS

A unit is always in one of the following states:

Good order

All units are in *good order* at the beginning of the battle. They are in formation, combat-ready and have their full cohesion (from 1 to 4 points).

Disordered

After being shot at or a melee, a unit may lose one or more cohesion points and find itself *disordered*. A disordered unit is penalised in melee and shooting, but this penalty is the same regardless of the number of cohesion points lost. The protection of a unit is not changed if it is disordered. A disordered unit can regain cohesion points by rallying. Disorder is best indicated by placing a marker behind the unit, bearing the number of lost cohesion points, i.e.: 1, 2 or 3. Coloured markers or tokens can also be used with the following meaning:

- Green = 1 cohesion point loss,
- Yellow = 2 cohesion points loss,
- Red = 3 cohesion points loss,
- Blue or Black = rout.

A unit could also become disordered following a difficult manoeuvre. In this case the unit loses a cohesion point, but cannot be routed. When it is down to only one cohesion point, the unit can perform the manoeuvre without losing another cohesion point.

Routed

When a unit has lost all its cohesion points, it is *routed*. It is no longer able to fight and will flee the battlefield. The rout is indicated by the placement of a "rout" marker behind the unit. A routed unit can no longer be rallied and is eliminated at the end of the current phase.

DEFINITIONS

Here are the definitions of some terms used throughout the rules.

Unit orientation

Each unit has an orientation that defines a front (or front edge), a rear and two flanks. By convention, in all of the diagrams you will see in these rules, the unit's front is indicated by a small triangle on its base.

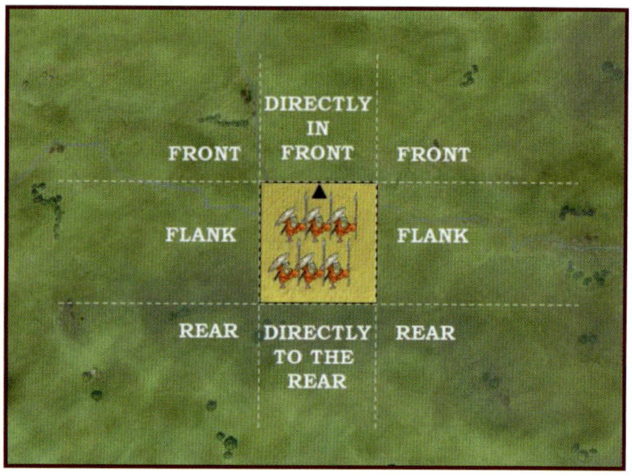

Units directly in front

An enemy unit *directly in front* of a unit is one whose base is situated in the zone measuring one UD wide that extends directly forward from the front edge of the player's unit.For shooting purposes only, a WWg or LH unit counts its shooting edge as its front edge.

Unit the most in front

The enemy unit that is the *most in front* is the one that has the greatest part of its base situated directly in front (see above) of the player's unit.

Nearest unit

The enemy unit that is the *nearest unit* is the one that has any point of its base located nearest to any point of the **front edge** of the player's unit.

Zone of control (ZoC)

Enemy troops are in a unit's *zone of control* if they are directly in front (see above) of the unit and **less than** one UD from its base. Enemies entering a unit's ZoC are restricted in their movement (see p 33).

Charge

This is a move allowing a unit to come into contact with the enemy, in order to fight in melee (see p 36). It can be spontaneous (see p 22) if it is made against an enemy directly in front (see above) at a distance of one UD or less, or uncontrolled in the case of impetuous troops (see p 40) in other circumstance.

Receiving a charge

A unit is considered to have *received a charge* if an enemy contacts it on its front edge. Some combat abilities apply only if the unit receives a charge on its front edge, but not if it has charged the enemy, nor if the enemy contacts it on its flank or rear.

Groups of units

In order to make movement easier, several units of the same corps can temporarily be joined together and moved as a *group*. The concept of a group is used only in the movement phase to allow units to move together.

The units comprising a group must be in contact with adjacent units of the group by their edges and must be aligned with them by their front corners. They must also be facing in the same direction.

Groups can be formed and dispersed at will during the movement phase. However to be activated and moved together, units must form a group both at the beginning and at the end of their movement (except when continuing a charge, see p 36; or due to adjusting positions after interpenetration, see p 43).

GROUPS OF UNITS

A1, A2 and A3 units form a group. B1 and B2 do not form a group because they are not oriented in the same direction. B1 cannot form a group with A2 because the units are not aligned corner to corner. C1 and C2 are not a group because they are not aligned corner to corner. Although units D1 and C2 are aligned, they cannot form a mixed group of cavalry and infantry. D1, E1 and E2 can form a group because LI can be grouped with mounted units.

A group can be formed with different types of units according to the following rules:

- A group cannot have a frontage of more than six units wide.
- A group can be as many units deep as desired. Each rank can have a different width (six units maximum).
- Only units belonging to the same corps can form a group.
- Mounted and foot units cannot be mixed within the same group except in the following two cases:
    - Light infantry can form a group with mounted units.
    - Elephants can form a group with foot units.
- Elephants cannot form a group with mounted units other than elephants.
- Camel units can only form a group with other camel units (LH, Cv or Kn) or light infantry.
- Artillery and war wagons can form a group with other foot units.
- Scythed chariots cannot form a group with any other types of troops.

Army composition

An army is composed of three corps: centre, right wing and left wing. One of the corps may be an allied contingent from another army list. Each corps has a commander and must include one or more units. It is up to each player to decide the exact composition of his army, and the organisation of its corps, prior to deployment. The second part of these rules presents army lists that specify the minimum and maximum numbers of each unit type available.

Each unit is assigned a points cost according to its type and special abilities. A standard army is built with a budget of 200 points. It is also possible to play larger battles with a budget of 300 or 400 points or smaller ones with 100 points (see p 75 & 76).

Game etiquette

One of the issues with miniatures gaming is that it is often difficult to accurately measure a distance or to verify precisely a line of sight. For example figures may be accidentally moved or the board may not be completely flat and this can lead to long discussions. To avoid tedious debates and disputes between players, here are a few tips that in our experience can greatly improve a game.

It is advisable to specify in advance the distance that a unit will move in order to avoid a measurement issue later. For example when a unit is moved you may specify that it is in charge range of a target unit or that it remains out of range of enemy shooting.

Normally, any movement performed cannot be undone unless the starting position of the unit was exactly marked. This may be the case, for example, if the unit was aligned with another one which has not moved or if the player has identified the starting position with a marker. It is therefore advisable to clearly identify the starting position of a unit before performing any movement with that unit.

L'Art de la guerre is a rule set that is meant to be both easy and fast to play. Despite all the care taken in the writing of rules, players can find themselves in an unanticipated or ambiguous situation. In this case, the situation must be assessed in the most logical way by considering the spirit of the rules rather than their wording.

Like all other sets of rules, it has not been possible to write *l'Art de la Guerre* in such a way as to cover every possible situation - however that does not mean that anything not covered by the rules is allowed!

If the players are unable to agree on a measurement or a rule issue, it is often simpler and faster to rely on the rolling of 1D6. One player chooses 1-3 and the other 4-6, leaving the decision of the dispute to the roll of the dice. After the game, the players can check the rules more closely and find the correct interpretation for the next game.

In tournaments the presence of a referee makes the resolution of disputes between players easier. In every case, the referee is ALWAYS right and the players must accept his judgment. His decision taken at the time, and in particular circumstances, can neither be questioned nor used as a precedent in subsequent adjudications. This ensures that the referee will be able to restrain players who seek to take advantage of a rule without regard to the logic and spirit of the game.

Players must agree before the game to define how a cocked die will be treated. Sometimes dice will stop rolling in a way that makes the result unclear, like when it stands on edge against other dice. When this happens, it is always better to re-roll the die that is in doubt. Purists may use a small cup and a dice tray, but it is not absolutely necessary.

RULES ORGANISATION

The rules are organised in chapters that follow the order of the normal sequence of play to make it easier to find specific rules.

The annexes of this rulebook include information that is not directly related to the rules, but which is essential to play a game; more specifically: the terrain rules, the battle set up and everything concerning army selection.

The choice was made to repeat and reinforce certain rule concepts in different chapters, so that the information can be easily found. While this may seem repetitive, it aids in finding and understanding individual rules.

The reference sheet supplied with this book gives a summary of the rules. It serves as a memory aid and should be sufficient to answer most questions that are asked during the course of a game. If there is any discrepancy, the rulebook takes precedence.

Greek hoplites

TROOPS

If you know the enemy and know yourself you need not fear the results of a hundred battles. Sun Tzu

TROOP ATTRIBUTES

In l'*Art de la guerre*, all troops have five attributes: *category*, *type*, *protection*, *cohesion* and *quality*. Troops may also have some specific abilities (see p 16).

Category

Foot and mounted units are divided into several categories (light infantry, cavalry, etc). This allows troops to be differentiated according to their manoeuvrability and their relative effectiveness compared to other troop categories. Troop categories consist of the following:

Foot: Light Infantry (LI), Medium Infantry (MI and LMI), Heavy Infantry (HI), War wagons (WWg) and Artillery (Art).

Mounted: Light Cavalry (LH), Cavalry (Cv), Knights (Kn), Scythed Chariots (SCh) and Elephants (El).

Note: The term "light troops" includes light infantry and light cavalry.

Type

Within the same category, there are different types of troops representing variations in fighting style or use of a specific primary weapon. For example, the heavy infantry (HI) category includes heavy swordsmen, heavy spearmen, foot knights, pikemen and levies.

Protection

This is a number between 0 and +3 which represents the unit's protection against missiles. Protection takes into account the armour worn, how densely packed the troops are and whether the unit is mounted. The level of protection can be increased by factors such as terrain, fortifications, and possession of *armour*, *heavy armour* and/or a *pavise*. The protection rating can also be adjusted when shot at by some weapons, such as longbows, crossbows and artillery. The *armour* and *heavy armour* ability of foot knights, medium knights, heavy knights, cataphracts and heavy cavalry is already taken into account in their protection value.

Cohesion

Cohesion represents the resistance of the unit during a battle. Heavy units in close order are stronger than those more lightly equipped. Each unit has between one and four cohesion points. When a unit has lost all its cohesion points it is routed.

Quality

The quality of troops is a measure of their training and the quality of their equipment. The majority of troops are of *ordinary* quality, but there are also troops of *mediocre* quality that suffer a disadvantage in combat and *elite* troops that are, in contrast, more effective.

Troop quality applies to:
- Melee
- Shooting
- Protection against shooting

Troop quality does **not** apply to:
- Rally tests
- Movement adjustment rolls during a charge or evade move.

The die result is modified by unit quality **before** applying any other modifier (such as *armour, heavy armour, two-handed weapon* or *missile support* abilities):
- Elite troops add 1 to the result if it is less than or equal to 3.
- Mediocre troops subtract 1 from the result if it is greater than or equal to 4.

Therefore the possible results are:
- Elite quality 2, 3, 4, 4, 5 or 6
- Ordinary quality 1, 2, 3, 4, 5 or 6
- Mediocre quality 1, 2, 3, 3, 4 or 5

TROOP DESCRIPTION

Light infantry (LI)

These troops are unprotected, fight in open order and are equipped with missile weapons (javelins, bows, slings, crossbows or firearms). Their main functions are to harass the enemy and occupy areas of rough or difficult terrain. They are able to fight effectively against elephants and scythed chariots, but cannot stand up to formed troops in melee. They must evade the charge of heavier troops or be destroyed if contacted in open terrain.

Medium infantry (MI and LMI)

These troops have light or partial armour and sometimes a shield. They fight in a loose formation that allows them to move more quickly and not be penalized in rough terrain. However their loose formation makes them more vulnerable against mounted troops. LMI primarily use missile weapons, whereas MI is more capable of fighting in melee.

Bowmen, crossbowmen (LMI): These troops have little or no armour and are equipped with bows, longbows, crossbows or firearms. They shoot at long-range in concentrated volleys rather shooting to harass. They are not effective in close combat and are at a particular disadvantage when it comes to fighting heavy infantry or when charged by mounted units.

Javelinmen (LMI): These troops are equipped with javelins and light spears but, unlike light infantry, their tighter formation allows them to withstand a frontal attack without being destroyed. They have the *javelin* ability and can shoot at distance and also evade as light infantry do. Examples of these units are peltasts or warriors of certain nomadic or mountain tribes that prefer to harass the enemy rather than make frontal attacks.

Medium swordsmen (MI): These are troops equipped with light armour, a shield and a hand weapon, or a polearm. Their focus is close combat and they can benefit from the *impact* ability if they have a missile weapon or if they are impetuous. Non-impetuous medium swordsmen cancel the *impact* ability of impetuous infantry if they receive the charge on their front edge. Roman Auxilia, Spanish Scutari and some Vikings are examples of medium swordsmen.

Medium spearmen (MI): Medium spearmen are equipped with a spear and fight in close formation, but one that is sufficiently flexible to avoid being penalised in rough terrain. Their use of spears combined with their close formation gives them an advantage when they face mounted units compared with other medium infantry units. In addition they cancel the *impact* ability of mounted troops if they receive the charge on their front edge. Examples are Greek Thureophoroi and medieval Welsh spearmen.

Heavy infantry (HI)

These troops represent those trained to fight in a deep, close formation. They may be equipped with sturdy armour or a large shield. Their tight formation puts them at a disadvantage in rough or difficult terrain.

Heavy swordsmen: These troops are equipped with hand weapons but could also have heavy two-handed weapons or polearms. Typical examples of heavy swordsmen are Roman legionaries, huscarls, Frankish warriors or medieval halberdiers. They favour close combat. Those with a heavy throwing weapon like the pilum, francisca or angon and those classified as impetuous benefit from the *impact* ability. Non-impetuous heavy swordsmen cancel the *impact* ability of impetuous foot units if they receive the charge on their front edge.

Foot knights: This represents the heavy dismounted knight of the Middle Ages. They all have the *heavy armour* and *two-handed weapon* abilities. Like other heavy swordsmen, they cancel the *impact* ability of enemy impetuous foot units.

Knights on foot

Heavy spearmen: These troops are equipped with a long spear and fight shoulder to shoulder in a shield-wall formation. They are at a great disadvantage in rough or difficult terrain. Their use of spears combined with their close formation gives them the *impact* ability when they face mounted units other than elephants. In addition they cancel the *impact* ability of mounted troops if they receive the charge on their front edge. Greek hoplites and most medieval spearmen fall into this category.

Pikemen: Pikemen are equipped with pikes or long spears over five meters in length and fight in very deep formations. They are very powerful in frontal combat, especially against mounted troops, but vulnerable on their flanks. They have the same advantages as spearmen against mounted. Their deep formation makes them *unmanoeuvrable* and they are at a great disadvantage in rough or difficult terrain. Petzaroi of Hellenistic armies, Swiss pikemen or German landsknechts are examples of pikemen.

Levy: These are civilians and combatants of little value or motivation, brought together in haste. They fight in close order with various weapons (hand weapons, spears, etc) as heavy infantry but have a lower cohesion and are *unmanoeuvrable*. Some levies can be impetuous to represent religious fanatics or revolting peasants.

War wagons (WWg)

These are wheeled wagons protected by wooden mantlets and are usually crewed by troops equipped with missile weapons (bows, crossbows or firearms). Some may also be equipped with artillery. War wagons are very tough and can block mounted troops. They are more vulnerable against heavy infantry, elephants and artillery. Some examples are the war wagons used by the Hussites, Poles and Hungarians in the later Middle Ages.

Artillery (Art)

Artillery represents all types of engines of war that used gunpowder or mechanical propulsion and were used on the battlefield. Light artillery and medium artillery can move while heavy artillery is fixed and can only rotate in place, but benefits from a longer range.

- **Light artillery:** Small ballista (scorpions), organ guns and Chinese rockets launchers.
- **Medium artillery:** Large ballistae mounted on wagons, culverins or small cannon.
- **Heavy artillery:** Trebuchets, catapults, bombards and heavy cannon.

Organ gun

Light cavalry (LH)

These are unprotected cavalry, usually equipped with missile weapons and used to harass the enemy. They fight in open order allowing them to move quickly and evade the enemy. Some riders have a light spear to drive away the enemy's light cavalry and they benefit from the *impact* ability. This category also includes light units mounted on camels (light camelry). Some armies like the Numidians, the Huns and the steppe tribes have numerous light cavalry.

Cavalry (Cv)

Cavalry may be protected or unprotected and fight with hand weapons, spears and possibly missile weapons. If cavalry have javelins, they use them for close combat and not for shooting. Cavalry is very manoeuvrable and has an advantage against medium foot in open terrain. However, cavalry fears close combat against heavy infantry or knights.

Medium cavalry: These are unarmoured or lightly armoured cavalry. They are equipped with hand weapons, light spears and possibly bows, crossbows or firearms. They are quite similar to light cavalry, but fight in a more compact formation. Those equipped with a long lance have the *impact* ability. Huns, Mongols, Arab lancers and mounted sergeants of the Middle Ages are typical examples of medium cavalry.

Heavy cavalry: These are better protected than the medium cavalry with some riding barded horses. Heavy Cavalry such as Alexander's Companions rely on the power of their charge, using lances or long spears that give them the *impact* ability. Others, such as Arab Ghulams, rely on missile weapons. Some use both lance and bow, such as Byzantine cavalry.

Light chariots: These are the chariots of the ancient period drawn by two horses, like those used by the Egyptians or the Hittites. They generally serve as a shooting platform for an archer or for transporting warriors.

Medium camelry: These are troops mounted on camels and can be armed with spears or bows, such as the Tuaregs or Bedouins. They have the advantage of panicking horses and ignore the effect of some terrain, such as sand dunes and scrub.

Knights (Kn)

The first knights appeared during the 11th century. We arbitrarily set the date of 1050 as a milestone. Before that date, troops are classified as heavy cavalry, after that date, they become knights. The knights of the Middle Ages are heavily armoured and move more slowly than other cavalry. They have tremendous shock power but are not equipped with missile weapons. Some knights, unaccustomed to the use of the lance when mounted, do not have the *impact* ability.

Medium knights: These are knights of the 11th, 12th and 13th centuries, equipped with chain mail or partial plate, on mounts either with or without cloth barding. They have the *armour* ability.

Heavy knights: These are knights of the 14th and 15th centuries with full plate armour mounted on horses with or without cloth or metal barding. They have the *heavy armour* ability.

Cataphracts: Cataphracts are warriors from the ancient period with full metal armour on heavily armoured horses. They have the *heavy armour* ability. They charge at a trot in a compact formation. They are super heavy cavalry, able to push through the ranks of foot troops, but they count as *unmanoeuvrable*. Cataphracts have the *impact* ability against infantry, but not against mounted units because of the slower pace of their charge is less powerful. This type includes the cataphracts of the Byzantines or Sassanidss and also includes the camel-mounted cataphracts of the Parthians and Arameans.

Heavy chariots: These are the chariots of the ancient period, each drawn by four horses and with several crew members, at least one of whom is equipped with a long weapon, as found amongst the Assyrians and Babylonians. They move more slowly than light chariots, but may have the *impact* ability and have the advantage in combat against cavalry. They have the *armour* ability.

Scythed chariots (SCh)

This troop type represents "suicide" scythed chariots used by the Persians and the Seleucids. The driver rushes his chariot into the enemy ranks to sow confusion. Scythed chariots are classed as *unmanoeuvrable* and *impetuous*, but they do not have the impact ability. They have only one cohesion point. In the first phase of a melee, the opponent of a scythed chariot has a combat factor of zero and cannot receive any support from friendly units. LI, LH, LMI, WWg and elephants retain their basic factor and their abilities against scythed chariots.

Also included in this category are stampeding animals and the flaming chariots used by some armies to disrupt the enemy, having an effect comparable to that of a scythed chariot.

Elephants (El)

Elephants are used as shock troops to break the enemy ranks. They are formidable against other mounted troops in that their mere presence can cause panic, but they are vulnerable to light infantry and javelinmen. African elephants, like those used by the Carthaginians, are small and are considered to be *mediocre*. Elephants protected by armour or accompanied by an escort of light infantry, such as those used by the Seleucids, are *elite*.

SPECIAL ABILITIES

Special abilities allow the differences between troop types to be represented in more detail. They can include such things as the possession of a throwing weapon, the ferocity of the charge, the nature of the main weapon used or other advantages that might only come into play when facing specific enemies.

Assigning specific abilities to historical troops or units inevitably involves a degree of subjectivity. However the intention has been to assign abilities in such a way as to best reflect historical effectiveness and encourage the use of troops on the tabletop as they were actually used on the battlefield.

For instance, many cavalry units were equipped with lance and bow, but those who are recorded as generally charging the enemy have the *impact* ability, whilst others who relied on archery do not. To keep a balanced game, only the main ability of the unit is used.

Missile weapons

Having missile weapons allows a unit to shoot with bows, longbows, crossbows, javelins, slings, atlatls or firearms. Javelins can also be used in melee by light troops and javelinmen.

> *Note: The Atlatl is a spear-thrower which can throw light javelins a great distance. It was used by the armies of Mesoamerica (Maya, Aztecs etc). Light javelins are too weak to be used in melee.*

Armour and heavy armour

Some troops are better protected by metal armour and / or a large shield. The *armour* ability gives a +1 bonus to the unit's protection value against shooting while the *heavy armour* ability gives a +2 bonus. This bonus is added to the base value of protection (0 for mounted, 1 for foot). This means that foot units with the *armour* ability have a protection of 2 and those with *heavy armour* a protection of 3. The protection bonus for knights on foot and mounted units is already included in the unit characteristics table.

If a unit with **heavier armour** than its opponent loses a melee, add one point to its die roll before determining the outcome of the combat. The armour advantage thus goes to the unit with the best ability:

Without armour → Armour → Heavy armour

During melee, *armour* and *heavy armour* abilities do not apply in the following cases:

- During the first phase of a melee if the enemy has *furious charge*,
- Fighting elephants frontally.

> *Example: A knight unit with heavy armour ability is fighting a cavalry unit with armour ability. The knight adds one point to the result of the die if it loses the melee because its armour is heavier than that of its opponent.*

Two-handed weapon (2HW)

These troops are equipped with two-handed swords or axes, polearms or anti-cavalry heavy maces. They have the ability to inflict greater damage, especially against units armed with spears or pikes.

If a unit with the *2HW* ability wins a melee when fighting to its front, it adds +1 to the die roll before determining the combat outcome. Moreover, in the case of tie in melee against spearmen or pikemen, a unit with the *2HW* ability adds +1 to the die roll and so wins the melee. The tie bonus is added after applying the quality modifier (elite or mediocre) but before applying the effect of the armour ability of the unit (if appropriate) with the 2HW ability.

In game terms the additional protection of armour and the extra force of two handed weapons offset each other.

> *Examples:*
> *a) Unit A has the 2HW ability and unit B has the 2HW and either the armour or heavy armour abilities.*
> *If A wins the melee, the effect of 2HW is negated by the effect of B's armour. If B wins it adds +1 to its die roll.*
>
> *b) Unit A has the heavy armour ability and unit B has the 2HW and armour abilities.*
> *The effect of B's 2HW is counteracted by the heavier armour of A. If B also had Heavy Armour, the effect of the 2HW would apply because no opponent would then have the armour advantage.*
>
> *c) If both units A and B have the 2HW ability and the same armour or heavy armour ability, the effects of 2HW apply to both sides.*

Camelry

Units mounted on camels (light camelry, medium camelry and cataphract camelry), panic mounted units using horses (n.b. elephants are not affected). All mounted units using horses (friends and enemies) in contact (even only by a corner) with a unit mounted on camels suffer a -1 penalty in melee. However they can still provide support to a friendly unit in melee. Mounted units that are panicked retain their *impact* ability against camels. The penalty is not cumulative if a unit using horses is in contact with more than one unit of camels and/or elephants.

Elephant

Elephants panic all other mounted units. All mounted units (friends and enemies) except elephants in contact (even only by a corner) with a unit of elephants suffer a -1 penalty in melee. However, they can still provide support to a friendly unit in melee. The penalty is not cumulative if a unit using horses is in contact with more than one unit of camels and/or elephants. All units (including other elephants) lose their *impact* ability if in melee against elephants.

ELEPHANTS CAUSING PANIC

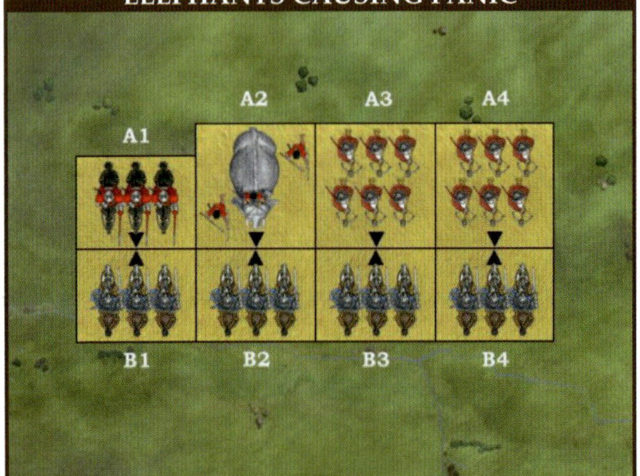

Cavalry A1, B1, B2 and B3 are panicked by the elephant.
A1 and B1 fight with no penalty as the *panic* applies to both units.
Units B2 and B3 are panicked by the elephant while their opponents are not affected.
A4 and B4 are not in contact with the elephant and therefore are not affected.

Impact

The *impact* ability corresponds to the use of a heavy throwing weapon just before contact (such as the Roman pilum) or to a very powerful charge. The unit has a +1 bonus in the first phase of a melee. This bonus is only applicable if the unit charges or receives the charge on its front edge and only for the first game-turn of combat. It does not apply for the rest of the melee. The *impact* ability of mounted troops (but not that of foot) is cancelled if they are fighting in rough or difficult terrain.

The *impact* ability can be valid only against foot units or only against mounted units. If nothing is specified, the *impact* ability applies against everyone. In all cases, the following rules apply:

- The *impact* ability of foot troops does not apply against mounted troops if the foot unit charges the mounted unit.
- The *impact* ability of foot troops does not apply against mounted troops with *impact* ability when the mounted unit charges the foot unit.
- Heavy spearmen and pikemen that cancel the *impact* ability of mounted troops keep their own *impact* ability if they receive a mounted charge.
- The *impact* ability never applies against elephants.

Impetuous

Some units are undisciplined and likely to charge without an order at any enemy within range. The undisciplined nature of such troops also has an adverse effect on their manoeuvrability. These units rely on the shock power of their charge to disrupt the enemy and so they have a similar ability to *impact* (except scythed chariots). However the *impact* of impetuous foot is cancelled when charging non-impetuous medium and heavy swordsmen that are contacted on their front edge, as they are better able to withstand this type of charge. The *impact* ability remains valid if these target troops are contacted on their flank or rear. The *furious charge* effect (see p 58) applies against all foot units.

<u>Example:</u> A barbarian (impetuous heavy swordsmen) charges a Roman legionary (heavy swordsmen with impact). The Roman legionary cancels the impact bonus of the barbarian on his front but applies its own impact bonus in the 1st phase. If the legionary charges the barbarian, the two adversaries get the impact bonus. If the barbarian charges the legionary on the flank, only the barbarian receives the bonus for impact. In all cases above, the effect of furious charge for barbarian is applied.

Javelin

The javelin may be used by light troops and javelinmen as a missile weapon or a melee weapon. For other types of troops the effect of javelin is already included in the combat factor. Units with the *javelin* ability gain a +1 bonus in the first phase of melee. This bonus is only applicable if the unit charges or receives a charge on its front edge and only for the first phase of melee. This does not apply for the rest of the melee.

The *javelin* bonus is cancelled if the opponent is contacted on its front edge and has either the *impact* ability or is *impetuous*. The *javelin* bonus applies against scythed chariots and elephants as they lose their *impact* ability against the front edge of light troops (LI and LH) and javelinmen.

Pavise

Units equipped with a large shield or *pavise* receive a +1 bonus to their protection against missiles, except when shot at by artillery. This protection cannot be added to that provided by additional cover (in woods for example).

Stakes

Some foot units, like English longbowmen, can be equipped with *stakes* capable of being placed in front of the unit. Stakes are represented by bases of one UD wide and 1 to 2 cm deep. The following rules apply to stakes:

- Placing or removing stakes requires an order and replace one complete movement. If the unit moves or is forced to turn as a result of an attack on its flank or rear without having previously removed its stakes, they are lost.
- When a unit places its stakes the unit is moved back the depth of the base of the stakes and the stakes are placed in front of it. The front of the stakes now becomes the front of the unit.
- Stakes can be placed even if the unit is in an enemy ZoC.
- Stakes have no effect on enemy foot troops.
- Stakes cancel the *impact* ability and *furious charge* of all mounted troops (including elephants).
- Mounted troops (other than elephants) charging enemy foot behind stakes suffer a -2 penalty.
- Stakes do not provide any protection against shooting.

Expendables

Expendable units do not count towards the cohesion of the army. Their loss does not therefore have any consequence. This applies to scythed chariots and some levy units that represent hostages or prisoners of war forced to fight.

Expendable units cannot be rallied.

Missile support

Some units include bowmen or crossbowmen in their rear ranks to improve their defence. When charged, these troops shoot at short range in an attempt to break the enemy's morale and momentum.

If a unit with *missile support* is charged on its front edge by an enemy unit and loses the melee, add +1 to its die roll before determining the outcome of the combat. This only applies when losing in the first phase of a melee. This bonus is cumulative with that of *armour* or *heavy armour*.

The *missile support* ability applies against any opponent except those with the *heavy armour* ability like cataphracts, heavy knights or knights on foot.

The *missile support* bonus is given to foot units partially equipped with bows or crossbows, i.e.:

- Foot with the *missile support* ability
- Medium swordsmen with bow
- Mixed units

Note: Bowmen and Crossbowmen do not have the *missile support* ability but have a special bonus against mounted troops in the first phase of a melee to represent their last shoot at close range.

Archers behind stakes

Mixed units

Mixed units represent those formations in which some troops are primarily equipped with melee weapons and others with missile weapons (e.g. heavy spearmen and archers).

- The unit moves at the rate of the slowest troop type involved and is considered as one level lower in quality in melee. Thus an ordinary mixed unit is treated as mediocre and an elite mixed unit is treated as ordinary.
- The unit keeps its quality when it shoots or is shot at.
- A mixed unit has the cohesion and the protection of the heaviest unit type.

Persian Sparabara

DISMOUNTED TROOPS

Mounted troops can dismount only after the deployment of all units. Medium and heavy knights unit can always dismount if their army list allows deploying these units on foot. Otherwise, mounted units can dismount only in the following cases:

- The enemy has deployed fortifications. A fortified camp is not sufficient to dismount.
- The enemy has deployed elephants, war wagons or bowmen with stakes (even if stakes are not already placed). Units in ambush or in flank march are not taken into account.

Once the troops have dismounted they cannot remount for the rest of the game.

The unit maintains the same quality and cohesion as it had when mounted.

Troops dismount as the following types unless otherwise specified in the army lists.

- **Light cavalry or light camelry:** Dismount as light infantry with the same equipment (bow, javelin etc). Light cavalry with *impact* ability dismounts as light infantry with *javelin* ability.
- **Medium cavalry, medium camelry and light chariots:** Dismount as bowmen or crossbowmen (if the mounted unit has the corresponding weapon); as medium spearmen if the mounted unit has the *impact* ability, otherwise as medium swordsmen, *impetuous* if the cavalry is *impetuous*. Cavalry with firearms dismounts as LMI with firearms, which is equivalent to crossbowmen.
- **Heavy cavalry:** Dismounts like medium cavalry but the dismounted unit has the *armour* ability. Heavy cavalry with *impact/bow* dismounts at the choice of the player's as bowmen or as medium spearmen.
- **Heavy chariots or Medium knights:** Dismount as heavy swordsmen or heavy spearmen with the *armour* ability.
- **Cataphracts:** Dismount as heavy spearmen with the *heavy armour* ability.
- **Heavy knights:** Dismounts as foot knights.

<u>Note:</u>

- Knights, heavy chariots and cataphracts that dismount keep their cohesion of 3 points.
- They lose their *impact* ability and are no longer considered *impetuous* as this ability is only valid when mounted.
- Elephants and scythed chariots can never dismount.

Roman equites

UNIT CHARACTERISTICS TABLES

Foot	Category	Protection	Cohesion	Basic factor and modifiers
Light infantry	LI	1	2	Destroyed in open terrain by LMI, MI, HI, Cv, Kn. Otherwise 0 vs. all
Javelinmen	LMI	1	3	+1 vs. LI, LH, El and SCh, *javelin*
Bowmen or crossbowmen	LMI	0	3	+1 vs. LI and LH, +1 in first phase vs. Mounted
Medium swordsmen **	MI	1	3	+1 vs. all except Kn
Medium spearmen *	MI	1	3	+1 vs. all except Kn *Impact* vs. Mounted except El
Heavy swordsmen **	HI	1	4	+2 vs. LMI in open terrain or vs. LH otherwise +1 vs. all
Foot knights **	HI	3	4	Same as heavy swordsmen *Heavy armour* and *2HW*
Heavy spearmen *	HI	1	4	+2 vs. LMI in open terrain or vs. LH otherwise +1 vs. all *Impact* vs. Mounted except El
Pikemen *	HI	1	4	+2 vs. all *Impact* vs. Mounted except El
Levies	HI	1	3	+1 vs. LI, LMI and LH
War wagons @	WWg	2	4	+1 vs. LI and Mounted except El +2 vs. LH
Artillery	Art	1	2	+1 if shooting against El or WWg +1 for the enemy except if LI or LH

* Cancels *impact* of Mounted except elephant if receiving the charge on its front. *Furious charge* is still applicable.
** Cancels *impact* of *impetuous* swordsmen if receiving the charge on its front. *Furious charge* is still applicable.
@ Cancels *impact*, *javelin* and *furious charge* except if attacked by elephants.
(1) Panic on Mounted units with horses if camels or horses and camels if elephants.

Mounted	Category	Protection	Cohesion	Basic factor and modifiers
Light cavalry Light camelry (1)	LH	1	2	+1 vs. LI if LI is in open terrain
Medium cavalry Light chariots Medium camelry (1)	Cv	0	3	+1 vs. Mounted, LI, LMI, MI and Levies +1 vs. HI if attacking flank or rear Add +1 in first phase vs MI except if cavalry already has *impact*
Heavy cavalry	Cv	1	3	Same as medium cavalry plus *armour*
Medium knights	Kn	1	3	+2 vs. LMI and Mounted except El, otherwise +1 vs. El and Foot except WWg, *armour*
Heavy knights	Kn	2	3	Same as medium knight plus *heavy armour*
Cataphracts Cataphract camelry (1)	Kn	2	3	+2 vs. LMI and LH, otherwise +1 vs. all except WWg *Impact* vs. Foot, *heavy armour*
Heavy chariots	Kn	1	3	+2 vs. LMI, LH and Cv, otherwise +1 vs. all except WWg, *armour*
Elephants (1)	El	0	3	+2 vs. Mounted and +1 vs. Foot *Impact* unless vs. LI, LH and javelinmen
Scythed chariots	SCh	0	1	Enemy factor is set to 0 in first phase except LI, LH, LMI, WWg or El, which keep their factors. Cancels enemy's support in the 1st phase.

Note: The protection value of foot knights, medium knights, heavy knights, heavy chariots, cataphracts and heavy cavalry already takes into account in their *armour* or *heavy armour* abilities.

COMMAND

The general who triumphs is one who is better informed. Sun Tzu

COMMANDERS

Each army must have a *commander-in-chief* (c-in-c) and two *sub-commanders*. One of the sub-commanders can be an *allied commander* from another army list. Sub-commanders can be *unreliable*. Each commander leads an army corps. The role of a commander in battle is crucial and can be summarised as follows:

- Giving orders to units,
- Rallying disordered units,
- Boosting a unit by fighting alongside it.

In *l'Art de la guerre*, a commander can be represented in two ways:

- Based separately and represented by a single figurine on a standard size base or a circular base. The figurine of the commander can also be accompanied by a standard bearer, musician, etc; or
- Included in a unit of a type permitted in the army list (indicated by *). A commander included in a unit follows particular rules described below in this chapter and must be distinguishable from ordinary units of the same type.

Greek Commander

Command value

The system of command in *l'Art de la Guerre* simulates the effectiveness of different armies according to their historical counterparts. For example, a Roman army differs from a barbarian one in its tactical flexibility as well as in its use of weapons and equipment. The command system simulates this.

Each army has a *command value* between +2 and +6 to represent the overall quality of the leadership and organisation. The armies that historically were well led and well organised have a good command value. This is the case for the Romans, the Byzantines and the Mongols for instance.

Conversely, barbarian armies have in general a low command value. Players can choose the quality of their commanders by dividing the command value of the army between them. There are three kinds of commanders:

Commander Quality	Value
Ordinary	0
Competent	+1
Brilliant	+2

For instance, an army with a command value of +4 can have two competent commanders (+1) and one brilliant commander (+2). Another possibility is to have one ordinary commander (0) and two brilliant (+2) ones. It is not mandatory to use all the army's command value - it is possible for example to only have ordinary commanders.

Each point of command value must be paid for from the budget of the army (see p 74). Consequently an army with more effective commanders will tend to have fewer or poorer units.

The quality of a commander has a direct impact on the number of command points and thus on the number or complexity of actions available each game-turn.

Strategists

Strategists are historical personalities that proved their ability on the battlefield. If you play, for example, the army of Julius Caesar, Hannibal or Alexander the Great, your commander-in-chief can be a strategist. In this case he has an advantage in terms of command and initiative.

Only some armies can have a strategist (and then only one) if it is allowed in their list. If chosen he must be the commander-in-chief of the army.

A strategist is considered a brilliant commander but he adds an extra point to his command value when determining the number of command points. A strategist also adds a +1 to the initiative of the army.

A strategist always represents 2 points of the command value of the army. For instance, an army with a command value of +4 can have two brilliant commanders one of which can be a strategist.

Army Initiative

Army initiative basically depends on the value of its overall command and the number of scouts. An army with a good initiative can choose to attack or to defend and will have an advantage during deployment on the battlefield. Army initiative is noted on the army sheet and is calculated as below:

- Total value of all commanders divided by two and rounded down.
- +1 if the commander-in-chief is a strategist
- +1 if the army contains 2 to 5 LH
- or +2 if the army contains at least 6 LH

Example: The initiative of an army with a strategist (+2), a competent commander (+1) and an ordinary commander (0) and 4 LH units is calculated in the following way: Commanders: (2+1+0) / 2 rounded down, which gives 1. Add +1 for the strategist and +1 for having at least 2 LH for a final initiative value of +3.

Orders

Command points

The main role of a commander is to give orders to his troops. To do that, commanders have command points (or CP) that can be used each game-turn to give orders to the units under their command.

The command point system allows the simulation of uncertainty during a battle in an easy and abstract way. Troops did not always obey an order because they may not have received it in time or the order was not understood or their leader has decided to do something else. Rather than do a test for each order to verify if it has been obeyed, the number of orders which can be issued is determined randomly each game-turn. In this respect, the player is never certain he can do everything he wants and may need to regroup his units and focus on essential actions.

When an army corps is activated, the player rolls 1D6 and adds to the result the command value of the corps' commander (0, +1, +2 or +3 if strategist). The total is divided by two and rounded up. The result is the number of command points (CP) for the commander to give orders to units under his command. The commander also gets a free order each game-turn which allows him either to rally a unit (see below) or to move.

Example: A player activates his c-in-c Hannibal who is a strategist. He rolls 1D6 and obtains a 4, to which he adds the command value of the strategist (+3) for a total of 7. This result divided by two and rounded up gives 4 CP.

Giving orders

Each CP allows one move order to be given to a unit or a group of units. A commander can only give orders to units under his command (i.e. those which belong to his army corps). A commander can issue up to three move orders per game-turn to the same unit or group of units. CPs can also be used to make difficult manoeuvres, to stop impetuous units from charging without orders, and in attempts to rally units.

Spontaneous charge

When a unit is very close to the enemy, it can decide to charge the enemy without any orders. In this case it is a *spontaneous charge*.

When a unit has an enemy situated at least partially directly in front of it at a distance of one UD or less, the unit, or the group that contains the unit, can charge this enemy without being given any orders. In this case the commander does not need to use any CP.

A spontaneous charge is still possible even if the unit has to interpenetrate friends (for example a LI unit) that are between it and the target.

Impetuous units may also charge without an order if the enemy is within charge range. However if the unit is not eligible to make a spontaneous charge, the charge will be uncontrolled (see p 40).

Command range

A commander sends his orders by signals or messengers. Units must be in command range to be able to receive orders from their commander without penalty.

- Ordinary commander — 4 UD
- Competent commander — 6 UD
- Brilliant commander — 8 UD
- Strategist — 8 UD

If a unit or group is out of command range, the commander must expend an extra CP to give an order to the unit. This simulates the additional difficulty of communicating with distant units.

Command range is measured by a straight line between the nearest points on the commander's base and that of the unit or group. Command range is not affected by enemy units or terrain (except impassable terrain). Command range is evaluated at the moment the order is given.

Light troops (LH and LI) are able to operate at longer range. The command range is doubled when the commander gives an order to a unit of light troops or a group entirely composed of light troops. For example, light troops up to 16 UD away from a brilliant commander are still within his command range.

Commanders engaged in melee

When a commander is engaged in melee, it is more difficult for him to give orders. He has to expend one extra CP for each order except if he tries to rally a unit to which he is attached.

This modifier is cumulative with the modifier for a unit being out of command range. So it takes 3 CP for a commander engaged in melee to give an order to a unit or a group out of command range.

Lost commander

When a commander is lost, the following rules apply:

- All units of his army corps are considered to be out of command range for the rest of the game.
- The player still rolls a die to determine CP each game-turn (without adding the command value of the lost commander) to represent the actions of his subordinates.
- Every order costs at least 2 CP except units can always conform or make spontaneous charges.

Commander without Units

A commander not included in a unit who is alone at the end of a combat phase because all units of his corps have been eliminated must flee. He is removed from the table but does not count towards the losses of the army. If the commander was attached to the last unit of his own corps, he must survive and be at 5 UD or less of another friendly unit otherwise he is captured and counts towards the losses of the army.

COMMAND RANGE

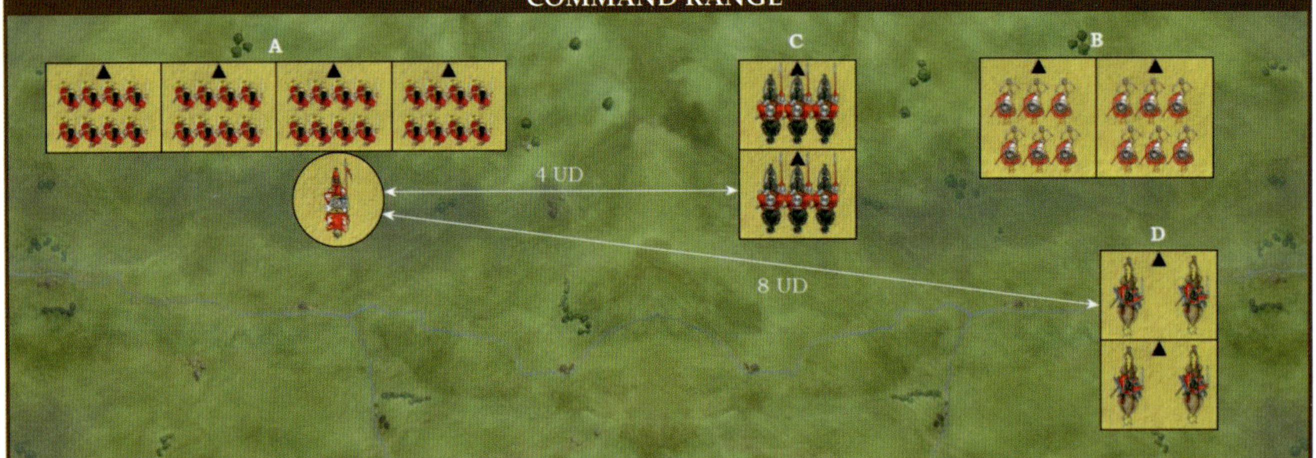

An ordinary commander has 2 CP for the game-turn. He can use his free command point (see below) to give a move order to group A of heavy foot.
If he wants to order group B of medium foot, he has to expend 2 CP because the group is out of command range (it is more than 4 UD).
Cavalry unit C can be given an order for only one CP, as can the light cavalry D because the command range is doubled for light troops and equals 8 UD in this case.

MOVEMENT OF COMMANDERS

A commander on his own can move up to 5 UD per game-turn without being restricted by terrain effects, except impassable terrain. Unlike other units a commander can rotate and move in any direction (sidewards or backwards for example).

A commander does not block movement and can pass through and be passed through by a friendly unit without restriction in any direction.

A commander can be displaced, by the minimum necessary, to make room for friendly or enemy units. This does not prevent the commander from moving later in the game-turn. If there is not enough room for the commander's base, it is temporarily replaced by a marker to indicate its position.

A commander on an individual base does not count as a unit and so does not form a group in the same way as a unit.

COMMANDERS AND GROUPS

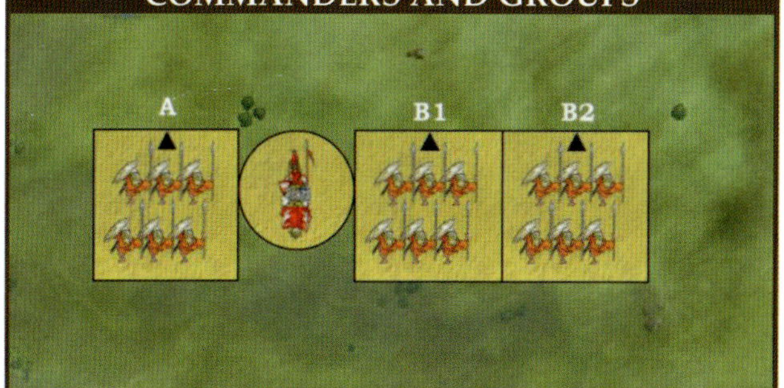

Units A, B1 and B2 do not form a valid group.

The commander can be attached to A or B1 and so must be placed behind the corresponding unit.

Attaching a commander to a unit

An individually based commander can be moved individually or be attached to a unit, which can be part of a group. In this case he moves and flees with the unit or the group.

During the movement phase, a commander can be attached to an adjacent unit either before or after he has moved. A commander that has moved individually cannot move with a unit or group in the same game-turn. When a commander is attached to a unit he stays attached to it until the end of the game-turn or until the end of the melee if it is engaged in combat.

To indicate that a commander is attached to a unit, he is placed behind the unit. A commander can be attached to only one unit at a time. This unit must be clearly identified by the player to avoid confusion.

Free command point

A commander does not require an order to move and can always move during a player's phase by using his free command point. Every commander receives a free CP every game-turn. This free CP however, can be used only in the following cases:

- To move a commander individually.
- To move or stop a unit or group if the commander is included in, or attached to, the unit or one of the units in the group.
- To rally a unit that the commander is included in, or attached to.

COMMANDER IN MELEE

An individually based commander cannot be attacked by enemy units in melee or by shooting. If an unattached commander is contacted by an enemy unit during the movement phase, he must flee up to his maximum distance (5 UD) towards the nearest friendly unit. If he cannot reach a friendly unit (even of another army corps), the commander is considered captured and counts as lost. It is therefore dangerous to move a commander further than 5 UD from his troops as he can be captured by the enemy.

A commander attached to a unit is not affected by shooting against this unit. He can engage in a melee but only if the player chooses to and says so to his opponent. Once engaged in melee the commander remains so until the unit is eliminated or flees, which can take several game-turns. During the melee, the engaged commander must spend one more CP for each order given, except to try to rally the unit in which he is included or to which he is attached. A commander attached to a unit in melee but not engaged is not at risk of being lost. If the unit to which he is attached is destroyed, he must flee as described above.

A commander engaged in melee gives a +1 bonus to his attached unit for combat (but not for shooting) but takes the risk of being lost. If the unit to which he is attached loses cohesion in melee, the opposing player rolls 1D6 and on a 1, the engaged commander is lost. The attached unit then loses another cohesion point for the loss of the commander. An engaged commander is only tested once per game-turn even if the unit he is included in, or attached to, loses more than one cohesion point.

If the unit to which he is attached is routed, the commander is lost on a result of 1, 2 or 3. If the commander survives, he must flee up to his maximum distance (5 UD) towards the nearest friendly unit. If he cannot reach a friendly unit (even of another corps) or if he is forced to move off the table, the commander is removed and counts as lost.

The presence of a commander does not affect the protection or the shooting capability of a unit.

COMMANDER INCLUDED IN A UNIT

It is possible to include a commander directly in a unit instead of having it based individually. This can represent a commander who prefers being engaged in combat alongside his troops rather than staying behind to direct the battle. Barbarian chiefs and Kings during the Middle Ages are good examples, as well as Alexander the Great, who fought in the front rank at the risk of being wounded or killed.

Whether or not to include a commander in a unit is left to the judgment of each player. The main advantage is to reduce the cost of the commander and to save points when budgeting for the rest of the army. It is only possible to include a commander in the troop types indicated by an asterisk (*) in each army list. The unit including the commander must be easily recognisable by using an appropriate figure, a standard bearer or a flag.

If a commander included in a unit is lost, the unit loses an additional cohesion point and becomes a normal unit. It is recommended to replace the unit with another one without a commander for clarity although it is not compulsory.

If a commander is included in a unit, the following rules apply:

- Command points are determined as usual and the commander still has his free command point.
- The commander moves with his unit and can never be detached.
- The commander can form a group with other units following the rules for groups which depend on the type of unit in which he is included. For example a commander included in a unit of Knights cannot form a group with Foot units except Light Infantry.
- The commander moves as the troop type of the unit in which he is included. For example a commander included in a pikemen unit moves only 2 UD.
- If the unit in which the commander is included is engaged in melee, the commander is also engaged and runs the risk of being lost.
- When engaged in melee, the commander must spend one extra CP for each order given except to try to rally the unit in which he is included.
- If the unit loses cohesion in melee, the commander is lost on a roll of 1.
- Commanders cannot be lost as a result of shooting unless the unit is routed by losing its last cohesion point.
- If the unit which includes the commander is routed (in melee or by shooting), the commander is lost.

ALLIED AND UNRELIABLE COMMANDERS

Sub-commanders can be considered as unreliable to represent a rival commander or one who is likely to betray his commander-in-chief. In this case, it is necessary to verify at the beginning of each battle if the army corps led by this sub-commander is hesitant or not (see p 73).

Only one of the sub-commanders can be an allied commander and he is automatically classed as unreliable. An allied commander leads troops from another army list. An allied army corps must include at least half of the minimum number of units of each troop type from the corresponding army list (see p 78).

An allied commander can be ordinary, competent or brilliant but cannot be a strategist. The command value of an allied commander is calculated in the maximum command value of the army.

Roman commander

SEQUENCE OF PLAY

He will win who, prepared himself, waits to take the enemy unprepared. Sun Tzu

In a game of *l'Art de la guerre* time is divided into game-turns, each of which consists of two phases; one per player. The first player plays his entire phase of the game-turn and then the second player's phase follows. The player who is moving his units is called the *phasing player*.

At the beginning of the game, each player rolls a die and adds his army initiative. The player with the highest result decides if he wants to be the attacker or the defender.

The order of player phases in each game-turn then remains the same for the entire game. A player phase is composed of the following:

MOVEMENT

The player activates each of his army corps in succession until they have all been activated. He can do this in any order he chooses except that if he has any hidden corps (i.e. in ambush or making a flank march), they must be activated before the others.

For each corps the player nominates which one he is activating and rolls 1D6. To this he adds the value of the commander (0, +1, +2 or +3 for a strategist), divides the total by two and rounds up the result to give the number of command points (CP) available for this army corps for the game-turn.

He then performs, in the order of his choice, all the movement and rally attempts for units in that corps up to the CP available. Uncontrolled moves of impetuous units are performed after all other movements. The player does this corps by corps until all of his army corps have been activated.

N.B. each corps can only be activated once per game-turn and the activation of one corps must be completed before moving on to the next one.

SHOOTING

During the shooting phase both players' units can shoot. The phasing player shoots with his units first, followed by his opponent, but all results are applied simultaneously.

War wagons and artillery cannot shoot if they have moved or wheeled during the movement phase. Other units cannot shoot if they have made a second or third movement, are engaged in melee or are providing support to a friendly unit in melee.

MELEE

All units engaged in melee perform their combats during this phase. The order in which individual combats are resolved is decided by the phasing player. All results are applied simultaneously.

ROUT AND PURSUIT

Routs and pursuits are carried out after the resolution of all combats for all army corps. Units that have lost all their cohesion points are routed and removed from play. When doing this a check is made to see if routed units cause a loss of cohesion to nearby friendly units. Then, victorious units of the phasing player can (or must if they are impetuous) conduct a pursuit move of one UD (or less if they are not impetuous).

VICTORY

At the end of each player phase a check is made to see if one of the armies (or both) is demoralised. If so, this is the end of the game. If this is not the case a new player phase is started.

The game continues until the end of the phase in which one of the armies is demoralised or until the end of the current game-turn if the time allotted for the game is reached.

MOVEMENT

The clever general imposes his will on the enemy, but does not allow the enemy's will to be imposed on him. Sun Tzu

GENERAL RULES

The movement of units is carried out corps by corps by the phasing player. The rules below apply to all movement:

- Movement distance is expressed as multiples of the unit of distance (UD).
- A movement can be performed by a unit or a group of units.
- A group of units moves at the speed of the slowest unit. However, during a wheel, each unit of the group can move up to the maximum of its distance as long as all units remain in the group until the end of the wheel.
- For mixed units, the movement distance is that of the slowest troop type.
- To move together, a group of units must start and finish their movement as a group (see p 10).
- To move a unit or group of units, its commander must give it an order by spending one or more CP.
- One additional CP must be spent if the commander is engaged in melee, if the unit is out of command range or if it is a difficult manoeuvre. The modifiers are cumulative.
- There is no need to spend any CP if a unit charges an enemy at one UD or less *straight in front* of its front edge. It is then classified as a spontaneous charge that does not require the intervention of the commander or the use of CP.
- A unit or group can perform up to two movements per phase, or three if it is accompanied by its commander throughout the whole phase.

MOVEMENT DISTANCES

- A unit moves up to the maximum movement distance according to its type and terrain crossed during the move (see table below).
- If the unit moves, even partially, through different types of terrain, the unit can only move at the lowest distance allowed. For example, a unit, which at the beginning of its movement is in a wood and moves to open terrain, can only move up to the distance allowed in the wood.
- A unit or group of units moving its full movement distance in column along a road can advance up to its movement distance in open terrain regardless of the type of terrain crossed by the road. The unit can also add one UD to its movement allowance if the player chooses.

Note: Units with base deeper than one UD (pikemen 3 ranks deep and troop with the missile support ability) can ignore the additional base(s) when determining whether the unit is in the terrain. This is also applicable during the shooting and melee phases.

Troop categories/types	Movement distance (UD)		
	Open	Rough	Difficult
Light infantry	3	3	3
Medium infantry	3	3	2
Heavy infantry	2	2	1
Light cavalry or light camelry	5	4	2
Medium cavalry, medium camelry or heavy cavalry	4	3	1
Medium knights or heavy knights	3	2	1
Light chariots or scythed chariots	4	2	-
Heavy chariots, cataphracts or cataphract camelry	3	1	-
Elephants	3	3	1
War wagon or mobile artillery	2	1	-

How to measure distance

When a unit or group moves, only the distance travelled by the front edge is measured. No point on the front edge can move more than the allowed distance.

In the case of a wheel (see the diagram below), distance is measured in a straight line as the distance moved by the outside corner of the front edge of the unit, i.e. the front corner that moves the furthest.

Movement is measured in several parts if the unit performs more than one wheel.

MEASUREMENT OF DISTANCES

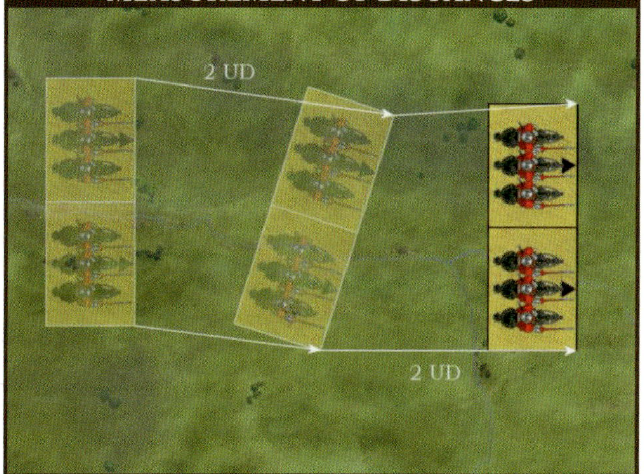

The two Cavalry units advance as a group a total of 4 UD by performing two wheels.

Types of movement

A unit or group can perform the following types of movement:

Advance

During an advance the unit moves straight forward. One or more advances can be combined with wheels and/or one slide, up to the unit's maximum movement distance.

Slide

To ease movement, a unit or group is allowed to perform a lateral slide of up to and including one UD (i.e. the width of one base). It can only be performed by advancing at least one UD straight ahead, this include when charging. Wheels are also allowed during the move, but do not count towards the minimum advance of 1 UD.

The unit can perform a slide at any time during its move: It can be made before, after or during its advance or before or after any wheel. The slide simplifies movements by avoiding the need for complicated wheels. For example it allows a unit to avoid a friendly unit or a terrain blocking its way forward or to align with a friendly unit.

- The slide is free: i.e. the extra distance travelled is not counted in the movement distance.
- If the slide is made during a charge, the extra distance must not allow an enemy unit out of range at the beginning of the movement to be reached.
- A unit can only perform a single slide per game-turn even if it performs 2 or 3 moves. A slide may occur in the 1st, 2nd or 3rd movement.
- A slide is prohibited during any manoeuvre with a quarter-turn, a half-turn or an extension or contraction. This applies even to LI and LH.
- A unit cannot slide when it is in an enemy zone of control except to conform to an enemy that it can engage in melee (see p 52).

EXAMPLES OF SLIDES

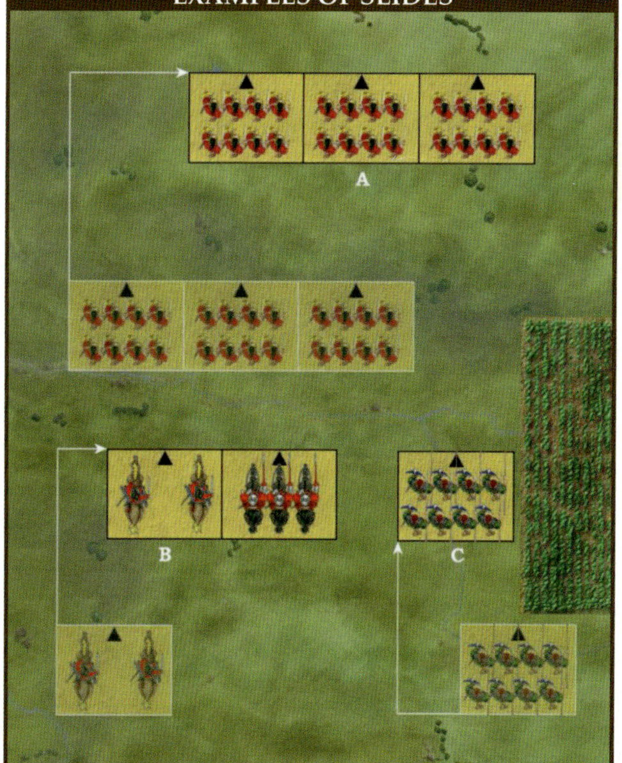

Group A moves 2 UD while performing a lateral slide of one UD. The light cavalry B advances and aligns itself with a friendly unit. Spearmen C advance while performing a slide to avoid an obstacle.

Wheel

During a wheel, one of the outermost front corners remains stationary while the unit or group pivots forward around it. The wheel is measured by the straight line distance moved by the front corner that moves furthest. A wheel is limited to 90°, which for simplicity equals 1.5 UD for a single unit.

- Units in a group maintain their relative positions and alignment when wheeling, pivoting as a single block. Units in a wheeling group must not exceed their maximum movement distance. It is possible that the outermost front corner of a group is not in its front rank.
- During an advance, one or more wheels can be made provided they do not total more than 90°.
- A wheel can be performed before or after a quarter-turn or a half-turn.
- A wheel cannot be performed during an extension or contraction manoeuvre.
- Units can temporarily overlap adjacent friendly units during a wheel provided they do not end their move overlapping them (see below).
- Artillery (fixed or mobile), can change its facing by wheeling on its central point up to a maximum of 90°. Only mobile artillery can perform a wheel on one of its front corners.

WHEEL EXAMPLES

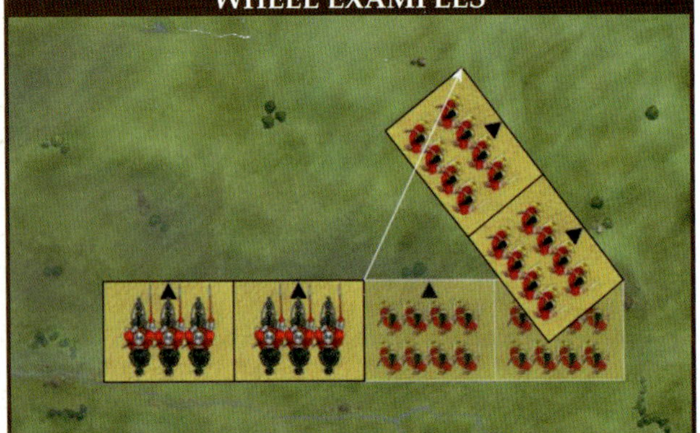

The infantry unit may temporarily overlap the cavalry unit to perform its wheel.

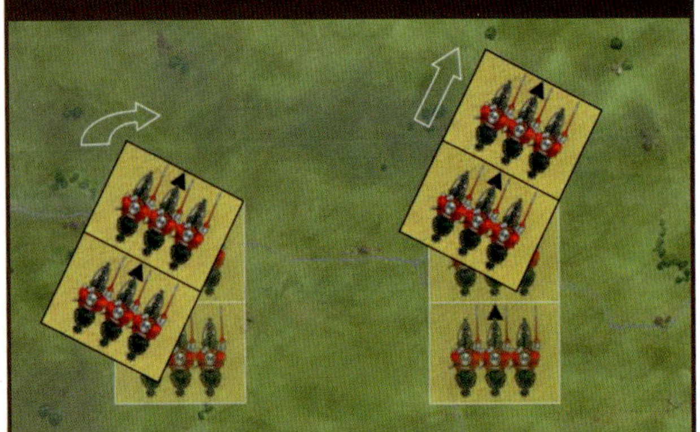

A wheel followed by an advance. The rear unit aligns itself behind the wheeling unit.

Half-turn or quarter-turn

Half-turn:

To perform a half-turn (or about face), the unit, or each unit of a group, turns in place by rotating 180° on its centre: its former rear edge becoming its new front edge. In the case of mixed units, the base positions are exchanged so that those at the front of the units remain at the front after the half-turn. In the case of a group of units with different base depths, they remain a group after the half-turn by aligning with the unit with the least deep base.

Half-turn

A half-turn on the spot: simply re-orientate the units by 180 °.

Quarter-turn:

A unit that performs a quarter-turn rotates 90° so that its front edge ends up occupying the position of the side edge before the manoeuvre. A group of units in line then becomes a column, and vice-versa.

Line to column

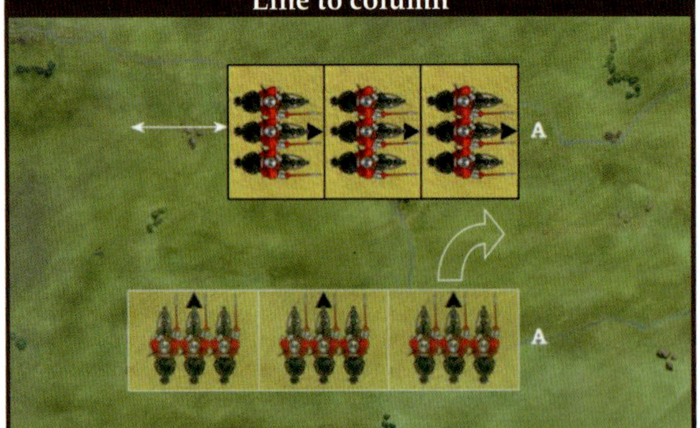

A 3 Cv line performs a quarter-turn to the right. Front Cavalry A is rotated so that its left front corner occupies the place of its former right front corner - notice that the unit does not advance or retreat.

The other cavalry units are aligned behind the front unit. In doing so, they gain a little distance. This additional distance is not considered as distance moved, and does not affect the rest of the movement.

When changing from line to column, the other units are rotated individually and aligned behind the end unit, closing up or making room as required.

When changing from column to line, the other units are rotated individually and aligned alongside the front unit, closing up or making room as required.

The change from a column to a line may be prevented due to lack of space in which to move the units. In this case, the units that cannot find a place in the first line are placed in the second line.

COLUMN TO LINE

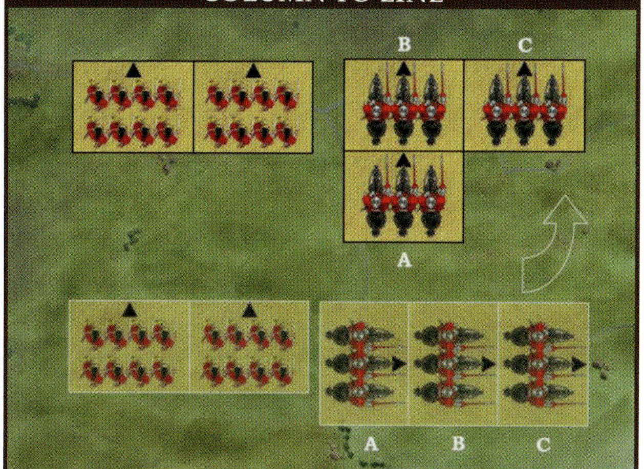

A column of 3 cavalry units try to make a quarter-turn to form a line. This manoeuvre is blocked by an obstacle (here a friendly unit). The cavalry unit A that did not have enough room to be placed in the first line is then placed in the second line.

Particular cases:

- It is possible to perform a simple advance (without a slide but with a wheel) before or after (or both) a quarter-turn or a half-turn if the unit has enough available movement.
- Performing a quarter-turn or a half-turn uses one UD of the unit's movement or 2 UD if the unit is *unmanoeuvrable* or is pikemen or cataphracts.
- Neither war wagons nor mobile artillery can perform a quarter-turn or a half-turn as a group. Each manoeuvre must be perform individually
- Only light troops can perform two quarter-turns or half-turns in the same movement.
- If the group contain units with different base depths, the entire group is aligned on the front of the units with the least deep base.

Example: A medium infantry unit can make a half-turn and advance 2 UD in the same movement. It cannot make a half-turn, advance one UD and then perform another half-turn. It would have to perform two separate movements and therefore pay twice the CP.

Extension

An extension can only be performed by a group of units which are deployed several ranks deep, in one or more columns. Its purpose is to extend the width of the front of the group by deploying units to the sides of units already in the front rank.

In this type of movement, the whole group is considered to be moving even if some of the units do not actually move. The distance of each unit's movement is not measured but the extension is performed simply by moving a number of units to the group's front according to their movement allowance. If the group is composed of units of different types, the extension is limited to that of the movement allowance of the slowest type of unit that moves.

Movement distance	Extension
1 UD	Impossible
2 UD (HI)	1 unit
3 UD (LMI, MI, Kn, El, LI)	2 units
4 UD and more (Cv, LH, SCh)	3 units

If the manoeuvre is performed in terrain that slows down the unit, the number of units the group can extend by changes. Thus a group of LH in a wood (movement 2 UD) can extend its front rank by one unit instead of the usual three.

EXTENSION EXAMPLE

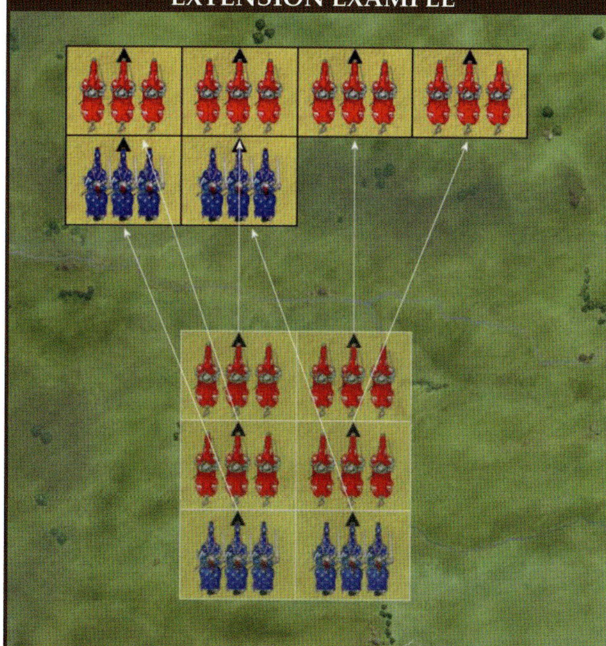

This is an extension of a group of Knights. The two units from the second rank can deploy to the right and/or left of the front units. Those occupying the back rank may conduct a slide on the left or right and be aligned behind the first line units.

Units can be added to the front rank of a group from its rear ranks, on its right or its left, or both. Units located on the ends of the second rank are deployed first. The units that cannot be extended to the front line are simply advanced and placed behind the units of the first line, sliding sideways by a maximum of one UD if desired.

It is possible to make an extension even if the front unit is in melee. The unit must have sufficient place to perform the extension. If the path of the units making the extension is blocked by friendly units, the normal interpenetration rules apply.

Restrictions:

- War wagons, artillery and units whose movement is reduced to one UD cannot make an extension.
- An extension cannot be combined with an advance, a wheel, a slide, a quarter-turn, a half-turn or a contraction.
- A unit moving to the front rank can only move to the end of the front rank it is closest to at the start of the extension (player's choice if equal).
- A unit moving to the front rank can only move sideways by up to its movement allowance (including terrain effects) minus one UD.

Contraction

This is the reverse movement of the extension, i.e. a contraction is a reduction in the width of the front of a group by advancing some front units straight forward and by moving the units located on the right and/or left behind the units which have advanced. The advance can include a wheel of the front units but cannot include a slide.

Advancing units must move in a way that allows other units to be placed behind, i.e. a minimum of one unit's depth and a maximum of their whole movement allowance. The movement distances of the other units are not measured, but the contraction of the front is simply completed by the allowed number of units according to their movement allowance while still forming a group.

If the group is composed of units of different types, the contraction is limited to that of the movement allowance of the slowest type of unit that moves.

Movement distance	Contraction
1 UD	Impossible
2 UD (HI)	1 unit
3 UD (LMI, MI, Kn, El, LI)	2 units
4 UD and more (Cv, LH, SCh)	3 units

If the manoeuvre is performed in terrain which slows down the unit, the number of units that the group can contract by changes. Thus a group of LH in a wood (movement 2 UD) can contract its front rank by only one unit instead of the usual three.

CONTRACTION EXAMPLES

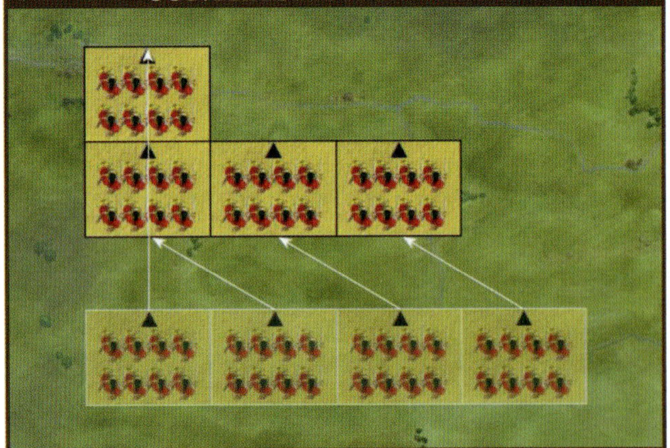

A line of heavy infantry contracting to the left.

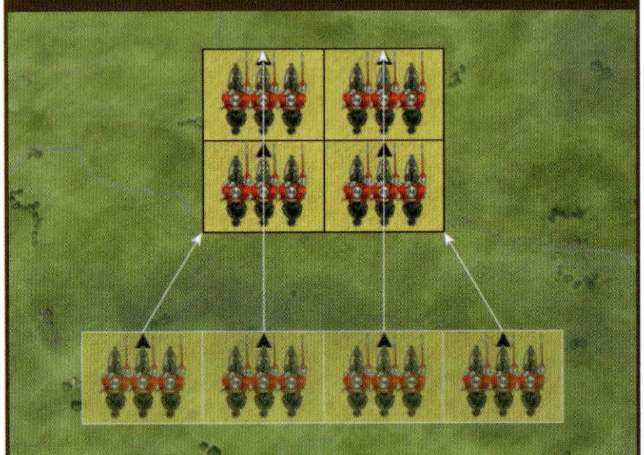

A line of cavalry contracting on both wings.

Restrictions:

- War wagons, artillery and units whose movement is reduced to one UD cannot make a contraction.
- A contraction cannot be combined with a slide, a quarter-turn, a half-turn or an extension.

Iberian warriors

SECOND AND THIRD MOVEMENT

A unit or group of units can perform a second or even a third consecutive movement in the same phase under the following conditions:

- During the entire movement phase the unit or group must remain **at least 4 UD** (i.e. at exactly 4 UD or more) away from all enemy units (including the enemy camp). A commander which is not included in a unit does not prevent such movement.
- Unmanoeuvrable troops (except impetuous cavalry) cannot perform a third movement.
- All other troops (including impetuous cavalry) can perform a third consecutive movement. This is treated as a difficult manoeuvre, except for light troops and non-impetuous cavalry.
- In order to perform a third consecutive movement, a commander must accompany the unit or group during all three movements. This also applies to light troops and cavalry.

MANOEUVRABILITY

Unmanoeuvrable units

Not all units perform equally well when manoeuvring. Some will have difficulty performing manoeuvres more complex than a simple advance. These units are referred to as *unmanoeuvrable*. This applies to the following units:

- Impetuous units
- Elephants
- Levies
- War wagons
- Artillery
- Scythed Chariots

Difficult manoeuvres

Manoeuvres can be easy or difficult. A difficult manoeuvre requires the commander to spend one additional CP.

The following are difficult manoeuvres:

- A third movement in the same phase except if the movement is performed by light troops or non impetuous cavalry.
- A retreat when the unit is in an enemy's zone of control (see next page) except if it is performed by light troops or troops that can evade.

For unmanoeuvrable units only, the following are also considered difficult manoeuvres:

- An advance of less than the unit's full movement distance (excluding any road bonus) unless the unit ends in contact with the enemy. An advance of full movement distance, with a wheel and/or a slide is still an easy manoeuvre.
- Any manoeuvre that includes a quarter-turn, a half-turn, an extension or a contraction, whether the unit ends in contact with the enemy or not.

If a group contains one or more unmanoeuvrable unit, the penalty in CP for performing a difficult manoeuvre applies to the whole group.

It may happen that a unit does not have enough movement allowance to perform a difficult manoeuvre: for example an impetuous HI wanting to make a half-turn in a wood. In this case, the movement is permitted but causes the unit to become disordered. The unit loses a cohesion point unless the unit only has a single cohesion point left, in which case it retains its single cohesion point.

Persian scythed chariot

Particular Cases

Pikemen or cataphracts: Due to their very compact formations, when pikemen or cataphracts (including cataphract camelry) make a move that includes a quarter-turn or half-turn, it is considered a difficult manoeuvre for them.

Impetuous cavalry: Although unmanoeuvrable, impetuous cavalry can perform a third movement, which is treated as a difficult manoeuvre.

War wagons or mobile artillery: These units cannot perform contractions or extensions. Quarter-turns and half-turns are carried out individually.

Artillery: Heavy artillery cannot be moved but can change its orientation by wheeling on the centre point of the unit. The wheel must be done individually, is limited to a maximum of 90° and counts as a difficult manoeuvre. Light and medium artillery can wheel in the same manner without counting it as a difficult manoeuvre.

Scythed chariots: Scythed chariots can only perform advances including wheels and slides. All other manoeuvres are not allowed.

Impetuous: When an impetuous unit or group is within charge distance of an enemy, any manoeuvre other than a charge or a movement to support a friend in melee costs 3 CP (see p 40). It also costs 3 CP to prevent the unit or group charging the enemy even if the player does not intend to move the unit or group.

LIGHT TROOPS

Light troops are light infantry and light cavalry units. Due to their relatively loose formation, these troops manoeuvre more easily than other units:

- They can make a half-turn or a quarter-turn for free at the beginning or end of an advance move. This half-turn or quarter-turn is not counted in the movement distance.
- They can make an additional half-turn or a quarter-turn during their move but their movement distance is reduced by one UD.
- Thanks to the free half-turn, they are the only units that can retreat to their rear while remaining facing the enemy.
- They can perform a third movement that is not considered a difficult manoeuvre. To do this the commander must accompany the unit or group during all three movements.
- The command range is doubled for light troops.

ZONE OF CONTROL

Definition

A unit that is located close to the front of an enemy risks being charged at any time and no longer tries to manoeuvre.

Troops are in an enemy unit's *zone of control* (ZoC) if they are directly in front (see above) of the unit and **less than** one UD from its front edge. All units with at least part of their base in the ZoC of an enemy unit are limited in their movements (see below).

Units exert a ZoC through friendly units that they can interpenetrate (e.g. HI through LI).

To accurately measure if a unit is in the ZoC of an enemy or not, it is easiest to place a marker one UD square adjacent to, and aligned with, the front edge of the enemy's base. If the marker covers at least a part of the unit's base, then the unit is in the ZoC. If the marker merely touches the unit's base then the unit is not in the ZoC as it is exactly one UD from the enemy.

ZONE OF CONTROL

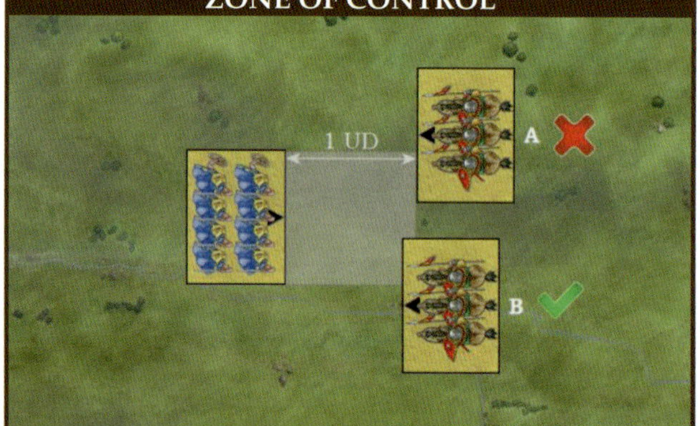

Cavalry unit A is outside the ZoC of the infantry. Cavalry unit B is in the ZoC and must restrict its movements accordingly.

Abbasid infantry

Movements allowed in a ZoC

When a unit is in or enters one or more enemy ZoC (including in conforming see p 52), the only movements permitted are to:

- Stay in place.
- Advance, make a wheel, a quarter-turn or a half-turn in order **to align with the most threatening enemy**, move closer to it or charge it. The unit cannot end its movement being less aligned than at the beginning. The unit cannot exit the most threatening enemy's ZoC or move away from it. No point on its front edge must move further from the enemy than at the beginning of the move (except in special cases below). It cannot slide except to conform just after contact.
- Perform an extension or contraction as long as no units of the group leave the enemy's ZoC.
- Retreat to leave a ZoC (see below).

The **most threatening enemy** is:

- The enemy in front of the unit whose ZoC covers the largest part of the front of the unit.
- If no enemy exerts a ZoC on the front edge of the unit, the nearest enemy whose ZoC covers a portion of the flank or rear edge of the unit.

If a unit is in the ZoC of several enemy units, only the ZoC of the most threatening enemy unit is considered. The unit ignores the ZoC of other units when making its move. If several units are equally threatening, the choice is left to the player whose unit is inside those ZoCs.

MOVEMENTS IN A ZOC

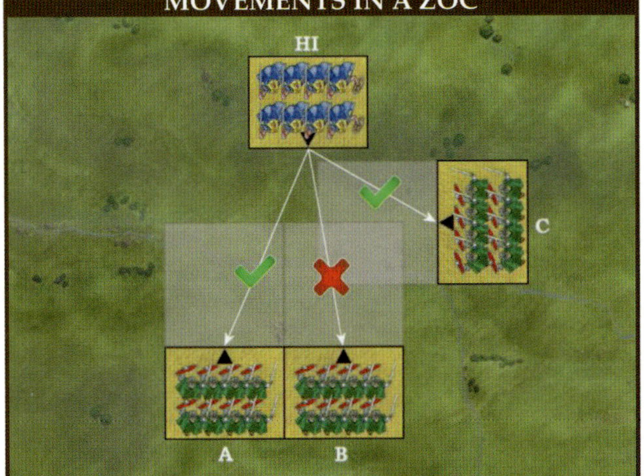

The HI unit can charge unit C by wheeling and then advancing into C's ZoC, which is then the most threatening unit. It can also charge unit A by sliding in order to avoid C's ZoC and advancing straight ahead. It will conform to unit A, which is then the most threatening. It cannot charge unit B without first entering the ZoC of A or C, which would then be the most threatening enemies.

Exiting a ZoC

A unit cannot voluntarily leave an enemy ZoC except in the following circumstances:

- A unit or group capable of evading (see p 37) must make a half-turn if the enemy is to its front or a quarter-turn if the enemy is on its flank. If the unit is in more than one ZoC, only take account that of the **most threatening enemy**. This manoeuvre is counted in the distance moved. The unit or group then advances its remaining movement distance (or until it meets an obstacle) straight forward without changing orientation. Contacting an enemy or shooting are not allowed in this case.
- Light troops can turn to face the enemy by using their free half-turn. They can therefore retreat while facing the enemy. They are not allowed to contact the enemy, but they can shoot.
- Other units that cannot evade must make a retreat move without turning away from the enemy. To do this, they retreat directly to their rear, without changing orientation. They move one UD for foot or 2 UD for mounted troops or until they meet an obstacle. This is considered a difficult manoeuvre (i.e. it costs 2 CP) and **the unit is disordered**. However, a unit already in disorder does not lose another cohesion point. This retreat cannot be made by a group; it must be performed individually, unit by unit. A unit that performs a retreat move is not allowed to contact the enemy or shoot.

<u>Particular case:</u> It is possible that a unit could leave an enemy ZoC involuntarily. For instance, if another friendly unit, also in front of the enemy, slides in order to align with the enemy exerting the ZoC. This can also occur when switching from column to line or while conforming.

INVOLUNTARY EXIT FROM A ZOC

Cavalry units A and B are in an enemy ZoC.
A and B can perform a quarter-turn which results in A exiting the enemy ZoC.

Exceptions to ZoC

- Light troops in open terrain only exert a ZoC on other light troops.
- Light infantry completely in rough or difficult terrain exert a ZoC against all enemy units (including non light troops) that are at least partially in the rough or difficult terrain.
- The camp, artillery and war wagons do not exert a ZoC.
- War wagons ignore an enemy ZoC and can move freely without having to charge.
- An enemy ZoC is ignored by a unit located completely behind a friendly fortification or entirely behind an intervening friendly unit.
- A ZoC is ignored by units making an evade move (see p 37)
- A unit does not exert a ZoC when engaged in melee even if it is attacked only on its flank or rear.
- A unit does not exert a ZoC when in terrain that penalises it during combat.
- A unit's ZoC is not blocked by friendly units it can interpenetrate in normal circumstances.

Example: A cavalry unit in rough terrain does not exert a ZoC on a MI unit in open terrain or rough terrain. On the other hand the MI exerts a ZoC on the cavalry as it is not penalised when in melee in rough terrain.

EXAMPLE OF ZOC

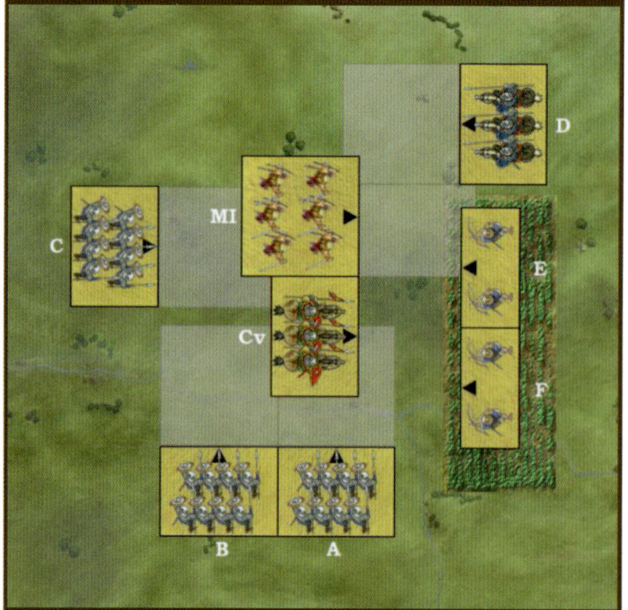

The cavalry unit Cv does not exert a ZoC on the light infantry units E and F because they are in rough terrain that penalises Cv.
The most threatening unit to Cv is the heavy infantry unit A. Cv can therefore wheel or make a quarter-turn to align with A or charge it.
Note: If A was not there, Cv would take into account the ZoC of B which is closer than C.

The medium infantry unit MI exerts a ZoC on the light infantry E in front of it because MI is not penalised by the rough terrain.
MI also exerts a ZoC on the cavalry unit D and vice versa. MI can perform a wheel and/or a slide to align with D or charge it.
Note: MI cannot make a half-turn to charge C because D exerts a ZoC to its front and is therefore more threatening.

Aztec warriors

Special Movements

Hold out baits to entice the enemy. Feign disorder, and crush him. Sun Tzu

Charge

Definition

A charge is a move in which a unit contacts an enemy, which is not already in melee, with its front edge (even by single corner). It stops once contact with the enemy is made. The charging unit must then conform (see p 52).

A group can charge if at least one of its units is able to contact an enemy. This contact can take place on the enemy's front, back or flank. Measuring the distance to see if you can charge an enemy is allowed.

Apart from when charging, contact with the enemy is onlypossible only in the following cases:

- If the unit is already in contact at the beginning of its movement (even by a single corner) with that enemy. The unit can conform by aligning to fight in melee. In this case, charge specific abilities (e.g. *impact, javelin, furious charge*, etc) do not apply.
- If the unit has just contacted an enemy **already engaged in melee** in order to give support (see p 50) to a friendly unit.
- If the unit has just contacted an enemy following a pursuit after a melee.
- If the unit charges an enemy (including camp) and has to contact another enemy by a single corner or slide along the flank or rear of this new enemy. The charging unit can choose to conform to this new enemy if its primary target chooses to evade.

Charge movement

A charge consists of an advance directly forward towards the enemy. At the beginning of a charge, it is also possible to wheel, slide (not both) or make a half-turn or quarter-turn followed by an optionnal wheel. An extension or contraction that brings the front of one or more units in contact with the enemy is also considered a charge.

Before charging, the player must indicate to his opponent the exact direction of his charge. This is particularly important when the target can evade. A small ruler indicating the direction of the charge can be used. Once the charge has started, the group advances straight ahead in the specified direction and only stops if it encounters an enemy, an obstacle or the edge of the table.

Changing the direction of a charge once it has started is prohibited.

Continuing a charge

When one or more units of a charging group contact the enemy, the other units of the group who have not contacted an enemy can continue their charge up to their maximum movement. The charge stops at the moment an ennemy is contacted. This could cause the group to become separated but the CP cost does not change.

Once the units are in contact with an enemy, they must each conform (see p 52). Continuing a charge is optional except for impetuous units making an uncontrolled charge, in which case it is compulsory.

CONTINUING A CHARGE

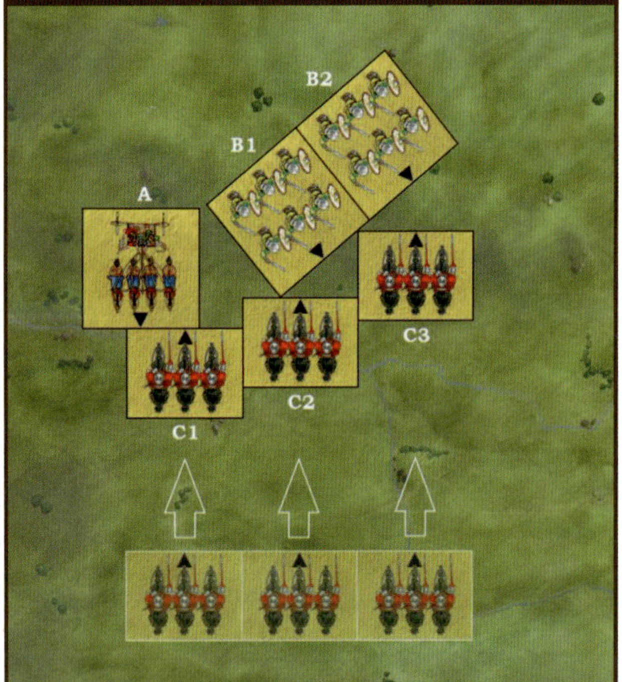

The 3 cavalry units C1, C2 and C3 form a group and charge together. The enemy unit A is contacted first, but the player chooses to continue his charge against B1 and B2. During conformation, C1 will conform with A, C2 with B1 and C3 with B2.

Melee after a charge

Combat immediately following a charge allows the units to use certain capabilities (e.g. *impact, javelin,* etc) which only apply in the first phase of a melee. A unit that is charged is always assumed to counter-charge unless it is attacked on its flank or rear. Thus, a unit always benefits from its specific abilities (e.g. *impact, javelin,* etc.) if it receives a charge on its front edge. Some units also benefit from a *furious charge* (see p 58) allowing them to inflict more cohesion losses on their opponent if they win the combat in the first phase of a melee.

Illegal charge

There are two particular cases in which a charge is not allowed.

- Due to the difference in base size or the inability to align correctly, it is possible a part of the front edge of a unit already in melee could be contacted. However it is not allowed to charge a unit already in melee on its front edge by contacting it on the same edge. A move to provide support or to charge the flank or rear of such an enemy is still allowed.

ILLEGAL CHARGE

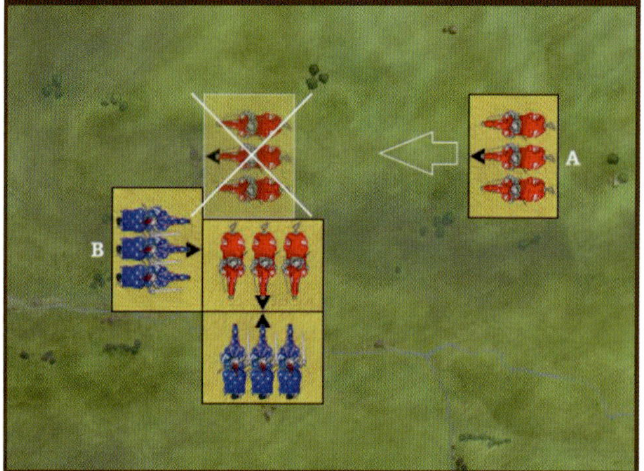

The knight unit A is not allowed to charge the front of knight unit B, because it is already in melee to its front edge.

- A charge on the flank or rear of an enemy is not allowed if the charging unit cannot conform properly as a result of obstacles or the ZoC of an enemy (see p 52).

EVADE MOVE

The evade move allows some troops to avoid contact because they would not want to fight in melee, either because they were too lightly equipped or because they preferred to shoot at the enemy from a distance.

A unit can evade as many times as it is charged by different enemies but in practice a unit rarely evades more than once per game-turn.

Troops that can evade

Only the following types of troops can evade:

- Light troops (light infantry and light cavalry),
- Javelinmen,
- Cavalry (including camelry and light chariots) provided that they do not have the *Impact* ability and are not impetuous. *Impact/bow* cavalry can still evade.

Evading is not allowed in the following cases:

- The unit is engaged in melee, including supporting a friendly unit, with its front edge in contact with an enemy.
- The unit is blocked by an obstacle within one UD in the direction of the evade move (see point 3 of the evade procedure, below).

However, the evade move remains possible for units in support that are in contact with the enemy only by a corner or a side edge.

Troops that must evade

Light infantry units must evade the charge of heavier troops (i.e. Cv, Kn, LMI, MI, LMI, HI) if they are in open terrain. If they cannot evade or they are still contacted by the charger after an evade move, they are eliminated immediately. The unit that destroyed the light infantry ends its movement at the point of contact with no conformation.

Evade procedure

An evade move can be attempted by a unit or by all or part of a group in which at least one of the units would be contacted by the enemy's charge. The procedure is as follows:

1 -Charge direction

The target and the exact path of the charging unit or group are indicated (for example by placing a ruler).

2 - Evading unit's orientation

The evading unit is reoriented as follows. If the unit is charged on its front edge, it makes a half-turn. If it is attacked from flank, it performs a quarter-turn. If it is attacked from the rear, it remains facing in the current direction (see p 51). Any change in the orientation is free and does not decrease the distance of the evade move.

EVADING UNIT'S ORIENTATION

A LH is charged by a Cv on its flank. It must make a quarter-turn.

3 - Blocked evade move

An evading unit may be blocked by an enemy or an obstacle that prevents its manoeuvre. If this is the case, the evade move is cancelled. The player may decide to not evade if it finds that it is impossible. Evading is blocked in one of the following two cases:

- After any change in orientation, the unit has an enemy at least partially located less than one UD directly ahead (i.e. in its ZoC). This enemy, regardless of its orientation, blocks the evade move of the unit. A LI unit can only block LI or LH units. A LH unit can block all units.

AN EVADE MOVE BLOCKED BY AN ENEMY

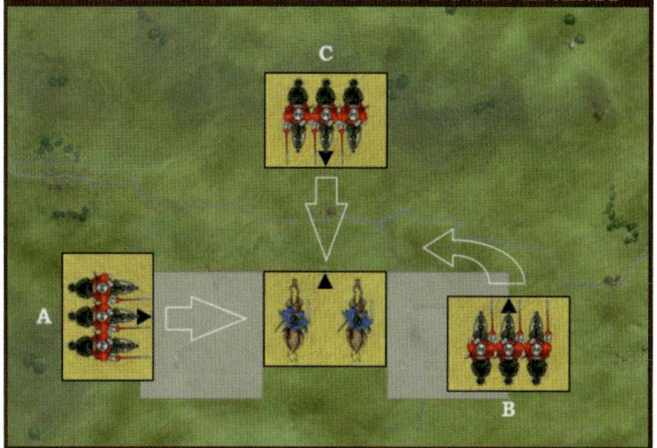

If unit A charges, the LH cannot evade since it will have B in its ZoC. The same applies if B performs a quarter-turn and charges, since the LH will have A in its ZoC.
If C charges the LH, the LH can evade towards its rear ignoring the ZoC of A.

- After any change in orientation, the unit has an obstacle (a friendly unit that it cannot interpenetrate or impassable terrain) located less than one UD directly ahead (i.e. in its ZoC) that cannot be avoided by a sideways slide of one UD or less. This slide to avoid an obstacle is not free and is deducted from the distance of the evade move. If the obstacle in the evading unit's ZoC is rough or difficult terrain, it must enter the terrain and its movement distance is reduced accordingly.

EVADE BLOCKED BY AN OBSTACLE

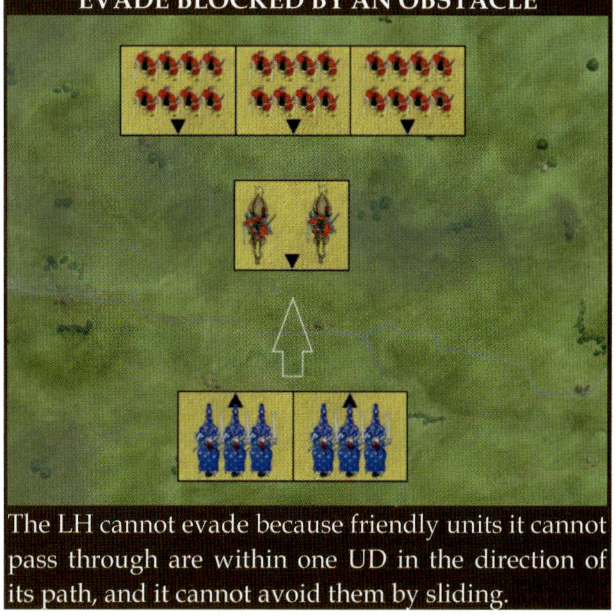

The LH cannot evade because friendly units it cannot pass through are within one UD in the direction of its path, and it cannot avoid them by sliding.

4 - Evade move direction

If the evade move is not blocked, an evading unit can, if the player wishes, wheel to exactly match the direction of the charge. This wheel is not free in that it does decrease the evading distance. It cannot be used to avoid an obstacle as defined in point 3 above.

EVADE MOVE DIRECTION

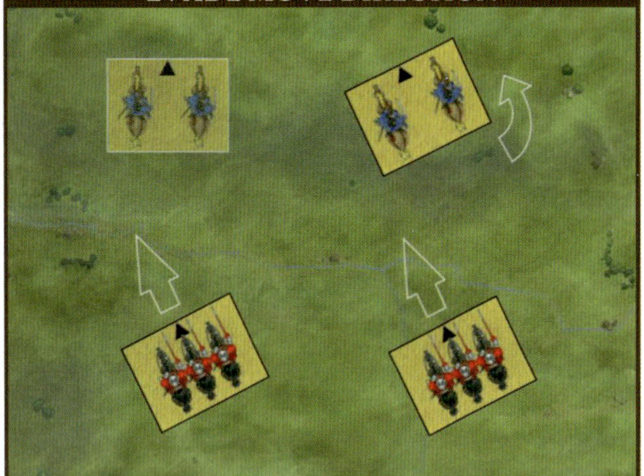

The LH can, if the player wishes, realign itself to exactly match the direction of the enemy's charge.

5 - Adjusted movement distance

The unit or group that evades rolls 1D6 and adjusts its movement distance accordingly. It then moves the remainder of its move (the full evade distance less any realign move) in a straight line directly forward.

D6	Evade distance
1 - 2	Normal movement distance - 1 UD
3 - 4	Normal movement distance
5 - 6	Normal movement distance + 1 UD

If the evading units form a group, a single adjustment roll is made for the entire group or the part of the group which evades. However, if the units of a group that evades do not all have the same movement distance (such as Cv with LH), a separate adjustment roll is made for each sub group with the same movement distance.

6 - Evade move

After having verified that no obstacle within one UD can block the evade move, the unit makes its evade move (including the adjustment) in a straight line directly forward. If during the evade move, the unit encounters a new obstacle in its way (other than the edge of the table), it must manoeuvre to avoid it when it arrives within one UD of the obstacle. First, it can slide by a maximum of one UD to avoid the obstacle, reducing its move distance by the distance of the slide. If the obstacle cannot be avoided by a slide, then it can wheel by a maximum of 90°. This wheel must be the minimum necessary to avoid the obstacle and must deviate as little as possible from the direction of the initial line of charge. During an evade move (as in a normal advance), the unit can only make only one slide together with several wheels (up to a maximum of 90° in total). Any wheel or slide reduces the distance of evade move by the relevant amount.

During an evade move, a unit cannot perform a quarter-turn or a half-turn other than the turn to initially reorient itself (see point 2).

The following rules apply to the evade procedure:

- An evading group may be compelled to perform a contraction to avoid obstacles and risks being caught.
- All enemy ZoC are ignored.
- The enemy camp is regarded as an obstacle and cannot be contacted.
- Friendly units that can be interpenetrated are not considered as obstacles and therefore can be passed through without cohesion loss.
- An enemy LI is not an obstacle in open terrain for heavy units. If an enemy LI would be contacted by an evading unit, it must itself evade.

EVADE MOVEMENT

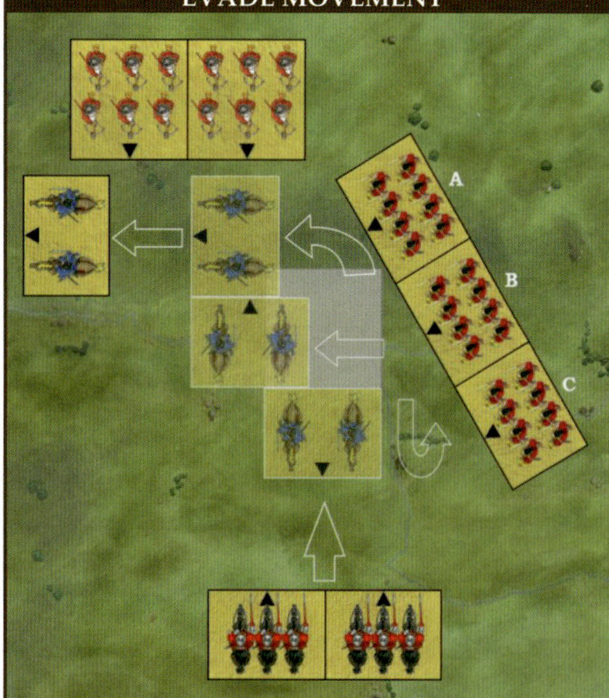

The light cavalry can evade because it has no enemy within one UD behind it. It makes a half-turn and advances directly to its new front, making a slide to avoid the enemy infantry A. It then meets other enemies in its path and at 1 UD from them it wheels 90° to the left before finishing its evade move.

7 - Charge movement

A charging unit or group performs its charge straight forward in the direction indicated in point 1. A D6 is rolled to adjust its movement distance (see point 5) only if **all target** units have evaded.

Once begun, it is not possible to change the direction of a charge or to make a slide or wheels to contact units other than the initial target.

A charging unit must move at least one UD for foot or 2 UD for mounted units towards its target if its adjusted move allows. A preliminary half-turn or quarter-turn does not count towards this minimum. A non-impetuous unit can then stop, but an impetuous unit must continue its charge for the full adjusted distance, unless it meets the edge of the table or terrain that penalises it in combat.

If a new enemy is in the path of the charge, it can be contacted and can also evade in turn if possible. The procedure is identical except that the charging unit does not perform further movement.

If contact with this new enemy is not allowed (i.e. LI on HI) then the unit or group concerned must stop at one UD of the new enemy. The others units can continue their charge.

If an evading unit is contacted by the charging enemy despite of it's evade move, it loses a cohesion point (unless the charging unit consists of light troops) and fights as if being attacked from its rear.

Leaving the table

A unit that leaves the table while evading is lost and will not return to the game. It counts as one point of loss towards the demoralisation of the army. Pursuers who reach the edge of the table do not leave it even if their adjusted move would allow it.

Hoplite Phalanx

Uncontrolled Charge

Some troops are very eager to fight and tend to attack even if they do not receive orders to do so. This, for example, is the case for most barbarian warriors and many mounted knights of the Middle Ages. Troops that are subject to an uncontrolled charge are:

- Impetuous units and,
- Scythed chariots.

When a unit subject to an uncontrolled charge is within its charge distance of an enemy (see exceptions, p 41), the following rules apply:

- Any action other than a charge or a movement to bring support to a friend in melee costs **3 CP**. Staying in place or rallying also cost 3 CP. This represents the difficulty of restraining troops that want to charge.
- Charge moves or moves in order to support (or continue to support) a friend already in melee cost 1 CP, or 2 CP if it is a difficult manoeuvre.
- If the unit or group receives no orders, all impetuous units that are within their charge range of an enemy (see exceptions, p 41) must make an uncontrolled charge.
- If several enemies provoke an uncontrolled charge, the target is chosen according to the following priorities:
  1. The nearest valid enemy target among those who are directly in front of its front edge
  2. The nearest valid enemy target among those who are not directly in front of its front edge.
- Only enemies (including those already in melee) situated in front or to the flank of the unit are considered. Enemy units located behind the unit (i.e entirely behind its rear) are ignored and do not provoke an uncontrolled charge.
- Units making an uncontrolled charge are moved in the order chosen by the owning player after all others movements of the corps have been made.
- Each unit advances by the shortest route towards its target in order to contact it. If the target is already in melee, the unit making an uncontrolled charge tries to place itself in support, choosing the closest option as priority.
- If contacting enemy is not possible, the unit do not make an uncontrolled charge.
- If friendly units are between the charging unit and its target, they will be interpenetrated (if allowed, see p 43) or burst through (see p 42).
- Units making an uncontrolled charge must continue their charge until they are in melee with the enemy, are in position to support a friendly unit in melee or have moved their full distance.
- Movements of units that make an uncontrolled charge are still restricted by enemy ZoC.

The Patrician Romans took the offensive

Uncontrolled charges and melee

- Units that make an uncontrolled charge lose effectiveness due to their disorganised attack. Thus they fight with a penalty of -1 in the first phase of the combat.
- The uncontrolled charge penalty is cumulative with any disorder penalty. Units still benefit from their *impact* and *furious charge* abilities (see p 58) if they are applicable.
- If the target of the charge is directly in front, and one UD or less from the front edge of the charging unit, it is a *spontaneous charge* (see p 22), which does not incur any combat penalty.

Timing of an uncontrolled charge

The check to see if a unit is subject to an uncontrolled charge is made at the beginning of its movement, or at the end of the movement phase if it did not move.

After friendly units have charged and enemy units have evaded, an impetuous unit may become subject to an uncontrolled charge even though it was not subject to it at the start of the phase. Conversely, if an enemy unit that provokes an uncontrolled charge is forced to evade by the charge of another friendly unit, an impetuous unit may no longer be subject to an uncontrolled charge even though it was subject to it at the start of the phase. Uncontrolled charges are made after all others movements of the corps .

Exceptions to uncontrolled charge

An enemy does not provoke an uncontrolled charge in the following cases:

- If the impetuous unit is already in melee or providing support to a friendly unit in melee.
- If the impetuous unit is restricted by the ZoC of an enemy unit that cannot be reach by a charge. For instance a impetuous HI with an enemy to its rear.
- If the impetuous unit is in ambush.
- If the impetuous unit or its enemy is behind a fortification (including stakes if the charging unit is a mounted unit) or a river, or in a village.
- If the only target unit is an elephant or a WWg,
- If the charge would cause a mounted unit to contact an elephant, even only by a corner (see note).
- If the enemy unit is light troops and the impetuous unit would interpenetrate or burst through friendly troops to reach it.
- If the impetuous unit is foot and the target is the front edge of enemy mounted troops (see note).
- If the impetuous unit is a cavalry or camelry unit and the target is the front edge of an enemy heavy infantry unit (HI except levy) that is not disordered (see note). However these enemy units remain valid targets for Kn and SCh units.
- If the charge would cause the unit to enter terrain that inflicts a combat penalty on it.

Note: Before making a charge move, if the target unit can evade, any other enemy unit located behind the target unit that could be contacted (up to the full movement distance of the charging unit, plus one UD) must be taken into account. For example, an impetuous HI unit facing LI units will not have to make an uncontrolled charge if there is a mounted unit behind the LI, within 3 UD.

Burst through

If a unit making an uncontrolled charge or fleeing due to the arrival of a flank march meets friends in its path, it must pass through them. If the unit is not normally allowed to interpenetrate these friends, given the troop types or the directions in which the units are facing, it must burst through them.

Units that are burst through lose one cohesion point and can no longer move or rally during the phase. This can cause them to rout if they had only one cohesion point left. If necessary, burst through units are moved by the minimum necessary to make room for units making an uncontrolled charge.

Units cannot be burst through in the following cases:

- The unit to be crossed is in melee with the enemy or provides support to a friend in melee.
- The unit to be crossed is pikemen.
- The unit to be crossed is an elephant.

If a unit is burst through by several units in the same phase, the effects are not cumulative and it only loses one cohesion point.

EXAMPLE OF AN UNCONTROLLED CHARGE

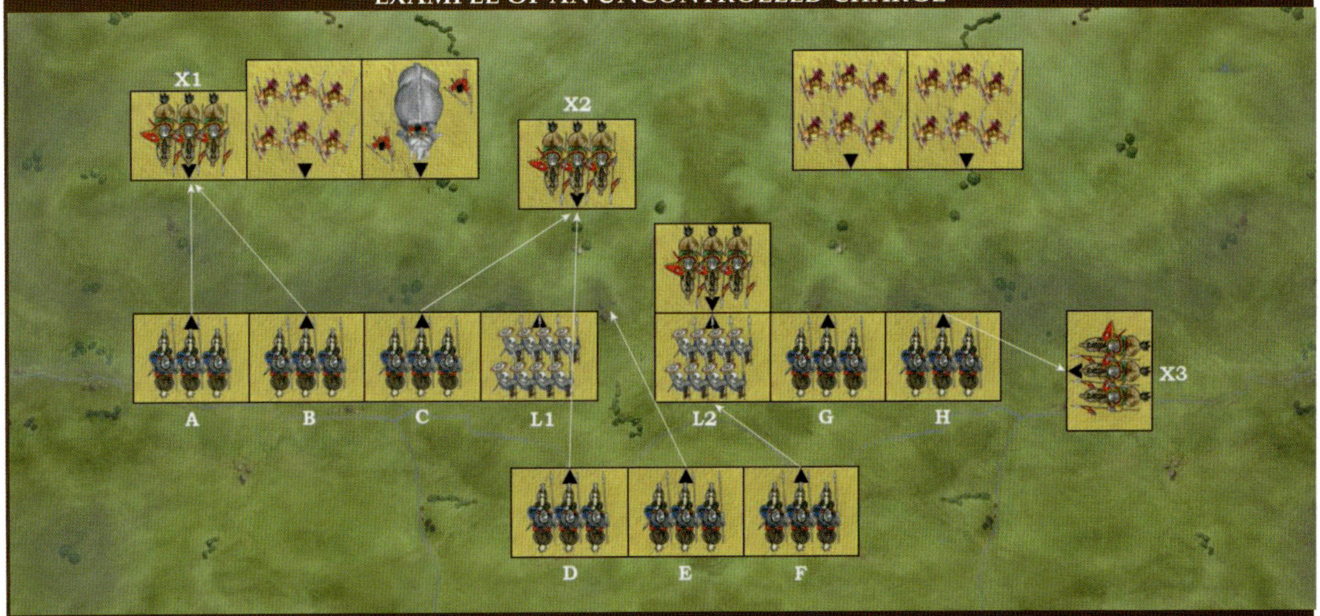

All cavalry units A to H are impetuous and are left without orders.

A and **B** have the same target, i.e the cavalry unit X1.
B does not make a charge against the infantry in front as it would result in contacting the elephant. Units A and B slide to the left to allow B to contact X1 with the support of A.
C ignores the elephant as it is not a valid target and must make an uncontrolled charge against the nearest valid target, which is the enemy cavalry X2, by bursting through the spearmen L1. L1 loses a cohesion point.
D has the cavalry to its front as a valid target. It makes an uncontrolled charge and bursts through the spearmen L1. Spearmen do not lose another cohesion point as they have already lost one because of cavalry C.
E has the cavalry to its front as a valid target. L2, being already in melee, cannot be burst through, so instead it advances in order to place itself in support next, and in support of, the spearmen L2. In doing so it bursts through L1 which must fall back to make place for it, but without losing any cohesion (the loss for being burst through is limited to one cohesion point per game-turn).
F also has the cavalry to its front as a valid target, but it cannot contact it or move to place itself in support, so instead it moves behind the spearmen L2, so to be as close to its target as possible.
G does is not subject to an uncontrolled charge because it is already in position to give support.
H has the enemy infantry to its front as a valid target. Since it is in the ZoC of enemy cavalry on its flank, it ignores the infantry and charges the enemy cavalry X3 as it is within charge range.

INTERPENETRATION

Interpenetration allows some troops to pass through others.

Interpenetrations allowed

The only allowed interpenetrations are:

- Separate commanders (i.e. those not included in a unit) can pass through and be passed through by all friendly troops in any direction.
- Light infantry can pass through all other friendly troops in any direction.
- All troops can pass through friendly light infantry in any direction.
- Light cavalry can pass through other friendly mounted troops, provided they are oriented in the same or opposite direction.
- All mounted troops can pass through friendly light cavalry, provided they are oriented in the same or opposite direction.
- Knights on foot and heavy or medium swordsmen that are non impetuous, can pass through friendly bowmen or crossbowmen (but not vice versa) provided they are oriented in the same or opposite direction. Mixed units and javelinmen cannot be interpenetrated.
- Foot units can pass through friendly artillery in any direction or through war wagons by the latter's long edge (i.e. across the narrowest part).

Special cases:

- Interpenetration is not allowed if the friendly unit to be passed through is in melee or is providing support to a friendly unit in melee.
- Mounted units cannot interpenetrate mounted that cause them panic. If mounted units are interpenetrated by other mounted that cause panic they are disordered and lose one cohesion point.
- Interpenetration is allowed during a charge or evade.

Adjusting positions

During interpenetration, the movement distance of the unit passing through friends must allow it to at least partially reach the other side of those friends. If the unit passed through cannot be fully crossed, the positions of the units are adjusted in the following way:

- If the unit passing through is light troops or a separate commander (i.e. one not included in a unit), it can advance the minimum distance necessary to fully cross the friendly unit.
- In the other cases the unit passing through makes its normal move and it is the unit being crossed that is displaced the minimum necessary to make room for them. This happens unless the unit passed through is artillery or war wagons, in which case the crossing unit must have enough movement to completely clear the base of the artillery or the war wagons, otherwise the interpenetration is not allowed.

If the movement distance is too short to cross the unit at least partially, or if there is not enough space to adjust the positions of the units, the interpenetration is not allowed. This can result in a group being broken up.

INTERPENETRATION

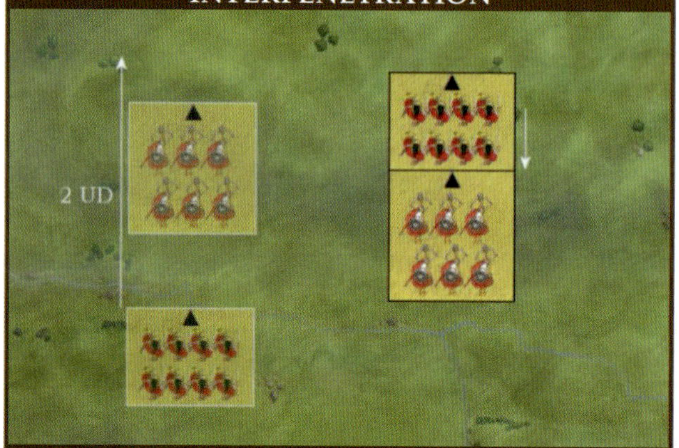

The swordsmen can only partially cross the bowmen. They therefore advance by 2 UD and the bowmen are moved back by the minimum distance needed to make room for the swordsmen.

Cataphracts on camels

DISENGAGE

This move allows a unit or a group that is in melee with the enemy to disengage from combat and fall back. It is possible only in the following cases:

- Light infantry fighting foot or elephant units.
- Light infantry fighting mounted units in terrain that penalises the mounted unit in combat.
- Mounted units, except elephants and scythed chariots, fighting foot or slower mounted units.
- Javelinmen fighting against heavy infantry or elephants.
- Any unit fighting against war wagons, artillery or fighting an enemy across a fortification.
- Any unit providing support by fighting against the flank or the rear of an enemy.

Disengaging is not allowed if:

- The front of an enemy is in contact with the unit's flank or rear.
- The unit is in the ZoC of another enemy unit to its flank or its rear.
- An obstacle (either a friend or enemy that cannot be interpenetrated or impassable terrain) is less than on UD directly behind the unit.

The disengage move is considered to be a difficult manoeuvre by unmanoeuvrable units and so the commander must then spend 2 CPs to make it.

A unit or group that disengages moves its full move minus one UD directly backwards while still facing towards the enemy. It must however stop if meets an obstacle or enemy ZoC excluding that of the enemy from which it is disengaging. It is possible to interpenetrate friendly units while disengaging.

The enemy with which the disengaging unit was in melee remains in place and neither unit is allowed to shoot.

Battle between Greeks and Persians

RALLYING

Securing ourselves against defeat lies in our own hands, but the opportunity of defeating the enemy is provided by himself.
Sun Tzu

PROCEDURE

Disordered units can try to regain one cohesion point by rallying during the movement phase. A disordered unit can attempt to rally instead of moving. It can still shoot or fight in melee.

RALLY TEST

Rally tests are made by rolling 1D6. If successful, the unit regains one cohesion point. If the attempt to rally fails, the amount of cohesion points remains the same. Only one rally attempt can be made for each unit per game-turn.

Rallying attempts are dealt with as follows:

- A unit more than 4 UD from all enemies will rally on a result of 3+. The corps commander does not need to spend a CP even if the commander is lost, engaged in a melee and/or the unit is out of command range.
- A unit 4 UD or less from an enemy unit, even if it is supporting a friend in combat by virtue of corner-to-corner or edge contact with the enemy, will rally on a result of 4+. The corps commander must spend 1 CP to make the rally attempt.
- A unit engaged in melee with an enemy will rally on a result of 5+. The corps commander must spend 2 CPs to make the rally attempt.
- Elephants and expendable units, due do their nature, cannot be rallied.

The quality of the unit does not affect the result of the die roll in a rally attempt.

PARTICULAR CASES

- If the unit is 4 UD or less from an enemy unit and is out of command range, the commander must spend one additional CP for the rally attempt.
- If the commander is attached to or included in a unit, the unit gains a bonus of +1 on the die roll for the rally attempt. A commander can only give a bonus to a single unit in each game-turn.
- The commander can move and be attached to the unit before the rally in order to give it a bonus.
- A commander can use its free command point to rally the unit it is included in or attached to.
- A commander engaged in melee must spend one additional CP to attempt to rally a unit other than the one it is attached to or included in.
- When a group with impetuous troops is held by spending 3 CPs, one rally attempt for one unit in the group is permitted at no extra CP cost. Other units can also attempt to rally for one additional CP for each rally attempt.

EXAMPLE OF RALLY

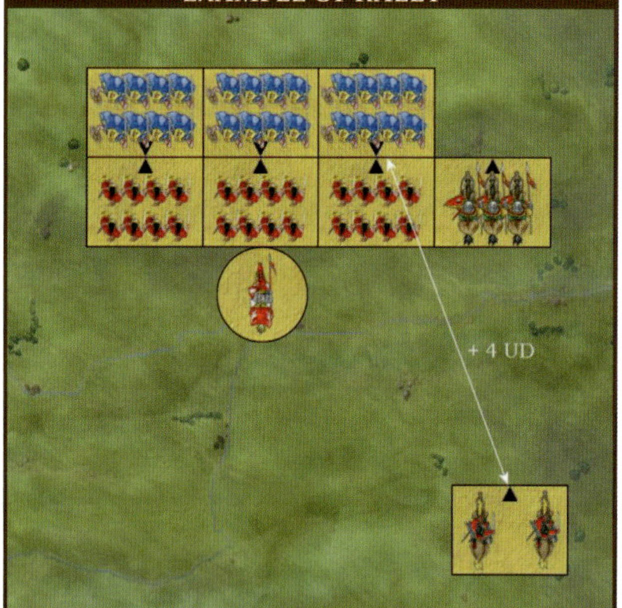

The Commander must spend 2 CP to attempt to rally one of the three heavy swordsmen units that are engaged in melee. It will be a success on a result of 5+. The unit situated in front of the commander has a +1 bonus and can therefore be rallied on a 4+.

The cavalry unit is supporting a friend in combat and can be rallied on a result of 4+ if the commander spends 1 CP.

The light cavalry unit can rally itself on a result of 3+without spending CP as it is situated at more than 4 UD of all enemies, even if it is also out of command range.

SHOOTING

The success of an operation lies in its preparation. Sun Tzu

OVERVIEW

Units equipped with missile weapons can fight at distance without risk, except from shooting. Those units are:

- Light infantry,
- Javelinmen,
- Bowmen or crossbowmen,
- Medium swordsmen equipped with bows or spear-throwers (atlatl),
- Mixed units with bows or crossbows,
- Light cavalry or light camelry with bows, crossbows, javelins or firearms,
- Medium cavalry, medium camelry, heavy cavalry or chariots with bows, crossbows or firearms,
- Light, medium and heavy artillery,
- War wagons.

Units can shoot during both the player's phase and during the opponent's phase. The order of shooting is chosen by the phasing player but all shots are considered simultaneous. Enemy units that were disordered or eliminated by shooting earlier in the phase can shoot back without taking those effects into account.

SHOOTING LIMITATIONS

- Artillery and war wagons that have moved or wheeled cannot shoot during the player's phase.
- Other units can shoot after they have moved as long as they have not made a second or third move.
- A unit that has charged, evaded, disengaged, pursued or retreated out of an enemy ZoC cannot shoot in the same player phase.
- A unit engaged in melee or supporting a friend in melee cannot shoot.
- A unit cannot shoot at an enemy engaged in melee or one supporting another unit in melee (even if only by corner-to-corner contact).
- A unit cannot shoot at an enemy unit it cannot see: i.e. in ambush, hidden behind a hill or out of *line of sight* (see below).

SHOOTING RANGES

The table below gives shooting ranges for each type of missile weapon. The effective range depends on both the weapon and the type of troops using it. For example, LI or LH shoots at shorter range than foot bowmen. This is because the former tended to rely on individual accuracy whereas the latter relied more on the volume of shooting.

Missile weapon	Range
LI or LH with javelins, Javelinmen MI with atlatls	1
LI or LH with slings, bows, crossbows or firearms	2
Cv with bows, crossbows or firearms	2
LMI, MI or HI with bows or crossbows	4
War wagon, Light artillery	4
Medium artillery	6
Heavy artillery	8

A unit can only shoot at a target that is at maximum range or less. Simply measure the shortest straight-line distance between the unit's shooting edge and the nearest part of the target's base, including optional stands (e.g. pikemen).

TARGET SELECTION

Target priority

If several targets are eligible, the shooter must choose the target using following priorities:

- Firstly, the nearest target directly in front of the shooter (even partially).
- Otherwise, the nearest target in the shooter's arc of fire but not directly in front of the shooter.

Special cases:

- If multiple targets are at equal distance, the player must choose the target *most in front* if there is one, otherwise any target.
- As light cavalry/camelry shoot with an arc of 360°, they always choose the nearest target.
- Heavy and medium artillery shooting at more than 4 UD can choose any target in the arc of fire.

Arc of fire

A unit can shoot at a target at maximum range or less and in its arc of fire. The arc of fire of a unit is a rectangle directly in front of its shooting edge (normally its front), which is the unit's shooting range long and the width of the shooting edge plus 1 UD on either side wide (see below).

ARC OF FIRE

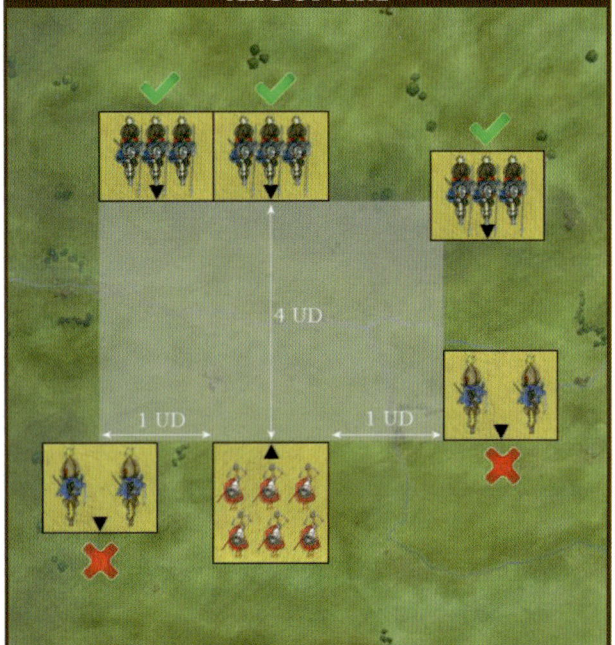

Targets with a red cross are not included in the arc of fire of the bowmen.

Special cases:

- Light cavalry and light camelry can shoot 360°, which means that their arc of fire extends all around them. The arc of fire, the line of sight and range measurement can be taken from any side of the unit's base, not just the front edge.
- Light chariots can also shoot from the rear edge with a -1 penalty.
- War wagons shoot only from one flank which is one of the long edges. They cannot shoot from their front.
- Heavy and medium artillery shooting at more than 4 UD has its width of arc of fire increased to 2 UD on either side of its base.

Line of sight (LoS)

To shoot, a unit must be able to see its target and be able to trace straight lines between the two corners of its shooting edge and a single point on one edge of the target's base. These lines must not cross any obstacle, i.e. terrain that blocks LoS or other units, whether friends or enemies (see diagram).

LINE OF SIGHT

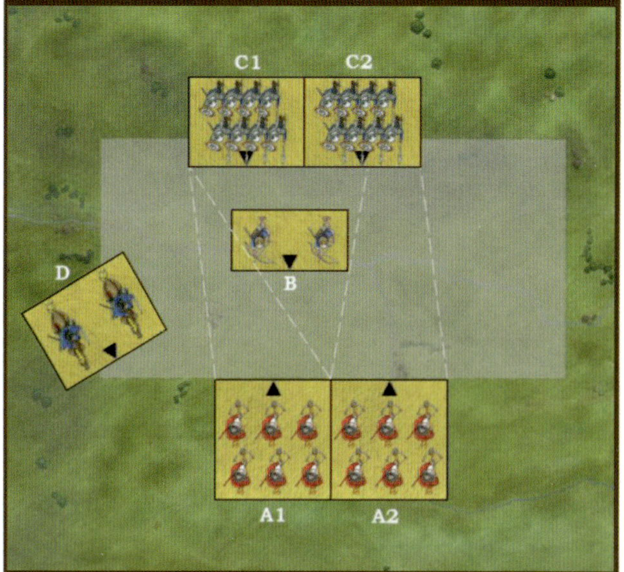

Unit B blocks the line of sight of bowmen A1 and A2 to C1. By contrast C2 is in the line of sight of bowmen A2.

Unit D is the nearest target to A1 but it is not directly in front of the bowmen.

Unit B is situated directly in front of the two units of bowmen and so it is the priority target for both A1 and A2.

Multiple shooters at the same target

A unit can only be shot at once per phase. Therefore the shooting of all units against the same target must be resolved together in one calculation.

If several shooters have the same target, the player can choose which unit will be the main shooter. Additional units that shoot at the same target give support to the main shooter. Each unit gives a +1 bonus on the die roll. This bonus cannot exceed +3.

In the example above, the two bowmen units A1 and A2 concentrate their shooting on the light infantry B. The main shooter will be choosen by the player.

Shooting resolution

The players controlling the main shooter and the target each roll 1D6, which is modified by the quality of the units. The target adds its protection value (0 to +3) to its result.

The main shooter adds to its result the relevant modifiers from the following table:

Circumstance	Mod.
LI or LH shooting	-1
Target in cover or behind a fortification	-1
Shooter is disordered	-1
Shooting from cover or in difficult terrain except if shooter is LI	-1
For each supporting unit (max +3)	+1
LMI, MI, HI with bows or crossbows shooting at mounted (see Note)	+1

Note: Units of LMI, MI or HI armed with bows or crossbows and shooting at mounted unit have a +1 bonus. This simulates the greater vulnerability of mounted units to the massed volleys of medium and heavy infantry. Light troops, javelinmen and WWg do not get this bonus.

Shooting results

If the result of the shooter is higher than that of the target, the target loses one cohesion point. The cohesion loss by shooting is limited to just one point per phase. This represents the lesser effectiveness of shooting, compared to the melee. If the result of the shooter is equal to or less than the result of the target, then there is no effect.

When two units shoot at each other, shooting is resolved in two steps: A shoots at B and then B shoots at A. The results are applied simultaneously after the two steps are resolved. Therefore it is possible that both units lose one point of cohesion or that they each rout during the same shooting phase.

Protection modifiers

Crossbows and firearms: These weapons are capable of piercing heavy armour. However they have a slower rate of fire than bows. They are less effective against targets with little or no protection because their slow rate of fire is not offset by any extra penetrating power. Therefore all units are considered to have a basic protection value of 1 against crossbows and firearms, except war wagons and elephants.

War wagons: Their crews can be armed with bows, crossbows, firearms or light artillery as indicated in the army list. The corresponding modifier should be applied.

Longbows: This powerful weapon is very effective against most kinds of target. All units except war wagons, artillery and all light troops reduce their basic protection by one. However their protection cannot be lower than zero.

Artillery: Armour is useless against artillery. All units (including artillery, war wagons and those equipped with pavises) have a protection value equal to zero if they receive artillery fire. Light troops are the only exception and keep their protection value of 1, which is due to their dispersion rather than their armour.

Pavises: Pavises add +1 to the protection of the unit after the crossbows, firearms or longbows modifier is applied. Pavises offer no protection against artillery. The protection of pavises plus the protection of armour cannot exceed 3 points in total. The protection bonus of pavises cannot be added to those of terrain cover or fortifications.

Terrain cover and fortifications: The cover given by terrain or fortifications is effective only if the line of sight of the shooter goes through the terrain or the fortification. If the two units are separated by more than one UD of terrain that gives cover (in a wood for example) shooting is not possible. Stakes do not give any protection.

Light troops and shooting support

Light troops have a slower rate of shooting than other shooting units. Therefore they are less effective when they shoot in support. Each unit of light troops that shoots in support of another unit, counts only as half a unit. The number of supports is then rounded up to give the final modifier.

Thus, one unit of light troops gives a +1 bonus to the main shooter, but there must be at least three units of light troops units for a bonus of +2 and at least five units for a bonus of +3.

Longbowmen

EXAMPLE OF SHOOTING

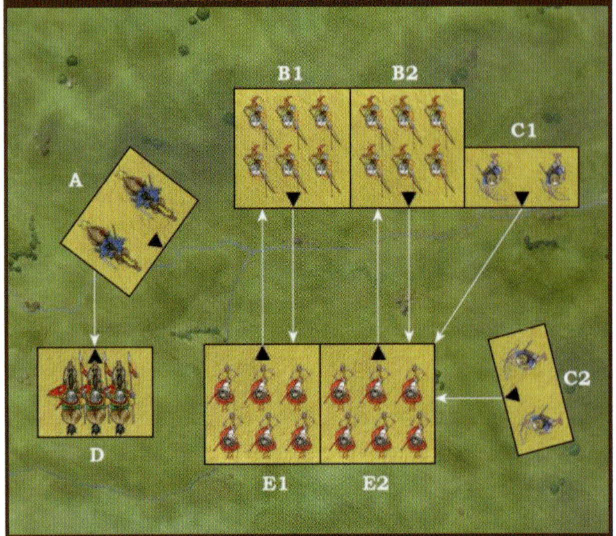

Light cavalry unit A must shoot at the nearest target which is the heavy cavalry D. The player rolls a dice modified by -1, as it is LH shooting, and has a final result of 3. The target rolls a 2 modified by +1 for its protection with a result of 3. The shot has no effect.

Bowmen unit B1 can shoot at E1 or E2 but as E1 is the most directly in front, this target takes priority. B1 rolls 1 and E1 rolls a 6. The shot has no effect.

Bowmen unit B2 shoots at E2 with the support of C1 and C2. As C1 and C2 are both light troops, the total bonus for support is only +1. The player rolls a 4 modified by the support bonus of +1 to a final result of 5. E2 rolls only 4 and so loses one cohesion point.

Shots are simultaneous thus the enemy units shoot before losses take effect: E1 shoots at B1 and E2 at B2.

SPECIFIC CASES

Shooting overhead

It is possible to shoot over intervening friendly units in the following cases:

- Troops situated on higher ground can shoot over friends if the target is more than one UD away from these friendly units.
- Artillery can shoot over friendly light infantry and light cavalry on the same level if the target is more than one UD away from the light infantry or cavalry.
- Artillery can shoot over enemy light infantry and light cavalry without any restriction.
- LH can shoot in support of another LH with the same armament if it is aligned corner to corner and in contact just behind. The shooting range is measured from the front edge of the front unit.

Mixed units

Mixed units have the same shooting ability as units of bowmen or crossbowmen. The normal quality of the unit is used for shooting, unlike melee where the quality is downgraded by one level. This represent that mixed unit have less melee fighters than others units.

In mixed units, shooters that are located in the rear rank shoot over the front rank without penalty. The shooting range is measured from the front edge of the unit's base. Indeed these units are trained to exchange their ranks. The shooters go back to the rear ranks only with the threat of melee.

French ordonnance archers are ready to shoot

Melee

Invincibility lies in the defence; the possibility of victory in the attack. Sun Tzu

General Principles

The melee phase occurs after all movement and shooting has been made. Units in contact with an enemy will fight in melee. The following section describes the concepts used for resolving the melee.

Charge

A charge is a movement that allows a unit to initiate a melee with a new enemy by contacting it with its front edge. A unit that starts its movement already in contact with an enemy (e.g. only by a corner) cannot charge it, but can move into melee with it by simply conforming. A move into contact with an enemy already in melee, in order to provide support to a friend, is not a charge.

Melee

A unit is considered in melee in the following cases:

- It is in contact with an enemy's front edge (i.e. not just by the enemy's front corner).
- It is in contact with at least part of its front edge (i.e. not just by its front corner) against the flank or the rear of an enemy.

A melee can last one or more phases and ends when all units of the same side are routed or disengage.

Main unit

A melee is always resolved using the melee factors and modifiers of only one friendly unit and one enemy. When several friendly units are in contact with the same enemy, only the main unit fights, while other units give support to it. The main unit is the one in contact with the enemy's front edge, or the first unit that contacted the enemy if the enemy is only contacted on its flank or rear.

Support

A unit engaged in melee can receive support from other friendly units **that are not engaged in melee with another enemy**. Each supporting unit adds a +1 bonus to the melee die roll. Support can be provided by a unit in one of the following situations:

- The unit is in contact with its front edge (i.e. not just by its front corner) against the flank or the rear of the enemy.
- The unit is aligned and in front corner to front corner contact with a friendly unit that is **engaged in melee on its front edge** against an enemy unit other than a WWg.
- The unit is in contact with a part of its flank edge (i.e. not just by a single corner) against all or a part of the flank edge of an enemy unit other than a WWg, which is engaged in a melee on its front edge. A supporting unit must be oriented either in the same direction as the enemy or in the opposite direction.

Special cases:

- A unit in contact with its flank edge against the rear edge of an enemy cannot provide support against that enemy.
- A unit can be supported by a maximum of three units: one on each flank and one on the rear of the enemy. Each supporting unit adds a +1 bonus to the melee die roll.
- A unit can provide support to a maximum of two friendly units, one on each flank.
- Panic caused by camels or elephants does not cancel mounted support. Only units **engaged in melee** with an enemy are affected by the panic from contact with camels or elephants, even if that contact is only by a single corner.
- War wagons follow special rules (see p 60).

Byzantine cavalry

EXAMPLE OF SUPPORT N°1

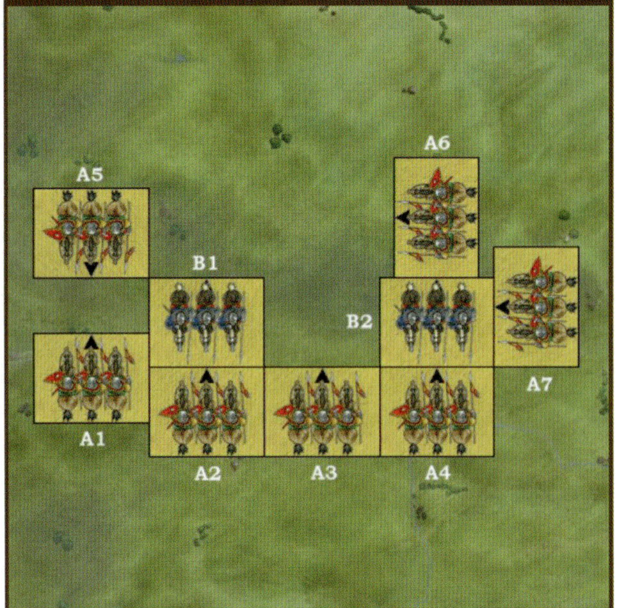

A2 and B1 are engaged in a melee.
A1 and A3 provide support to A2 against B1.
A5 does not provide support as it is only in contact with a single corner.

A4 and B2 are engaged in melee.
A3 and A7 provide support to A4 against B2.
A6 does not provide support as it is in contact, with its flank, against the rear of an enemy.

EXAMPLE OF SUPPORT N°2

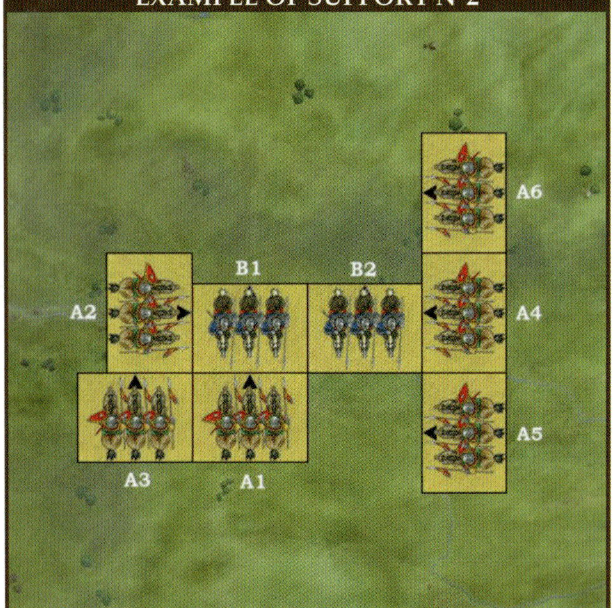

A1 and B1 are engaged in a melee.
A2 and A3 can provide support to A1 but as they are on the same flank, only one support is counted.

B2 does not provide support to B1 as it is already engaged in a melee with A4.

A5 and A6 each provide support to A4 against B2.

TYPES OF CONTACT

A unit can contact an enemy on its front edge, on its flank or on its rear.

Front contact

An attacking unit can contact the front edge of an enemy if it begins its movement with its front edge either entirely or partially in front of the straight line extending the enemy's front edge.

Flank contact

An attacking unit can contact the nearest flank edge of an enemy if it begins its movement with its front edge either entirely or partially directly to the flank of the enemy (i.e. in the zone between the straight lines extending the enemy's front and rear edges) provided no part of the attacking unit's front edge is directly in front of the enemy's front or rear edge.

Rear contact

An attacking unit can contact the rear edge of an enemy if it begins its movement with its front edge either entirely or partially behind the straight line extending the enemy's rear edge.

TYPES OF CONTACT

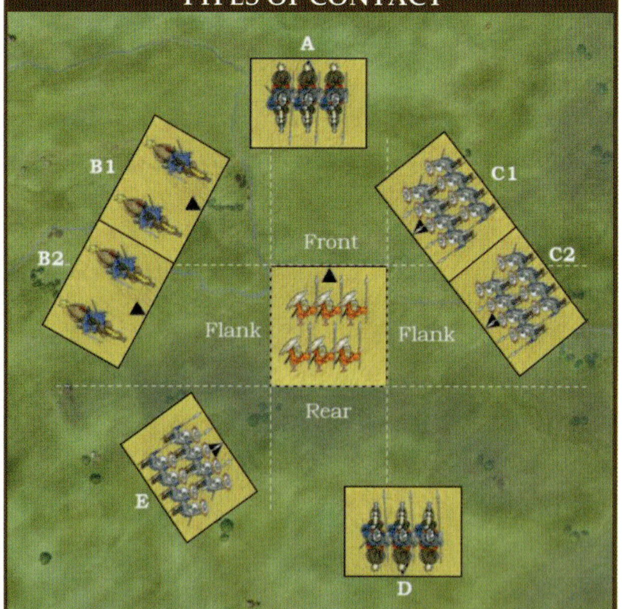

A can contact the enemy's front.
B1 can contact the enemy's front but not its flank.
B2 can contact either the enemy's front or its flank.

C1 can only contact the enemy's front as part of its front edge is directly in front of the enemy.
C2 can contact the enemy's flank only.
D can contact the enemy's rear only.
E can contact either the enemy's flank or rear.

Contact restrictions

Some units are not intended to engage in melee and can only contact the enemy under certain conditions:

- Bowmen, crossbowmen and light cavalry can only charge an enemy if:
    - The target is light troops, artillery or the enemy camp, **or**
    - Contact is made on the flank or rear of the enemy, **or**
    - The target is a foot unit that is providing support to a friend in melee.
- LH can also charge an enemy frontally if the LH has the *impact* ability or if the enemy is disordered.
- Mixed unit can charge foot unit with no restriction. They can contact mounted units that are in melee or charge them in flank or rear.
- Light infantry can only charge an enemy if:
    - The target is light infantry, artillery, scythed chariots, elephants or the enemy camp **or**
    - The target is in rough or difficult terrain **and** one of the following cases apply:
        - Penalised in melee in such terrain, **or**
        - Attacked in the flank or on the rear, **or**
        - Disordered.
- War wagons and artillery can never charge an enemy or enter into contact to provide a support.

A unit (except WWg and Art) can always contact an enemy to provide support if this enemy is already engaged in melee when the unit makes contact. For instance, a LI can contact an enemy in open terrain to provide support.

Illegal contact

In some situations (after an evade move or a pursuit for instance), a unit is able to contact an enemy that it is not normally allowed to contact because of its type or its position. This is called an illegal contact. The unit must stop its movement just before contacting the enemy.

Destruction of light infantry

If a light infantry unit is contacted at least partially in open terrain by a charging unit of LMI, MI, HI, Cv or Kn whose front is entirely in open terrain, it is destroyed unless the light infantry unit can evade. Light infantry is also destroyed if contacted in open terrain by an opponent other than light troops or elephants during the pursuit phase. LI is not destroyed by camels in sand dunes or brush.

A light infantry unit that is destroyed due to being contacted in open terrain is removed from the table after the resolution of all melees. The attacking unit stops its movement at the point of contact without conforming.

Following a rout or a disengagement from melee, if a light infantry unit would remain in contact (even by a single corner) with an enemy which could destroy it automatically (for example heavy infantry), it is immediately moved back one UD to break contact. If this move is blocked by another enemy, the light infantry is destroyed.

German knights

Conforming

Conforming is used to align opposing units corner to corner in order to simplify the resolution of melee.

Conforming is mandatory unless it forces a friendly or enemy unit to leave the table or to enter terrain **in which the unit is penalised in melee**. In the last case the player may choose whether to conform his units or not. Only the phasing player can conform his troops.

After initial contact is made, the unit continues to move by sliding and/or wheeling up to one UD in order to align corner to corner with the enemy the most in front:

- In the case of front or flank contact, the unit must be aligned with its front corner against the enemy's front corner.
- In case of rear contact, unit must be aligned with its front corner against the enemy's rear corner.

The bonus of one UD distance is only for conforming and is not added to the movement distance. If the unit or group does not have sufficient distance to make the initial contact, it cannot charge the enemy.

If the conforming unit is part of a group, the entire group can, if the player wishes, be moved a maximum of one UD by sliding and/or wheeling, thus maintaining the integrity of the group. Units that had not originally contacted the enemy can therefore become engaged in melee.

CONFORMING TO THE ENEMY

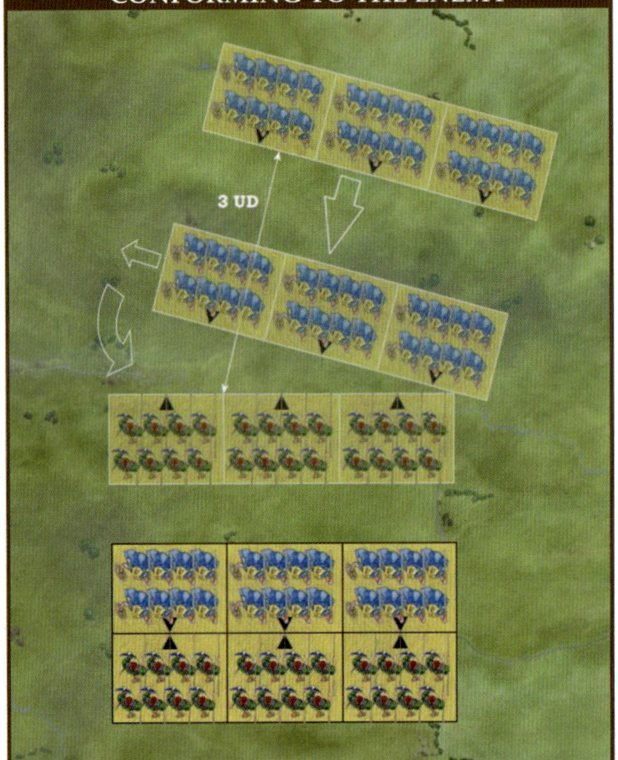

A group of medium swordsmen contacts an enemy group of heavy swordsmen at 3 UD.

After the first contact, the group is conformed to the enemy by sliding and wheeling in order to be aligned corner to corner with the enemy.

Conforming and ZoC

During a conform move, a unit must consider an enemy ZoC that may prevent attacks on the flank or rear because the unit cannot conform correctly due to not being allowed to enter a ZoC.

CONFORMING AND ZOC

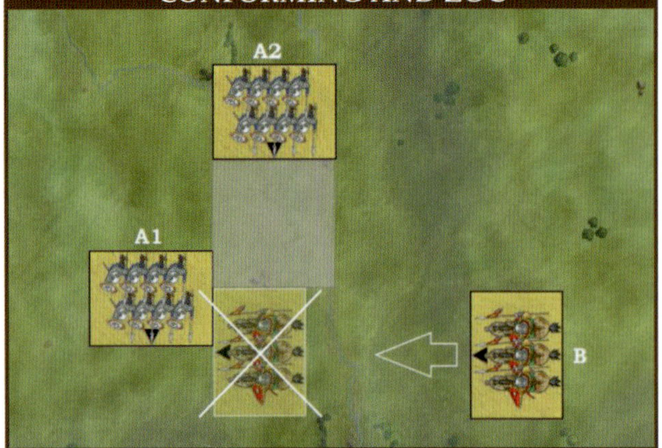

The unit B cannot attack A1 on its flank because it will enter in the ZoC of A2 during the conformation. A slide inside an enemy ZoC is not allowed.

Conforming and displacing units

If necessary to allow room for units to conform, it is allowed to displace **friendly and/or enemy troops that are not already engaged in melee.** Moving units must respect the following rules:

- In priority friendly units, then enemy units
- The minimum number units (one if possible)
- Units are moved the minimum space necessary in priority to the rear or to the flank.

A unit in support can be displaced only if it remains in the position of support. This displacement can lead to a unit either leaving or entering an enemy ZoC unintentionally. A unit displaced in this way can move as usual during its movement phase.

Gallic warriors

DISPLACING A UNIT

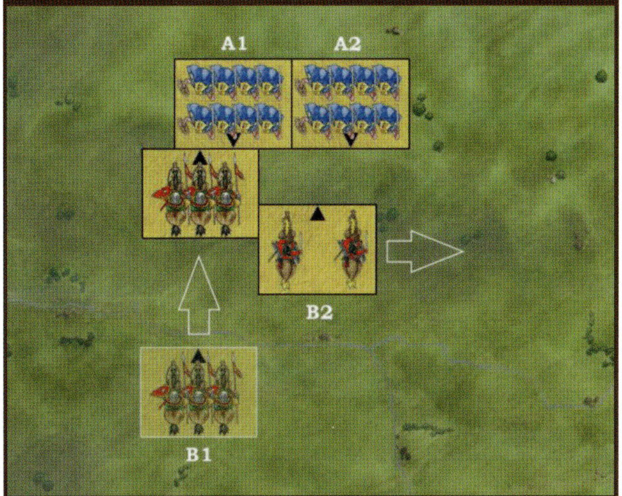

Cavalry unit B1 charges A1 and conforms. Unit B2 is displaced to the right and leaves the ZoC of A1.

Unable to conform

In some situations it may be impossible for a unit contacting the front of an enemy to conform. This does not prevent the melee, which is resolved normally. The main opponents are those units that are most in front of each other. The units must conform as soon as possible.

If a unit attacks an enemy on the flank or the rear, it must conform correctly so that it can be considered a valid *attack on the flank or rear*, with all its advantages (see p 56). If a unit is unable to conform, the contact is illegal and therefore not allowed.

CONFORMING AND TERRAIN

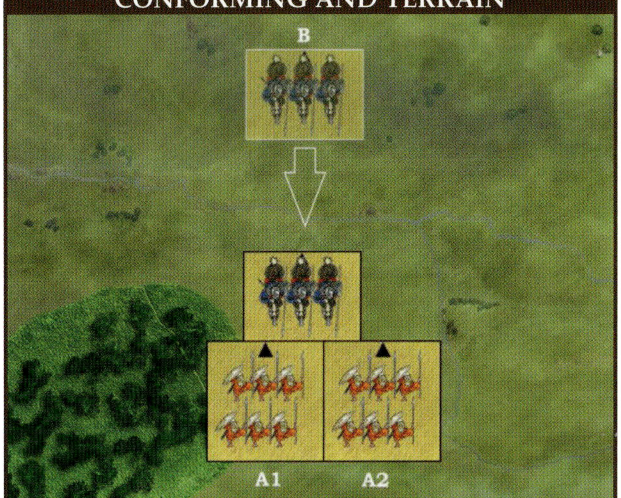

Unit B does not have to conform to A1 as this would move it into terrain that penalises it in a melee. Combat occurs between B and A1, which will be supported by A2. During its phase A1 must conform to B because the open terrain does not give a combat penalty to MI. A2 will be displaced to the right and will remain in position to support A1.

IMPOSSIBLE TO CONFORM

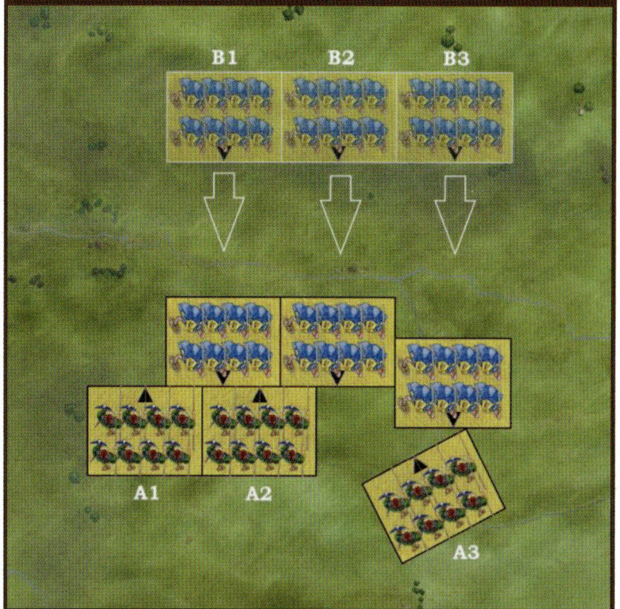

B1, B2 and B3 are aligned and charge straight ahead. They contact enemies A1 and A2 but as they are impetuous, B3 continues and contacts A3

B1 is in melee with A2 which is the enemy that is the most in front but it cannot conform.

There will be a melee between B1 and A2, respectively supported by B2 and A1

B3 is in melee with A3 but cannot conform because it would require displacing B2 which is supporting B1 in melee against A2.

During the next phase, A2 will conform to B1 by displacing A1 to the left and A3 will conform to B3.

Units more than one UD deep

Units with a depth greater than one UD (pikemen and units with *missile support*) can be difficult to conform. If necessary, it is possible to temporarily remove the rear stand to allow the unit to conform or to make a move as a flank attack, for example.

Conforming after a flank attack

Units, except WWg, that are contacted on the flank or rear must be turned and conformed at the end of the melee phase unless they are already in melee with another enemy on their front edge.

If a unit that has been contacted on both its front and its flank or rear routs the enemy to its front, it cannot pursue. Instead it must conform at the end of the phase to the enemy whose front edge is contacting it, at the player's choice if there is more than one.

Conforming after a melee

After a rout or disengage move a unit may still be in contact with the enemy without being in melee or in a position to support a friend in melee: front corner against front corner or side by side for example.

The phasing player is allowed to conform such units without expending CP. Conforming in this manner is not considered a charge. Abilities like *impact* or *javelin* and the effect of *furious charge* do not apply. The enemy unit that is contacted can evade if it is allowed to (see p 37).

Conforming like this is not compulsory except for impetuous units that are subject to an uncontrolled charge against the enemy unit concerned. For other units the player can choose to make another move (including a charge against another enemy) or not to move his units at all. The rules for contacting the side or rear of an enemy and the restrictions on contact remain valid for this particular kind of conformation.

CONFORMING: EXAMPLE 1

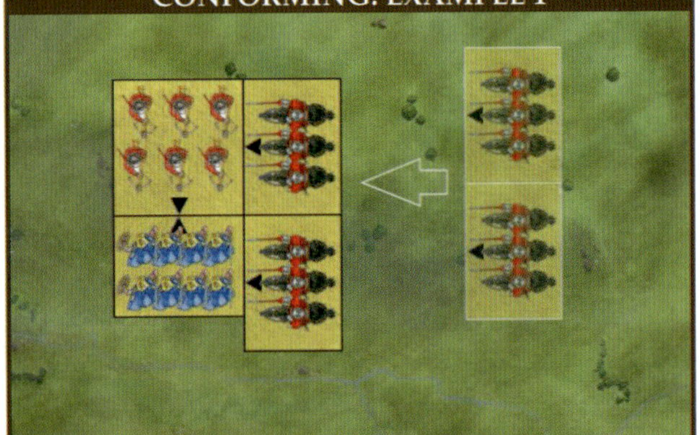

Two cavalry units contact the flank of a heavy infantry unit already in melee. They conform to the heavy infantry by aligning front corner to front corner.

CONFORMING: EXAMPLE 2

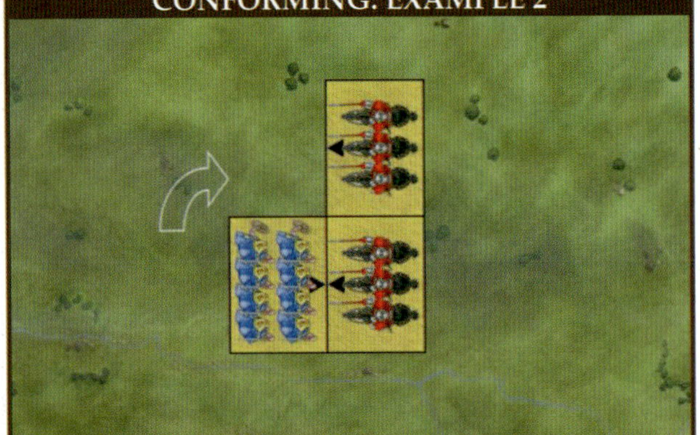

The heavy infantry destroys its opponent. It has to conform to the cavalry in contact with its flank. The infantry make a quarter-turn and align front corner to front corner. The cavalry cannot evade as it is in contact with enemy by its front edge.

CONFORMING: EXAMPLE 3

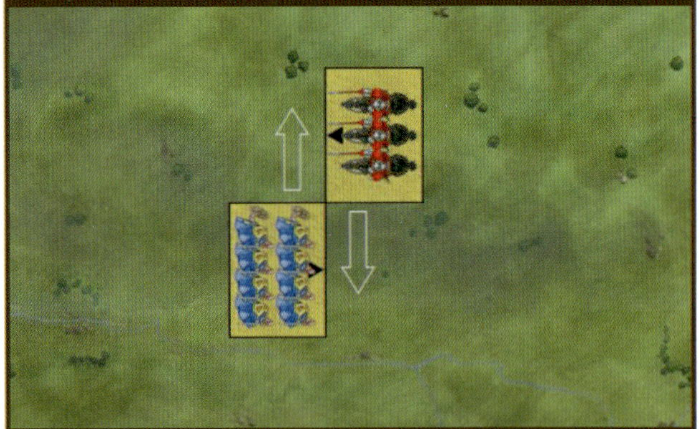

The heavy infantry then destroys the cavalry. The two remaining units can therefore conform to each other. The cavalry can evade as it is not in contact with enemy by its front edge.

MELEE RESOLUTION

The phasing player determines the order in which to resolve all of the melees during the melee phase. As in the shooting phase, effects of melees are considered simultaneous.

To resolve a melee, each player throws a die, modifies it by the unit's quality, and adds all other melee factors and modifiers. The two results are then compared:

- The unit with the highest result wins the melee.
- If a unit wins by 1 or 2 points, its opponent loses 1 cohesion point.
- If a unit wins by 3 or 4 points, its opponent loses 2 cohesion points.
- If a unit wins by 5 or 6 points, its opponent loses 3 cohesion points.
- If a unit wins by 7 points or more, its opponent is automatically routed.
- In the case of a tie, no cohesion points are lost.

MELEE MODIFIERS

Quality modifier

The Quality modifier is applied **before** all other melee factors and modifiers.

- Elite troops add 1 point to the result if the die roll is 3 or less.
- Mediocre troops subtract 1 point from the result if the die roll is 4 or more.

Basic factor

Each troop type has a basic factor according to the main opponent it faces. These modifiers are displayed in the unit characteristics tables on p 20. For instance, heavy spearmen have a basic factor of +1 against all foot units.

The basic factor is reduced to zero if the unit is attacked on its flank or rear by an enemy unit other than light troops (see p 56).

Some abilities *(impact, javelin* or *missile support*) are only effective during the first round of a melee (e.g immediately after a charge) and only against an enemy in melee on the unit's front edge. If the melee continues, these modifiers are not applied in subsequent rounds.

Mixed units: A mixed unit always fights as swordsmen or spearmen depending on the unit's troop type. This is the case even if the unit is attacked on the flank or rear. During a melee, a mixed unit is always considered to be one level lower in quality (e.g. mediocre instead of ordinary).

Support modifier

A unit may be supported by up to three friendly units: one on each flank and one to the rear of the enemy. There are specific rules for some troop types:

Scythed chariots: A unit in melee with the front edge (other than by a single corner) of an enemy scythed chariot cannot be supported by friendly units during the first round of a melee after a charge. If the melee continues after the first phase, support modifiers do apply. Scythed chariots can support a friendly unit normally.

War wagons: Only those units in contact by their front edge (other than by a single corner) with a war wagon count as supporting a friendly unit in melee with that war wagon (see p 60).

Disorder modifier

If a unit has lost one or more cohesion points, it is disordered and has a -1 modifier to all its melee and shooting rolls. The modifier is limited to -1 even if it has lost more than one cohesion point.

Situation modifier

If the main unit of a melee is situated on the flank or rear of the enemy, it has a +1 modifier for the melee.

Attacked on the flank or the rear

A unit (except WWg) charged on its flank or rear by an enemy other than light troops, has its basic factor **reduced to zero**. If the unit is also disordered, its basic factor will be equal to -1.

The same applies to a unit in melee with several enemies, except if all the enemies attacking the unit's flank or the rear are light troops (see p 59).

Spartan warriors with Leonidas

When a unit is attacked on its flank or rear, the following rules apply:

- *Impact, javelin, 2HW* and *missile support* abilities are cancelled (even if attacked by light troops),
- The unit cannot benefit from the effect of a *furious charge,*
- The unit cannot cancel the abilities of enemies that are in melee against its flanks or its rear (e.g. troops with *impact* cancelling the *javelin* ability or spearmen cancelling the *impact* ability of mounted units).
- *Armour* and *heavy armour* abilities, as well as the *panic* caused by elephants and camels, still apply.

The effects of being attacked on the flank or rear are effective as long as the unit has an enemy in melee against its flank or its rear.

In order for an attack on a flank or rear to be valid, the attacking unit must be able to conform and be aligned corner to corner with the enemy (see p 52). If, for whatever reason, conforming is not possible, then the attack on the flank or rear is illegal.

Terrain modifiers

Some troops are at a disadvantage in rough or difficult terrain and so are penalised during the melee. A unit receives the penalty for being in the terrain if any part of its base (excluding optional stands for pikemen or *missile support*) is situated in the terrain. If a melee occurs just on the edge of a terrain, both units are considered to be in the terrain.

Foot units

- HI or WWg: -1 in rough terrain or -2 if heavy spearmen or pikemen. -2 for all types in difficult terrain.
- MI or LMI: -1 in difficult terrain.

Mounted units

- -2 in rough terrain and -3 in difficult terrain.

Special cases

- Camels consider brush as open terrain. They are not penalised in melee when they are in sand dunes but count such terrain as rough for movement.
- Light camelry in melee against LI in sand dunes or brush have a basic factor of zero. The *furious charge* ability applies in this case.
- Cavalry does not automatically destroy LI in rough and difficult terrain. It has a basic factor of +1 plus terrain modifiers.
- Elephants count fields and brush as open terrain.
- Mounted units that are in a terrain that results in a penalty in melee cannot use the *impact* ability or the effect of *furious charge.*

Height advantage

Units that are on a hill and are higher than their opponents receive a +1 bonus in combat for the height advantage.

A unit receives the height advantage if it is entirely on the hill and if the highest point (or ridge) of the hill is located behind the line that extends its front edge. If two opposing units are at the highest point or ridge line, then none has the height advantage.

HEIGHT ADVANTAGE

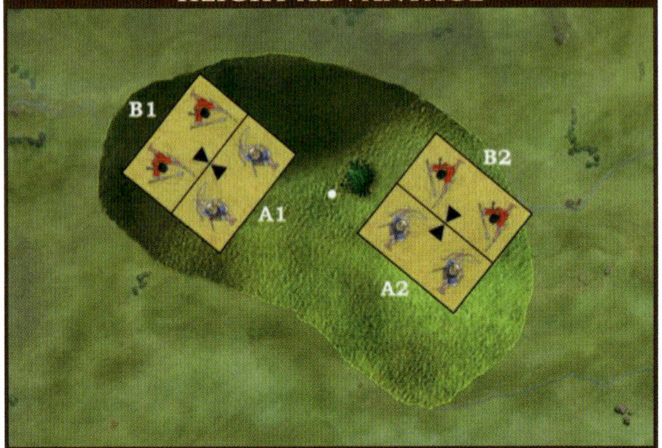

Units A1 and A2 have the height advantage against their opponents relative to the top of the hill (indicated by the white point).

Riverbank

A unit defending a riverbank gets a +1 bonus in combat if it is not itself in the river (even partially) and if it is fighting against an enemy that is at least partially in the river.

Edge of a gully

A unit defending a gully edge gets a +1 bonus in combat if it is not itself in the gully (even partially) and if it is fighting against an enemy that is at least partially in the gully.

Presence of a commander

When a commander is attached to a unit, he can choose to be engaged in the melee. The player must clearly state the decision before rolling the dice for the melee. If in doubt the commander is not engaged. If the commander is engaged in melee, the unit receives a +1 bonus in combat but the commander risks being lost if the unit loses the melee (see p 24). Commanders included in a unit are automatically treated as engaged in a melee involving their unit.

COMBAT EXAMPLE 1

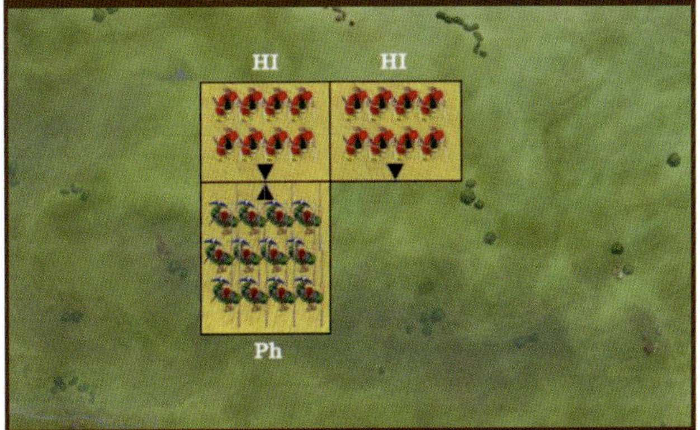

A unit of pikemen opposes two units of heavy swordsmen with the *armour* ability.

Heavy swordsmen have a +1 factor in combat against other foot units whereas pikemen have a +2 factor. The heavy swordsmen unit is supported by the friendly unit on the right bringing both to equal factors. The Heavy swordsmen roll a die and get a 2 while the pikemen get a 5. As the swordsmen have the *armour* ability, their final result is equal to 3. With a final difference of (5-3) = 2 points, the swordsmen lose the melee and one cohesion point (instead of two points if they had not had *armour*).

COMBAT EXAMPLE 2

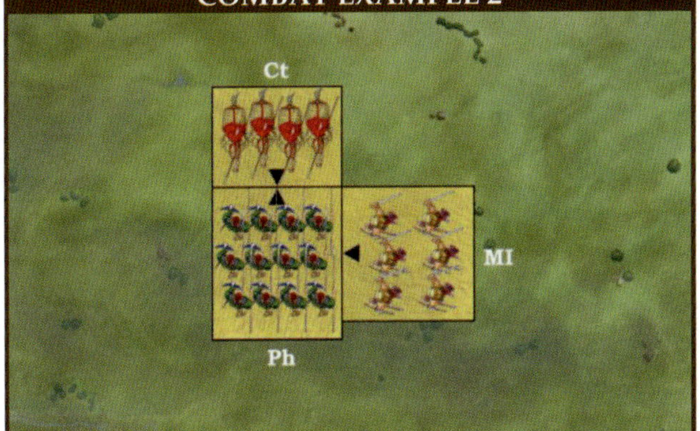

A unit of pikemen unit is attacked by a unit of elite cataphracts and a unit of medium swordsmen.

Cataphracts have a +1 factor in combat against foot units and are supported by the swordsmen which bring them to a factor of +2. Their *impact* ability is cancelled by the pikemen having been charged on their front edge. The pikemen are attacked by multiple opponents with one of them on their flank and so are disordered and lose one cohesion point. Thus, the basic factor of pikemen is equal to zero (instead of +2) and they also lose their *impact* ability. The final modifier for the pikemen is -1 as they are disordered. The cataphracts roll a die and get a 1 modified to 2 as they are elite and then to 4 with their +2 factor. The pikemen get a 6 modified by -1 to 5 and so win the melee! However, the cataphracts have +1 for their *heavy armour* which makes the results equal, so they do not lose any cohesion.

FURIOUS CHARGE

Some units rely on a particularly powerful charge to rout their opponents swiftly. This is particularly true when mounted units charge foot units. This is called a *furious charge*.

If a unit with the *furious charge* ability wins the first round of a melee (i.e. after a charge), it inflicts the loss of one additional cohesion point to the enemy.

<u>Example:</u> Impetuous heavy swordsmen charge heavy spearmen. The heavy swordsmen unit has a +1 bonus for impact. It rolls a 5 modified to 6 and its adversary a 4. The difference is 2 points and so the heavy spearmen lose one cohesion point. With the furious charge ability, the loss is increased to 2 cohesion points.

The *furious charge* ability only applies against foot units and has no effect against mounted units. It only applies during the first round of a melee if the unit charges or is charged on its front edge. If the combat takes place due to conforming after a melee (see p 55) or because of a pursuit, the *furious charge* does not apply as there was no charge.

Troops with the *furious charge* ability are:

- Impetuous foot (including levies) against all foot units,
- Cv and Kn that are impetuous or have the *impact* ability against all foot units,
- Other Cv and Kn, but only against LMI,
- LH against LI
- Elephants and Scythed chariots against all foot units except LI and Javelinmen.

Furious charge does not apply in the following cases:

- Against WWg except if it is an elephant charging,
- Against units behind a fortification,
- Against units behind stakes if they are charged by mounted unit,
- If the opponents are foot units in frontal melee and if both units have the *furious charge* ability,
- If the unit with the *furious charge* ability is attacked on the flank or in the rear,
- If the unit with the *furious charge* ability is in terrain that penalises it in melee.

Heavy and medium swordsmen units that cancel the *impact* ability of impetuous foot units do not cancel their *furious charge* ability.
The *armour* and *heavy armour* abilities do not apply during the first round of a melee if the opponent has the *furious charge* ability.

Multiple opponents

The following rule is used to simulate the devastating effect that can result from coordinated attacks on a single unit.

When a unit, already in melee with an enemy on its front edge, is engaged in melee by a new enemy (other than light troops) on its flank or rear edge, it immediately loses one cohesion point, except if it is a WWg. It is not necessary for the new enemy to make a charge. It can engage the melee with a simple move, or by conforming if it was already in contact with the unit. The new enemy must conform and align properly, corner to corner, otherwise the contact is illegal and no cohesion is lost.

A unit also loses a cohesion point if it is contacted during the same phase on two different sides by two different enemy units. At least one of the enemy units must be a non-light troop unit contacting the flank or the rear and all must conform properly.

A unit in melee with an enemy in contact with its flank or rear loses a cohesion point only during the phase in which it is contacted on its flank or its rear.

The cohesion loss is applied **before** the melee is resolved. The cohesion loss is limited to only one point per phase. Therefore, a unit attacked on both flanks and from the rear during the same phase only loses one cohesion point. However, if it is attacked on the flank in one game-turn, then on the rear in the next, it loses one cohesion point each time.

The same rules are applied to basic factors and combat abilities as when attacked on the flank or the rear (see p 56).

Specific cases:

- If a unit loses its last cohesion point following an attack by multiple opponents, the player places a rout marker on the unit. There is no combat during the melee phase and this unit will not give any support. The routed unit is removed at the end of the melee phase, after the resolution of all melees.
- If a unit moves to a position where there is an enemy unit on its flank or on its rear, it does not lose a cohesion point.
- If a unit that pursues after a melee contacts the flank or the rear of an enemy, that enemy does not lose a cohesion point.

Attacking a camp

The camp, whether fortified or not, is considered a unit without a ZoC. Therefore, an enemy unit cannot contact the camp during its second or third movement. The camp is a valid target for the *uncontrolled charge* of impetuous units. No unit can pass through a camp.

If an unfortified camp is contacted by an enemy unit, it is automatically captured and looted. The camp is then lost but it is not removed and is still an obstacle to movement.

A fortified camp has guards who are supposed to fight off any attackers. A fortified camp cannot be attacked by light troops. Other troops can attack a fortified camp but the fight is resolved in a simplified way. Every attacking unit (other than light troops) in contact with the camp rolls a die. The camp is captured on a 5 or 6 by foot troops and only on a 6 by mounted troops. No factors or modifiers (including quality) are applied during the attack of the camp. The defenders of the camp can never inflict losses to the attackers.

A unit attacking the enemy camp is considered to be engaged in melee. Therefore it cannot be shot at and the unit cannot evade if it is charged. If it is attacked by another unit, it is no longer involved in attacking the camp and the melee is resolved as normal. The camp provides no support and does not cause cohesion loss like an attack by multiple opponents.

When an enemy camp is captured, all units that have participated in the attack, start looting the camp. To represent this, before giving an order to a unit engaged in looting the camp, the commander needs to get a 4+ on 1D6. If it fails, no CP is spent but the unit continues looting the camp and remains immobile. A unit engaged in looting the camp is no longer subject to an *uncontrolled charge*.

A camp

FORTIFICATIONS

Fortifications are prepared positions such as ditches, embankments, palisades or a wagon laager. The fortifications are placed at the beginning of the battle and remain fixed. They are represented by bases of one UD wide and 1 to 2 cm deep and should have a defined front and rear. The following rules apply for fortifications:

- Moving through a fortification costs one UD for foot units and two UD for mounted.
- A unit with front edge in contact and aligned with the rear edge of a fortification element counts the front edge of the fortification as its own front edge, including when determining range for shooting.
- A unit attacked by its main opponent across a fortification has an advantage in melee. This advantage applies even if the unit is also attacked on its flank or rear at the same time.
- A foot unit, other than WWg and LI, has a +1 bonus in melee if it is behind the fortification.
- The *impact* and *furious charge* abilities do not apply (for either attackers or defenders) if the combat takes place across a fortification.
- Mounted units that attack an enemy behind a fortification suffer a -2 penalty in melee.
- A light infantry unit can defend a fortification without having to evade heavier troops. It avoids destruction in open terrain and fights with a basic factor equal to zero.
- WWg units cannot defend a fortification and thus have no basic factor.
- All units placed behind fortifications, other than WWg, count as being in cover if shot at from their front, except if they are being shot at by artillery.
- Artillery placed behind a fortification can rotate on itself and is still considered protected by the fortification if it remains in contact it. An attacker must conform to the fortification to attack the artillery.

WAR WAGONS

War wagons follow specific rules for combat

- When a WWg is attacked on its long edge by a **single** enemy unit, it is considered supported and thus has a +1 bonus in melee. If there are two enemy units on the same long side, only one unit fights. The effect of the second unit is only to cancel the support bonus of the WWg.
- A WWg can never be attacked on its flank or rear because all its edges are considered as a front edge for combat purposes. Therefore a WWg cannot lose cohesion points in case of an attack by multiple opponents.
- A WWg has no ZoC and its movement is not restricted by an enemy ZoC. It cannot contact enemy units by its own movement.
- A WWg can only be attacked once in each melee phase. The phasing player decides which unit in contact with the WWg is considered the main unit for that melee phase.
- Units in contact by their front edge with the other sides of an enemy WWg give support to the main unit in melee (+1 bonus for each **side**). Units that are in corner to corner contact or units in flank contact cannot support the attack.
- Friendly units can be supported in melee by a WWg on any side of the WWg, whatever orientation. However, like every unit, a WWg can support a maximum of two friendly units (one on each side).
- A light infantry unit can contact a WWg to support another heavier unit engaged in melee with the WWg. If, after the outcome of combat, a LI unit is alone in contact with the WWg, it must fall back one UD.

WAR WAGONS

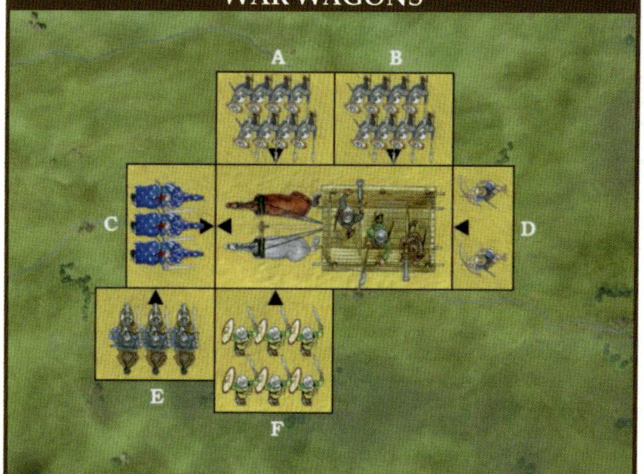

If unit A is the main unit in melee with the WWg, it is supported by units C, D and F and thus has a +3 bonus.

If unit F is the main unit in melee with the WWg, the WWg counts +1 for support as F is alone in contact on the long side of the WWg. F is supported by units C, D and either A or B and thus has a +3 bonus. In total, unit F will have a net advantage of +2 in melee against the WWg.

Due to its position (corner to corner), unit E never gives any support in melee against the WWg.

ROUT AND PURSUIT

He who knows when he can fight and when he cannot, will be victorious. Sun Tzu

ROUTED UNITS

When a unit has lost all its cohesion points, by whatever cause (melee, shooting or other), it is routed and removed from play.

When a unit is routed, its flight can affect any friends less than one UD from it and in its path. It risks passing through them and causing them to lose cohesion. Enemy units are not affected.

Routs and pursuits are conducted at the end of the player's phase after the end of all combats.

The following rules apply:

- If the unit is **in melee** and only being attacked on its flanks and/or rear when routed, the unit is reoriented to face the main enemy.
- All friends directly behind the routing unit after its reorientation (except if it is an elephant, for which see below) and within one UD of it lose one cohesion point and will in turn rout if reduced to zero cohesion points. This can result in a "cascade" of routs.
- Routing artillery and war wagons do not affect nearby friendly units. They are immediately removed from the table.
- Routing light infantry only affect other light infantry units making them lose one cohesion point as normal.
- A commander not included in the unit, but engaged in melee and attached to a unit that routs may be caught in its flight and is lost on a 1, 2 or 3 on 1D6. If he survives, then he must flee to the closest friendly unit up to a maximum distance of 5 UD. If he is not able to reach a friendly unit (even from another corps) the commander is lost (see p 24).
- A commander **included** in a routing unit is automatically lost.

ELEPHANT RAMPAGE

Instead of always affecting friends behind it, a routing elephant will rampage in a random direction. After reorienting it as above (if applicable) roll 1D6 and consult the following chart:

1D6	Direction
1	Forward
2	90° on the left
3	90° on the right
4-5-6	On the rear

All friends or enemies, except light infantry, lose one cohesion point if they are less than one UD from a rampaging elephant in the indicated direction.

ROUTING EXAMPLE

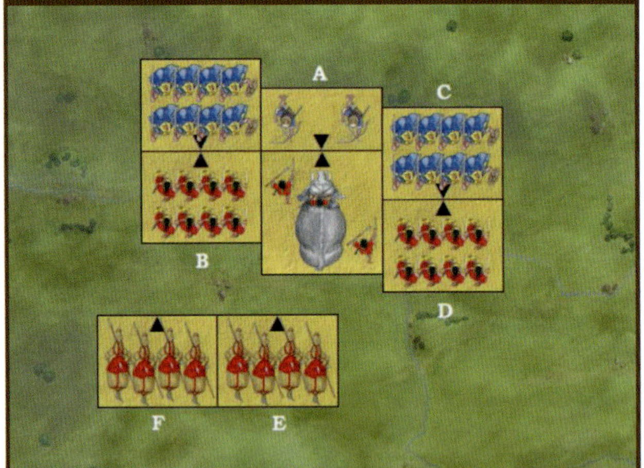

The elephant is routed. 1D6 is rolled, if the result is:

1: The elephant rampages through unit A, which does not lose cohesion because it is light infantry
2: The elephant rampages through unit B, which then loses one cohesion point
3: The elephant rampages through units C and D, which each lose one cohesion point
4, 5 or 6: the elephant rampages through unit E, which loses one cohesion point

If unit B is routed, it causes units E and F to both lose one cohesion point.

If unit D is routed, no friendly units are affected.

Pursuit

When a unit has routed all its opponents in melee, it can perform an advance at the end of the melee phase to pursue a routed unit. A pursuit is a move directly forward of a maximum of one UD ignoring enemy ZoC. Only the phasing player's units can perform a pursuit.

Pursuit is optional for non-impetuous units. Pursuit is mandatory for impetuous units which must pursue one complete UD except in the following cases:

- The impetuous unit destroyed artillery, war wagons or elephants,
- Pursuit would result in the impetuous unit exiting the table or entering terrain that would penalise it in combat,
- The impetuous unit is defending fortifications or the bank of a river,
- It is an impetuous foot unit pursuing mounted troops.

Supporting friendly units can also advance the same distance providing that they are aligned corner to corner with the pursuing unit and have the same facing.

If several units are in melee with the same enemy, only one of the units can pursue. The unit that pursues is chosen by the controlling player.

If the pursuit movement brings the unit into contact with a new enemy it does not result in a new combat. The units remain in contact (an evade move is not permitted) and combat will be resolved in the next round melee phase. A unit contacted on its flank or rear may conform prior to combat. Contact following a pursuit is not considered a charge. Abilities available only in the 1st round of a melee (*impact, javelin, missile support* and *furious charge*) are therefore not allowed, and there is no loss of cohesion due to multiple attacks.

If a pursuing unit of LMI, MI, HI, Cv or Kn contacts a light infantry unit, the light infantry unit is immediately eliminated as an evade move is not permitted. If the enemy camp is contacted, it is immediately taken or attacked in the following game-turn if it is fortified.

Note: A unit which routs its opponent but is still in contact with the front edge of one or more ennemies on its flank or rear does not pursue and must immediately conform to one of the enemies of its choice.

Demoralisation

The battle continues until one of the armies is demoralised. This occurs when the army's losses are equal to or greater than its demoralisation value.

The total demoralisation value of an army is equal to the number of units of which it is made up. A **fortified camp** counts as one unit. If a part of the army is not on the table (on flank march or in ambush for example) then these units do not count towards the demoralisation value of the army. Losses are counted as follows:

Situation	Losses
Per disordered unit	1 pt
Per unit that has fled the table	1 pt
Per routed unit	2 pts
Per lost commander	1 pt +Value *
If the camp is lost	4 pts
If a fortified camp is lost	6 pts

* Command Value (0, +1, +2 or +3)

Expendable units, namely scythed chariots and some levy units, are not counted in either the demoralisation value of the army or its losses.

Army losses are checked at the end of each player-phase. Once an army has suffered losses greater than or equal to its total demoralisation value, the army routs and the game ends. It is possible that two armies rout at the same time (though this is quite rare) and in this case the game is a draw.

Example: An army of 24 units in total has a corps with 6 units on a flank march that has not yet arrived on the table. It therefore has a total of 18 units. It has 3 units that have been routed, 5 units in disorder and 1 unit of light cavalry that fled off the table following an enemy charge. It has therefore lost 12 of its demoralisation value of 18.

Greek warriors

TERRAIN

Topographic setting is a valuable aid in military operations. Sun Tzu

Terrain is an important part of any battle. According to the strengths or weaknesses of his army, a player might prefer open terrain allowing cavalry manoeuvres or dense terrain in which he can hide his light infantry.

The advantage of choosing the most effective terrain is therefore essential and a good general must take it into account.

TERRAIN SIZE AND SHAPE

Some terrain is linear, like roads or rivers, but most of the time terrain consists of elements covering an area of the battlefield. The shape of an element of terrain must be appropriate to its type. Fields, plantations and villages must be rectangular in shape. Other terrain elements are of irregular shape with rounded corners.

A valid terrain element must be able to fit inside a circle of 6 UD in diameter and it must be able to enclose a rectangle with a size of 2 UD x 3 UD.

TYPES OF TERRAIN

Terrain is classified as open, rough, difficult or impassable:

Open

Open terrain is clear, flat or gently sloping terrain that has no effect on movement. Any part of the table not covered by terrain elements is considered open terrain.

Rough

Rough terrain is flat or gently sloping terrain covered with brush, scrub, rocks, gullies, orchards or cultivated fields with hedges or irrigation ditches. This kind of terrain impedes the movement of most troops except light and medium infantry.

Difficult

Difficult terrain consists of dense woods, marshes, sand dunes and steep hills with or without cover. Villages are also considered difficult terrain. Only light infantry can move through this kind of terrain without penalty.

Impassable

Impassable terrain is terrain that cannot be crossed or occupied by any type of troops. It can be, for example, a small lake, or a canyon. This type of terrain does not block visibility or shooting but blocks lines of command.

VISIBILITY & AMBUSH

For simplicity all units physically present on the table are considered to be visible and known to the enemy. It is therefore possible to charge a unit behind a hill even though the charging unit has no line of sight to it at the beginning of its movement.

However certain types of terrain block visibility and allow troops to hide in them. In this case a marker representing the units waiting in ambush is placed. Light infantry is often used in this role, but other troops can also hide in woods or in villages for example. An ambushing unit must be entirely in or behind the terrain which conceals it. It is detected if the enemy advances beyond the terrain which hides it or approaches to one UD from its position (see Ambushes p 70).

COVER FROM SHOOTING

Some terrain can also provide cover, for example trees will stop or deflect missiles. A unit benefits from cover if the line of sight of the shooter passes through the terrain (see the terrain table on p65).

In some cases troops protected by terrain may also be penalised for shooting. A unit, except light infantry, is penalised when shooting if part of the edge of the unit from which it is shooting is in cover.

TERRAIN DESCRIPTION

River or coastal zone

A river or stream will slow down the movement of units crossing it or even block the movement altogether. The difficulty of a river is determined at the time of its placement on the following table:

1D6	River Difficulty
1	Open terrain (dried river)
2-3	Rough terrain
4-5	Difficult terrain
6	Impassable terrain (flooded river)

A river must be between 1 and 2 UD wide and always extends from one long edge (player's base edge) to the other. River elements must be placed entirely between 2 and 6 UD of one short edge (side edge) of the table. If a road crosses the river, a bridge or a ford is considered present at this location, allowing units to cross without penalty.

A river has the following effects on movement and combat:

- A unit must cross a river at an angle of 90° (i.e. at right angles) relative to its course, except if the river is dried. The unit's movement allowance is adjusted according to the difficulty of the river.
- A unit cannot shoot if part of its base is located in the river. Units located in a river have no cover.
- When a unit defends the bank of a river, it has a bonus of + 1 in combat against units located at least partially in the river.

A coastal zone represents the edge of a large river, lake or sea and is always 4 UD wide. It is completely impassable and completely blocks the short edge of the table.

Gentle or steep hills

A hill can be modelled with either a crest line or with a central point and contour lines. The hill gives a bonus of + 1 in combat for units that are located higher than their opponent. It blocks visibility and units hidden behind it are only visible if the enemy crosses beyond the crest line or approaches to within one UD. Units placed on a hill can, under certain conditions, shoot over lower units.

A gentle hill is regarded as open terrain. It can count as rough terrain if it is covered with fields, brush or a plantation or as difficult terrain if it is covered with woods. The choice of covering is free but must take into account the terrain available in the region. For example a wooded hill cannot be placed in the Steppes. Choosing the covering for a hill does not count as choosing an additional item of terrain. Thus it is possible in a Forest region to place 3 elements of woods and 2 steep hills covered with woods.

Steep hills are identical to gentle hills except that their steep slopes mean they are difficult terrain regardless of what vegetation covers them. A unit, except LI, that shoots from a steep hill does so with a penalty of -1.

Brush

Flat land covered with rocks, shrubs or small trees is considered brush and is treated as rough terrain. Only light infantry can be placed in ambush inside it. Elephants and camels treat brush as open terrain.

Plantations

These are cultivated areas with small trees placed in rows close together like orchards, palm groves and olive groves. They are considered rough terrain and offer cover to the units located in them. All troops except elephants may be placed in ambush in them. A unit, except LI, that shoots from a plantation does so with a penalty of -1.

Fields

These are areas of cultivated land with ditches, hedges, low walls or vines. They are considered rough terrain but offer no cover. Only light infantry can be placed in ambush inside them. Elephants treat fields as open terrain.

Woods

These are areas covered with trees and undergrowth or jungle. They are considered difficult terrain and offer cover for the units located there. All troops can be placed in ambush inside them. A unit, except LI, that shoots from a wood does so with a penalty of -1.

Marsh

Marsh is wetland or bogs sparsely populated with trees and bushes. It is considered difficult terrain but offers no cover. Only light infantry can be placed in ambush inside it. A unit, except LI, that shoots from a marsh does so with a penalty of -1.

Sand Dunes

These are areas of soft sand with dunes. They are considered difficult terrain, except for camels, and offer no cover. Camels treat this terrain as rough for the movement, but are not penalised in combat. Only light infantry can be placed in ambush inside them. A unit, except LI and Camelry that shoots from sand dunes does so with a penalty of -1.

Gully

This is a depression below the level of the surrounding terrain. It is considered rough terrain but offers no cover. All troops except elephants may be placed in ambush inside it. The units defending the edge of a gully against enemies located at least partially in the gully have a bonus of + 1 in combat. Note that a gully is not the inverse of a hill as there is no height advantage in a gully.

Road

A road must be 1 UD wide and between 10 to 30 UD in length. It can pass through all other types of terrain (except a coastal zone and impassable terrain) and allows troops to move more quickly. However it does not change the type of terrain crossed in regards to combat. For example, a unit fighting on a forest road is considered to be in difficult terrain. A road must go from one table edge to another table edge, a village or another section of road.

Village

A village is an area with buildings, walls and a road passing through or ending in it. A village is considered difficult terrain and offers cover to the units. All troops except elephants and WW g may be ambushed inside a village. A unit, except LI, shooting from a village does so with a penalty of -1. It is possible to place a village on the top of a gentle or steep hill.

TERRAIN TABLE

Terrain	Category	Ambush	Cover
River	Variable	Not possible	-
Coastal zone	Impassable	Not possible	-
Hill	Variable	All if behind the crest	Variable
Steep hill	Difficult	All if behind the crest	Variable
Brush	Rough	LI	-
Field	Rough	LI	-
Plantation	Rough	All except elephants	Yes, -1 if shooting
Wood	Difficult	All	Yes, -1 if shooting
Marsh	Difficult	LI	-
Sand dune	Difficult	LI	-
Gully	Rough	All except elephants	-
Road	Same as the terrain crossed	Not possible	-
Village	Difficult	All except elephants	Yes, -1 if shooting
Impassable	Impassable	Not possible	-

SETTING UP

He, who has no goals, will not achieve them. Sun Tzu

GAME PREPARATION

Each player must first organise his army according to the corresponding army list. He chooses his units and allocates them to an army corps, each of which is led by a commander.

Players should have a table covered by a gaming mat or some suitable terrain boards to represent the battlefield. The battlefield must be of the correct dimensions relative to the scale of figures used:

- 120 x 80 cm for 6-15 mm (UD of 4 cm)
- 180 x 120 cm for 20-25 mm (UD of 6 cm)
- 240 x 160 cm for 28-32 mm (UD of 8 cm)

SET UP

To set up a game, follow the steps below:

- Initiative to determine the attacker and region
- Choosing and placing terrain elements
- Placing camps and fortifications
- Preparing battle plans
- Deploying troops
- Dismounting troops
- Starting battle

INITIATIVE

Each army has an initiative value that corresponds to the quality of its command and the number of scouts. Army initiative is noted on the army sheet and is calculated as below:

- Total value of all commanders divided by two and rounded down.
- +1 if the commander-in-chief is a strategist
- +1 if the army contains 2 to 5 LH
- or +2 if it contains at least 6 LH

At the beginning of the game, each player rolls 1D6. The player with the highest initiative value adds to his die roll the difference between the two initiative values limited to +4. Whoever gets the highest score can choose the region for the battle and decide to be the attacker or the defender. Each role (attacker or defender) has its advantages and disadvantages.

The attacker deploys his army corps after the defender, but he is more limited in the placement of ambushes. He always starts to play.

The defender deploys his army corps first. He has the advantage of choosing and placing the terrain elements first (including the additional compulsory element). He can also deploy ambushes further forward - up to halfway across the table in the flank sectors.

Once the battlefield is in place and all troops are deployed, the attacking player starts to play.

REGIONS

The player with initiative selects the region for battle. If he chooses to be the attacker, he selects a region from defender's army list. If he chooses to be the defender, he selects a region from his own list. Each region has a compulsory terrain element. The defender places one element of the required type in addition to its other terrain choices.

Region	Compulsory terrain
Plain	Field
Forest	Wood
Mountain	Steep hill
Desert	Sand dune
Steppes	Gentle hill

The following table shows the types of terrain available in each region. Indicated in the table is the maximum number of elements (including the compulsory element in brackets) that can be chosen.

Example: If the region chosen is "Plain", the defender must take a field (as it is the compulsory terrain) and then chooses 2 to 4 other elements. If he selects two plantations, his opponent cannot choose this type of terrain because the maximum number has been reached.

Terrain type	Plain	Forest	Mountain	Desert	Steppes
River or coastal zone	1	1	1	-	1 River only
Gentle hill (G) or steep hill (S)	1 G	2	3 (1) S	2	3 (1) G
Field	3 (1)	-	-	-	-
Brush	-	2	2	2	3
Plantation	2	-	-	1	-
Wood	-	3(1)	2	-	-
Marsh	-	2	1	-	-
Sand dune	-	-	-	3 (1)	-
Gully	1	1	1	1	1
Road	1	1	1	-	-
Village	1	1	1	-	-
Impassable	-	1	1	1	-

Placing terrain

Choosing and placing terrain elements takes place in the following order:

- Defender takes the compulsory terrain element and chooses 2 to 4 other terrain elements.
- Attacker chooses 2 to 4 terrain elements.
- Defender places the compulsory element on its own side of the table.
- If a river or a coastal zone is chosen by one of the players, this player places it on the table.
- Defender places the village if there is one.
- Players; starting with the defender, place all other terrain elements, except the road.
- A road is always placed on the table last.
- Attacker tries to *adjust* some terrain elements.
- Defender tries to *adjust* some terrain elements.

A player cannot choose more than two identical terrain elements (for example 2 fields in plain).
A player must place at least two terrain elements on the battlefield.

Placing a river or coastal zone

There can be only one element of this type on the table. If the defender has not successfully selected a river or coastal zone, the attacker can try to select one or the other. The selection of a river or a coastal zone is not guaranteed; the player must get a 4 + on 1D6 to select the terrain element. If unsuccessful the player can choose another terrain element other than a river or a coastal zone.

The river or coastal zone must be placed along the short edge (side edge) of the table, on the right or left at the player's choice, providing it will fit there. The river must be between 1 and 2 UD wide and form a straight line. It must be placed to be between 2 and 6 UD from the chosen table edge. The difficulty of the river is determined when it is placed (see p 64).

A coastal zone is completely impassable and extends 4UD in from the chosen edge.

The battle start around the village

Placing the village

Only the defender can choose a village. This is not automatic; he must get a 4 + on 1D6 to select the element. If unsuccessful the player can choose another element of terrain.

The village must be placed in a flank sector (i.e. within 10 UD of one short edge). The village must touch a river or coastal zone, if any; otherwise the player chooses the right or left sector on his side of the table. He then rolls a die to determine the position of the village relative to his base edge (the long edge of the table). On a result of 1-4 the village must touch the player's long edge; otherwise the village must be at least at 2 UD from all edges of the table. The player must also place a road linking the village with one edge of the table. This road is free and does not count against the number of chosen elements.

If the player wishes, he may also choose a hill (steep or gentle) and put the village on top. In this case the hill counts as an extra selection but it is placed along with the village (one single placement die is rolled for both elements).

Placing others terrain elements

To help with laying out the terrain, the game table is divided into six areas of equivalent size (10 x 10 UD) called sectors:

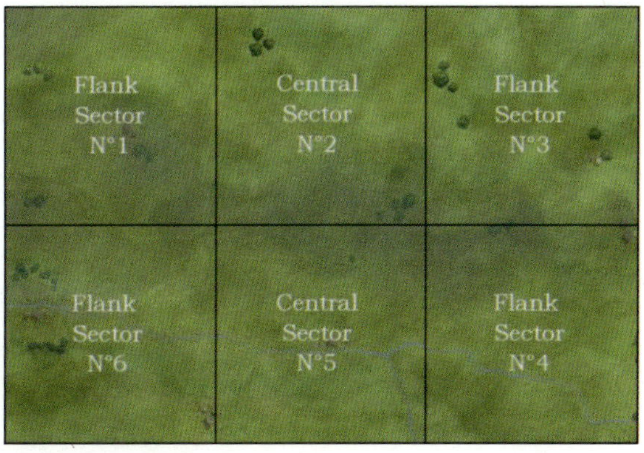

For each of the other terrain elements selected, except the road, the player rolls 2D6. One die is nominated to indicate the sector where the terrain must be placed; the other indicates its position relative to the edges of the table:

1D6	Terrain position
1-4	Must touch one edge of the table or a river or coastline.
5-6	Must be at least at 2 UD from all edges of the table.

If a terrain element cannot be placed on the table, it is simply discared.

Road

The road is the last element to be placed. A road must link two table edges or a table edge to a village or to another road. A road must be between 10 and 30 UD in length. The placement of the road is up to the player but if a road is placed along the table long edge it must be placed entirely 2 UD away from this table edge in order to allow placement of the camp.

A road is the only element that can be placed over other terrain; however it cannot be placed on top of a coastal zone or impassable terrain. If the road crosses a river, it is assumed there is a bridge or a ford at the crossing point.

Terrain adjustment

Once all terrain elements have been placed, players who chose fewer elements than the maximum allowed may attempt to move or remove terrain elements. Only elements other than roads, a river, a coastal zone and a village (including the hill on which it is placed) can be moved or removed. The compulsory element can be moved but not removed.

If a player has chosen only 2 elements of 4, he can attempt to move or remove two elements placed on the table. If he has chosen 3 of 4, he can attempt to move or remove a single element. The compulsory element placed by the defender does not count towards the maximum. The player can choose an element placed by himself or by his opponent. Only one attempt per player per element can be made (except by a Strategist). It is not mandatory to attempt to adjust the terrain element; this is the player's choice. The player selects an element and rolls a dice:

1D6	Terrain adjustment
1-2	Element stays in place
3-4	The player can either move the element up to a maximum of **4 UD** or rotate the element (but not both).
5	The player can either move the element up to a maximum of **6 UD** or rotate the element (but not both) or remove the element if it is impassable.
6	The player can either move the element up to a maximum of **6 UD** or rotate the element (but not both) or remove the element whatever its type (except the compulsory element).

- To rotate an element, simply place a finger on any point of the element and rotate it while keeping this point fixed.
- After being moved, no element can overlap another terrain element other than a road.
- Removing an element of impassable terrain from the table is allowed, but it cannot be moved.
- If the army is commanded by a Strategist, the player can try to move or remove one more element, or he can re-roll a dice (so he can have two attempts for the same terrain element).

CAMPS & FORTIFICATIONS

Starting with the defender, each player deploys his camp and his fortifications.

The camp must be placed in the deployment area, either next to the player table's edge or beside a river or a coastal zone. If the camp is fortified, it can be deployed anywhere in the deployment area. The camp can only be deployed in open terrain and must be accessible by a passage at least one UD wide. The camp cannot be placed over a road.

Fortifications are placed in the player's deployment area for heavy troops in any type of terrain except marshes, a river or a coastal zone. The fortifications must touch and be aligned with each other or separated by at least one UD to allow the movement of a unit between them.

BATTLE PLAN

Each player now indicates the disposition of his army in a battle plan. Writing the battle plan is an important phase because it is at this point that the player defines his strategy and how he will deploy his army.

The battle plan can be a simple sheet of paper but you can find a ready to use deployment sheet on the *l'Art de la Guerre* website. On his battle plan, the player must indicate the following:

- The position of each army corps not making a flank march relative to the others.
- Which corps, if any, is making a flank march and on which flank it will arrive.
- The composition of each ambush.

There is no need to specify the exact disposition of all the units on the plan. The player only has to indicate the position of his army corps relative to each other: e.g. which corps is deployed in the centre, which is on the right wing and which is on the left.

Macedonian camp

Ambush

Each player can place units in ambush. To do this, players place ambush markers on the table. These markers must be one UD square. They are placed on the table **after** the players have made their battle plans but before they start deploying their units. The defender places his ambush markers first.

Galloglaich near the village

Placing ambushes

The players can place their ambush markers up to 5 UD in from their own table edge. The defender can also place his ambush markers up to halfway across the table in his two flank sectors (i.e. up to 10 UD from the short edges of the table). The defender's ambush markers in the central sector can only be placed up to 5 UD from his table edge. Ambush markers must be placed in terrain that allows troops to make an ambush or behind an obstacle that blocks the line-of-sight of the enemy, such as a wood, a plantation, a village or a hill.

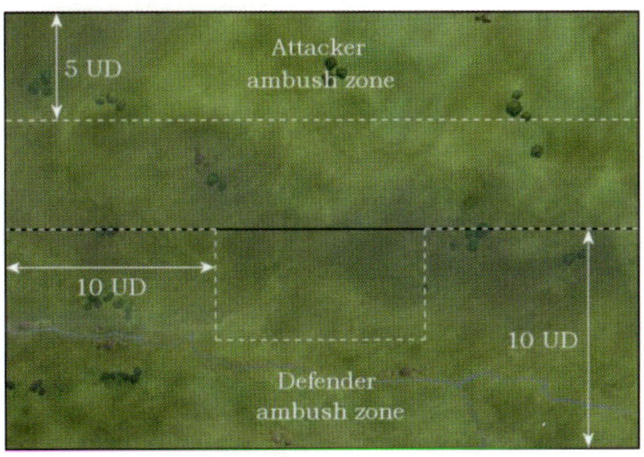

Each player can place two ambush markers or three if the commander-in-chief is a strategist. The player indicates on his battle plan which units are placed in ambush. Each ambush can contain up to 4 units. These units are not deployed on the table until the ambush has been revealed. The player can place a fake ambush containing no units to deceive his opponent. It is possible to place a commander in an ambush but only if it is not the commander-in-chief.

Discovering an ambush

Until it has been revealed, an ambush is treated as an enemy unit, even if it is a fake ambush. The enemy cannot make a second or third move if it moves to within 4 UD of an ambush marker.

An ambush is automatically revealed when an enemy unit is one UD from the marker, even if there is no clear line-of-sight. It is also revealed if the enemy is further than one UD, but has a clear line-of-sight to the marker (e.g. having moved round a hill).

An enemy unit must stop its movement when it moves to one UD from the marker. It is not possible to charge units in ambush. The opponent must then indicate if the ambush contains units or not. If it is a fake ambush, the marker is removed and the enemy unit can finish its move. Otherwise, all units placed in the ambush are deployed on the table respecting the following rules:

- All units of the ambush must form a valid group and must be inside the terrain or out of sight of the enemy when the ambush is placed.
- One of the units in ambush must be placed entirely on the ambush marker.
- Others units in ambush cannot be deployed less than one UD from any ennemy unit.

If some units cannot be deployed on the table, they are considered to have fled the battlefield. These units are not counted as losses but are deducted from the demoralisation value of the army.

A player can reveal an ambush during his own movement phase by deploying units on the table. It is not necessary to spend CP as long as the units do not move. A player can also reveal his units in ambush during the opponent's movement phase as soon as an enemy unit comes within 4 UD of the marker. The enemy unit can continue its move but cannot charge the units that were in ambush.

If an entire army corps is placed in ambush, the player can roll the die each game-turn to determine CP (even if it is not used). This can confuse the opponent who does not then know if the corps is in ambush or on a flank march.

Battle between Egyptian army and Hittite army

DEPLOYING ARMY CORPS

Sequence of deployment

Once the players have made their battle plans and placed their ambushes, they begin to deploy their corps on the table. Starting with the defender, the players each deploy one corps in turn until all corps are on the table. All units except those in a corps on a flank march or those placed in ambush must be deployed on the table. The player describes his troops to his opponent at the time of placement on the table.

During deployment, a player must follow his battle plan. All units belonging to the same corps (even if in ambush) must be deployed inside a rectangular zone and must be in command range of their commander. The zones of the various corps cannot overlap and their relative positions must match those defined in the battle plan.

It is very important to understand that only the *relative position* of each corps to the others must be respected. For example, it does not prevent a player from placing his army entirely in the left half or entirely in the right half of the table, as long as all corps are deployed in the same relative positions as shown on his battle plan.

Deployment area

All units must be placed in the deployment area on the army's own half of the table (see below). Light troops (LI and LH) can be deployed right up to the short/flank edges and no closer to the halfway line than 3 UD. All other units (including the camp) must be deployed no closer to the short/flank edges of the table than 4 UD and no closer to the halfway line than 5 UD (except if in the defender's ambushes).

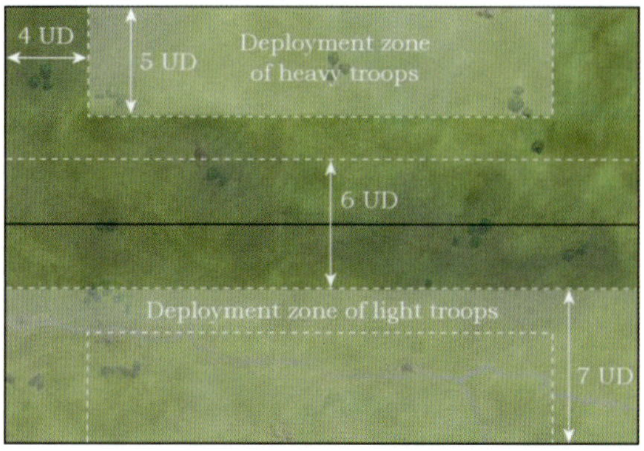

The depths of the deployment area must be adjusted if the table size is not exactly the size required (for example 120 x 80 cm for 15 mm). The zone between the light troops of the two armies should be at least 6 UD deep. Other troops must deploy 4 UD or more from the short/flank edges and the zone between the non light troops of each side must be at least 10 UD.

No unit can be deployed in a coastal zone, a river or in a terrain element in which it cannot move (e.g. artillery in difficult terrain) unless it is on a road.

Charging knights

Dismounting troops

- Medium and heavy knight units can always dismount if their army list allows deploying these units on foot.
- Other mounted troops can be dismounted only if the enemy has deployed fortifications, elephants, war wagons, or bowmen with stakes on the table. Enemy units in ambush or on a flank march are not considered.
- Elephants and scythed chariots can never be dismounted.
- The choice to dismount troops is made after all corps have been deployed on the table. The defending player chooses first, then the attacker.
- Once troops have been dismounted they cannot remount during the game. It is not allowed to dismount troops during the course of the game.
- The player must note on his battle plan if his troops placed in ambush or sent on a flank march have been dismounted or not. If nothing is specified, the units are considered to be mounted.

Flank marches

A corps sent on a flank march is not placed on the table during the deployment phase. It will instead arrive at a randomly determined time on the specified short/flank edge of the table. This tactic is risky because of the random time of arrival but it can give spectacular results if the enemy does not position troops to counter it. The player must indicate on his battle plan which corps has been sent on the flank march and on which flank it will arrive.

- Neither army can have more than one flank march.
- A flank march cannot be made on a flank that is blocked by a coast zone or an impassable river.
- The corps that includes the commander-in-chief cannot be sent on a flank march.
- A corps sent on a flank march cannot include war wagons, scythed chariots or artillery as these troops lack the necessary manoeuvrability.

Arrival of a flank march

At the beginning of each movement phase, the player rolls 1D6 for the corps sent on a flank march. A score of 6 on the first roll or a 5 or 6 on subsequent rolls means that the flank march will arrive during next game-turn.

The player declares to his opponent the table edge on which the flank march will arrive according to what is noted on his battle plan. If both sides have a flank march on the same flank, it is necessary to check which one is driven back (see below).

In the game-turn following the successful die roll, **all the units** in the flank march must move onto the table during the player's movement phase or be lost. Units can enter from anywhere along the chosen short/flank edge.

The first move is measured from the table edge and must be an advance in a straight line (i.e. perpendicular to the edge of the table). All rules of movement and command apply as normal to the units entering on a flank march.

If some units cannot enter the table, e.g. because the commander does not have enough CP to move them, they are considered lost and removed from play. However they do not count towards the army's demoralisation value and are not counted as losses when calculating army demoralisation.

Fleeing from a flank march

When the units of a flank march move onto the table, all enemy units (including those in ambush) that are 4 UD or less from the entry points will panic and flee as follows:

- If the unit is not engaged in melee, it makes an evade move in a direction perpendicular to the entry edge of the flank march. If the unit is not normally allowed to evade, it still makes the move but becomes disordered.
- If the unit is engaged in melee, it continues the fight but may risk being attacked on the flank or on the rear.
- Artillery units and war wagons are automatically eliminated. It is assumed the crews have become demoralised by the unexpected arrival of enemies and fled.
- Units that flee from a flank march can *burst through* friends if their path is blocked (see p 42).

Syrian chariots

Driving back a flank march

If both players have ordered a flank march on the same edge of the table, the corps with fewest units is driven back. When comparing the size of the corps, light units are counted as half a unit each. If the two corps are the same size, both are driven back. If one of the flank marches is hesitant (see below), it immediately becomes reliable at the moment the enemy flank march enters.

A flank march that is driven back enters the table during the next movement phase of the owning player. It must enter from the side/flank edge up to 5 UD from the player's base edge (i.e. the long edge on the player's side of the table). It does not cause enemy units to flee. Where possible a unit must not move to within 4 UD from an enemy. If it is forced to do so, the unit is disordered.

In the movement phase following the arrival of the flank march that was driven back, the corps making the opposing flank march moves onto the table. Its effects are those described on p 72.

ALLIED OR UNRELIABLE COMMANDERS

During the first game-turn of the game, it must be determined if any corps led by an allied or unreliable commander is able to join in the battle. If the result of the first activation die roll for a corps led by an allied or unreliable commander is equal to 1 (without any modifier), it means the corps is hesitant.

The troops of a hesitant corps, or those of an unreliable or allied corps that has not yet tested, cannot shoot or move and are not subject to uncontrolled charges.

In following game-turns, if an activation roll is a 6, it indicates that the corps has become reliable and can join in the battle. When a corps becomes reliable a new die roll is used to determine the command points for the game-turn.

The commander-in-chief can spend 2 CPs (and only 2 CPs) to give a +1 bonus to the activation die roll of a hesitant corps (even if it is on a flank march or is in ambush). This corresponds to sending messengers to negotiate, threaten or promise rewards.

If troops belonging to a hesitant corps are attacked or are shot at by the enemy or if the enemy moves to within **4 UD** (i.e. closer than 4 UD), the corps immediately becomes reliable.

If a hesitant corps is in ambush, it becomes reliable only if an enemy moves to **1 UD** from it and discovers the ambush.

If a corps on a flank march is hesitant, it cannot enter the table; it must first become reliable. Starting with the game-turn in which the corps becomes reliable, the player rolls 1D6 to see if it will arrive in the following game-turn: a 6 on the first attempt or a 5 or 6 on subsequent attempts means success, just as it would normally.

BUDGET

When the world is at peace, a wise man keeps his sword by his side. Sun Tzu

ARMY BUDGET

In a standard format game the budget for an army is 200 points and its units are organised into three corps, each led by a commander. Allied or unreliable commanders, as well as those included in a unit, are less expensive. Refer to the army list for the number of command points and the types of troops available.

Commander and camp	Budget 100	200	300
Strategist commander	+ 5	+ 10	+ 15
Brilliant commander	+ 3	+ 6	+ 10
Competent commander	+ 2	+ 3	+ 5
Ordinary commander	+ 0	+ 0	+ 0
Allied or unreliable cdt	- 2	- 3	- 5
Commander included	- 2	- 3	- 5
Fortifications	1	1	1
Fortified camp	3	6	9

Foot units	Type	Cost of units M	O	E	Options
Light infantry	LI	-	4	5	
Javelinmen	LMI	5	7	9	
Bowmen, crossbow	LMI	5	7	9	+1 if pavise, +1 if stakes, +2 if longbow
Medium swordsmen	MI	5	7	9	+1 if impact, +1 if 2HW, +1 if missile support, +1 if atlatl +2 if mixed unit, +2 if armour, +3 if bow
Medium spearmen	MI	5	7	9	+1 if missile support, +1 if pavise, +2 if armour +2 if mixed unit
Heavy swordsmen	HI	6	8	10	+1 if impact, +1 if 2HW, +1 if missile support +2 if armour, +2 if mixed unit
Heavy spearmen	HI	6	8	10	+1 if missile support, +1 if pavise, +2 if armour, +2 if mixed unit, +4 if mixed unit with longbow
Foot knights	HI	-	12	14	Already includes heavy armour and 2HW
Pikemen	HI	8	11	13	+1 if pavise
Levies	HI	2	3	-	-1 if expendable, +1 if impetuous
War wagons	WWg	8	10	-	+2 if light artillery, -2 if cannot shoot
Light artillery	Art	-	6	-	
Medium artillery	Art	-	10	-	
Heavy artillery	Art	-	10	-	

Mounted units	Type	Cost of units M	O	E	Options
Light cavalry	LH	4	6	7	+1 if light camelry
Medium cavalry Light chariots	Cv	5	7	9	+2 if missile weapon, +1 if impact +1 if medium camelry
Heavy cavalry	Cv	7	9	11	+2 if missile weapon, +1 if impact
Medium knights	Kn	-	10	12	+1 if impact
Heavy knights	Kn	-	12	14	+1 if impact
Cataphracts	Kn	-	11	13	+1 if cataphract camelry
Heavy chariots	Kn	8	10	12	+1 if impact
Scythed chariots	SCh	-	3	-	
Elephants	El	10	13	16	+2 if artillery

M = Mediocre, O = Ordinary, E = Elite

OPTIONAL RULES

Do not repeat the same tactics; adapt to circumstances. Sun Tzu

REDUCED FORMAT

For beginners or those who want to play faster games, here is a reduced format version of *l'Art de la Guerre*. All the standard format rules apply but the budget is reduced and the deployment is simplified.

The armies

The budget for a reduced format game is **100 points** with all the units in a single corps led by the commander-in-chief. This commander cannot be unreliable or an ally. The minimums and maximums in army lists are divided by 2 and rounded up.

The points costs remain the same except the costs of all commanders and the fortified camp are modified (see Budget page 74). For instance a strategist commander costs 5 points instead of 10.

Area of play

The area of play is reduced as follows:
- 60 x 80 cm for 6-15 mm (UD of 4 cm)
- 90 x 120 cm for 20-25 mm (UD of 6 cm)
- 120 x 160 cm for 28-32 mm (UD of 8 cm)

It is also possible to play on a larger table to allow more room for manoeuvre.

Initiative

The initiative bonus is equal to the commander's value (0 to +3). Add +1 if the army contains 1 or 2 LH or +2 if it contains at least 3 LH.

Terrain setup

The maximum size of terrain elements is reduced. A valid terrain element must now be able to fit inside a circle of **4 UD** in diameter and it must be able to enclose a rectangle with a size of 2 UD x 3 UD.

The defender places the compulsory terrain as well as 1 or 2 other terrain elements. The attacker places 1 or 2 terrain elements.

- A river must be from 1 to 2 UD wide and is placed 1D6 UD from one short/flank edge.
- A coastal zone must be 2 UD wide.
- It is not possible to choose impassable terrain together with a river or a coastal zone.

Roll 2D6 for each terrain element:

- The 1st die indicates the side of the table: even the side of the player, odd the side of the opponent.
- The 2nd die indicates if the element is placed against a table edge (1-4) or at 2 UD or more from all table edges (5-6).

The procedure for terrain adjustment is the same as that used for a standard format game except each player has just one attempt if he only placed one optional element.

Army deployment

There is no need for a battle plan and flank marches are not allowed.

Only the defender can place a single ambush marker (of 4 units or less) in his deployment zone, regardless of the value of his C-in-C.

- The defender deploys all of his army first. Light troops can be deployed right up to the short/flank edges and up to 5 UD from the player edge. All other units must be deployed no closer to the short/flank edges of the table than 3 UD and up to 3 UD from the player edge.
- The attacker then deploys all his army.
- The attacker starts playing first.

Demoralisation

Losses are recorded as usual except that a captured enemy camp only counts 2 points or 3 points if it is a fortified camp.

Big battles

Players may want to play with more miniatures and on larger tables. For this we propose the following adjustments to play with 300 or 400 point armies.

The armies

With a budget of 300 or 400 points, the minimum and maximum troop allowances (except the fortified camp) of each army list are multiplied by 1.5 or by 2, respectively, and rounded down.

The cost of commanders and fortified camps is also modified so that the points remain the same relative to those used in standard games.

With 300 points, the army can have 4 commanders which allows playing in teams of two players, each player controlling two army corps. A 300 point game lasts about 3 hours to 3h30.

At 400 points, a game lasts more than 4 hours. It is possible to play in teams, each player having a standard army of 200 points with 3 commanders.

Area of play

The area of play for larger battles is increased proportionately as shown below:

Budget	6-15 mm UD 4 cm	20-25 mm UD 6 cm	28-32 mm UD 8 cm
300 points	100 x 150	150 x 230	200 x 300
400 points	120 x 180	180 x 280	240 x 360

Terrain and deployment

Terrain is placed in the same way as a standard game, but the size of terrain elements is increased to 7 UD for a 300 pts game and 8 UD for a 400 pts game

The number of LH required to get a bonus to the army initiative is increased proportionately:

- 300 pts game: +1 for 3-8 LH and +2 for 9+ LH
- 400 pts game: +1 for 4-11 LH and +2 for 12+ LH

The deployment area is calculated in the usual way; 5 UD from the halfway line and 4 UD from the flank edges for both 300 and 400 point games.

Demoralisation

Losses are recorded as usual except that if the camp is taken, it is equivalent to 6 demoralisation points for a 300 point game and 8 points for 400 points.

Rerolls

This rule allows players to re-roll some bad dice.

- Each player has 3 rerolls that can be used during the game. It is possible to use tokens or special dice to represent the number of re-rolls.
- Each reroll allows the player to roll one die again during shooting or melee. It is only possible to reroll once and the second result must be kept even if it is inferior to the first one. The phasing player chooses first if he wants to reroll.
- It is not allowed to reroll a die to attack the camp or to try to kill a commander.
- It is not necessary that the unit is in command range to reroll a die.

Average dice

To reduce the random aspect in the game it is possible to use average dice.

- Average dice are 6-sided dice marked 2, 3, 3, 4, 4 and 5.
- Average dice are used during melee resolutions only. For shooting and rallying, standard dice are still used.
- Elite troops count a result of 2 as 5 with average dice.
- Mediocre troops count a result of 5 as 2 with average dice.

Demoralisation rules

This alternative rule takes into account the relative importance of each troop type for army demoralisation.

The army's demoralisation value is calculated as follows:

- Units of Expendables 0
- LI, Levies ½
- Elite LMI, MI, HI, Cv or Kn units 2
- All others units 1

Losses are calculated as follows:

- 1 point per unit in disorder except LI or Levies
- The value of the unit (as detailed above) if it is routed or leaves the table
- Command value +1 for each commander lost
- 4 points if the camp is taken by enemy
- 6 points if the fortified camp is taken by ennemy

The loss of LI and Levies becomes negligible for the army while elite troops (nobles, guards) are now very important. This can make some armies very difficult to demoralise.

ARMY LISTS

The enemy should never know how you intend to fight. Sun Tzu

LIST DESCRIPTION

In the following pages you will find army lists for use with *l'Art de la Guerre*. Each list is designed for a standard 200 points game and it includes a header with the following information:

Number of the list (e.g. 40)
Name of the list (e.g. Alexander the Great)
Period (e.g. 330 – 320 BC)
Regions : Plain, Forest, Mountain, Desert, Steppes
Command bonus (+2 to +6)
Strategist (e.g. Alexander)

COMMANDERS

Every army has three commanders, each one leading an army corp. The player distributes the command points available between the commanders and pays the corresponding points. The commander-in-chief of the army may be a strategist only if the army list allows it. A strategist counts as a brilliant commander in terms of command bonus points (value +2).

Roman Commander

The player can choose one or two sub-commanders to be unreliable to save points at the risk of them being hesitant at the beginning of each battle. One sub-commander can be an ally taken from another list, and in this case is also unreliable. You can only include a commander in a unit type marked with an asterisk (*).

TYPES OF TROOPS

A table for each army list details all the available troop types together with the minimum and maximum number of units allowed and their cost. The title in italics above the troop type gives the usual name, origin or description of the troops.

Troop type	Pts	Units
Companions * Heavy cavalry impact elite	12	2-4
Sogdian, Scythian or Bactrian Light cavalry bow Upgrade to elite (max 1)	6 +1	1-3
Macedonian Phalangites Pikemen	11	2-6
Replace some Phalangites by Medium spearmen	8	0-4
Hypaspists Heavy spearmen elite Medium spearmen elite Pikemen elite	10 10 13	1-2

In the example above:

- The army must have at least 2 units of Companions and not more than 4 of them. This type of unit can include a commander (*).
- The army must have at least 1 unit of light cavalry with bow and not more than 3 of them. One of these units can be upgraded to elite.
- The army must have at least 2 units of pikemen and not more than 6 of them. It is possible to replace up to 4 pikemen with medium spearmen.
- The army must have either 1 or 2 units of Hypaspists. Each one can be an elite pikemen, elite heavy spearmen or elite medium spearmen.

In some army lists there are different options corresponding to varying time periods and/or geographic areas. It is possible to combine options if the armies are compatible in terms of the dates and areas. Some troops can be partially replaced or upgraded, others entirely so, in which case *All* appears in the Units column.

If the troops available change to a different type at a certain date the numbers allowed to be upgraded to elite is not cumulative

Troop type	Pts	Units
Xystophoroi * Heavy cavalry impact Upgrade to elite (max 2)	10 +2	1-4
After 205 BC		
Replace all the Xystophoroi * Cataphract Upgrade to elite (max 2)	11 +2	All

In the example above:

- The army must have at least 1 unit of Xystophoroi and not more than 4 of them. Up to 2 of these units can be upgraded to elite.
- If the period chosen is up to 205 BC, all Xystophoroi must be heavy cavalry impact, whereas if the period chosen is after 205 BC they must all be cataphracts.
- In both cases the maximum number of units allowed to be upgraded to elite is two.

Mixed units represent units with two different types of troops. These are noted as follows:

Troop type	Pts	Units
Militia Heavy spearmen mediocre	6	0-2
Militia Crossbowmen mediocre Light infantry crossbow	5 4	0-2
Florence option		
Replace the Militia ½ Heavy spearmen ½ Crossbowmen	10	All

In the example above:

- The army can have up to 2 militia units of heavy spearmen mediocre and up to 2 militia units of either crossbowmen mediocre or light infantry with crossbow.
- If the Florence option is chosen, all militia units must be replaced by mixed units with one stand of spearmen and one stand of crossbowmen. The army can up to 4 of these mixed units.

ALLIED CORPS

Many army lists can have allies. If the player wishes, he can replace one of his army corps with an allied corps taken from another list. It is not possible to have an allied corps from the same army list, but it is possible to have an unreliable commander from it.

Only one allied corps is allowed and its commander is unreliable by default. To use an allied corps the player refers to the corresponding army list and chooses units from it with the following restrictions:

- If the minimum for the troop type is zero, it remains zero. Otherwise it is divided by two and rounded down, but it cannot be less than one.
- The maximum of each troop type is divided by two and rounded down. This may result in zero, in which case the troop type cannot be chosen.
- Units or fortifications that are not mandatory in the list can be chosen.
- A fortified camp cannot be chosen.
- Only units that correspond to the time period and/or the geographical area of the main army list can be chosen.
- An allied corps cannot exceed 40% of the total points cost of the army.

Troop type	Pts	Units
Noblemen * Cataphract Upgrade to elite (max 3)	11 +2	3-6
Followers Heavy cavalry impetuous	9	0-3
Horse archers Light cavalry bow	6	4-12
Warriors Medium swordsmen Medium spearmen	7 8	2-8
Bowmen mediocre Light infantry bow	5 4	2-5
Heavy artillery	10	0-1

Example of an allied corps taken from the above list:

- 1 to 3 Cataphracts of which the maximum of 1 unit can be upgraded to elite,
- 0 to 1 Heavy cavalry impetuous
- 2 to 6 Light cavalry bow
- 1 to 4 Medium swordsmen or medium spearmen
- 1 to 2 Bowmen mediocre or Light infantry bow
- No artillery is allowed

LISTS CLASSIFICATION

The lists are split into two eras, which are themselves each subdivided into three periods:

Antiquity

- **Ancient period**: Sumer, Babylon, Egypt and Middle East until the rise of the Achaemenid Persians.
- **Classical period**: The Greco-Persian wars, Alexander the Great and his successors, the rise of Rome and the Punic wars.
- **Roman period**: Rome and its enemies, from Julius Caesar until the fall of Rome.

Middle Ages

- **Dark Ages**: Byzantine Empire, Arab conquest, Viking invasions and Carolingian Frankish.
- **Feudal Ages**: Frankish knights, crusades, Mongol invasions.
- **Late Middle Ages**: Hundred Years' War, fall of Byzantine Empire and the rise of the Ottomans.

Lists for the Americas armies have been grouped together and effectively form a seventh period. For a tournament the organisers are free to include them in the most appropriate of the other periods.

Within each period the lists are grouped by geographical area. This method of classification is preferred to a strictly chronological one because it allows the armies belonging to the same time and area to be listed together.

This classification of army lists allows matches or tournaments to be easily organised, whether the choice of armies is unrestricted or it is limited to a theme, for example to armies connected in time and/or by geography. Because the list for some armies covers several periods it is also possible to simply set a start date and an end.

For a tournament, the theme could be:

- Open, i.e. armies from all periods,
- One era, either Antiquity or the Middle Ages,
- Only one or two periods, for example the Feudal Age and the Late Middle Ages,
- All armies between two dates, for instance between 450 AD and 1150 AD,
- Only one period with some restrictions, for instance the Roman period without armies from Africa and Asia.

Burgundian Ordonnance army

LIST INDEX

ANCIENT PERIOD 83

Sumer & Babylon 83

1 - Sumer and Akkad 83
2 - Sumerian Successor 83
3 - Amorite Highlanders 84
4 - Elamite 84
5 - Old Assyrian and Babylonian 85
6 - Kassite Babylonian..85
7 - Assyrian 86
8 - Neo-Babylonian 86
9 - Assyrian Empire and Sargonid 87

Ancient Egypt 88

10 - Old and Middle Kingdom Egyptian 88
11 - Nubian 88
12 - Libyan 88
13 - Hyksos 89
14 - New Kingdom Egyptian 89
15 - Libyan Egyptian 90
16 - Kushite Egyptian..90

Middle East 91

17 - Ancient Bedouin...91
18 - Syrian City States 91
19 - Oman and Gulf States 91
20 - Hittite 92
21 - Hurri-Mitanni 92
22 - Syria, Canaan and Ugarit...........................93
23 - Ancient Hebrew 93
24 - Sea Peoples...93
25 - Philistine..94
26 - Aramaean and Neo-Hittite 94
27 - Urartu 95
28 - Medes 95
29 - Phrygian 95

Early Europe.. 96

30 - Mycenaean 96
31 - Geometric Greek 96
32 - Phoenicians of Cyprus 97
33 - Celts 97

Early Asia... 97

34 - Indus Valley..97
35 - Vedic Indian...98
36 - Shang Chinese 98
37 - Spring and Autumn Chinese.....................98

CLASSICAL PERIOD 99

Macedonian.. 99

38 - Early Macedonian 99
39 - Alexandrian Macedonian 99
40 - Alexander the Great 100
41 - Early Successors 100
42 - Seleucid 102
43 - Ptolemaic 103
44 - Pyrrhic 103
45 - Later Macedonian 104
46 - Graeco-Bactrian and Graeco-Indian........104

Rome and Italy 105

47 - Italian Tribes...105
48 - Etruscan 105
49 - Tullian Roman...106
50 - Syracusan 106
51 - Campanian, Lucanian, Apulian and Bruttian 107
52 - Camillan Roman 107
53 - Republican Roman 108

Carthage and Africa...109

54 - Early Carthaginian 109
55 - Carthaginian...109
56 - Numidian..110
57 - Saitic Egyptian..111
58 - Cyrenian Greek 111
59 - Meroitic Kushite...112

Greece and Danube 112

60 - Classical Greek 112
61 - Hellenistic Greek..113
62 - Illyrian 114
63 - Thracian 114

Asia minor...115

64 - Achaemenid Persian..................................115
65 - Lydian 115
66 - Lycian 116
67 - Bithynian...116
68 - Later Achaemenid Persian 117
69 - Cappadocian...117
70 - Bosporan Kingdom....................................118
71 - Armenian 118
72 - Galatian 119
73 - Pergamon 120

East and Steppes 120

74 - Aramaean...120
75 - Early Arab...121
76 - Scythian 121
77 - Sarmatian 122

Classical Asia...122

78 - Vietnamese 122
79 - Classical Indian 123
80 - Warring States 124
81 - Ch'iang and Ti..124

ROMAN PERIOD......................................125

Roman Empire..125

82 - Triumvirate Roman 125
83 - Spartacus...125
84 - Early Imperial Roman 126
85 - Middle Imperial Roman...........................126
86 - Late Imperial Roman...............................127
87 - Patrician Roman..128

Barbarian 129

88 - Gallic...129
89 - Ancient Spanish 130
90 - German...130
91 - Dacian and Carpi 130
92 - Visigoth 131

93 - Vandal 131
94 - Ostrogoth 132
95 - Gepid, Herul and Taifali 132
96 - Franks, Alemanni, Burgundi, Suevi 133
97 - Visigoths in Spain 133

Great Britain 134

98 - Ancient British 134
99 - Caledonian, Irish, Scots and Pictish 134
100 - Saxon, Anglo-Saxon, Frisian, Jutes 135
101 - Romano-Britsh 135

East Roman 136

102 - Parthian 136
103 - Judaean Jewish 136
104 - Commagene 137
105 - Mithridatic 137
106 - Palmyran 138

Steppes 139

107 - Kushan 139
108 - Alan 139
109 - Sassanid Persian 139
110 - Huns 140
111 - Hephthalite Huns 141

Ancient Africa 141

112 - Blemmyes and Nobatae 141
113 - Moors 142
114 - Kingdom of Axum 142
115 - African Vandal 142

Ancient Asia 143

116 - Hsiung-Nu 143
117 - Han Chinese 143
118 - Hsien-Pi 144
119 - Three Kingdoms Chinese 144
120 - Chinese North. and South. Dynasties 145
121 - Tamil Indian 146
122 - Three Kingdoms Korean 146
123 - Japanese 147
124 - Emishi 147

DARK AGES 148

Byzance and Armenia 148

125 - Justinian Byzantine 148
126 - Maurikian Byzantine 148
127 - Thematic Byzantine 149
128 - Nikephorian Byzantine 150
129 - Armenian Principality 150
130 - Bagratid Armenian 151

Arab Empire 151

131 - Arab Conquest 151
132 - Umayyad Arab 152
133 - North African Arab 153
134 - Andalusian Arab 153
135 - Abbasid Arab 154
136 - Arab Indian 154
137 - Khurasanian 155
138 - Tulunid and Iqshidid Egyptian 156
139 - Dynastic Bedouin 156

Central Asia 157

140 - Sogdian and Central Asia City States 157
141 - Central Asian Turkish 157

Western Europe 158

142 - Lombard 158
143 - Italian Ostrogoth 158
144 - Merovingian Frankish 158
145 - Armourican Breton 159
146 - Welsh 159
147 - Anglo-Saxon 160
148 - Feudal Spanish 160
149 - Carolingian Frankish 161
150 - Viking and Leidang 161
151 - Feudal Irish 162
152 - Pre-Feudal Scots 163

Eastern Europe 163

153 - Slav 163
154 - Avar 164
155 - Bulgar 164
156 - Khazar 165
157 - Serbo-Croatian 165
158 - Magyar 166
159 - Pecheneg 166
160 - Rus 166

Sudan 167

161 - Christian Nubian 167
162 - Beja 167

Far East 168

163 - Burmese 168
164 - Hindu Indian 168
165 - Sui and Tang Chinese 169
166 - Tibetan 170
167 - Khmer Empire and Champa 170
168 - Nan-Chao and Dali 171
169 - Tang and Five Dynasties Chinese 171
170 - Shatuo Turkish 172
171 - Tribal Mongol 172

FEUDAL AGES 173

Feudal Europe 173

172 - Norman or Frankish 173
173 - Anglo-Danish 173
174 - Anglo-Norman 174
175 - Feudal French 174
176 - Feudal English 175
177 - Feudal Scots 175
178 - Anglo-Irish 176
179 - Scots Isles and Highlanders 176
180 - Normans in Sicily 177
181 - Communal Italian 178
182 - Imperial Frankish 178
183 - Feudal German 179

Crusades 179

184 - Komnenan Byzantine 179
185 - Cilician Armenian 180
186 - Crusader 180
187 - Later Crusader 181
188 - Frankish Cyprus 182
189 - Eastern Latin Empire 182
190 - Order of St John 183

Muslims 183
191 - Buyid 183
192 - Dynastic Kurdish 184
193 - Ghaznavid 184
194 - Fatimid Egyptian 185
195 - Seljuk Turk 186
196 - Berber 186
197 - Syrian 187
198 - Ghurid 188
199 - Ayyubid Egyptian 188
200 - Khwarazmian 188
Africa 189
201 - Sahelian Empire 189
202 - Tuareg 189
Feudal Eastern Europe 190
203 - Feudal Polish 190
204 - Feudal Hungarian 190
205 - Georgian 191
206 - Feudal Russian 191
207 - Cuman 192
208 - Prussian and Estonian 192
209 - Teutonic Knights 192
Feudal Asia 194
210 - Samurai 194
211 - Khitan-Liao 194
212 - Koryo Korean 195
213 - Medieval Vietnamese 195
214 - Song Chinese 196
215 - Xi-Xia 196
216 - Jurchen-Chin 197
217 - Qara-Khitan 197
218 - Mongol Empire 198

LATE MIDDLE AGES 199

Medieval Europe 199
219 - Granadine 199
220 - Swiss 199
221 - Medieval Scandinavian 200
222 - Medieval Scots 200
223 - Medieval Irish 201
224 - Condottieri 202
225 - Hundred Years War English 203
226 - Hundred Years War French 203
227 - Medieval German 204
228 - Medieval Spanish 205
229 - Navarrese 206
230 - Free Company 206
231 - Burgundian 207
232 - Low Countries 208
233 - Medieval Welsh 208
234 - French Ordonnance 208
235 - Burgundian Ordonnance 209
236 - Wars of the Roses 210
Medieval Eastern Europe 211
237 - Lithuanian 211
238 - Medieval Hungarian 211
239 - Muscovite Russian 212
240 - Golden Horde 213
241 - Medieval Polish 213
242 - Hussite 214
Turks and Balkans 214
243 - Serbian Empire 214
244 - Later Bulgarian 215
245 - Later Byzantine 215
246 - Turkoman 216
247 - Ottoman Turkish 216
248 - Catalan Company 217
249 - Vlach and Moldavian 217
250 - Albanian 218
251 - Ottoman Empire 218
252 - Besieged Byzantine 219
Medieval Egypt 220
253 - Mamluk 220
Central Asia 220
254 - Islamic Persian 220
255 - Ilkhanid Mongol 220
256 - Steppes Mongol 221
257 - Jalayirid 221
258 - Timurid 221
259 - Black Sheep & White Sheep Turkoman 222
Medieval Asia 223
260 - Delhi Sultanate 223
261 - Indonesian and Malay 224
262 - Siam 224
263 - Yuan Chinese 224
264 - Later Samurai 225
265 - Ming Chinese 226
266 - Yi Korean 226

AMERICA 227

Central America 227
267 - Maya 227
268 - Zapotec and Mixtec 228
269 - Toltec 228
270 - Chinantec 228
271 - Tarascan 229
272 - Aztec 229
273 - Texcala 230
South America 231
274 - Inca 231
275 - Chanca 231
276 - Chimu 231
277 - Tupi 232
278 - Mapuche 232
North America 232
279 - Chichimec 232
280 - Pueblos 232
281 - Forest Indian 233
282 - Mississippi Indian 233
283 - Plains Indian 233

ANCIENT PERIOD

SUMER & BABYLON

1 - SUMER AND AKKAD

3000 - 2004 BC
Plain
Command +4
Strategist: King Agga (2700 BC), Sargon of Akkad (2334-2279 BC)

Sumerians occupied Mesopotamia between the Tigris and the Euphrates, in the current region of Iraq. They lived in city-states such as Ur, Eridu, Nippur, Umma or Larsa. These city-states of Mesopotamia were at war to control water and irrigation canals. A very ancient account tells the story of the conflict between the powerful king Aga of Kish and the hero Gilgamesh, defender of the city of Ur. The greatest warrior monarch was Sargon of Akkad who, circa 2330 BC, unified the city-states and extended his influence as far as Syria, Anatolia and the Gulf of Oman. In 2193 BC, a great revolt caused the fall off the Akkadian Empire. The country was reunited again during the 3rd dynasty of Ur, between 2112 and 2004 BC.

Troop type	Pts	Units
4-wheeled battle cars * Heavy chariot Downgrade to mediocre	 10 -2	2-4
Scouts on equids Light cavalry bow mediocre	4	0-1
Royal guardsmen * Medium swordsmen 2HW elite Bowmen pavise elite	10	0-2
Warriors and militia Medium spearmen mediocre Heavy spearmen mediocre Add pavise Upgrade to ordinary (max ½)	 5 6 +1 +2	8-24
Militia Bowmen mediocre	5	2-6
Amorites mercenaries Medium swordsmen	7	0-4
Zagros hillmen Javelinmen mediocre	5	0-4
Nomads Light infantry javelin Light infantry bow	4	0-4
Shepherds Light infantry sling	4	0-2
Levy	3	0-4
Fortifications	1	0-6
Fortified camp	6	0-1

Note

- Elamite allies (List #4 Elamite)
- Bedouin allies (List #17 Ancient Bedouin)
- Syrian allies (List #18 Syrian City States)
- Indian allies (List #34 Indus Valley)

2 - SUMERIAN SUCCESSOR

2028 - 1460 BC
Plain
Command +4

After the collapse of the 3rd Dynasty of Ur, city-states emerged in the south of Mesopotamia. The main ones were the cities of Eshunna, Isin and Larsa. These kingdoms preserved part of the military tradition of Sumer and were ruled by Amorite or Elamite dynasties.

Troop type	Pts	Units
4-wheeled battle cars * Heavy chariot Downgrade to mediocre	 10 -2	0-3
Scouts on equids Light cavalry bow mediocre	4	0-1
Royal guardsmen * Heavy spearmen elite Medium swordsmen 2HW elite	10	0-2
Warriors and militia Medium spearmen mediocre Heavy spearmen mediocre Add pavise Upgrade to ordinary (max ½)	 5 6 +1 +2	12-24
Elamites mercenaries Bowmen Downgrade to mediocre	 7 -2	0-6

Amorites mercenaries Medium swordsmen	7	0-4
Zagros hillmen Javelinmen mediocre	5	0-2
Light infantry javelin	4	1-3
Light infantry bow	4	1-3
Light infantry sling	4	1-3

Note

- Elamite allies (List #4 Elamite)
- Assyrian allies (List #5 Old Assyrian and Babylonian)
- Bedouin allies (List #17 Ancient Bedouin)

3 - Amorite Highlanders

3000 – 1000 BC
Mountain
Command +2

The Amorites were a people that Sumerian texts refer to as *Martu* and are called *Amurru* in Akkadian. The Amorites were fierce enemies of the Sumerian cities and caused the fall of the 3rd Dynasty of Ur around the end of the 21st century BC. Amorite dynasties developed in many cities of the Near East, particularly in Babylon. The Gasgans were regular opponents of the Hittites. They were the ones who overthrew the Hittite Empire circa 1180 BC. The Guti seized power in the city-states after the great revolt in 2193 BC against the Akkadian Empire.

Troop type	Pts	Units
*Guardsmen ** Medium swordsmen 2HW elite Bowmen elite (max 2)	10 9	0-4
Warriors Medium swordsmen Downgrade to mediocre	7 -2	6-16
Bowmen Downgrade to mediocre	7 -2	0-8
Hill tribesmen Javelinmen Downgrade to mediocre	7 -2	0-12
Light infantry javelin	4	4-8
Light infantry sling	4	2-6
Light infantry bow	4	0-4
Gasgans		
Replace all warriors Medium swordsmen impetuous	7	All
Chariots with 2 horses Light chariot impetuous elite	9	0-2

Gutis and The Great Revolt 2193 BC Sumerian allies (List #1 Sumer and Akkad) Elamite allies (List #4 Elamite) Syrian allies (List #18 Syrian City States)		
Makkans mercenaries Medium swordsmen impetuous	7	0-2
Melukhkans Mercenaries Medium spearmen Bowmen	7	0-2
Sumerians and Akkadians subjects (between 2193 and 2112 BC) Medium spearmen mediocre Heavy spearmen mediocre Add pavise Upgrade to ordinary (max ½)	5 6 +1 +2	0-8

4 - Elamite

3000 – 539 BC
Plain, Mountain
Command +3

The Elamites occupied the south west of Iran around the regions or Susa and Anshan. They waged war against the Mesopotamian powers (Sumerians, Babylonians and Assyrians). After a long struggle against Assyria, the last Elamites were integrated into the Achaemenid Empire.

Troop type	Pts	Units
Only before 800 BC		
*4-wheeled battle cars ** Heavy chariot Downgrade to mediocre	10 -2	0-4
Scouts on equids Light cavalry bow mediocre	4	0-2
*Guardsmen ** Medium swordsmen impact elite Bowmen pavise elite	10	0-2
Militia from 2600 to 2100 BC Medium spearmen Heavy spearmen	7 8	0-4
Warriors from 2100 BC Medium swordsmen impact	8	
Bowmen Bowmen Downgrade to mediocre	7 -2	12-24
Light infantry bow (max 6)	4	
Hill tribesmen Javelinmen Downgrade to mediocre	7 -2	0-4
From 1400 BC		
*Chariots with 2 horses ** Light chariot bow	9	2-6

From 800 BC (Later period)		
*Chariots with 2 horses ** Light chariot bow Upgrade to elite (max 4)	 9 +2	2-12
Horsemen Medium cavalry bow Light cavalry bow	 9 6	2-6
Militia with mixed units ½ Medium swordsmen ½ Bowmen	9	0-4
Archers Bowmen Downgrade to mediocre	 7 -2	8-16
Light infantry bow (max 6)	4	

Note

- Babylonian allies (List #8 Neo-Babylonian)
- Bedouin allies (List #17 Ancient Bedouin)
- Indian allies (List #34 Indus Valley)

5 - OLD ASSYRIAN AND BABYLONIAN

1900 – 1595 BC
Plain, Mountain, Desert
Command +4

Following the fall of the 3rd Dynasty of Ur, the Amorites became civilised and founded the Assyrian and Babylonian states. This list also covers the states of Syria until their conquest by the Hittites. Babylon was attacked by the Hurrians and the Kassites and finally razed and destroyed by the Hittites in 1595 BC.

Troop type	Pts	Units
*Chariots with 2 horses ** Light chariot bow Upgrade to elite	 9 +2	0-2
Scouts Light cavalry bow mediocre	4	0-1
Warriors Medium swordsmen impact	8	6-16
Warriors with bow Bowmen	7	0-2
Nomads Medium swordsmen mediocre	5	0-4
Sabum qullatum Javelinmen Light infantry javelin	 7 4	2-8
Sabum qullatum Light infantry bow Light infantry sling	4	2-8
Levy	3	0-2
Fortified camp	6	0-1

6 - KASSITE BABYLONIAN

1595 – 750 BC
Plain
Command +5
Strategist: Nebuchadnezzar I (1124-1103 BC)

This list covers the Kassite dynasty that was on the Babylonian throne until it was overthrown by the Elamites. In turn they were driven out by the King of Isin, who reinstalled the dynasty in Babylon in 1130 BC. Nebuchadnezzar I was considered the greatest king of the dynasty of Isin due to his victory over the Elamites. From 1050 BC, Babylon suffered from the incursions of the Arameans and the Chaldeans and fell into chaos. Afterwards the country entered into a long war against Assyria.

Troop type	Pts	Units
*Chariots with 2 horses ** Light chariot bow Upgrade to elite (max 2)	 9 +2	4-10
Scouts Light cavalry bow mediocre	4	0-1
Militia Medium spearmen Add support	 7 +1	4-12
Militia Bowmen mediocre Upgrade to ordinary (max 4)	5	4-12
Arameans and hillmen Javelinmen Downgrade to mediocre	 7 -2	0-10
Light infantry javelin	4	0-4
Light infantry bow Light infantry sling	4	0-4
Fortified camp	6	0-1
From 890 BC		
*Replace some chariots with 2 horses by chariots with 4 horses ** Heavy chariot impact Upgrade to elite (max 2)	 11 +2	0-4
Horsemen Medium cavalry mediocre	5	0-2

Note

- Only two elite chariots in total
- Assyrian allies (List #7 Assyrian) from 890 BC
- Bedouin allies (List #17 Ancient Bedouin) from 890 BC
- Aramean allies (List #26 Aramean and Neo-Hittite)

7 - Assyrian

1365 – 745 BC
Plain, Mountain
Command +5
Strategists: Shalmaneser I (1274-1245 BC), Tukulti-Ninurta (1274-1245 BC), Tiglath-pileser I (1116-1077 BC)

The Assyrian kingdom expanded during the 14th century BC and became as powerful as those of Babylon and the Hittites. It was at its peak under the kings Shalmaneser and Tukulti-Ninurta. Afterwards, the kingdom was considerably weakened under the pressure of the Arameans despite Tiglath-Pileser's victories. From the 10th century BC the Assyrian dynasty started a reconquest and became the main power of the Middle-East.

Troop type	Pts	Units
*Chariots with 2 horses **		
Light chariot bow	9	4-12
Upgrade to elite (max 4 in total)	+2	
*Chariots with 3 horses (after 890) **		
Heavy chariot impact (max ½)	11	
Upgrade to elite (max 4 in total)	+2	
Scouts		
Light cavalry bow mediocre	4	0-1
Pethalle horsemen (after 890)		
Medium cavalry bow mediocre	7	0-4
Upggrade to ordinary	+2	
Asharittu warriors		
Medium swordsmen impact elite	10	2-6
Add support	+1	
Hupshu warriors		
Medium swordsmen	7	0-10
Add support	+1	
Downgrade to mediocre	-2	
Hupshu warriors		
½ Medium swordsmen	9	
½ Bowmen		
Bowmen mediocre	5	0-6
Arameans		
Javelinmen	7	0-4
Downgrade to mediocre	-2	
Light infantry bow Light infantry sling	4	0-4
Light infantry javelin	4	0-2
Levy	3	0-2
Fortified camp	6	0-1

Note

- Neo-Hittite allies (List #26 Aramean and Neo-Hittite)

8 - Neo-Babylonian

750 – 482 BC
Plain
Command +5
Strategist: Nebuchadnezzar II (604-552 BC)

This list covers the period when Babylon was under Assyrian domination until the creation of the Neo-Babylonian Empire by Nebuchadnezzar II. Helped by the Medes, the Babylonians detroyed the Assyrian power in 609 BC. in turn they fell to the mighty Achaemenid Persians in 539 BC. The list also comprises the period of the last revolts in 522-521 and in 482 BC.

Troop type	Pts	Units
*Chariots with 4 horses **		
Heavy chariot impact	11	2-4
Upgrade to elite (max 2)	+2	
Guard horsemen		
Medium cavalry bow	9	2-4
Heavy cavalry bow	11	
Chaldeans and Arameans		
Medium cavalry bow	9	2-4
Downgrade to mediocre	-2	
Scythians		
Light cavalry bow	6	0-4
Bedouins		
Medium camelry	8	0-4
Medium camelry bow	10	
Foot guardsmen		
Heavy spearmen elite	10	0-2
Add armour	+2	
Greek mercenaries		
Heavy spearmen	8	0-2
Add armour	+2	
Chaldeans and Arameans		
Bowmen	7	6-16
Downgrade to mediocre	-2	
Upgrade to mixed units (max 6)		
½ Medium swordsmen	9	
½ Bowmen		
Light infantry bow Light infantry sling	4	0-4
Chaldeans		
Javelinmen	7	0-2
Light infantry javelin	4	
Levy	3	0-2
Fortifications	1	0-6

Note

- Elamite allies (List #4 Elamite)
- Bedouin allies (List #17 Ancient Bedouin)
- Medes allies (List #28 Medes)

9 - Assyrian Empire and Sargonid

745 - 609 BC
Plain, Mountain
Command +6
Strategists: Tiglath-pileser III (744-727 BC), Sargon II (721-705 BC), Sennacherib (704-681 BC) and Assurbanipal (669-627 BC)

From Tiglath-Pileser III the Assyrians reformed their Empire and their army and expanded like never before. Under the great Sargonid kings the Assyrian Empire pushed its borders through Anatolia and Egypt. After the death of Assubanipal a revolt broke out. The Babylonians and the Medes took advantage to defeat the Assyrian Empire in 609 BC.

Troop type	Pts	Units
*Chariots with 4 horses **		
Heavy chariot impact	11	2-4
Upgrade to elite (max 4)	+2	
*Horsemen **		
Medium cavalry bow	9	2-8
Heavy cavalry bow	11	
Upgrade to elite (max 4)	+2	
Scythians and Cimmerians		
Light cavalry bow	6	0-2
Bedouins		
Light camelry bow mediocre	5	0-2
Medium camelry bow mediocre	8	
Guardsmen		
Medium swordsmen elite	9	1-2
Heavy swordsmen elite	10	
Add armour	+2	
Add support	+1	
Line infantry		
Medium swordsmen	7	2-6
Heavy swordsmen	8	
Add support	+1	
Line infantry		
½ Medium swordsmen	9	
½ Bowmen		
Line infantry		
½ Heavy swordsmen	10	
½ Bowmen		
Poor infantry		
Medium swordsmen mediocre	5	0-6
Heavy swordsmen mediocre	6	
Add support	+1	
Egyptians and Kushites		
Bowmen	7	0-2
Downgrade to mediocre	-2	
Light infantry bow	4	1-4
Light infantry sling		
Javelinmen	7	0-2
Light infantry javelin	4	
Levy	3	0-2
Fortifications	1	0-6
Fortified camp	6	0-1

Note

- Elamite allies (List #4 Elamite)
- Egyptian allies (List #15 Libyan Egyptian)
- Bedouin allies (List #17 Ancient Bedouin)
- Hebrew allies (List #23 Ancient Hebrew)
- Philistine allies (List #25 Philistine)
- Aramean allies (List #26 Aramean & Neo-Hittite)
- Medes allies (List #28 Medes)
- Phrygian allies (List #29 Phrygian)
- Phoenician allies (List #32 Phoenician of Cyprus)
- Scythian allies (List #76 Scythian)

Assyrian infantry

ANCIENT EGYPT

10 - Old and Middle Kingdom Egyptian

3000 - 1550 BC
Plain, Desert
Command +4

This list covers the armies of ancient Egypt over the periods of the Ancient Empire (3000 to 2260 BC) and Middle Empire (2260 to 1550 BC). Around 1650 the Hyksos, a Semitic people, invaded the north of Egypt. They were only driven back about a hundred years later by the 17th Egyptian Dynasty who had kept control over the southern part of the country.

Troop type	Pts	Units
Guardsmen and Sherden *		
Medium swordsmen 2HW elite	10	2-4
Heavy swordsmen 2HW elite	11	
Warriors		
Medium swordsmen impact	8	4-10
Archers		
Bowmen mediocre	5	4-12
Upgrade to ordinary (max 6)	+2	
Conscripts		
Medium swordsmen mediocre	5	2-12
Nubians		
Bowmen	7	0-4
Light infantry bow	4	
Libyans and Egyptians		
Javelinmen	7	0-4
Light infantry javelin	4	
Bedouins		
Light infantry sling	4	0-2
Levy	3	0-2

Note

- Commanders can be represented by a two-horse chariot or in a litter.

Egyptian javelinmen

11 - Nubian

3000 - 593 BC
Plain, Desert
Command +2

Nubia spreads south of Egypt after the 1st cataract of the Nile and corresponds to modern day Sudan. The Egyptians were often at war with the Nubians, whom they subjugated in 1898 BC. Nubia became independent again around 1080 BC. The Kushites, descendants of Egyptians who had settled in Nubia, ruled the country afterwards.

Troop type	Pts	Units
Warriors with bow *		
Bowmen	7	16-32
Upgrade to elite (max 4)	+2	
Downgrade to mediocre	-2	
Light infantry bow	4	
Fanatics warriors *		
Medium swordsmen impetuous	7	0-6
Upgrade to elite	+2	
Javelinmen	7	0-6
Light infantry javelin	4	

12 - Libyan

3000 BC - 70 AD
Desert
Command +2

Libyans represented the most serious and constant threat to Egypt. During the 13st century BC the threat grew bigger because of the alliance between the Libyans and the Sea Peoples. The Libyans conquered northern Egypt around 945 BC and had founded the Libyan dynasty.

Troop type	Pts	Units
Libyan warriors *		
Javelinmen	7	12-30
Downgrade to mediocre	-2	
Fanatics warriors *		
Medium swordsmen impetuous	7	0-12
Upgrade to elite (max 4)	+2	
Bowmen	7	0-8
Downgrade to mediocre	-2	
Light infantry javelin	4	2-12
Light infantry bow	4	0-4
From 1250 BC		
Chariots with 2 or 4 horses *		
Light chariot bow	9	1-4
Heavy chariot	10	

Only Garamantes after 200 BC		
*Replace all chariots ** Light cavalry Javelin	6	All

Note

- Sea People allies (List #24 Sea Peoples)

13 - Hyksos

1650 - 1546 BC
Plain, Desert
Command +4

Hyksos had taken control of northern Egypt between 1650 and 1546 BC. They founded the 15th and 16th Egyptian Dynasties before being driven out by their Egyptian vassals, who had remained masters of the southern part of the country.

Troop type	Pts	Units
*Chariots with 2 horses ** Light chariot bow Upgrade to elite (max 4)	9 +2	2-8
Scouts Light cavalry bow mediocre	4	0-1
Warriors Medium swordsmen impact	8	4-12
Bowmen	7	0-2
Canaanite and Amorite warriors Medium swordsmen Javelinmen	7	2-12
Libyan Light infantry javelin	4	0-3
Aamu and Libyan skirmishers Light infantry bow Light infantry sling	4	0-3
Egyptian levies Levy	3	0-2

Note

- Egyptian allies (List #10 Old and Middle Kingdom Egyptian)

14 - New Kingdom Egyptian

1550 - 1070 BC
Plain, Desert
Command +5
Strategist: Tutmosis III (1479-1425 BC), Ramesses III (1184-1153 BC)

Following the expulsion of the Hyksos, the pharaohs of the 18th dynasty tried to control Palestine and Syria. Thutmosis III was considered the greatest military leader of his time. The 19th Dynasty was that of Seti I and Ramesses II who fought the battle of Kadesh against the Hittites. Circa 1180 Egypt was invaded by the Libyans and by the Sea Peoples, who were driven back by Ramesses III, first ruler of the 20th dynasty. His successors were weaker and Egypt fell under the control of a Libyan chief named Sheshonk.

Troop type	Pts	Units
*Chariots with 2 horses ** Light chariot bow Upgrade to elite (max 4)	9 +2	4-10
Scouts Light cavalry bow mediocre	4	0-1
Guardsmen Heavy swordsmen 2HW elite	11	0-2
Sherden guardsmen Heavy swordsmen impetuous elite	10	
Warriors (all of the same type) Medium swordsmen impact Medium spearmen	8 7	2-8
Warriors with two handed axe Medium swordsmen 2HW	8	0-2
Sherden warriors Medium swordsmen impetuous	7	0-6
Libyan warriors Medium swordsmen impetuous	7	0-4
Egyptian archers Bowmen Downgrade to mediocre	7 -2	2-6
Syro-Canaanites Javelinmen Light infantry javelin	7 4	0-4
Nubians or Egyptians Light infantry bow	4	0-2
Bedouins Light infantry sling Light infantry javelin	4	0-2
Fortified camp	6	0-1

Note

- Sea Peoples allies (List #24 Sea Peoples)

Pharaoh's Chariot

15 - Libyan Egyptian

945 - 700 BC
Plain, Desert
Command +3

After the Libyan takeover, three succeeding Libyan dynasties of Egyptian culture, the 22nd, 23rd and 24th, ruled the land. Only the north was controled, while the south remained under influence of the Kushites from Nubia. In the end, the Kushites took control of the whole country and installed the 25th Nubian dynasty.

Troop type	Pts	Units
*Chariots with 2 horses ** Light chariot bow Upgrade to elite (max 2)	 9 +2	2-10
Medium cavalry mediocre	5	0-3
Light cavalry bow	6	0-2
Light cavalry javelin	6	0-2
Sherden guardsmen Heavy swordsmen 2HW elite	11	0-2
Egyptian guardsmen Heavy spearmen elite	10	
Meshwesh Libyan warriors Medium swordsmen impetuous Heavy swordsmen impetuous Upgrade to elite (all or none)	 7 8 +2	2-8
Egyptian warriors Medium swordsmen mediocre	5	2-4
Egyptian archers Bowmen mediocre	5	2-4
Bedouins and Palestinians Javelinmen mediocre Light infantry javelin	 5 4	0-8
Nubians and Libyans Light infantry bow	4	0-4

16 - Kushite Egyptian

850 - 660 BC
Plain, Desert
Command +3

Nubia, which corresponds to modern Sudan, was controlled over a long period by Egypt, which brought its culture and its gods. Nubia became independent circa 1080 BC. It was ruled by the Kushites, who were descendants of the Nubian people and the Egyptian immigrants. In 730 BC, the Kushites started a crusade against the Libyan dynasty in the north of the country and conquered the whole of Egypt in 712 BC. A series of wars against Assyria for the control of Syria resulted in the defeat of the Kushites. They were driven out of Egypt but continued to reign over Sudan and founded the kingdom of Meroe in 593 BC.

Troop type	Pts	Units
*Chariots with 2 or 4 horses ** Light chariot bow Heavy chariot impetuous Upgrade to elite	 9 10 +2	2-4
*Kushite horsemen ** Medium cavalry Heavy cavalry (max ½) Upgrade to elite (max 4)	 7 9 +2	2-8
Light cavalry javelin	6	0-4
Kushite Bowmen Bowmen	7	2-10
Kushite warriors Medium swordsmen	7	0-4
Libyan warriors Javelinmen Light infantry javelin	 7 4	0-4
Kushite slingers Light infantry sling	4	0-4
Light infantry bow	4	0-4
Egyptian troops (730 to 660 BC)		
*Chariots with 2 or 4 horses ** Light chariot bow Heavy chariot impact	 9 11	1-4
Medium cavalry mediocre	5	0-2
Light cavalry bow Light cavalry javelin	6	0-1
Egyptian warriors Medium swordsmen mediocre	5	1-4
Egyptian archers Bowmen mediocre	5	1-2

Note

- Egyptian allies (List #15 Libyan Egyptian) before 730 BC
- From 730, Egyptian troops can be included in the army. They must be all in the same corps under the command of an Egyptian commander.
- One sub commander can be included in a Kushite horsemen unit.

MIDDLE EAST

17 - Ancient Bedouin

3000 – 300 BC
Desert
Command +2

This list includes all peoples and tribes from the eastern part of the Middle East and the edges of the steppe before the introduction of the horse. This is in particular the first Aramean people, the Midianites and the Amalekites.

Troop type	Pts	Units
Warriors on camels * Medium camelry bow Downgrade to mediocre	 10 -2	8-16
Scouts on camels Light camelry bow Downgrade to mediocre	 7 -2	0-4
Warriors on foot * Medium swordsmen Downgrade to mediocre	 7 -2	0-12
Javelinmen Light infantry javelin	7 4	0-8
Bowmen Downgrade to mediocre	7 -2	0-6
Light infantry bow Light infantry sling	4	0-4

Note
- Mesopotamian allies (List #1 Sumer and Akkad)
- Assyrian allies (List #9 Assyrian Empire and Sargonid)
- Syrian allies (List #18 Syrian City States)

18 - Syrian City States

2800 – 2200 BC
Plain, Mountain, Desert
Command +2

This list presents the armies of the ancient states of Syria, such as the cities of Mari and Elba. At that time, Syria was divided into city-states who maintained close ties with Mesopotamia. Located on major commercial routes, the cities were in turn independent or submitted to the influence of a powerful neighbor.

Troop type	Pts	Units
4-wheeled battle cars * Heavy chariot Downgrade to mediocre	 10 -2	0-2
Scouts Light cavalry javelin mediocre	4	0-1
Guardsmen with axes * Medium swordsmen impact	8	0-4
Militia * Medium spearmen mediocre Heavy spearmen mediocre Add pavise Upgrade to ordinary (max ½)	 5 6 +1 +2	4-8
Nomads Bowmen mediocre Upgrade to ordinary (max 4)	 5 +2	4-12
Nomads Javelinmen Downgrade to mediocre	 7 -2	4-12
Light infantry sling Light infantry bow	4	0-8
Light infantry javelin	4	0-4

Note
- Sumerian allies (List #1 Sumer and Akkad)
- Bedouin allies (List #17 Ancient Bedouin)

19 - Oman and Gulf States

2800 – 312 BC
Plain, Desert
Command +2

In the Arabian Peninsula some brilliant, though little known, civilizations had emerged very early. Thus in Yemen, cities maintained vast irrigation networks and navigators from Oman traded with Sumer and Vedic India.

Troop type	Pts	Units
Warriors Javelinmen Medium swordsmen Downgrade to mediocre	 7 7 -2	6-24
Warriors with sword * Medium swordsmen impact Upgrade to elite (max 2)	 8 +2	0-8
Scouts Light cavalry javelin mediocre	4	0-1
Light infantry javelin Upgrade to elite	4 +1	2-6
Light infantry bow	4	0-6
Makkan option from 1300 BC		
Replace all warriors and warriors with sword * Medium swordsmen impetuous Upgrade to elite (max 2)	 7 +2	All
Bowmen mediocre	5	4-12

From 1000 BC Bedouin allies (List #17 Ancient Bedouin)		
Horsemen * Medium cavalry mediocre	5	1-3
Warriors on camels Medium camelry Medium camelry bow	 8 10	0-8
Scouts on camels Light camelry bow Downgrade to mediocre	 7 -2	0-2

Note

- Babylonian allies (List #6 Kassite Babylonian) before 1000 BC and not with Makkan option.

20 - Hittite

1680 – 1180 BC
Plain, Mountain
Command +5
Strategists: Mursili I (1620-1590 BC), Suppiluliuma (1380-1336 BC)

The Hittites came from Anatolia and were one of the major powers of the ancient world. King Mursili I destroyed the power of the Amorites in Syria and overthrew the 1st Babylonian dynasty. After a period of decline, the Empire was restored by Suppiluliuma circa 1380 BC. Mitanni and Syria were reduced to the state of vassals. The Hittites fought the armies of Ramesses II in the famous battle of Kadesh in 1247 BC. After having been sorely weakened by the invasions of the Sea Peoples, the Hittite Empire collapsed under the blows of the Gasgans, a people from the mountains of Pontus.

Troop type	Pts	Units
Hittite chariots (before 1380 BC) * Light chariot Light chariot bow Upgrade to elite	 7 9 +2	2-4
Scouts Light cavalry bow mediocre	4	0-1
Guardsmen Medium spearmen elite Medium swordsmen impact elite	 9 10	0-2
Hittites warriors Medium spearmen	7	6-16
Syro-Canaanites and Bedouins Javelinmen mediocre Light infantry javelin	 5 4	2-6
Bowmen mediocre Light infantry bow	5 4	0-4
Light infantry sling	4	0-2
Levy	3	0-2

Hittite Empire from 1380 BC Mitanni allies (List #21 Hurri-Mitanni)		
Replace all Hittite chariots * Light chariot Light chariot bow Heavy chariot impact Upgrade to elite (max 4)	 7 9 11 +2	4-8
Syro-Canaanite chariots Light chariot bow Heavy chariot impetuous (max 2)	 9 10	0-4
Replace all Hittites warriors Medium spearmen Medium swordsmen	7	4-12
Anatolians Javelinmen	7	0-2
Gasgans Medium swordsmen impetuous	7	0-4

21 - Hurri-Mitanni

1600 – 1250 BC
Plain, Mountain
Command +3

After the fall of the Amorite dynasties, the Hurrian rapidly extended their influence over Mesopotamia, Syria and Asia Minor and established the powerful kingdom of Mitanni. They revolutionised the art of war with their chariots both rapid and well protected, serving as a platform for a warrior armed mainly with bows. This type of warrior ruled the battlefields for many centuries.

Troop type	Pts	Units
Chariots with 2 horses * Light chariot bow Upgrade to elite (max ½)	 9 +2	6-16
Scouts Light cavalry bow mediocre	4	0-1
Spearmen Medium spearmen Add support	 7 +1	2-6
Bowmen Light infantry bow	7 4	2-6
Javelinmen mediocre Light infantry javelin	5 4	0-4
Light infantry sling	4	0-2
Levy	3	0-2

Note

- Bedouin allies (List #17 Ancient Bedouin)
- Hittite allies (List #20 Hittite)
- Canaanite allies (List #22 Syria, Canaan & Ugarit)

22 - Syria, Canaan and Ugarit

1595 - 1100 BC
Plain, Desert
Command +3

This list covers the armies of the city-states of Syria and Canaan. These cities were usually vassals of one of the powerful kingdoms of the time: Egypt, Assyria, the Hittites or Mitanni. Among these small cities, Ugarit was the most famous and was successively under Egyptian and Hittite influence. It was destroyed by the invasion of Sea Peoples.

Troop type	Pts	Units
Chariots with 2 horses * Light chariot bow Upgrade to elite (max 6)	 9 +2	6-16
Scouts Light cavalry bow mediocre	4	0-1
Royal guardsmen * Medium swordsmen impact elite Bowmen pavise elite	10	0-2
Sherden and mercenaries Medium swordsmen impetuous	7	0-4
Hupshu warriors Medium swordsmen	7	0-4
Apiru javelinmen Javelinmen mediocre Light infantry javelin (max 6)	 5 4	4-12
Hupshu archers Bowmen Downgrade to mediocre	 7 -2	0-6
Light infantry bow	4	
Bedouins Light infantry javelin Light infantry sling	4	0-4
Levy	3	0-2
Only Ugarit after 1275 BC		
Replace some chariots with 2 horses * Heavy chariot impetuous Upgrade to elite	 10 +2	0-4
Medjergelem guardsmen Heavy swordsmen elite	10	0-2

Note

- A maximum of 6 light and/or heavy chariots can be upgraded to elite.
- Egyptian allies (List #14 New Kingdom Egyptian)
- Mitanni allies (List #21 Hurri-Mitanni) before 1340 BC

23 - Ancient Hebrew

1250 - 587 BC
Plain, Mountain
Command +2 or +3 after 1000 BC

This list represents the Jewish armies during the whole period of the Old Testament. After the rise of David chariots began to be used, but their use only became widespread under King Solomon.

Troop type	Pts	Units
Chariots with 2 or 4 horses * Light chariot bow Heavy chariot impact (after 800) Upgrade to elite (max 4)	 9 11 +2	0-8
Gibborim warriors * Medium swordsmen elite Add armour	 9 +2	0-4
Jewish warriors Medium swordsmen	7	4-24
Light cavalry javelin Medium cavalry	6 7	0-1
Bedouins Medium camelry bow Downgrade to mediocre	 10 -2	0-2
Philistine mercenaries Medium spearmen Heavy spearmen	 7 8	0-2
Bowmen mediocre Light infantry bow	5 4	2-4
Light infantry sling	4	2-4
Light infantry javelin	4	0-4

Note

- Egyptian allies (List #15 Libyan Egyptian)
- Egyptian allies (List #16 Kushite Egyptian)
- Philistine allies (List #25 Philistine)
- Aramean allies (List #26 Aramean & Neo-Hittite)
- Phoenician allies (List #32 Phoenicians of Cyprus)
- Egyptian allies (List #57 Saitic Egyptian)

24 - Sea Peoples

1210 - 1175 BC
Plain
Command +3

During the 13th century BC, the Middle East suffered the attacks of tribes from Anatolia grouped under the name of *Sea Peoples*. The Hittite Empire collapsed under their blows and Egypt suffered two invasions in 1179 and 1176 BC. After that, the Sea Peoples settled in Syria and Palestine.

Troop type	Pts	Units
*Warriors on chariots **		
Light chariot elite	9	0-4
Heavy chariot elite	12	
*Retinue warriors **		
Heavy swordsmen impetuous elite	10	0-6
Medium swordsmen impet. elite	9	
Common warriors		
Medium swordsmen impetuous	7	8-16
Javelinmen	7	0-6
Light infantry javelin	4	
Migrant families		
Levy mediocre	2	0-3
Fortified camp	6	0-1

Note

- Libyan allies (List #12 Libyan)

25 - Philistine

1165 – 600 BC
Plain
Command +3

The Philistines originated from the Peleset, one of the Sea Peoples, and gave their name to Palestine after being settled in that region by Ramesses III. They extended their influence over the region and gradually adopted chariots crewed with archers.

Troop type	Pts	Units
*Chariots with 2 horses **		
Light chariot	7	2-10
Light chariot bow	9	
Upgrade to elite (max 4)	+2	
*Nobles warriors **		
Heavy swordsmen impetuous elite	10	0-2
Other warriors		
Medium swordsmen impetuous	7	6-12
Javelinmen	7	2-10
Light infantry javelin	4	
Bowmen	7	0-2
Light infantry bow	4	
Light infantry sling	4	0-2
From 1100 BC		
*Replace all nobles warriors **		
Heavy spearmen elite	10	All
Replace all other warriors		
Medium spearmen	7	All
Gibborim mercenaries		
Medium swordsmen elite	9	0-2

Note

- Egyptian allies (List #15 Libyan Egyptian)
- Egyptian allies (List #16 Kushite Egyptian)
- Canaanite allies (List #22 Syria, Canaan & Ugarit)
- Aramean allies (List #26 Aramean & Neo-Hittite)
- Phoenician allies (List #32 Phoenicians of Cyprus)

Sea Peoples Warriors

26 - Aramaean and Neo-Hittite

1100 – 710 BC
Plain, Mountain
Command +3

After the ruin of the Hittite Empire, the Arameans settled in northern Mesopotamia, in Syria, in Palestine and in Lebanon. Some of these kingdoms continued to perpetrate Hittite traditions, but gradually fell under the attacks of the Assyrians.

Troop type	Pts	Units
*Chariots with 2 or 3 horses **		
Light chariot bow	9	4-12
Heavy chariot impact (max ½)	11	
Upgrade to elite (max 4)	+2	
Horsemen		
Medium cavalry mediocre	5	0-2
Bedouins		
Light camelry bow	7	0-2
Medium camelry bow	10	
Guardsmen		
Medium spearmen elite	9	0-2
Heavy spearmen elite	10	
Aramean spearmen		
Javelinmen	7	4-16
Medium spearmen (max 4)		
Bowmen mediocre	5	2-6
Light infantry bow	4	
Light infantry sling	4	0-4

Note

- Hebrew allies (List #23 Ancient Hebrew)
- Phoenician allies (List #32 Phoenicians of Cyprus)

27 - URARTU

900 – 590 BC
Mountain
Command +3

Urartu was an ancient kingdom located around Lake Van in the easternmost part of Turkey. At its apogee, the kingdom extended to Armenia and to the north of Iran and Syria. The kingdom of Urartu was influenced by Assyria which was its main opponent. As of 800 BC Urartu started an expansionist policy towards Armenia and northern Syria. The Assyrian kings Tiglath-Pileser III and then Sargon II inflicted serious defeats on the kingdom which considerably weakened it. The Medes put an end to Urartu kingdom in 590 BC.

Troop type	Pts	Units
Chariots with 2 horses *		
Light chariot bow	9	0-4
Upgrade to elite (max 2)	+2	
Chariots with 4 horses *		
Heavy chariot impact	11	0-2
Upgrade to elite	+2	
Medium cavalry bow mediocre	7	2-8
Upgrade to ordinary (after 750)	+2	
Scythians and Cimmerians		
Light cavalry bow	6	0-2
Qurbuti guardsmen		
Medium swordsmen elite	9	0-2
Heavy swordsmen elite	10	
Add armour	+2	
Royal and provincial infantry		
½ Medium swordsmen	9	6-24
½ Bowmen		
Other infantry		
Medium swordsmen	7	0-6
Light infantry bow	4	0-4
Light infantry javelin	4	0-2
Levy	3	0-2
Fortified camp	6	0-1

Note

- Aramean allies (List #26 Aramean & Neo-Hittite)
- Median allies (List #28 Medes)
- Scythian allies (List #76 Scythian)

28 - MEDES

835 – 550 BC
Plain, Mountain
Command +4

The Medes were an Iranian people and were related to the Persians. They were mentioned by the Assyrian king Shalmaneser III who subdued the Median kings in 835 BC during a campaign in the Zagros Mountains. The Medes intervened in the war between the Babylonians and the Assyrians and hastened the ruin of the latter by occupying several of their main cities between 614 and 610 BC. The Medes were then defeated by the Achaemenid Persians in 550 BC.

Troop type	Pts	Units
Horsemen *		
Medium cavalry bow	9	4-16
Heavy cavalry bow (max 6)	11	
Upgrade to elite (max 6)	+2	
Light cavalry bow	6	0-4
Spearmen		
Medium spearmen	7	4-12
Heavy spearmen	8	
Add support	+1	
Armenians and hillmen		
Javelinmen	7	0-6
Downgrade to mediocre	-2	
Median and parthian archers		
Bowmen	7	0-6
Downgrade to mediocre	-2	
Light infantry bow	4	0-4
Light infantry javelin	4	0-2

Note

- Babylonian allies (List #8 Neo-Babylonian)
- Assyrian allies (List #9 Assyrian Empire and Sargonid)
- Scythian allies (List #76 Scythian)

29 - PHRYGIAN

800 – 696 BC
Plain, Mountain
Command +3

Upon the fall of the Hittites, the Phrygians dominated eastern Asia Minor from their capital Gordion. They fought against the Assyrians before Phrygia was conquered by the Cimmerians who were related to the Scythes. Gordion fell in 696 BC and power in the region passed to Lydia. Phrygia became a satrapy of the Persian Empire.

Troop type	Pts	Units
Chariots with 2 horses * Light chariot Heavy chariot Upgrade to elite	 7 10 +2	0-4
Horsemen Medium cavalry	7	2-8
Light cavalry javelin Light cavalry bow	6	0-4
Spearmen Medium spearmen	7	8-24
Bowmen	7	0-4
Light infantry javelin	4	0-4
Light infantry bow Light infantry sling	4	0-4

Note

- Scythian allies (List #76 Scythian)

Mycenaean Spearmen

EARLY EUROPE

30 - MYCENAEAN

1600 – 1150 BC
Plain, Mountain
Command +4

The Mycenians were the inhabitants of pre-hellenic Greece at the end of the Bronze Age. They took their name from the city of Mycenae, located in the Peloponnese, but the civilisation encompassed Pylos and Knossos in Crete as well. The War of Troy related in the Iliad and the Odyssey took place during this period.

Troop type	Pts	Units
Mycenaean chariots * Light chariot Heavy chariot Upgrade to elite (max 4)	 7 10 +2	2-12
Horsemen Medium cavalry mediocre	5	0-2
Spearmen Medium spearmen Heavy spearmen Add support Add pavise	 7 8 +1 +1	6-16
Light infantry javelin	4	2-6
Bowmen Light infantry bow	7 4	0-6
Light infantry sling	4	0-2
Only Greek		
Achilles' Myrmidons * Medium swordsmen impact elite Add armour	 10 +2	0-2
Fortified camp	6	0-1
Only Trojan		
Thracian mercenaries Javelinmen	7	0-3
Sarpedon's Lukka warriors Medium swordsmen impact	8	0-2

Note

- One commander can be included in a Myrmidon unit to represent Achilles.

31 - GEOMETRIC GREEK

1100 – 650 BC
Plain, Mountain
Command +2

Between the end of the Mycenaean civilization and the introduction of the hoplite system, Greece was in the period called *geometric*. Most warriors fought on foot with swords and javelins, but there were also warriors on horseback. Chariots seem to have been used only for the transport of the highest ranking noble warriors.

Troop type	Pts	Units
Nobles warriors * Light chariot	7	0-3
Medium cavalry mediocre	5	2-6
Warriors Javelinmen Medium swordsmen	7	8-24
Bowmen	7	0-2
Light infantry javelin	4	2-6
Light infantry bow Light infantry sling	4	0-4
After 725 BC		
Replace all warriors Heavy spearmen mediocre	6	All

32 - Phoenicians of Cyprus

1000 – 330 BC
Plain, Forest
Command +3

The first Phoenicians settled in Cyprus circa 1000 BC. The island fell under the control of the Assyrians during the reign of the Sargonids and subsequently passed under Egyptian influence. Then the Persians made Cyprus a dominion of their Empire before the island passed under the control of the armies of Alexander the Great in 332 BC.

Troop type	Pts	Units
Chariots with 2 horses * Light chariot bow Upgrade to elite (max 4)	9 +2	2-6
Medium spearmen	7	6-16
Bowmen Light infantry bow	7 4	2-6
Light infantry javelin	4	0-3
Light infantry sling	4	0-3
Only after 900 BC		
Replace all chariots with 2 horses * Heavy chariot impact Upgrade to elite (max 4)	11 +2	All
Cavalry Medium cavalry bow mediocre	7	0-3
Sardinian and Spanish mercenaries Medium swordsmen Upgrade to impetuous	7	0-4
Greek mercenaries from Egypt * Heavy spearmen	8	
Heavy artillery	10	0-2

Note

- Egyptian allies (List #57 Saitic Egyptian)
- Asiatic Greek allies (List #60 Classical Greek)

33 - Celts

1300 – 400 BC
Plain, Mountain, Forest
Command +2

The Celts migrated all over Europe and were antecedents of numerous peoples such as the Gauls, the Galatians of Asia Minor, the Celtiberians of Spain, the Ancient Britons and the Welsh. Around 1300 BC, bronze began to be used by Celts for the fabrication of metal weapons. Circa 900 BC a new revolution occurred with the introduction of iron-working.

Troop type	Pts	Units
Mounted nobles * Light chariot elite Medium cavalry elite	9	0-6
Nobles on foot * Medium swordsmen impetuous elite	9	
Scouts Light cavalry javelin	6	0-2
Celtic warriors Medium swordsmen impetuous	7	8-24
Light infantry bow Light infantry sling	4	2-6
Women and children Levy mediocre	2	0-2

EARLY ASIA

34 - Indus Valley

2700 – 1500 BC
Plain, Forest
Command +3

This list represents the pre-Vedic civilization of the Indus Valley. The Harappans (from the name of the great city of Harrapa) were known by the Sumerians under the name of Melukhan. An Indian contingent had participated in the revolt of Sumerians against the Akkadians. The Harappan civilisation declined and disappeared circa 1500 BC due to Aryan invasions.

Troop type	Pts	Units
Elephant	13	0-1
Scouts Light cavalry bow mediocre	4	0-1
Guardsmen * Medium swordsmen 2HW elite Medium spearmen elite	10 9	0-2
Spearmen Medium spearmen Downgrade to mediocre	7 -2	4-12
Archers Bowmen Downgrade to mediocre	7 -2	4-12
Hill tribesmen Javelinmen Light infantry javelin	7 4	0-6
Light infantry sling Light infantry bow	4	0-8

35 - Vedic Indian

1500 – 500 BC
Plain, Forest
Command +3

This list represents the armies of the Vedic civilisation which dominated India after the Aryan invasions. The Aryans first occupied Punjab then took possession of all of northern India. At that time war chariots were the favourite weapon.

Troop type	Pts	Units
*Chariots with 2 horses ** Light chariot bow Upgrade to elite (max 6)	9 +2	6-12
Elephant *	13	0-2
Medium cavalry mediocre	5	0-4
*Guardsmen ** Medium swordsmen 2HW elite	10	0-2
Archers Bowmen mediocre Upgrade to ordinary (max 6)	5 +2	6-16
Warriors Medium swordsmen 2HW Downgrade to mediocre	8 -2	0-6
Light infantry bow	4	0-4
Levy	3	0-2

36 - Shang Chinese

1700 – 1045 BC
Plain, Forest
Command +3

The Shang dynasty is the earliest Chinese dynasty of which archaeological evidence has been found. Occupying the valley of the Yellow River, the Shang dynasty had an advanced culture and mastered bronze metallurgy and the use of war chariots. The Jungs were barbarian tribes who lived in northern China.

Troop type	Pts	Units
*Nobles ** Light chariot bow elite Bowmen elite	11 9	2-4
Warriors with long spear Medium spearmen	7	4-12
Bowmen Downgrade to mediocre	7	4-12
Royal guardsmen Medium swordsmen 2HW elite	10	0-4
Light infantry bow	4	0-4
Armed slaves Levy	3	0-4

Jung allies		
*Jung warriors ** Medium swordsmen impetuous	7	4-8
Bowmen mediocre Light infantry bow	5 4	0-4

Note

- Jung allies (see list above)
- Zhou allies (List #37 Spring and Autumn Chinese)

37 - Spring and Autumn Chinese

1100 – 480 BC
Plain, Forest
Command +4
Strategist: Duke Wen (Jin in 632 BC)

The Shang dynasty was overthrown by the Zhou, who came from the valley of the Wei river in the 11th century BC. Supported by a very centralised bureaucratic system, the Zhou sovereigns entrusted the management of fiefs to important noble families. As of 770 BC, the power of the king was fragmented and there began an era called the "Spring and Autumn Period". This period saw the rise of many conflicts and the emergence of seven principal kingdoms.

Troop type	Pts	Units
*Chariots with 4 horses ** Heavy chariot impetuous Upgrade to elite (max 4)	10 +2	4-10
Guardsmen with halberds Medium swordsmen 2HW elite	10	0-2
Halberdiers and spearmen Medium swordsmen 2HW Medium spearmen Add support	8 7 +1	4-12
Archers Bowmen Downgrade to mediocre	7 -2	2-8
Tribal auxiliaries Medium swordsmen impetuous	7	0-4
Light infantry bow	4	0-4
Levy	3	0-4

Note

- Jung allies (see list above for Shang Chinese)
- Shang allies (List #36 Shang Chinese)

CLASSICAL PERIOD

MACEDONIAN

38 - EARLY MACEDONIAN

650 - 355 BC
Plain, Mountain
Command +3

This list describes the armies of Macedonia before the reforms of Philip II, father of Alexander. The army relied on powerful shock cavalry and infantry equipped as hoplites. Hoewer, the majority of troops were provided by peasant levies with poor fighting abilities.

Troop type	Pts	Units
*Companions **		
Heavy cavalry impact	10	2-4
Upgrade to elite (max 2)	+2	
Scouts		
Light cavalry javelin	6	0-2
Macedonian hoplites		
Heavy spearmen	8	2-6
Medium spearmen	7	
Mercenaries hoplites		
Heavy spearmen mediocre	6	0-4
Illyrian mercenaries		
Medium spearmen	7	0-2
Macedonian peasants		
Medium swordsmen mediocre	5	6-24
Javelinmen mediocre	5	
Upgrade to ordinay (max 4)	+2	
Light infantry javelin	4	0-4
Light infantry bow	4	0-2

Note

- Spartan or Thessalian allies (List #60 Classical Greek)

39 - ALEXANDRIAN MACEDONIAN

355 - 330 BC
Plain, Mountain
Command +5
Strategists: Philip II (360-336 BC), Alexander (338-330 BC)

King Philip II of Macedonia reorganized the army to make it a tool for his conquests. The soldiers fought in a phalanx of 24 ranks deep and used the sarissa, a pike over 5 meters long. With this army, Philip made Greece surrender and intended to attack Persia. His untimely death gave power to his son, Alexander, who pursued his father's project. He won decisive victories over the Persians at Granicus, Issus and Gaugamela.

Troop type	Pts	Units
*Companions **		
Heavy cavalry impact elite	12	2-4
*Greek and Thessalian cavalry **		
Medium cavalry	7	0-3
Heavy cavalry	9	
Prodromoi		
Light cavalry impact	6	0-2
Thracians and Paionians		
Light cavalry javelin	6	0-2
Macedonian phalangites		
Pikemen	11	2-8
Replace some Macedonian phalangites		
Medium spearmen	7	0-4
*Hypaspists **		
Pikemen elite	13	1-2
Heavy spearmen elite	10	
Medium spearmen elite	9	
Greek hoplites		
Heavy spearmen	8	0-4
Thracian peltasts		
Javelinmen	7	0-4
Medium swordsmen	7	
Medium swordsmen 2HW	8	
Greek Peltasts		
Javelinmen	7	0-2
Agrianian or Thracian javelinmen		
Light infantry javelin	4	2-4
Upgrade to elite	+1	
Light infantry bow	4	0-4
Upgrade to elite (max 2) if Cretan	+1	
Light infantry sling	4	
Heavy artillery	10	0-1
Fortified camp	6	0-1

Note

- Phalangites and Hypaspists can be deployed as lighter troops with spears instead of pikes.
- Commander in chief can be included in a unit of Hypaspists.
- Thessalian allies (List #60 Classical Greek)

40 - Alexander the Great

330 - 320 BC
Plain, Mountain
Command +6
Strategist: Alexander (330-323 BC)

After subjugating the Achaemenid Persian Empire, Alexander turned to India. His army had less heavy infantry because many Greeks returned home but he had now more light cavalry and elephants than before. Alexander recruited more and more Persian soldiers for his army. He died in 323 BC.

Troop type	Pts	Units
*Companions ** Heavy cavalry impact elite	12	2-4
Sogdians, Scythians or Bactrians Light cavalry bow Upgrade to elite (max 1 Bactrian)	6 +1	1-3
Hippakontistai Light cavalry javelin	6	1-3
Macedonian phalangites Pikemen	11	2-6
Replace some Macedonian phalangites Medium spearmen	7	0-4
Hypaspists Pikemen elite Heavy spearmen elite Medium spearmen elite	13 10 9	1-2
Greek hoplites Heavy spearmen	8	0-2
Thracian peltasts Javelinmen Medium swordsmen Medium swordsmen 2HW	7 7 8	0-3
Greek peltasts Javelinmen	7	0-2
Agrianian or Thracian javelinmen Light infantry javelin Upgrade to elite	4 +1	2-4
Light infantry bow Upgrade to elite (max 2) if Cretan	4 +1	0-4
Light infantry sling	4	
Elephant	13	0-2
Heavy artillery	10	0-1
Fortified camp	6	0-1

Only after 324 BC		
Persian Companions Heavy cavalry impact Upgrade to elite	10 +2	1
Replace all Hypaspists by Persian guardsmen Bowmen pavise elite	10	All
Persian archers Bowmen Light infantry bow	7 4	0-4

Note

- Indian allies (List #79 Classical Indian) before 324 BC

Macedonian Phalanx

41 - Early Successors

320 - 260 BC
Plain, Mountain
Command +5
Strategists: Lysimachus (322-281 BC) or Eumenes (321-316 BC)

After Alexander's death, his former generals fought wars without mercy for the control of the Empire. The successors of Alexander are called the Diadochi. In Asia the main ones were Antigonus the One-eyed, Eumenes and Demetrius. In Macedonia there were the regent Perdiccas, Antipater, Polyperchon, Queen Olympias, Cassander, Ptolemy Keraunos and Antigonus Gonatas. Lysimachus was the governor of Thrace. The armies of Seleucus and Ptolemy are described in different lists.

Troop type	Pts	Units
Xystophoroi * Heavy cavalry impact Upgrade to elite (max 2)	 10 +2	 1-3
Greeks, Thracians or Persians Medium cavalry Heavy cavalry	 7 9	0-2
Thracians or Paionians Light cavalry javelin	6	0-2
Greek and Macedonian phalangites * Pikemen	11	2-6
Greek peltasts Javelinmen	7	0-4
Light troops Light infantry bow Light infantry sling	4	2-4
Cretan archers Light infantry bow elite	5	0-2
Greeks or Persians Light infantry javelin	4	0-4
Elephant	13	0-1
Heavy artillery	10	0-1
Fortified camp	6	0-1

Only for Asiatic Successors		
Asiatic horsemen Medium cavalry Heavy cavalry	 7 9	0-2
Asiatic mercenaries Pikemen	11	0-2
Antigonus the One-Eyed (Asiatic)		
Tarentines Light cavalry javelin	6	0-3
Medes and Persians Light cavalry bow	6	0-1
Macedonian phalangites Pikemen	11	1-2
Lycians and Pamphylians Javelinmen mediocre	5	0-2
Demetrius (Asiatic)		
Greek hoplites Heavy spearmen	8	0-4
Heavy artillery	10	0-1
Eumenes (Asiatic)		
Argyraspids * Pikemen elite	13	1-2
Arachosians and Pisidians Medium cavalry Light cavalry javelin	 7 6	0-3
Eudamos' Elephants Elephant	13	0-2

Only for Macedonian Successors		
Replace some Greek and Macedonian phalangites by veteran troops Pikemen elite	13	0-2
Mercenary peltasts Javelinmen Light infantry javelin	 7 4	2-4
Thracian mercenaries Javelinmen Medium swordsmen Medium swordsmen 2HW	 7 7 8	0-2
Antigonus Gonatas (Macedonian) Spartan or Argos allies (List #61 Hellenistic Greek)		
Medes or Parthians Light cavalry bow	6	0-2
Replace some Greek peltasts by Thureophoroi Medium spearmen	7	0-4
Galatians Heavy swordsmen impetuous Upgrade to elite	 8 +2	0-3
Cassander (Macedonian)		
Greek hoplites allies Heavy spearmen Downgrade to mediocre	 8 -2	0-4
Ptolemy Keraunos (Macedonian)		
Mount a Commander on elephant * Elephant	13	0-1
Polyperchon (Macedonian) Aetolian allies (List #61 Hellenistic Greek)		
Lysimachus (Thracian) Thracian allies (List #63 Thracian)		
Thracians Javelinmen Medium swordsmen Medium swordsmen 2HW	 7 7 8	2-8
Greek hoplites Heavy spearmen Downgrade to mediocre	 8 -2	0-4
Lycians and Pamphylians Javelinmen mediocre	5	0-2
Alliance between Lysimachus and Seleucus at Ipsos in 301 BC Lysimachus list options with no Thracian allies		
Replace all Xystophoroi Heavy cavalry impact Upgrade to elite (max 2)	 10 +2	2-5
Replace all Greek and Macedonian phalangites * Pikemen Upgrade to elite	 11 +2	2-10
Replace all elephants Elephant	13	0-3

42 - Seleucid

320 - 64 BC
Plain, Mountain, Desert
Command +5
Strategist: Antiochus III (220-190 BC)

General Seleucus, former companion of Alexander, built an Empire in the eastern territories from Syria to the Indus. His capital was Antioch in Syria. The Seleucids also controlled Mesopotamia and Babylonia. In 250 BC the province of Bactria seceded to form the Greco-Bactrian kingdom and later it was the turn of the province of Parthia to rebel. The Parthians extended their influence gradually from the eastern provinces of the Empire. After their defeat at Magnesia in 189 BC against the Romans, the Seleucids lost their provinces in Asia Minor to the benefit of Pergamon. The Seleucid dynasty ended in 64 BC when Pompey conquered Syria.

Troop type	Pts	Units
*Xystophoroi ** Heavy cavalry impact Upgrade to elite (max 2)	10 +2	1-4
Scythians Light cavalry bow	6	1-2
Bedouins Light camelry bow mediocre Medium camelry bow mediocre	5 8	0-2
Scythed Chariot	3	0-2
Seleucid pikemen Pikemen	11	2-6
*Argyraspids ** Pikemen elite	13	1-2
Thracians Javelinmen Medium swordsmen Medium swordsmen 2HW	7 7 8	0-2
Asiatic archers Bowmen Downgrade to mediocre	7 -2	0-2
Light infantry bow Light infantry sling	4	1-4
Cretan archers Light infantry bow elite	5	0-2
Cappadocians Light infantry javelin	4	0-2
Levy	3	0-2
Heavy artillery	10	0-1
Fortified camp	6	0-1
Before 280 BC		
Elephant	13	0-3
Asiatic horsemen Light cavalry javelin	6	0-3
Peltasts Javelinmen	7	0-2
After 280 BC		
Thureophoroi or Thorakitai Medium spearmen Add armour	7 +2	0-2
Until 205 BC Elephant	13	0-2
After 245 BC		
Galatian horsemen Medium cavalry elite Heavy cavalry elite	9 11	0-1
Galatian infantry Heavy swordsmen impetuous Upgrade to elite	8 +2	0-2
After 205 BC		
*Replace all Xystophoroi ** Cataphract Upgrade to elite (max 2)	11 +2	All
Until 167 BC Elephant elite	16	0-2
After 167 BC		
Militia Medium cavalry mediocre	5	0-2
Militia Medium swordsmen mediocre	5	0-4
Replace all Argyraspids Heavy swordsmen impact Add armour	9 +2	2-4
Elephant mediocre	10	0-2

Note

- One commander can be included in a unit of Argyraspids
- Aetolian allies (List #61 Hellenistic Greek)
- Elymaien allies (List #102 Parthian)
- Jewish allies (List #103 Judaean Jewish)

Xystophoroi

43 - Ptolemaic

320 - 30 BC
Plain, Desert
Command +4

The general Ptolemy took possession of Egypt after Alexander's death and founded the Ptolemaic dynasty. This was a time of rebirth for Egypt and its ancient traditions accompanied by an opening to Greek civilisation. The dynasty ended with the death of Queen Cleopatra.

Troop type	Pts	Units
Xystophoroi * Heavy cavalry impact Upgrade to elite (max 1)	10 +2	1-3
Greeks, Nubians or Galatians Medium cavalry Heavy cavalry Upgrade to elite (*if Galatian*)	7 9 +2	0-2
Nubians or Egyptians Light cavalry javelin	6	0-2
Bedouins Light camelry bow mediocre Medium camelry bow mediocre	5 8	0-2
Greek or Thracian peltasts Javelinmen Medium swordsmen Medium swordsmen 2HW	7 7 8	0-2
Border guards Medium swordsmen mediocre	5	0-2
Nubian warriors Medium swordsmen impetuous	7	0-3
Cretan or Pisidian javelinmen Light infantry javelin Upgrade to elite	4 +1	1-4
Light infantry bow Upgrade to elite (*if Cretan*)	4 +1	0-2
Light infantry sling	4	0-2
Heavy artillery	10	0-1
Before 55 BC		
Elephant Downgrade to mediocre	13 -3	0-2
Macedonian phalangites * Pikemen Upgrade to elite (max 2)	11 +2	4-8
Only from 274 to 55 BC		
Egyptian phalangites Pikemen mediocre	8	0-6
Galatian infantry Heavy swordsmen impetuous Upgrade to elite	8 +2	0-2
Thureophoroi or Thorakitai Medium spearmen Add armour	7 +2	0-4
Only after 167 BC		
Imitation legionaries Heavy swordsmen impact	9	0-4
From 54 BC		
Phalangites Pikemen Downgrade to mediocre	11 -3	0-4
Veteran legionaries Heavy swordsmen impact Add armour	9 +2	0-4

44 - Pyrrhic

300 - 272 BC
Plain, Mountain
Command +5
Strategist: Pyrrhus (301-272 BC)

Pyrrhus, who was a distant relative of Alexander, became King of Epirus in 306 BC. He attempted to conquer the whole of Macedonia but was expelled by Lysimachus. He then targeted Italy and won victories over the Romans at Heraclea (280) and then Ausculum (279) which were the origin of the expression "Pyrrhic victories". He left Italy for Sicily and drove off the Carthaginians. He was crushed by the Romans at the battle of Beneventum (275) and died in Greece during an expedition against Sparta. Pyrrhus was a brilliant general who was unable to politically exploit his victories.

Troop type	Pts	Units
Xystophoroi * Heavy cavalry impact elite	12	1-2
Greek horsemen * Medium cavalry Heavy cavalry	7 9	1-4
Aetolians, Paionians or Thracians Light cavalry javelin	6	0-2
Epirotes and Macedonians Pikemen	11	4-12
Greek hoplites Heavy spearmen Downgrade to mediocre	8 -2	0-4
Hypaspists or guards Medium spearmen elite Pikemen elite	9 13	0-2
Rhodian slingers Light infantry sling	4	1-2
Light troops Light infantry bow	4	1-2

Oscans Light infantry javelin	4	0-4
Elephant	13	0-2
Fortified camp	6	0-1
Pyrrhus in Italy from 280 to 275 BC		
Tarentine horsemen Light cavalry javelin	6	1-2
Replace half Epirotes & Macedonians by Tarentine phalangites Pikemen mediocre	8	2-6
Bruttian or Samnite mercenaries Medium swordsmen Add impact (max 2) Upgrade to elite (max 2)	7 +1 +2	1-4
After 274 BC		
Replace all Xystophoroi Heavy cavalry	9	All
Galatian infantry Heavy swordsmen impetuous Upgrade to elite	8 +2	0-2

Note

- If Pyrrhus in Italy, at least half of pikemen must be of mediocre quality with a maximum of 6.

45 - Later Macedonian

260 – 168 BC
Plain, Mountain
Command +4
Strategist: Philip V (221-179 BC)

King Philip V came to power in 221 BC. Allied to the Greeks, he victoriously fought the Aetolians in 217 and then allied with Hannibal against Rome in 215. Philip fought on all fronts and after signing a pact with the Seleucids, was engaged in various wars against Ptolemies of Egypt, Rhodes and Pergamon. The Romans, after winning the war against Carthage, turned against the Macedonians and defeated them at the battle of Cynocephalus in 197 BC. Macedonia had to submit to Rome but remained independent. The son of Philip V, Perseus, was defeated at the battle of Pydna in 168 BC and Macedonia became a Roman province.

Troop type	Pts	Units
*Macedonians, Greeks or Thracians ** Medium cavalry Heavy cavalry Upgrade to elite (max 2)	7 9 +2	1-4
Illyrians Light cavalry javelin	6	0-2
Agema Pikemen elite	13	1-2
Macedonian phalangites Pikemen	11	2-8
Thureophoroi or Thorakitai Medium spearmen Add armour (max 2)	7 +2	1-4
Thracians Javelinmen Medium swordsmen Medium swordsmen 2HW	7 7 8	0-4
Illyrians Medium spearmen	7	
Galatians Heavy swordsmen impetuous Upgrade to elite	8 +2	0-2
Light infantry javelin Upgrade to elite (*If Agrianian*)	4 +1	1-3
Light infantry bow Upgrade to elite (*If Cretan*)	4 +1	1-3
Heavy artillery	10	0-1
Fortified camp	6	0-1

Note

- Achaean League allies (List #61 Hellenistic Greek) from 222 to 202 BC.

46 - Graeco-Bactrian and Graeco-Indian

250 – 55 BC
Graeco-Indian: Plain, Mountain, Forest
Graeco-Bactrian: Plain, Desert, Steppes
Command +4

In 250 BC the satrap Diodotus I revolted against the Seleucids and declared independence. The Greco-Bactrian kingdom was located around the province of Bactria, which corresponds to modern Afghanistan as well as southern Turkmenistan and Uzbekistan. The successors of Diodotus extended the kingdom eastward towards India to form the Greco-Indian kingdom.

Troop type	Pts	Units
Arachosians and Paropamisadae Light cavalry javelin	6	0-3
Scythians Light cavalry bow	6	0-3
Greek phalangites Pikemen	11	1-3
Cretan archers Light infantry bow elite	5	0-2

Colonists and peltasts Javelinmen Light infantry javelin	 7 4	0-2
Indian spearmen Medium spearmen Downgrade to mediocre	 7 -2	0-4
Fortified camp	6	0-1
Graeco-Bactrian Saka allies (List #76 Scythian)		
Greek horsemen * Heavy cavalry impact	10	0-2
Iranian lancers Heavy cavalry impact Upgrade to elite (max 3)	 10 +2	3-6
Iranian lancers Cataphract Upgrade to elite (max 3)	 11 +2	
Bactrians Light cavalry bow Upgrade to elite	 6 +1	2-6
Elephant elite	16	0-2
Indian archers Bowmen Downgrade to mediocre	 7 -2	0-4
Graeco-Indian Indian allies (List #79 Classical Indian) Kushan allies (List #107 Kushan)		
Greek horsemen * Heavy cavalry	9	0-2
Indian horsemen Medium cavalry mediocre	5	1-2
Elephant elite	16	1-3
Indian warriors Medium swordsmen Downgrade to mediocre	 7 -2	0-4
Indian archers Bowmen Downgrade to mediocre	 7 -2	2-8
Replace some Indian archers by mixed units ½ Medium swordsmen ½ Bowmen	9	0-8

Note

- Player must choose one of the two options between Graeco-Bactrian and Graeco-Indian.
- In a Graeco-Indian army, at least half of units (others than allied units) must be Indian units.
- Only a total of 3 Iranian lancers can be upgraded to elite.

ROME AND ITALY

47 - Italian Tribes

1000 – 290 BC
Mountain
Command +2

This list brings together all the peoples who occupied Italy before their absorption by the Romans and the Etruscans. They were Samnites, Umbrians, Sabines, Volsci, Hernici and Aequi.

Troop type	Pts	Units
Horsemen * Medium cavalry Upgrade to elite (max 2)	 7 +2	1-4
Warriors * Medium swordsmen impetuous Upgrade to elite (max 4)	 8 +2	8-24
Replace some warriors Medium swordsmen Javelinmen Downgrade to mediocre	 7 7 -2	0-6
Light infantry sling	4	0-4
Light infantry javelin	4	0-4
Fortifications	1	0-6
Fortified camp	6	0-1
Samnites Volscian or Hernician allies (List #47 Italian Tribes) Etruscan allies (List #48 Etruscan) Campanian or Apulian allies (List #51 Campanian, Lucanian, Apulian and Bruttian) Roman allies (List #52 Camillan Roman) Gallic allies (List #88 Gallic)		
Replace all horsemen * Medium cavalry Upgrade to elite (max ½)	 7 +2	2-6
Replace all warriors * Medium swordsmen impact Upgrade to elite (max ½)	 8 +2	All

48 - Etruscan

600 – 280 BC
Plain, Mountain
Command +4

The Etruscans occupied Etruria, an area corresponding to current day Tuscany and the centre of the Italian peninsula. First they were allied to the Carthaginians. They dominated the peninsula and the peak of their influence was between 300 and 350

BC. Rome was liberated from their control as well as other Latin people. In 295 BC the Etruscans were defeated by the Romans at the battle of Sentinum and shortly after became completely controlled by Rome.

Troop type	Pts	Units
*Nobles before 500 BC ** Light chariot Upgrade to elite	7 +2	2-4
*Nobles after 500 BC ** Medium cavalry Upgrade to elite (max 4)	7 +2	2-6
Guardsmen Heavy spearmen armour elite	12	0-2
Hoplites of 1st class Heavy spearmen Add armour *(all or none)*	8 +2	2-4
Other hoplites Heavy spearmen mediocre	6	6-20
Light infantry javelin	4	2-6
Light infantry sling	4	0-4
Light infantry bow	4	0-2
Levy	3	0-2
Fortified camp	6	0-1

Note

- Samnite, Sabine or Umbrian allies (List # 47 Italian Tribes)
- Roman allies (List #49 Tullian Roman)
- Greeks in Italy allies (List #60 Classical Greek)
- Gallic allies (List #88 Gallic)

49 - TULLIAN ROMAN

578 – 400 BC
Plain, Mountain
Command +4

This list presents the Roman army after the reform of Servius Tullius until the reform of Camillus. The Roman infantry was organized into five classes and fought in the style of the hoplites. The plebeians, the poorest citizens, were less well equipped and were the fourth and fifth classes. The Romans often used Latin allies as auxiliary troops.

Troop type	Pts	Units
*Equites ** Medium cavalry Upgrade to elite (max 4)	7 +2	2-6
*1st Class ** Heavy spearmen armour Upgrade to elite	10 +2	2-4
2nd and 3rd Class Heavy spearmen	8	4-8
4th Class Javelinmen	7	2-4
5th Class Light infantry sling Light infantry javelin	4	0-4
Fortified camp	6	0-1

Latin allies		
Medium cavalry Upgrade to elite (max 2)	7 +2	1-4
*Hoplites ** Heavy spearmen mediocre	6	4-8
Light infantry sling Light infantry javelin	4	0-2

Note

- Hernician allies (List #47 Italian Tribes)
- Latin allies (see List above)

50 - SYRACUSAN

481 – 210 BC
Plain, Mountain
Command +5
Strategist: Timoleon (341-337 BC), Agathocles (317-289 BC)

The Greeks founded colonies in Sicily from the eighth century BC. Numerous wars were fought against the Carthaginians who arrived for the first time in 481 BC. During these wars Timoleon and Agathocles managed to re-unify the whole of Sicily by defeating the Carthaginians. Agathocles also made several expeditions against Carthage on African soil.

Troop type	Pts	Units
*Greek horsemen ** Medium cavalry Heavy cavalry (max 2) Upgrade to elite (max 2)	7 9 +2	2-6
Tarentines Light cavalry javelin	6	0-4
*Guard mercenaries ** Heavy spearmen elite	10	0-2
*Greek and Campanian hoplites ** Heavy spearmen	8	2-8
*Syracusan and allied hoplites ** Heavy spearmen mediocre	6	2-8
Gallic mercenaries Medium swordsmen impetuous Heavy swordsmen impetuous	7 8	0-3

Spanish scutarii Medium swordsmen impetuous	7	0-2
Ligurian and Sardinian Javelinmen Medium swordsmen	7	0-4
Peltasts mercenaries Javelinmen Light infantry javelin	7 4	0-2
Balearic slingers Light infantry sling elite	5	0-2
Light infantry javelin	4	0-4
Light infantry bow	4	0-2
Heavy artillery	10	0-2
Only Agathocles in Africa (310 to 307 BC) Libyan allies (List #12 Libyan) Numidian allies (List #56 Numidian) Greek allies (List #58 Cyrenian Greek) No Spanish, Ligurian, Sardinian or artillery		
Rowers dressed as hoplites Levy	3	0-2
Only after 275 BC		
Replace all peltasts mercenaries by Thureophoroi Medium spearmen	7	All

Note

- Carthaginian allies (List #55 Carthaginian)

51 - Campanian, Lucanian, Apulian and Bruttian

420 - 203 BC
Plain, Mountain
Command +3

These peoples occupied parts of southern Italy and were cousins of the Samnites. The Campanians submitted to the Romans in 340 BC and provided important contingents to the Roman army. This did not prevent them from fighting against Rome alongside Carthage. The Bruttians occupied the region of Calabria and fought against Agathocles the King of Syracuse and the Romans alongside Pyrrhus. Then they assisted Hannibal during his expedition to Italy. The Lucanians and Apulians also supported Carthage before being subjugated circa 200 BC.

Troop type	Pts	Units
*Horsemen ** Medium cavalry	7	0-4
Warriors Medium swordsmen	7	8-24
Javelinmen Light infantry javelin	4	0-6
Campanian Samnite allies (List #47 Italian Tribes) Roman allies (List #52 Camillan Roman)		
*Replace all horsemen ** Medium cavalry Upgrade to elite (max 2)	7 +2	0-6
Hoplites Heavy spearmen	8	2-8
*Replace all warriors ** Medium swordsmen Downgrade to mediocre	7 -2	4-16
Only from 337 BC Heavy swordsmen impact Downgrade to mediocre	9 -2	
Lucanian Bruttian allies (List #51 Campanian, Lucanian, Apulian and Bruttian)		
Upgrade some warriors to elite Medium swordsmen elite	9	0-6
Apulian		
*Replace all Horsemen ** Medium cavalry Upgrade to elite (max 4)	7 +2	4-10
Bruttian Carthaginian allies (List #55 Carthaginian) in 215 BC Lucanian allies (List #51 Campanian, Lucanian, Apulian and Bruttian)		
Upgrade some warriors to elite Medium swordsmen elite	9	0-6
Peasants Levy	3	0-2

52 - Camillan Roman

400 - 275 BC
Plain, Mountain
Command +4

This list represents the Roman army from the reforms of Camillus until the beginning of the Punic Wars. The army was organized into legions and supplemented by Latin auxiliaries. The legion fought in four lines: Velites, Hastati, Principes and Triarii.

Troop type	Pts	Units
*Equites ** Medium cavalry Upgrade to elite (max 2)	7 +2	1-4
Triarii Heavy spearmen armour elite	12	1-3
Hastati Heavy swordsmen impact Add armour *(all or none)*	9 +2	2-6

Principes Heavy spearmen Add armour *(all or none)*	8 +2	2-6
Velites Light infantry javelin	4	2-6
Accensi Heavy spearmen mediocre Medium spearmen mediocre	6 5	0-4
Rorarii Light infantry javelin	4	0-2
Fortified camp	6	1
Latin auxilliaries		
Medium cavalry Upgrade to elite (max 2)	7 +2	0-4
Medium swordmen elite (max 2) Medium swordsmen Javelinmen Downgrade to mediocre	9 7 7 -2	0-8
Light infantry javelin Light infantry sling	4	0-2

Note

- Roman army is organised in legions that each contains 2 units of Hastati, 2 units of Principes, 2 units of Velites and 1 unit of Triarii.
- Samnite allies (List #47 Italian Tribes) in 340 BC.

53 - Republican Roman

275 - 105 BC
Plain, Mountain
Command +4
Strategist: Scipio Africanus (210-202 BC) and Marius (100-105 BC)

After the wars against Pyrrhus the Roman army was reorganized. The Legion still fought in four lines and this army ensured the domination of Rome around the Mediterranean. The Romans were victorious against the Carthaginians, Macedonians and Seleucids. Scipio Africanus defeated Hannibal at Zama in 202 BC and Marius pushed back the Cimbri and the Teutones. He then began a reform of the Roman army.

Troop type	Pts	Units
*Roman and Gallic horsemen ** Medium cavalry Heavy cavalry Upgrade to elite (max 1)	7 9 +2	0-3
*Hastati and Principes ** Heavy swordsmen impact Add armour *(all or none)* Upgrade to elite (max 4)	9 +2 +2	4-12
Triarii Heavy spearmen armour elite	12	1-3
Velites Light infantry javelin Upgrade to elite (max 2)	4 +1	2-6
Fortified camp	6	1
Newly recruited legions		
Replace some Hastati and Principes Heavy swordsmen impact mediocre Add armour *(all or none)*	7 +2	0-8
Replace some Triarii Heavy spearmen armour Downgrade to mediocre	10 -2	0-2
Replace some Velites Light infantry javelin	4	0-4
Auxilliary troops		
Numidian or Illyrian horsemen Light cavalry javelin	6	0-2
Italian allies : Extraordinarii Medium swordsmen elite Add armour	9 +2	0-2
Others Italian allies Medium swordsmen Downgrade to mediocre	7 -2	0-4
Only from 202 BC Elephant mediocre	10	0-1
Cretan archers Light infantry bow elite	5	0-2
Syracusan slingers Light infantry sling	4	
Other auxilliaries		
Gallic warriors Medium swordsmen impetuous Heavy swordsmen impetuous	7 8	0-2
Spanish scutarii Medium swordsmen impetuous	7	
Greek or Illyrian thureophoroi Medium spearmen	7	
Ligurian Javelinmen Medium swordsmen	7	

Note

- The Roman army is organised in legions that each contains 4 units of Hastati-Principes, 2 units of Velites and 1 unit of Triarii.
- One legion can be upgraded to elite and two others downgraded to mediocre.
- Numidian allies (List #56 Numidian)
- Aetolian allies (List #61 Hellenistic Greek)
- Pergamon allies (List #73 Pergamon)
- Iberian allies (List #89 Ancient Spanish)

CARTHAGE AND AFRICA

54 - EARLY CARTHAGINIAN

550 - 275 BC
Plain
Command +4

Carthage was founded by the Phoenicians. The city became independent and gradually extended its influence over North Africa, Spain, the Balearic Islands, Corsica and Sardinia. Carthage disputed control of Sicily against the Greeks and Syracusans in three major wars in 480, 410 and 315 BC. Between 280 and 275 BC Pyrrhus, king of Epirus, undertook two great expeditions, one against Rome and the other against Carthage. After Pyrrhus withdrew, the period of the Punic Wars opened.

Troop type	Pts	Units
Carthaginian chariots * Heavy chariot impact Upgrade to elite	11 +2	2-4
Punic horsemen * Medium cavalry Downgrade to mediocre	7 -2	0-4
Numidians Light cavalry javelin	6	0-4
Sacred phalanx * Heavy spearmen armour elite	12	0-2
African spearmen Medium spearmen Heavy spearmen	7 8	2-6
Greek mercenaries Heavy spearmen Add armour *(all or none)*	8 +2	0-4
Punic levy Medium spearmen mediocre	5	0-6
Gallic warriors Medium swordsmen impetuous Heavy swordsmen impetuous	7 8	0-2
Spanish scutarii Medium swordsmen impetuous	7	0-2
Greeks, Ligurians or Sardinians Javelinmen Medium swordsmen (max 2)	7	2-6
Balearic slingers Light infantry sling elite	5	0-3
Libyans and Moors Light infantry javelin	4	0-3
Heavy artillery	10	0-1

Note

- Libyan allies (List #12 Libyan)
- Numidian allies (List #56 Numidian)
- Sicilian allies (List #60 Classical Greek)
- Only one commander can be included in the sacred phalanx unit.

55 - CARTHAGINIAN

275 - 146 BC
Plain
Command +5
Strategist: Hannibal (221-202 BC)

This list represents the armies of Carthage during the Punic Wars. The main cause of Punic Wars was the rivalry between the Carthaginian Empire and the Roman Republic for control of the Mediterranean, especially Sicily. During the second Punic War, the Carthaginian general Hannibal crossed the Pyrenees with his army and elephants and inflicted crushing defeats against the Romans before being himself defeated at Zama by Scipio Africanus. Finally the Romans destroyed Carthage in 146 BC.

Troop type	Pts	Units
Punic, Gallic or Spanish cavalry * Medium cavalry Heavy cavalry (max 2) Upgrade to elite	7 9 +2	0-6
Numidians or Spanish * Light cavalry javelin Upgrade to elite (max 2)	6 +1	2-6
African spearmen Heavy spearmen	8	2-6
Militia Medium spearmen mediocre	5	0-6
Spanish scutarii Medium swordsmen impetuous Medium swordsmen impact	7 8	0-2
Gallic warriors Medium swordsmen impetuous Heavy swordsmen impetuous	7 8	0-6
Ligurians Javelinmen Medium swordsmen	7	0-3
Elephant mediocre	10	0-3
Balearic slingers Light infantry sling elite	5	0-4
Numidians, Libyans or Spanish Light infantry javelin Upgrade to elite	4 +1	2-6
Heavy artillery	10	0-1
Fortified camp	6	0-1

Before 235 BC Syracusan allies (List #50 Syracusan) Sicilian Greek allies (List #60 Classical Greek)		
Hoplite mercenaries * Heavy spearmen	8	0-4
Thureophoroi Medium spearmen	7	0-2
Campanians and Italians Heavy spearmen Medium swordsmen Downgrade to mediocre	 8 7 -2	0-2
From 235 to 201 BC Iberian allies (List #89 Ancient Spanish)		
Celtiberian scutarii Heavy swordsmen impetuous	8	0-2
Hannibal in Italy from 216 to 203 BC Bruttian, Lucanian, Apulian or Campanian allies (List #51 Campanian, Lucanian, Apulian and Bruttian) Only one Elephant. No artillery, no impetuous Scutarii, no Numidian or Iberian allies.		
Replace all African spearmen Heavy spearmen armour elite	12	2-4
Replace all Gallic warriors Medium swordsmen impact Heavy swordsmen impact	 8 9	All
Replace all Campanians and Italians Heavy swordsmen impact Add armour *(all or none)*	 9 +2	0-2
Hannibal in Africa in 202 BC		
Replace all African spearmen Heavy spearmen armour elite	12	1-2
Bruttian veterans Medium swordsmen elite Add armour	 9 +2	1-2
Moors Light infantry bow	4	0-2

Note

- One Commander can be included in a hoplite unit before 235 BC.
- Numidian allies (List #56 Numidian) until 200 BC.

Carthaginian African spearmen

56 - Numidian

215 BC - 25 AD
Plain, Mountain
Command +3

Numidians were a semi-nomadic people of North Africa. During the 2nd Punic War the Numidians commanded by Syphax were allied with Carthage while those of Massinissa supported the Romans. At the end of the war Massinissa received many territories as a reward. In 148 BC, at the death of Massinissa, the Romans obliged his son Micipsa to divide the kingdom. In 113 BC Jugurtha rebelled and inflicted severe defeats on the Romans but was betrayed and delivered to his enemies. King Juba the 1st, a supporter of Pompey, lost his kingdom in 46 BC before it was finally restored to his son Juba II.

Troop type	Pts	Units
Numidian cavalry * Light cavalry javelin Upgrade to elite (max 4)	 6 +1	8-24
Javelinmen Javelinmen Light infantry javelin	 7 4	4-16
Light infantry bow Light infantry sling	4	0-4
Elephant mediocre	10	0-2
Before 55 BC		
Trained infantry Medium swordsmen	7	0-4
From 55 BC		
Imitation legionaries Heavy swordsmen impact Downgrade to mediocre	 9 -2	2-8
Bogud in 47 BC		
Spanish mercenaries Medium swordsmen impetuous	7	0-2
Juba the 1st from 55 to 46 BC		
Gallic and Spanish guardsmen Medium cavalry elite	9	0-2

Note

- Roman allies (List #84 Early Imperial Roman) for Juba II from 3 to 6 AD.
- Numidian can be used as allies before 215 BC.

57 - Saitic Egyptian

660 - 335 BC
Plain, Desert
Command +4

In 670 the Assyrian king Esarhaddon invaded Egypt and expelled the Kushites. He founded the 26th Egyptian dynasty as a vassal to himself. The Assyrians were eventually repulsed, but Egypt came under Persian control in 525 BC. There followed a turbulent period punctuated by revolts against the Persians. The Saitic army relied heavily on greek mercenaries who were more and more plentiful.

Troop type	Pts	Units
*Horsemen ** Medium cavalry mediocre Light cavalry javelin	 5 6	2-6
Egyptian guardsmen Bowmen Heavy spearmen Upgrade to elite	 7 8 +2	0-2
Egyptian Menfat Medium spearmen mediocre Heavy spearmen mediocre	 5 6	4-16
Egyptian archers Bowmen mediocre	5	2-6
*Greek mercenaries ** Heavy spearmen Add armour *(before 460)* Upgrade to elite (max 1)	 8 +2 +2	0-6
Nubians Bowmen Light infantry bow	 7 4	0-4
Libyans Light infantry javelin	4	0-2
Only 26th dynasty (664 - 525 BC) Assyrian allies (List #9 Assyrian Empire and Sargonid) before 650 BC		
*Replace some horsement with 4 horses chariots ** Heavy chariot impact Upgrade to elite	 11 +2	0-4
Scythian mercenaries Medium cavalry bow Light cavalry bow	 9 6	0-2

Note

- One commander can be included in a Greek mercenaries unit classed as elite. He can only command Greek mercenaries.
- Libyan allies (List #12 Libyan) after 360 BC
- Greek allies (List #58 Cyrenian Greek) after 570 BC

58 - Cyrenian Greek

630 - 96 BC
Plain, Desert
Command +3

The Greeks founded numerous colonies in Mediterranean. Cyrene was the largest in North Africa in the region of modern Libya. Cyrene became an independent kingdom under the reign of King Battus the first. In 321 BC, Cyrenaica became a province of the Ptolemaic Empire before coming under Roman control in 96 BC.

Troop type	Pts	Units
*Horsemen ** Medium cavalry mediocre	5	0-2
*Hoplites and mercenaries ** Heavy spearmen Downgrade to mediocre (max 8) *Only before 460 BC :* Add armour	 8 -2 +2	8-16
Greek peltasts Javelinmen	7	0-2
Libyans Light infantry javelin Light infantry bow (max 2) Light infantry sling (max 2)	4	2-12
Only before 275 BC		
*Chariots with 4 horses ** Heavy chariot	10	2-6
Only after 321 BC		
*Replace all horsemen ** Heavy cavalry impact Upgrade to elite	 10 +2	All
Macedonian garrison Pikemen	11	0-3
Thureophoroi Medium spearmen	7	0-2
Cretan archers Light infantry bow elite	5	0-2

Note

- Libyan allies (List #12 Libyan)
- Carthaginian allies (List #54 Early Carthaginian) in 322 BC

59 - Meroitic Kushite

590 BC - 350 AD
Plain, Desert
Command +3

After the Kushites were driven out of Egypt, they moved their capital further south to Meroe in modern day Sudan. The new kingdom was heavily influenced by Egyptian culture and supported the Egyptians in the revolts against the Ptolemies. From 300 AD the kingdom was weakened by attacks from Nobatae and then fell under the control of the Axum kingdom in 350 AD.

Troop type	Pts	Units
Meroitic horsemen * Medium cavalry Heavy cavalry (max ½) Upgrade to elite (max 4)	 7 9 +2	2-8
Light cavalry javelin	6	0-2
Elephant (*from 300 BC*)	13	0-1
Medium camelry Medium camelry bow	8 10	0-4
Meroitic archers * Archer Upgrade to elite (max 4)	 7 +2	4-12
Tribal spearmen Medium spearmen mediocre	5	4-24
Tribal swordsmen or axemen Medium swordsmen Downgrade to mediocre	 7 -2	0-4
Tribal archers Bowmen mediocre Light infantry bow	 5 4	0-4
Javelinmen Light infantry javelin	7 4	0-2

Note

- Blemmye allies (List #112 Blemmyes and Nobatae)

Greek hoplites

GREECE AND DANUBE

60 - Classical Greek

680 - 275 BC
Plain, Mountain
Command +3 or +4 if Spartan or Theban
Strategists: Brasidas (Spartan 431-422 BC), Epaminondas (Theban 371-362 BC)

This list represents the armies of the Greek cities during the classical period. The main warrior of this period was the hoplite. He was heavily protected by bronze armour and fought in a tight formation. The hoplites were supported by cavalry and light troops. The Spartans were the best trained fighters and were deemed elite. The Spartan general Brasidas won many victories. Epaminondas of Thebes ensured the supremacy of his city by beating the Spartans at Leuctra in 371 BC. From 275 BC the Greek cities replaced the hoplites with thureophoroi or a phalanx following the Macedonian model.

Troop type	Pts	Units
Hoplites * Heavy spearmen Add armour (*only before 460 BC*) Up. to elite (max 2 or 8 if Spartan)	 8 +2 +2	6-24
Horsemen Medium cavalry Downgrade to mediocre	 7 -2	0-3
Thracians Javelinmen Medium swordsmen Medium swordsmen 2HW	 7 7 8	0-2
Peltasts Javelinmen Light infantry javelin	 7 4	0-4
Skirmishers Light infantry sling Light infantry bow Upgrade to elite (max 2) if Cretan	 4 4 +1	0-4
Spartan		
Replace all horsemen Medium cavalry mediocre	5	0-2
Paphlagonians and Thracians Light cavalry javelin	6	0-2
From 431 to 422 BC with Brasidas *Replace some hoplites* Medium spearmen elite	9	0-2
From 369 to 368 BC, Gallic and Spanish mercenaries from Syracuse Medium swordsmen impetuous Heavy swordsmen impetuous	 7 8	0-4

Athenian		
Paphlagonians and Thracians Light cavalry javelin	6	0-2
Light cavalry bow	6	0-1
Theban		
*Replace all horsemen ** Medium cavalry	7	1-4
Light cavalry javelin	6	0-2
Sacred Band Heavy spearmen elite Add armour *(only before 460 BC)*	10 +2	0-1
Thessalian		
*Replace all horsemen ** Medium cavalry (max 4) Upgrade to elite	7 +2	2-8
Light cavalry javelin	6	
Replace all peltasts Javelinmen Light infantry javelin	7 4	4-8
Greek from Asia, Italy or Sicily		
Light cavalry javelin	6	0-2
Downgrade some hoplites Heavy spearmen mediocre	6	0-24
Aetolians and Phocaeans		
Replace all hoplites Javelinmen Light infantry javelin	7 4	All
Other hoplites Heavy spearmen	8	0-8
Heavy artillery	10	0-2

Note

- Each army corps may have a different origin (Athenian, Spartan ...). Each corps of a different origin to that of the commander in chief is considered as an allied corps with an unreliable general.

61 - Hellenistic Greek

275 - 146 BC
Plain, Mountain
Command +3 or +4 if Spartan
Strategist: Philopœmen (Achaean League in 222-183 BC)

From 275 BC the hoplite system was gradually abandoned in Greece to be replaced either by phalanxes on the Macedonian model or by thureophoroi who were more lightly armed than the hoplites. Greece became a Roman province in 146 BC.

Troop type	Pts	Units
*Horsemen ** Medium cavalry Heavy cavalry	7 9	1-2
Tarentines or Aetolian Light cavalry javelin	6	0-3
Hoplites Heavy spearmen	8	0-4
Thureophoroi Medium spearmen	7	6-24
Light infantry bow Light infantry sling	4	2-4
Peltasts Javelinmen Light infantry javelin	7 4	0-6
Heavy artillery	10	0-1
Spartan		
*Replace all hoplites ** Heavy spearmen elite	10	All
Replace all thureophoroi Heavy spearmen Pikemen (max 12)	8 11	All
Achaean League		
*Replace some horsemen ** Heavy cavalry impact	10	0-2
Replace some Thureophoroi Pikemen	11	0-12
Thracian horsemen Light cavalry javelin	6	0-3
Thorakitai Medium spearmen armour	9	0-3
Illyrian Medium spearmen	7	0-3
Freed slaves (only in 146 BC) Pikemen mediocre	8	0-4
Aetolian		
*Replace all horsemen ** Light cavalry javelin	6	All
Replace at least half thureophoroi Javelinmen Light infantry javelin	7 4	½ to All

Note

- Each army corps may have a different origin (Athenian, Spartan ...). Each corps of a different origin to that of the commander in chief is considered as an allied corps with an unreliable general.

62 - Illyrian

385 BC - 10 AD
Mountain
Command +3

The Illyrians occupied the coast of the eastern shore of the Adriatic Sea corresponding to today's Croatia and Slovenia. They were divided into tribes and were proud of their fighting abilities. Around 385 BC, King Bardylis first unified the country but was defeated by Philip II of Macedonia who incorporated Illyria into his Empire. In 229 BC the Romans took the city of Dyrrachium to end piracy in the region. The province of Illyria was created in 9 BC and was then divided into Dalmatia and Pannonia in 10 AD.

Troop type	Pts	Units
Noble Horsemen * Medium cavalry Upgrade to elite	 7 +2	0-3
Warriors and slaves * Medium swordsmen Medium spearmen (max 6) Upgrade to elite (max 6)	 7 7 +2	8-24
Light infantry javelin Upgrade to elite	4 +1	2-6
Light infantry bow	4	0-3
Light infantry sling	4	0-3
Only in 385 BC Syracusan allies (List #50 Syracusan)		
Illyrians equiped as Hoplites Heavy spearmen	8	0-4

Paionian allies		
Light cavalry javelin *	6	2-4
Warriors * Javelinmen Light infantry javelin	 7 4	4-8
Light infantry bow Light infantry sling	4	0-2

Note

- Paionian allies (see list above)

63 - Thracian

700 BC - 45 AD
Mountain, Forest
Command +3

The Thracians were an Indo-European people whose territory stretched from the Black Sea to the Danube River Basin. The Thracians south of the Danube were somewhat divided whilst those of the north founded a powerful kingdom in Dacia. They were often recruited as mercenaries due to their good fighting abilities. Thrace became a Roman province in 46 AD.

Troop type	Pts	Units
Nobles * Medium cavalry Heavy cavalry Upgrade to elite	 7 9 +2	0-4
Light infantry javelin Upgrade to elite	4 +1	2-6
Light infantry bow	4	0-3
Light infantry sling	4	0-3
Women, children and slaves Levy mediocre	2	0-1
Fortified camp	6	0-1
Plains tribes Greek mercenaries allies (List #60 Classical Greek) from 400 to 357 BC Roman allies (List #84 Early Imperial Roman) from 25 to 45 AD		
Light cavalry javelin Light cavalry bow (max ½)	6	4-12
Warriors Javelinmen Medium swordsmen (max 8)	7	8-24
Only from 350 to 250 BC Medium spearmen (max 8)	7	
Mountains tribes		
Light cavalry javelin	6	0-4
Warriors * Medium swordsmen Upgrade to elite (max 8)	 7 +2	8-24
Javelinmen	7	
From 250 BC (plains or mountains tribes)		
Upgrade warriors with rhomphaia * Medium swordsmen 2HW	8	0-12

Thracian warriors

ASIA MINOR

64 - Achaemenid Persian

550 – 420 BC
Plain, Mountain
Command +5
Strategist: Cyrus II (550-530 BC), Mardonius (492-479 BC)

The Achaemenid Persian Empire extended over much of the Middle East, Asia Minor, Thrace and along the Black Sea coast. To the east it extended to Afghanistan and Pakistan and to the south it included Syria and Egypt. Cyrus II, known as Cyrus the Great, was the first Persian emperor. He defeated the Medes in 550 BC who were thereafter integrated into the Empire. Darius I attacked Greece but was defeated at Marathon in 490 BC. Xerxes succeeded his father and continued the war against the Greeks (Battle of Thermopylae in 480 BC). After the naval defeat at Salamis he left the command to his general Mardonius. Mardonius ravaged Attica and Athens but he was killed at the Battle of Plataea in 479 BC.

Troop type	Pts	Units
*Persian Guardsmen ** Heavy cavalry bow elite	13	0-1
*Persians and Medes ** Medium cavalry bow Heavy cavalry bow Upgrade to elite	9 11 +2	3-6
Indians Medium cavalry mediocre	5	0-2
Arachosians and Paropamisadae Light cavalry javelin	6	0-2
Scythians and Bactrians Light cavalry bow Upgrade to élite (max 2 Bactrians)	6 +1	0-6
Bedouin scouts Light camelry bow mediocre	5	0-1
Immortals, mixed units ½ Medium swordsmen elite ½ Bowmen elite	11	0-3
Sparabara, mixed units ½ Medium swordsmen ½ Bowmen	9	2-6
Assyrians and Chaldeans Medium spearmen	7	0-2
Lydians or Ionians hoplites Heavy spearmen mediocre Add armour *(all or none)*	6 +2	0-2
Armenians or Thracians Javelinmen Medium swordsmen	7	0-2
Parthians, Scythians or Indians Bowmen	7	0-3
Arabs or Scythians Light infantry bow	4	0-4
Mysians, Lydians Javelinmen Light infantry javelin	7 4	0-4
Libyans, Colchians Light infantry javelin	4	0-2
Levy	3	0-2
Fortified camp	6	0-1
Only Cyrus in Lydia in 546 BC		
Improvised camelry Light camelry bow mediocre Medium camelry bow mediocre	5 8	1-2
Scythed chariot	3	0-2
Mobile Tower War wagon bow	10	0-2

Greek allies (only in 479 BC)		
Medium cavalry * Downgrade to mediocre	7 -2	0-1
*Hoplites ** Heavy spearmen Downgrade to mediocre Add armour *(all or none)*	8 -2 +2	2-4
Light infantry javelin	4	0-2

Note

- Greek allies (see list above)
- Saka allies (List #76 Scythian)

65 - Lydian

687 – 546 BC
Plain, Mountain
Command +3

The Lydians occupied a part of Asia Minor along the Aegean Sea. They were first under the rule of the Phrygians but pushed back the Cimmerians when they invaded Phrygia. This was the beginning of the Lydian Empire, culminating with the reign of Croesus, which extended its influence over much of Asia Minor. Lydia was conquered by the Persians of Cyrus the Great in 546 BC. It became part of the Seleucid kingdom, then that of Pergamum and finally was incorporated in the Roman Empire in 129.

Troop type	Pts	Units
*Lydian nobles ** Heavy cavalry Upgrade to elite (max 4)	9 +2	4-8

*Lydian chariots ** Light chariot	7	0-2
Phrygians or Paphlagonians Light cavalry javelin	6	2-6
Scythians Light cavalry bow	6	0-2
Lydians, Phrygians and Mysians Medium spearmen	7	4-16
Heavy spearmen (max 8) Add armour *(all or none)*	8 +2	
Bithynians or Thracians Javelinmen Medium swordsmen	7	0-2
Lydians, Phrygians and Mysians Javelinmen Light infantry javelin	7 4	2-8
Light infantry bow Light infantry sling	4	0-2

Note

- Asiatic Greek allies (List #60 Classical Greek)

66 - Lycian

546 – 300 BC
Mountain
Command +3

Lycia was a small state in Asia Minor in the south of Lydia. It was conquered by the Persians as well as all regions of Asia Minor. Lycia was associated with Xerxes during his first campaign against the Greeks. Then Lycia passed under the control of the Seleucids.

Troop type	Pts	Units
*Nobles horsemen ** Medium cavalry Heavy cavalry (max 2) Upgrade to elite (max 4)	 7 9 +2	2-6
Warriors Medium swordsmen	7	6-16
Warriors with drepanon Medium swordsmen impact	8	0-4
Hoplites mercenaries Heavy spearmen Add armour *(all or none)*	 8 +2	0-4
Peltasts mercenaries Javelinmen	7	0-2
Light infantry bow	4	2-4
Light infantry javelin	4	0-4
Light infantry sling	4	0-2

Note

- Asiatic Greek allies (List #60 Classical Greek)

67 - Bithynian

435 – 74 BC
Forest, Mountain
Command +4

The Bithynians were people of Thracian origin. They occupied a kingdom in northwest Asia Minor. Bithynia was annexed by King Croesus of Lydia before passing under the domination of the Persians. Bithynia regained its independence with King Nicomedes the 1st (278-243 BC) and became a prosperous kingdom. The last King - Nicomedes IV - bequeathed his kingdom to Rome in 74 BC.

Troop type	Pts	Units
*Nobles horsemen ** Medium cavalry Heavy cavalry Upgrade to elite	 7 9 +2	0-3
Light cavalry javelin	6	2-4
Warriors Javelinmen Medium swordsmen	7	8-24
Javelinmen Light infantry javelin Upgrade to elite	 4 +1	2-6
Light infantry bow Light infantry sling	4	0-4
Only before 335 BC		
Persians Medium cavalry bow	9	0-2
Only after 278 BC		
Galatians Heavy swordsmen impetuous Upgrade to elite	 8 +2	0-2
Only after 265 BC		
Citizens Medium spearmen Heavy spearmen Pikemen mediocre	 7 8 8	0-4
Thracians Javelinmen Medium swordsmen Medium swordsmen 2HW	 7 7 8	0-4

Paphlagonian allies after 176 BC		
Light cavalry javelin *	6	1-3
Medium swordsmen	7	1-4

Note

- Paphlagonian allies (see list above) after 179 BC
- Galatian allies (List #72 Galatian) in 278 BC

68 - Later Achaemenid Persian

420 - 329 BC
Plain, Mountain
Command +4

This list represents the army of the Achaemenid Empire from the time when the Immortals and Sparabara were no longer the backbone of the army. The cavalry were no longer using the bow as opposed to previous eras. The Persians regularly called for Greek mercenaries. The Empire was in a phase of turmoil and in the war of succession, when Alexander invaded Asia Minor in 334 BC. The Persian army suffered a first defeat by the Granicus. It was followed by the defeat of Issus and that of Gaugamela in 332 BC, before the capture of Babylon in 331 BC. The Last Emperor Darius III fled and was murdered by his own satraps. The satraps had pledged allegiance to Alexander who then became the master of the Persian Empire.

Troop type	Pts	Units
*Persian Guardsmen ** Heavy cavalry impact Upgrade to elite	 10 +2	0-1
*Persian, Median, Indian, Armenian and Cappadocian horsemen ** Medium cavalry Heavy cavalry Downgrade to mediocre	 7 9 -2	4-16
*Other horsemen with bow ** Medium cavalry bow Heavy cavalry bow Downgrade to mediocre	 9 11 -2	0-4
Paphlagonians Light cavalry javelin	6	2-4
Bactrians Light cavalry bow elite	7	0-2
Scythians and Parthians Light cavalry bow	6	0-4
Scythed chariot	3	0-2
Elephant	13	0-1
Guardsmen (Apple Bearer) ½ Heavy swordsmen elite ½ Bowmen elite	12	0-1
*Greek or Ionian mercenaries ** Heavy spearmen Downgrade to mediocre	 8 -2	0-6
Babylonian and Mardian archers Bowmen mediocre	5	0-6
Cardaces, Carian and Egyptian Medium spearmen Heavy spearmen mediocre	 7 6	0-6
Chalybes Medium spearmen mediocre	5	0-2
Persian, Greek or Thracian Peltasts Javelinmen Medium swordsmen (max 2) Medium swordsmen 2HW (max 2)	 7 7 8	0-8
Hill tribesmen Javelinmen Light infantry javelin	 7 4	0-2
Light infantry bow Light infantry sling	4	0-4
Levy	3	0-4
Fortifications	1	0-6
Heavy artillery	10	0-1

Note

- One commander can be included in a Greek Mercenaries unit
- Lycian allies (List #66 Lycian)
- Saka allies (List #76 Scythian) in 329 BC

Darius in his chariot

69 - Cappadocian

330 BC - 17 AD
Plain, Mountain
Command +3

Cappadocia lies in central Asia Minor and it was part of the Persian Empire. At the fall of the Persian Empire, King Ariarathes I pledged allegiance to Alexander and formed an independent state. His army comprised Greek mercenaries. One of Alexander's successors, Perdiccas, took control of Cappadocia in 322 BC. The region became independent under Ariarathes II with the help of the Armenians. The Cappadocians became allies of the Romans and supported them in the wars against the

Seleucids and Mithridates. In 17 AD, the region became a province of the Roman Empire.

Troop type	Pts	Units
*Nobles horsemen ** Heavy cavalry Upgrade to elite	 9 +2	 0-4
Other horsemen Medium cavalry	7	2-8
Light cavalry javelin	6	2-6
Warriors Medium swordsmen	7	4-16
Archers Bowmen (max 4) Light infantry bow	 7 4	 2-6
Thracian mercenaries Javelinmen Medium swordsmen Medium swordsmen 2HW	 7 7 8	 0-2
Light infantry javelin	4	0-4
Ariarathes I (330 - 322 BC)		
*Hoplites mercenaries ** Heavy spearmen	8	0-6

Note

- Armenian allies (List #71 Armenian) after 300 BC

70 - Bosporan Kingdom

310 BC - 375 AD
Plain, Steppes
Command +2

The Bosporan kingdom was a Greek kingdom established on the banks of the Strait of Kerch in Crimea. The kingdom's population was largely made up of Scythians and Sarmatians who were more or less Hellenized. Around 115 BC the kingdom was given to the King of Pontus, Mithridates VII and his son who reigned until 47 BC. The kingdom was then incorporated into the Roman sphere of influence but remained an independent vassal. The kingdom was conquered by the Huns in 375 AD.

Troop type	Pts	Units
*Horsemen with spear ** Medium cavalry impetuous Heavy cavalry impetuous Upgrade to elite (max 4)	 7 9 +2	 4-12
Horse archers Light cavalry bow Medium cavalry bow (max 6)	 6 9	 2-12
Greek militia Medium spearmen	7	2-4
Greek mercenaries Heavy spearmen	8	0-2
Sindi and Maeotians Bowmen Light infantry bow	 7 4	 0-4
Sindi and Maeotians Javelinmen Light infantry javelin	 7 4	 0-4
Light infantry sling	4	0-2
Fortifications	1	0-6
Fortified camp	6	0-1
Before 115 BC Scythian allies (List #76 Scythian)		
Celtic or Thracian mercenaries Javelinmen Medium swordsmen Medium swordsmen impetuous Medium swordsmen 2HW	 7 7 7 8	 0-4
After 41 AD Roman allies (List #84 Early Imperial Roman)		
Replace all Greek militia Medium swordsmen Heavy swordsmen	 7 8	 All
Roman auxiliaries Medium swordsmen impact Upgrade to elite	 8 +2	 0-2
Heavy artillery	10	0-1

Note

- Sarmatian allies (List #77 Sarmatian) before 41 AD

71 - Armenian

300 BC - 428 AD
Plain, Mountain
Command +3 or +4 with Tigranes the Great
Strategist: Tigranes the Great (83-69 BC)

The Armenian Kingdom reached its peak during the reign of King Tigranes II known as Tigranes the Great (95-55 BC). It extended from the Caucasus to the centre of present day Turkey, Lebanon and the north west of Iran. Defeated by the Roman general Pompey, Armenia submitted to Rome. In 301 AD it was the first kingdom to adopt Christianity. Armenia was divided between the Byzantines and the Persians in 428 AD and lost its independance.

Troop type	Pts	Units
*Nobles ** Cataphract Upgrade to elite (max 2)	 11 +2	 2-8

Horse archers Light cavalry bow Medium cavalry bow (max 4)	 6 9	4-12
Georgians or Albanians Heavy cavalry impetuous	9	0-2
Javelinmen	7	2-8
Bowmen Light infantry bow	7 4	2-6
Albanians Light infantry sling Light infantry javelin	4	0-4
Only Tigranes the Great from 83 to 69 BC Arab nomad allies (List #75 Early Arab) Atropatene allies (List #102 Parthian)		
Imitation legionaries Heavy swordsmen impact	9	0-2
Seleucid phalangites Pikemen mediocre	8	0-2
Levy	3	0-2

Note

- Allied contingent taken from this list need not to include Javelinmen or Bowmen.
- Following allies are only from 226 to 228 AD :
- Alan allies (List #108 Alans)
- Roman allies (List #85 Middle Imperial Roman)

72 - Galatian

280 - 25 BC
Plain, Mountain
Command +2

The Galatians were a Celtic people who originally came from Gaul. They crossed the Balkans and Greece, ravaging as they went. Some of them returned home and others settled in central Asia Minor. They were allied to the Bithynians against the Seleucids but were defeated by them. Then they served as mercenaries and fought against Pergamon, Mithridates king of Pontus and the Romans. Galatia became a Roman province in 25 BC.

Troop type	Pts	Units
*Horsemen ** Medium cavalry Heavy cavalry (max 3) Upgrade to elite	 7 9 +2	3-9
*Chariots with 2 horses before 62 BC ** Light chariot elite	9	0-3
*Warriors before 62 BC ** Heavy swordsmen impetuous Upgrade to elite (all or none)	 8 +2	8-24
*Warriors from 62 BC ** Heavy swordsmen impetuous Heavy swordsmen impact (max 8)	 8 9	
Light infantry javelin	4	0-2
Only in 273 BC Scythed chariot	3	0-2
Cappadocians in 189 BC Medium swodsmen	7	0-2
Greece invasion in 279 BC Paionian allies (see list below)		
Greeks Heavy spearmen Medium spearmen	 8 7	0-2

Paionian allies in 279 BC		
Light cavalry javelin *	6	2-4
*Warriors ** Javelinmen Light infantry javelin	 7 4	4-8
Light infantry bow Light infantry sling	4	0-2

Galatian warriors

73 - Pergamon

262 – 133 BC
Plain, Mountain
Command +4

Pergamon or Pergamum was a city of Asia Minor situated north of Smyrna. Initially, Pergamon was under the tutelage of the Seleucids. King Eumenes I defeated Antiochus in 262 BC and gained the independence of Pergamon. Allied with the Romans against Philip V of Macedonia, Pergamum extended its influence over a large part of Asia Minor. King Eumenes II (197-159) led Pergamon to its apogee and made it a great centre of Hellenism in Asia Minor. After the Roman victory at Magnesia in 190 BC, Seleucid troops joined the ranks of Pergamon. The last ruler, Attalus III, was without an heir. He chose to bequeath his kingdom to Rome in 133 BC.

Troop type	Pts	Units
Xystophoroi * Heavy cavalry impact Upgrade to elite (max 2)	 10 +2	1-4
Galatian horsemen Medium cavalry Heavy cavalry Upgrade to elite	 7 9 +2	0-2
Pergamon horsemen Light cavalry javelin	6	0-3
Thureophoroi and spearmen Medium spearmen Heavy spearmen	 7 8	4-12
Galatians Heavy swordsmen impetuous Upgrade to elite	 8 +2	0-2
City militia Medium spearmen mediocre	5	0-2
Mysians Javelinmen Light infantry javelin	 7 4	0-6
Cretan archers Light infantry bow elite	5	1-4
Light infantry sling	4	1-2
Heavy artillery	10	0-2
Fortified camp	6	0-1
After 190 BC : Ex Seleucids		
Cataphract	11	0-2
Elephant	13	0-1
Pikemen	11	0-2
Thracians Medium cavalry Light cavalry javelin	 7 6	0-1

Note

- Thureophoroi and Spearmen must be all of the same type
- Achaean League (List #61 Hellenistic Greek)
- Cappadocian allies (List #69 Cappadocian)
- Galatian allies (List #72 Galatian) in 218 BC

EAST AND STEPPES

74 - Aramaean

312 BC - 240 AD
Plain, Mountain, Desert
Command +3

This list represents the armies of the Aramaean cities of Syria and Mesopotamia such as Hatra, Edessa, Emesa, Characene, Nabataea or Adiabene. These cities were mostly influenced by the Parthians. The Roman Emperor Trajan forced several of these cities to submit during his expeditions in the East. The city of Palmyra has its own list.

Troop type	Pts	Units
Horsemen * Medium cavalry Heavy cavalry Upgrade to elite	 7 9 +2	1-3
Horse archers Light cavalry bow Medium cavalry bow (max 4)	 6 9	2-12
Bedouins Light camelry bow Downgrade to mediocre	 7 -2	0-2
Medium camelry bow Downgrade to mediocre	10 -2	
Bowmen Downgrade to mediocre	7 -2	4-16
Warriors with sword Heavy swordsmen	8	0-4
Warriors with javelin Javelinmen Light infantry javelin	 7 4	2-6
Light infantry bow	4	0-6
Light infantry sling	4	0-4
Only Nabataea		
Replace all horsemen * Heavy cavalry impact Upgrade to elite	 10 +2	All
Stampeding herd Scythed chariot	3	0-1
Fortifications	1	0-6

Only Hatra Parthian allies (List #102 Parthian)		
Cataphracts on camels Cataphract camelry	12	0-3
Roman auxiliaries Medium swordsmen impact	8	0-2
Heavy artillery	10	0-1
Only Emesa		
*Replace some horsemen ** Cataphract Upgrade to elite	11 +2	0-3
*Guardsmen ** Medium swordsmen impact elite	10	0-2

Note

- Arab nomad allies (List #75 Early Arab) only if Characene

75 - Early Arab

312 BC - 630 AD
Plain, Mountain, Desert
Command +2

This list covers the cities and nomadic tribes of Arabia before their conversion to Islam. This was especially the cities of Mecca, Medina and Oman; the Yemenite kingdom as well as the Ghassanid, Lakhmid and Kindah tribes. These tribes were often allied to the Byzantines or to the Sassanid Persians.

Troop type	Pts	Units
*Nomads chiefs ** Medium cavalry	7	0-3
*Other nomads ** Light cavalry javelin	6	2-8
Scouts on camels Light camelry bow	7	0-4
Nomads warriors on camels Medium camelry bow Downgrade to mediocre	10 -2	0-6
Nomads javelinmen Medium swordsmen Javelinmen Downgrade to mediocre	7 7 -2	6-16
Nomads warriors with swords Medium swordsmen impetuous	7	0-6
Nomads archers Bowmen Light infantry bow	7 4	0-4
Light infantry sling	4	0-4
Light infantry javelin	4	0-4
Women and children Levy mediocre	2	0-1

Bedouin Tribe		
Replace all Nomads javelinmen Light cavalry javelin Medium cavalry	6 7	All

Note

- Sassanid allies (List #109 Sassanid Persian)
- Byzantine allies (List #126 Maurikian Byzantine)

76 - Scythian

750 BC - 50 AD
Steppes
Command +2

The Scythians were a group of nomadic people coming from a large steppe area that extended from the Ukraine to Altai. They included the Cimmerians, Scythians, Saka, Massagetae and the Hu on the Chinese border. Seleucid pikemen units in 129 BC were part of the army of Antigonus VII who, after being captured by the Parthians, changed sides when the Parthians attacked the Scythians.

Troop type	Pts	Units
*Scythian nobles before 300 BC ** Heavy cavalry bow Upgrade to elite	11 +2	0-4
*Scythian nobles from 300 BC ** Heavy cavalry impetuous Upgrade to elite	9 +2	
*Saka nobles from 250 BC ** Cataphract Upgrade to elite	11 +2	
Horse archers Light cavalry bow Medium cavalry bow	6 9	8-24
Tribal militia Medium swordsmen mediocre	5	0-4
Archers Bowmen Downgrade to mediocre	7 -2	0-4
Light infantry bow	4	
Light infantry sling	4	0-2
Only Saka in 129 BC		
Captured Seleucid pikemen Pikemen mediocre	8	0-2

Note

- Asiatic Greek (List #60 Classical Greek) or Thracian allies (List #63 Thracian – plains tribes) for European scythians in 313 BC
- Mountain Indian allies (see list below) only if Saka or Massagetae.

Mountain Indian allies		
Elephant *	13	0-1
Light cavalry javelin *	6	0-4
Medium spearmen *	7	2-6
Bowmen Light infantry bow	7 4	2-6

77 - Sarmatian

310 BC - 375 AD
Steppes
Command +2

The Sarmatians were a people related to the Scythians and were originally established between the Don and the Urals. From the fourth century the Sarmatians pushed westward and replaced the Scythians in Ukraine. From the first century BC they dominated the steppes. They were divided into four groups: Lazyges, Roxolani, Aorsi and Siraces. Some groups were granted the status of federated tribes and settled in the Roman Empire. From the third century AD the Sarmatians were conquered by the Goths and then by the Huns.

Troop type	Pts	Units
Horsemen * Medium cavalry impetuous Heavy cavalry impetuous Upgrade to elite (max 6)	 7 9 +2	6-24
Scouts Light cavalry bow	6	0-3
Bowmen mediocre Light infantry bow	5 4	0-4
Light infantry sling	4	0-2
Peasants Medium swordsmen mediocre Levy	 5 3	0-3
Only Roxolani until 100 AD Scythian allies (List #76 Scythian)		
Replace all horsemen * Medium cavalry bow Heavy cavalry bow Upgrade to elite (max 6)	 9 11 +2	6-18
Other horsemen with long spear * Medium cavalry impetuous Heavy cavalry impetuous	 7 9	0-6

Note

- Herul allies (List #95 Gepid, Herul and Taifali) in 358 AD
- Quadi allies (List #96 Franks, Alemanni, Burgundi, Suevi) after 250 AD
- Alan allies (List #108 Alan) after 100 AD

CLASSICAL ASIA

78 - Vietnamese

700 BC - 938 AD
Plain, Forest
Command +3

This list corresponds to the armies of the ancient kingdoms of Vietnam, Van Lang, and Au Lac. In 208 BC a former Ch'in general founded the kingdom of Nam Viet that extended through southern China and Vietnam. In 111 BC the kingdom of Nam Viet was invaded by the Han Chinese and became a Chinese province, sometimes rebellious. In 938 AD Ngo Quyen founded an independent state and proclaimed himself as emperor.

Troop type	Pts	Units
Warriors * Medium swordsmen impetuous Upgrade to elite (max 6)	 7 +2	6-20
Bowmen Crossbowmen Downgrade to mediocre	7 7 -2	2-12
Light infantry bow Light infantry crossbow	4	2-6
Nam Viet Kingdom (206-111 BC)		
4 horses chariots * Heavy chariot impact Upgrade to elite	 11 +2	0-2
Ex Ch'in Medium cavalry crossbow	9	0-2
Ex Ch'in Medium spearmen Heavy spearmen Add support Downgrade to mediocre	 7 8 +1 -2	2-6
Ex Ch'in Crossbowmen mediocre	5	2-4
Imitation of Chinese troops after 135 AD		
Medium cavalry crossbow Heavy cavalry impact	9 10	0-2
Heavy spearmen Heavy swordsmen 2HW Add support Downgrade to mediocre	8 9 +1 -2	2-6
Bowmen mediocre Crossbowmen mediocre	5	2-4
Only after 200 AD		
Elephant *	13	0-2
Heavy artillery	10	0-1

Tribal allies		
Tribal warriors * Medium swordsmen * Javelinmen	7	2-6
Bowmen mediocre Light infantry bow	5 4	2-4

Note

- Tribal allies (see list above)
- Khmer or Cham allies (List #167 Khmer Empire and Champa) only en 722 AD. In this case, no *Imitation of Chinese troops* can be taken.

79 - Classical Indian

500 BC - 535 AD
Plain, Forest
Command +2 or +3 if Guptas or Mauryas

India had many Empires during the *Classical Period*. The Maurya Empire dominated much of the Indian subcontinent from the death of Alexander until 180 BC. This period was considered the golden age in India. The Guptas ruled the northern part of India from the third century until 535 AD.

Troop type	Pts	Units
War elephant * Elephant elite	16	2-6
Replace some elephant War wagon bow mediocre	8	0-3
Nobles * Light chariot bow Heavy chariot impetuous Upgrade to elite	9 10 +2	0-4
Horsemen * Medium cavalry mediocre	5	1-4
Light cavalry javelin	6	0-2
Guardsmen with two-handed sword or heavy mace Medium swordsmen 2HW elite	10	0-2
Indian archers Bowmen Downgrade to mediocre	7 -2	6-12
Indian archers in mixed unit ½ Medium swordsmen ½ Bowmen	9	
Indian warriors Medium swordsmen Downgrade to mediocre	7 -2	0-6
Light infantry bow Light infantry javelin (max 2)	4	0-6
Light artillery Heavy artillery	6 10	0-1
Stampeding herd Scythed chariot	3	0-1
Levy	3	0-4
Fortified camp	6	0-1
Only Guptas from 320 AD		
Replace all horsemen * Heavy cavalry impact Upgrade to elite	10 +2	All
Light cavalry bow	6	0-2

Classical Indian

80 - Warring States

480 - 206 BC
Plain, Mountain, Forest
Command +5
Strategist: Sun Pin (Ch'i in 351-341 BC)

After the *Spring and Autumn* period, only seven main states remained in China. This period of confrontation was called the Warring States period. Finally the king of Qin (or Ch'in) managed to conquer all the other kingdoms in 221 BC. This was the beginning of the Qin Dynasty that only lasted until 206 BC.

Troop type	Pts	Units
*4 horses chariots ** Heavy chariot impact Upgrade to elite	 11 +2	1-4
Horsemen Heavy cavalry Medium cavalry crossbow	9	0-4
Infantry Medium swordsmen 2HW Heavy swordsmen 2HW Downgrade to mediocre	 8 9 -2	6-16
Archers and crossbowmen Bowmen Crossbowmen Downgrade to mediocre	 7 7 -2	2-6
Fanatical warriors Medium swordsmen impetuous Upgrade to elite	 7 +2	0-2
Light infantry bow Light infantry crossbow	4	0-4
Light infantry javelin	4	0-2
Revolted peasants Levy Levy impetuous	 3 4	0-3
Light artillery Heavy artillery	6 10	0-2
Fortifications	1	0-8
Fortified camp	6	0-1
Yueh Option		
Tribal auxiliaries Medium swordsmen impetuous	7	0-3
Chao, Yen or Wei Option		
Light cavalry bow	6	0-6
Ch'u Option		
Light cavalry bow	6	0-1
Tribal auxiliaries Medium swordsmen impetuous	7	0-3
Guard crossbowmen Crossbowmen pavise elite	10	0-2
Han Option		
Light cavalry bow Medium cavalry bow	6 9	0-6
Qin Option		
Light cavalry bow	6	0-4
Replace all infantry Medium swordsmen impact Heavy swordsmen impact Upgrade to elite	 8 9 +2	All

81 - Ch'iang and Ti

315 BC - 417 AD
Mountain, Forest
Command +2 or +3 for Ch'in Kingdom

The Ch'iang and Ti were nomadic tribes situated west of China in the regions of Szechwan and Kansu. They frequently fought the Han Chinese and were allied with the Hsiung-Nu. Between 351 and 394 AD they founded the kingdom of Ch'in in northern China and incorporated Chinese troops.

Troop type	Pts	Units
*Horsemen ** Medium cavalry bow Light cavalry bow	 9 6	2-10
*Replace some horsemen ** Heavy cavalry impact Heavy cavalry bow Cataphract Upgrade to elite	 10 11 11 +2	0-4
Warriors Medium swordsmen 2HW Add armour (max 6)	 8 +2	6-16
Bowmen Light infantry bow	7 4	2-6
Ch'in Kingdom (351-394 AD) Hsien-Pi allies (List #118 Hsien-Pi)		
*Chinese horsemen ** Heavy cavalry impact	10	1-2
Med. swordsmen 2HW mediocre Heavy swordsmen 2HW mediocre	6 7	2-4
Bowmen mediocre Crossbowmen mediocre	5	2-4
Levy	3	0-3
Light infantry bow	4	0-2
Fortified camp	6	0-1

Note

- Hsiung-Nu allies (List #116 Hsiung-Nu)

ROMAN PERIOD

ROMAN EMPIRE

82 - TRIUMVIRATE ROMAN

105 – 25 BC
Plain, Mountain
Command +5
Strategists: Marius (105-100 BC), Pompey (77-48 BC), Lucullus (74-66 BC) or Caesar (62-45 BC)

This is the army of Rome after Marius' reforms. Marius won a victory over the Cimbri and the Teutones. Pompey, Caesar and Lucullus distinguished themselves on many battlefields and expanded the Roman Empire. The crisis of the first Triumvirate (Caesar, Pompey and Crassus) led to the civil war that saw the end of the republic and the rise of the Empire.

Troop type	Pts	Units
*Roman, Gallic, Greek or Spanish Horsemen ** Medium cavalry Heavy cavalry (max 2)	 7 9	1-4
*German horsemen ** Medium cavalry elite	9	
Numidians, Illyrians or Spanish Light cavalry javelin	6	0-2
Syrian horse archers Light cavalry bow	6	0-1
*Legionaries ** Heavy swordsmen armour impact Upgrade to elite Downgrade to mediocre	 11 +2 -2	4-12
Spanish scutarii Medium swordsmen impetuous	7	0-3
Thureophoroi Medium spearmen	7	
Thracians or Ligurians Javelinmen Medium swordsmen Medium swordsmen 2HW	 7 7 8	
Gladiators Heavy swordsmen elite Medium swordsmen elite	 10 9	0-2
Elephants if no Numidian Allies Elephant mediocre	10	0-1
Germans, Greeks or Numidians Light infantry javelin	4	0-3
Cretan archers Light infantry bow elite	5	0-2
Greeks, Numidians or Gauls Light infantry bow Light infantry sling	4	0-3
Light artillery (max 2) Heavy artillery	6 10	0-3
Fortifications	1	0-8
Fortified camp	6	1
Brutus and Crassus alliance No elephants or gladiators No Armenian or Numidian allies		
Oriental horse archers Light cavalry bow	6	2-8
Oriental archers Bowmen Light infantry bow	 7 4	0-2

Note

- Legionaries can be upgraded to elite if veterans or downgraded as mediocre for conscripts.
- Numidian allies (List #56 Numidian)
- Armenian allies (List #71 Armenian)
- Galatian allies (List #72 Galatian)
- Arab nomad allies (List #75 Early Arab)
- Dacian allies (List #91 Dacian and Carpi)
- Jewish allies (List #103 Judaean Jewish)

83 - SPARTACUS

74 BC – 71 BC
Plain, Mountain, Forest
Command +3
Strategist: Spartacus

Spartacus was a Thracian gladiator who led a slave revolt in southern Italy. He fled with his companions from the gladiator school in Capua. He was joined by many fugitive slaves and also by farmers and poor people. The Roman Senate neglected the threat and sent only a few troops against him. Spartacus defeated legions, one after the other and advanced on

Rome. The Senate assigned to Crassus the mission of eliminating the slaves who had revolted. With six legions Crassus managed to encircle the rebels in Bruttium and exterminated them. Spartacus died with sword in hand and 6,000 slaves were crucified on the Via Appia.

Troop type	Pts	Units
*Gallic and German horsemen ** Medium cavalry Upgrade to elite	 7 +2	0-2
*Gladiators ** Heavy swordsmen impact elite Add armour *(all or none)*	 11 +2	1-2
Slaves with weapons Medium swordsmen impetuous Heavy swordsmen impetuous	 7 8	4-12
Other slaves Medium swordsmen mediocre	5	0-8
Herdsmen Light infantry sling Light infantry javelin	4	2-6
Revolting peasants Levy impetuous	4	4-12

Note

- Army must be commanded by Spartacus.

84 - Early Imperial Roman

25 BC - 193 AD
Plain, Mountain, Forest
Command +5
Strategist: Trajan (98-117 AD)

This was the period of the Roman Empire from Augustus to Septimius Severus. The expansion of the Empire continued under the Julio-Claudian and the Flavian dynasties. The Empire reached its zenith with the emperor Trajan who conquered Dacia in 106 AD. Under the Antonine dynasty the Empire enjoyed a period of peace and prosperity. At the death of Marcus Aurelius in 180 AD, his son Commodus succeeded him. He promptly grew to be cruel and became an enemy of the Senate. The last of the Antonines was assassinated in 193 AD.

Troop type	Pts	Units
*Equites Alares or Singulares ** Medium cavalry Heavy cavalry (max 4) Upgrade to elite (max 2)	 7 9 +2	2-6
Numidians or Moors Light cavalry javelin	6	0-2
Equites Catafractarii after 100 AD Heavy cavalry impact	10	0-2
*Legionaries and Praetorians ** Heavy swordsmen armour impact Add support (max 4) Upgrade to elite	 11 +1 +2	4-12
Auxiliaries Medium swordsmen impact Add support (max 2) Upgrade to elite	 8 +1 +2	2-6
Auxiliaries archers Bowmen Light infantry bow	 7 4	0-2
Light infantry sling Light infantry javelin	4	0-4
Light artillery (max 2) Medium artillery (max 1) Heavy artillery	6 10 10	0-3
Fortified camp	6	1
Only Claude in Britain in 43 AD		
Eléphant mediocre	10	0-1
Western army Batavian allies (List #90 German)		
Sarmatians (not in Britain) Heavy cavalry impetuous	9	0-3
Eastern army Armenian allies (List #71 Armenians) Nabataean allies (List #74 Aramaean) Jewish allies (List #103 Judaean Jewish) Commagene allies (List #104 Commagene)		
Equites Sagittarii Light cavalry bow	6	0-2
Dromedarii Light camelry bow mediocre	5	0-1

85 - Middle Imperial Roman

193 - 307 AD
Plain, Mountain
Command +5
Strategists: Septimius Severus (193-211 AD), Claudius (268-270 AD), Aurelian (270-275 AD), Maximian (Eastern 285-309 AD), Galerius (Eastern 293-310 AD)

Severus took power in 193 by entering Rome with his legions which demonstrated the military nature of his power. He went to war against the Parthians and established the province of Mesopotamia. Between 235 and 268, the Empire suffered a period of military anarchy with not less than eight emperors. The Emperor Claudius Gothicus was the first of the Illyrian Emperors (268-284), all of whom were professional soldiers. Aurelian distinguished himself by ending the rebellion in Gaul and Palmyra. The Empire was increasingly under pressure from the barbarians. In 285 Diocletian appointed Maximian as co-emperor to defend the western part of the Empire while he took care of the eastern part. In 293 each emperor chose a Caesar to assist him. Diocletian chose Galerius who fought the Goths and Sarmatians on the Danube and campaigned in Mesopotamia.

Troop type	Pts	Units
Equites Alares and Singulares * Heavy cavalry (max 6) Upgrade to elite (max 2)	 9 +2	2-8
Equites Illyricani or Moors Light cavalry javelin (max 3)	6	
Equites Sagittarii Light cavalry bow (max 2)	6	
Legionaries and Praetorians * Heavy swordsmen impact Add armour *(all or none)* Upgrade to elite (max 6) Add support (max 6)	 9 +2 +2 +1	4-12
Auxiliaries and Lanciarii Medium swordsmen impact Add armour (Max 2 : *Lanciarii)* Upgrade to elite (Max 2 : *Lanciarii)* Add support	 8 +2 +2 +1	2-8
Auxiliary archers Bowmen Light infantry bow	 7 4	0-2
Light infantry sling Light infantry javelin	4	0-4
Light artillery (max 2) Medium artillery (max 2) Heavy artillery	6 10 10	0-3
Fortified camp	6	1
Western army Gothic allies (List #92 Visigoth) Frankish allies (List #96 Franks, Alemanni, Burgundi, Suevi)		
Catafractarii or Clibanarii Heavy cavalry impact Upgrade to elite	 10 +2	0-2
Eastern army Armenian allies (List #71 Armenian) Arab nomad allies (List #75 Early Arab) Sarmatian allies (List #75 Sarmatian)		
Catafractarii or Clibanarii Heavy cavalry impact Cataphract *(from 227 AD)* Upgrade to elite	 10 11 +2	0-2
Dromedarii Light camelry bow mediocre	5	0-1

86 - Late Imperial Roman

307 - 425 AD
Plain, Mountain, Forest
Command +5
Strategists: Constantius (306-323 AD), Valentinian (364-375 AD), Stilicho (394-408 AD)

The abdication of Diocletian and Maximian was followed by the Constantine dynasty. The Emperor Constantius I embraced Christianity. He reformed the Empire and fought the Goths and Sarmatians. The Emperor Valentinian retook Gaul, defeated the Alemanni and restored the Empire in Britain. Theodosius I was the last emperor to reign in both the East and the West. From 395 AD the Empire was split in two. Stilicho was a Vandal general who effectively defended Italy against the barbarian invasions.

Troop type	Pts	Units
Equites * Heavy cavalry Heavy cavalry impact (max 2) Upgrade to elite (max 2 in total)	 9 10 +2	2-6
Cataphract Upgrade to elite (max 2 in total)	11 +2	
Equites Sagittarii Light cavalry bow	6	0-3
Equites Illyricani Light cavalry javelin	6	0-3
Legionaries * Heavy swordsmen Heavy swordsmen impact Add armour *(all or none)* Add support Upgrade to elite (max 2)	 8 9 +2 +1 +2	2-8
Auxilia Palatina * Medium swordsmen impact Add support Upgrade to elite (max 2)	 8 +1 +2	2-8
Auxilia Pseudocomitatenses Medium swordsmen mediocre	5	0-2
Auxiliary archers Bowmen	7	0-2
Light infantry sling Light infantry bow Light infantry javelin	4	0-4
Light artillery Medium artillery Heavy artillery	6 10 10	0-3
Fortified camp	6	0-1

Only from 389 AD		
Foederati barbarians Heavy cavalry impact	10	0-2
Huns or Alans Light cavalry bow Upgrade to elite	6 +1	0-2
Goths Heavy swordsmen impetuous	8	0-4
Western army Visigoth allies (List #92 Visigoth or List #97 Visigoths in Spain) Frankish allies (List #96 Franks, Alemanni, Burgundi, Suevi) Alan allies (List #108 Alan)		
Eastern army Armenian allies (List #71 Armenian) Arab nomad allies (List #75 Early Arab) Visigoth allies (List #92 Visigoth)		
Dromedarii Light camelry bow mediocre	5	0-1

87 - Patrician Roman

425 - 493 AD
Plain, Mountain, Forest
Command +4 or +5 if Eastern army
Strategist: Aetius (Western army 425-454 BC)

While the Eastern part of the Empire continued to evolve into what would become the Byzantine Empire, the Western part suffered the barbarian invasions. The army was largely composed of barbarian foederati. Aetius was the last Roman leader to win victories against the barbarians. He pushed back the Huns at the Battle of Catalaunian Fields in 451 AD. The last emperors of the West were no more than puppets. In 476 AD Odoacer, king of the Heruli, deposed the last emperor Romulus Augustulus and was proclaimed king of Italy.

Troop type	Pts	Units
*Equites ** Heavy cavalry Add impact (max 2)	9 +1	0-4
Equites Illyricani Light cavalry javelin	6	0-2
Equites Sagittarii Light cavalry bow	6	0-2
Equites Clibanarii Cataphract	11	0-2
*Replace some Equites by horse archers after 450 ** Medium cavalry bow Heavy cavalry bow	9 11	0-6
Mounted foederati Medium cavalry impetuous Heavy cavalry impetuous	7 9	4-12
Foederati on foot Heavy swordsmen impetuous	8	
Huns or Alans Light cavalry bow Upgrade to elite	6 +1	0-3
Decadent Legionaries Heavy swordsmen Add support Downgrade to mediocre	8 +1 -2	0-4
Auxilia Palatina Medium swordsmen impact Add support Downgrade to mediocre	8 +1 -2	2-6
Auxilia Pseudocomitatenses Medium swordsmen mediocre	5	0-2
Auxiliary archers Bowmen Downgrade to mediocre	7 -2	0-2
Exculcatores Light infantry javelin Upgrade to elite	4 +1	0-2
Light infantry sling Light infantry bow	4	0-2
Heavy artillery	10	0-2
Fortifications	1	0-8
Western army Frankish or Burgundi allies (List #96 Franks, Alemanni, Burgundi, Suevi) Visigoth allies (List #97 Visigoths in Spain) Romano-British allies (List #101 Romano-British) Alan allies (List #108 Alan) Hunnic allies (List #110 Huns)		
Eastern army Arab nomad allies (List #75 Early Arab) Ostrogoth allies (List #94 Ostrogoth) Herul allies (List #95 Gepid, Herul and Taifali) Hunnic allies (List #110 Huns)		
Replace some foederati by Isaurians Javelinmen Light infantry javelin	7 4	0-6

Note

- Foederati barbarian can be all mounted or all on foot or can be a mix of both.
- Legionaries are now weaker and do not have *armour* or *impact* abilities.

BARBARIAN

88 - Gallic

400 – 50 BC
Plain, Forest
Command +2
Strategist: Vercingetorix (52 BC)

The Gauls were the descendants of Celts who controlled Northern Western Europe. During the Fourth and Third Centuries BC, the Gauls began expanding to the east and to the Mediterranean. In 390 BC they were in Rome; in 350 BC, they invaded Bulgaria, Thessaly and Athens. Delphi was plundered and the Gauls went to Syria. The Gallics were employed as mercenaries everywhere around the Mediterranean. The Gallic civilization ended with the conquest of Julius Caesar from 58 to 50 BC.

Troop type	Pts	Units
*Chariots or horsemen ** Light chariot Medium cavalry Heavy cavalry (max 1/3) Upgrade to elite (max 6)	 7 7 9 +2	2-12
Mounted scouts Light cavalry javelin	6	0-2
*Gallic warriors ** Medium swordsmen impetuous Heavy swordsmen impetuous	 7 8	8-24
*Gaestati (before 200 BC) ** Heavy swordsmen impetuous elite Medium swordsmen impet. elite	 9 10	0-6
*Soldurii (after 200 BC) ** Heavy swordsmen impetuous elite Add armour *(all or none)*	 10 +2	0-2
Light infantry javelin (max 3) Light infantry bow Light infantry sling	4	2-6
Women and children Levy mediocre	2	0-2
Wagon laager or plashed wood edge Fortifications	1	0-8
Fortified camp	6	0-1

Ariovistus German allies (from 71 to 61 BC)		
*German horsemen ** Medium cavalry Upgrade to elite	 7 +2	1-3
Light cavalry javelin	6	0-1
Heavy swordsmen impetuous Upgrade to elite	8 +2	4-8
Light infantry javelin	4	0-2

Ligurian allies (except with Vercingetorix)		
*Ligurian warriors ** Medium swordsmen Javelinmen	7	4-8
Light infantry javelin	4	0-2

Note

- Gaestati are going into battle entirely naked and are feared for their ferocity.
- Germanic allies (see list above)
- Ligurian allies (see list above)
- Iberian allies (List #89 Ancient Spanish) in 56 BC

Gaestati

89 - Ancient Spanish

240 - 20 BC
Plain, Mountain
Command +2 or +4 if Sertorius
Strategist: Sertorius (80-72 BC)

This list represents the armies of Spain from the Carthaginian expansion in this region until its complete submission to Rome. The list includes the Iberian, Lusitanian and Celtiberian tribes. Sertorius was a Roman general who rebelled against Rome and ruled Spain for 6 years. He defeated the Roman generals Sulla and Pompey who were sent to Spain to fight against him. He was assassinated at a banquet in 72 BC.

Troop type	Pts	Units
Spanish horsemen * Medium cavalry Upgrade to elite	7 +2	0-3
Light cavalry javelin	6	0-6
Iberian and Lusitanian Scutarii Medium swordsmen impetuous Upgrade to elite (max 4 in total)	7 +2	8-24
Celtiberian Scutarii Heavy swordsmen impetuous Upgrade to elite (max 4 in total)	8 +2	
Caetrati Javelinmen Light infantry javelin	7 4	4-12
Light infantry sling	4	0-4
Burning carts Scythed chariot	3	0-1
Sertorius from 80 to 72 BC - Only with Lusitanian		
Veteran legionaries * Heavy swordsmen armour impact Upgrade to elite	11 +2	0-4
Upgrade some Lusitanian Scutarii Medium swordsmen impact Upgrade to elite (max 4 in total)	8 +2	0-24

Note

- It is not allowed to mix different Scutarii nationalities within the same army corps.

90 - German

115 BC - 250 AD
Forest
Command +2
Strategist: Arminius (9-16 AD)

This list includes all the German barbarian tribes beyond the Rhine and Danube. These were especially the Cimbri, the Teutones, the Batavians, the Suevi, the Chatti and the Cherusci. The German tribes presented a constant threat to Rome. The Cimbri and Teutons destroyed four legions before being defeated by Marius. The Germanic chief Ariovistus invaded Gaul in 61 BC before being defeated by Julius Caesar. The greatest victory of the Germans was in the Teutoburg Forest in AD 9 when an alliance of Germanic tribes butchered three legions under the command of Publius Varus.

Troop type	Pts	Units
German horsemen * Medium cavalry Upgrade to elite	7 +2	0-6
Tencteri horsemen Light cavalry javelin	6	0-3
Sarmatian cavalry (after 25 av. JC) Heavy cavalry impetuous	9	0-2
Batavians or Cherusci * Medium swordsmen impetuous Upgrade to elite (all or none)	7 +2	8-24
Other german tribes * Heavy swordsmen impetuous Upgrade to elite (all or none)	8 +2	
Light infantry javelin	4	0-6
Light infantry bow	4	0-2
Wagon laager or plashed wood edge Fortifications	1	0-6
Fortified camp	6	0-1

Note

- All warriors must be of the same type and same quality (all medium or all heavy).
- Elite Cavalry represents horsemen supported by light javelinmen on foot.
- Gallic allies (List #88 Gallic)

91 - Dacian and Carpi

100 BC - 380 AD
Mountain, Forest
Command +3
Strategists: Burebista (70-44 BC) and Decebalus (87-106 AD)

The Dacians were related to the Thracians and occupied a territory between the Carpathians and the Black Sea. They often made raids against the Romans but became a great threat with two ambitious sovereigns: Burebista and Decebalus. The Dacians ravaged the Empire from 85 to 89 AD before accepting a treaty. The Emperor Trajan overcame the Thracians after two campaigns in 106 AD. The tribes that were not subjugated continued to cause trouble. In 256 AD, the Carpi (or free Dacians) allied to the Goths, regained control of the province.

Troop type	Pts	Units
Dacian horsemen * Light cavalry javelin	6	0-3
Dacian warriors * Medium swordsmen impetuous	7	8-24
Warriors with falx Medium swordsmen 2HW elite Medium swordsmen impet. elite	 10 9	0-6
Bowmen Light infantry bow	7 4	2-6
Light infantry javelin	4	0-6
Only Dacian before 107 AD Sarmatian allies (List #77 Sarmatian)		
Bastarnae cavalry Medium Cavalry Upgrade to elite	 7 +2	0-2
Captured Roman artillery Light artillery Heavy artillery	 6 10	0-1
Only Carpi from 256 AD Goth allies (List #94 Ostrogoth)		

92 - VISIGOTH

200 – 419 AD
Plain, Forest
Command +2

The Visigoths (or Western Goths) occupied and devastated Dacia about 235 AD. From 268 AD they attacked the Roman provinces of Pannonia and Illyria and threatened Italy. The Emperor Claudius Gothicus pushed them back beyond the Danube, but they remained in Dacia. In 376 the Emperor Valens welcomed the Visigoths into the Empire in order to protect it from the Huns. The following year famine broke out and the Visigoths revolted and inflicted a severe defeat upon the Romans at the battle of Adrianople in 378 in which the emperor Valens died. The Visigoth King Alaric I sacked Rome in 410 and his successor led the Visigoths into southern Gaul and Spain, where they founded a new kingdom.

Troop type	Pts	Units
Nobles * Medium cavalry impetuous Heavy cavalry impetuous Upgrade to elite (max 4)	 7 9 +2	0-8
Huns or Alans Light cavalry bow Upgrade to elite	 6 +1	0-4
Warriors * Heavy swordsmen impetuous Upgrade to elite (max 4)	 8 +2	8-24
Light infantry javelin (max ½) Light infantry bow	4	0-8
Fortifications	1	0-6
Fortified camp	6	0-1

Note

- Roman allies (List #86 Late Imperial Roman) after 416 AD
- Carpi allies (List #91 Dacian and Carpi)
- Ostrogoth allies (List #94 Ostrogoth)
- Taifali allies (List #95 Gepid, Herul and Taifali)

Visigoth Commander

93 - VANDAL

200 – 427 AD
Plain, Forest
Command +2

The Vandals originated from the Baltic coast and are related to the Gothic peoples. From 248 AD they started to attack the Roman Empire but were defeated by Aurelian in 271 AD. The Romans engaged the Vandals as auxiliary cavalry and allowed them to settle in the Empire. In the early fifth century, driven by the Huns, the Vandals crossed the Rhine and entered en masse into the Empire. They plundered Gaul and then migrated to Spain with the Alans in 409 AD.

Troop type	Pts	Units
Nobles * Medium cavalry impetuous Heavy cavalry impetuous Upgrade to elite	 7 9 +2	0-4

Alans remnant after 420 AD Light cavalry bow Upgrade to elite	6 +1	0-4
Warriors * Heavy swordsmen impetuous Upgrade to elite (max 6)	8 +2	8-24
Light infantry javelin	4	0-6
Fortified camp	6	0-1

Note

- Herul or Gepid allies (List #95 Gepid, Herul and Taifali) before 406 AD
- Suevi or Burgundi allies (List #96 Franks, Alemanni, Burgundi, Suevi) from 406 AD
- Alan allies (List #108 Alan) from 406 to 420 AD

94 - Ostrogoth

200 - 493 AD
Plain, Steppes
Command +2
Strategist: Theodoric (475-493 AD)

The Ostrogoths originated in the Ukraine and southern Russia. At first they were a single tribe with the Visigoths but separated into two distinct peoples in the third century. In 375 AD the Huns destroyed the Ostrogoth kingdom in Russia. The Ostrogoths then became vassals of the Huns. In 451 they fought under the command of Attila at the battle of the Catalaunian Fields. In 475 Theodoric became king of the Ostrogoths and then king of Italy in 488, after having reconquered the country on the orders of the Byzantine Emperor Zeno. He killed Odoacer, the king of the Heruli, and imposed his authority over Italy, the south of Gaul and most parts of Spain.

Troop type	Pts	Units
Nobles * Medium cavalry impetuous Heavy cavalry impetuous Upgrade to elite (max 6)	7 9 +2	6-16
Huns after 376 AD Light cavalry bow Upgrade to elite	6 +1	0-4
Warriors * Heavy swordsmen impetuous	8	0-8
Bowmen Downgrade to mediocre	7 -2	4-12
Light infantry bow (max 6)	4	
Fortifications	1	0-6
Fortified camp	6	0-1

Note

- Visigoth allies (List #92 Visigoth)
- Gepid allies (List #95 Gepid, Herul and Taifali)
- Rugian allies (List #96 Franks, Alemanni, Burgundi, Suevi)
- Hunnic allies (List #110 Huns)

Ostrogoth horsemen

95 - Gepid, Herul and Taifali

220 - 565 AD
Plain, Forest, Steppes
Command +2

This list presents the armies of the lesser barbarian tribes that participated in the invasions of the Roman Empire. The Gepids settled in Dacia and fought alongside the Huns of Attila. In 552, they suffered a disastrous defeat by the Lombards and their Byzantine allies and virtually disappeared from history. The Heruli appeared during the third century near the Danube and are best known for their king Odoacer who proclaimed himself king of Italy in 476 AD. The Heruli were chased from Italy by the Ostrogoths, but some still served as mercenaries in Byzantium. The Taifali were allies of the Goths and then the Huns. They were settled in northern Italy and in the south west of Gaul.

Troop type	Pts	Units
Nobles * Medium cavalry impetuous Heavy cavalry impetuous Upgrade to elite (max 6)	7 9 +2	6-16
Warriors Heavy swordsmen impetuous	8	0-8
Archers Bowmen Downgrade to mediocre	7 -2	2-6
Light infantry bow	4	
Fortified camp	6	0-1

Only Gepid		
Rugian, Thuringian or Vandal allied warriors * Heavy swordsmen impetuous Upgrade to elite (max 2)	8 +2	0-8
Only Gepid		
Replace all archers Javelinmen Light infantry javelin	7 4	All

Frankish warriors

96 - Franks, Alemanni, Burgundi, Suevi

250 - 534 AD
Plain, Mountain, Forest
Command +2
Strategist: Clovis (Franks 496 - 511 AD)

This list represents the barbarian tribes of Germania that gradually invaded the Roman Empire in the fifth century and settled in Gaul. In 506 AD, at the Battle of Tolbiac, the Frankish king Clovis defeated the Alemanni and became their overlord. The Burgundi kept their kingdom a little longer but it was finally annexed by the Merovingian Franks in 534 AD. The Suevi (including Quadi and Marcomanni) went through Gaul and settled in Spain. They settled there and were gradually assimilated by the Visigoths.

Troop type	Pts	Units
Nobles * Medium cavalry Heavy cavalry Upgrade to elite	7 9 +2	0-4
Warriors * Heavy swordsmen impetuous Upgrade to elite (max 4)	8 +2	8-24
Light infantry bow	4	0-4
Light infantry javelin	4	0-2

Only Franks Alemanni allies (List #96 Franks, Alemanni, Burgundi, Suevi)		
Replace all warriors * Heavy swordsmen impetuous elite	10	All
Only Alemanni Vandal allies (List #93 Vandal) Herul allies (List #95 Gepid, Herul and Taifali) Frank or Burgundi allies (List #96 Franks, Alemanni, Burgundi, Suevi) Alan allies (List #108 Alan)		
Bowmen Downgrade to mediocre	7 -2	2-6
Only Quadi Sarmatian allies (List #77 Sarmatian)		
Replace all Nobles * Heavy cavalry impetuous Upgrade to elite	9 +2	All
Only Suevi Roman allies (List #86 Late Imperial Roman) Ostrogoth allies (List #94 Ostrogoth) Alan allies (List #108 Alan)		

97 - Visigoths in Spain

419 - 711 AD
Plain, Mountain
Command +2

The Visigoths were settled in the south west of Gaul and Spain as allies of the Roman Empire. Then they fought against other barbarian tribes like the Suevi and the Vandals. The first capital of their kingdom was Toulouse before the Franks of Clovis drove them into Spain. After that their capital became Toledo. In 575 AD they conquered the kingdom of the Suevi in northern Portugal and Galicia. The Visigoth kingdom was finally conquered by the Muslims in 711 AD.

Troop type	Pts	Units
Bucellarii * Heavy cavalry impetuous Upgrade to elite (max 3)	9 +2	2-6
Gardingi Medium cavalry Light cavalry javelin (max 4)	7 6	4-12
Warriors Heavy swordsmen impetuous	8	4-16
Bowmen Light infantry bow	7 4	0-4
Roman militia Medium swordsmen mediocre Add support	5 +1	0-4
Light infantry sling	4	0-2

Fortified camp	6	0-1
Visigoths after 622 AD - No allies		
Replace all Warriors Heavy spearmen Add support	8 +1	All
Basques Light cavalry javelin	6	0-2
Basques Light infantry javelin	4	0-3

Note

- Burgundi or Suevi allies (List #96 Franks, Alemanni, Burgundi, Suevi)
- Ostrogoth allies (List #143 Italian Ostrogoth)
- Byzantine allies (List #125 Justinian Byzantine)

GREAT BRITAIN

98 - Ancient British

55 BC - 84 AD
Plain, Forest
Command +2
Strategists: Cassivellaunus (55-54 BC) and Boudicca (60-61 AD)

This list presents the armies of Britain after the first expedition of Julius Caesar until its complete pacification. Cassivellaunus opposed Caesar by using guerrilla tactics. He was forced to surrender in 54 BC but the Romans then withdrew to Gaul. Between 43 and 47 AD the Emperor Claudius ordered the conquest of the south of Britain. A revolt broke out in 60-61 AD led by Boudicca, the Queen of Iceni. Under Vespasian the Roman conquest resumed and extended Roman influence into Wales and over half of Scotland in 84 AD.

Troop type	Pts	Units
Chariots with 2 horses * Light chariot Upgrade to elite (max 4)	7 +2	0-8
British horsemen Light cavalry javelin	6	2-8
Warriors * Medium swordsmen impetuous Upgrade to elite (max 4)	7 +2	8-24
Light infantry javelin	4	0-4
Light infantry sling	4	0-8
Women and children Levy mediocre	2	0-2
Fortified camp	6	0-1

Cassivellaunus in 54 BC - No Roman allies		
Replace all Warriors Light chariot Upgrade to elite (max 4)	7 +2	All

Note

- Roman allies (List #84 Early Imperial Roman)

Britton horsemen

99 - Caledonian, Irish, Scots and Pictish

79 - 846 AD
Plain (except Picts), Mountain, Forest
Command +2

The north of Britain was occupied by various Celtic people such as the Caledonians and the Picts. In 79 AD the Roman forces came to Scotland and were faced with fierce resistance. The Caledonians were defeated in 83 AD by the Romans who decided to stop their conquest. Around 120 AD Emperor Hadrian ordered the construction of a fortified wall to mark the border of the Empire. After the withdrawal of the Romans in the fifth century various invasions took place in Britain: the Scots from Ireland, the Anglo-Saxons and finally Viking.

Troop type	Pts	Units
Caledonian		
Chariots with 2 horses * Light chariot Upgrade to elite (max 4)	7 +2	4-8
Caledonian warriors * Medium swordsmen impetuous	7	8-24
Atecotti warriors Medium swordsmen impet. elite	9	0-4
Light infantry javelin	4	0-6

Scots or Irish		
*Chariots with 2 horses ** Light chariot Upgrade to elite (max 4)	7 +2	0-8
*Scots warriors ** Medium swordsmen	7	8-24
Atecotti warriors Medium swordsmen impet. elite	9	0-4
Saxon mercenaries Heavy swordsmen impetuous	8	0-2
Light infantry javelin	4	0-6
Light infantry sling	4	0-2
Martyred monks (after 432 AD) Levy mediocre expendable	1	0-1
Fortifications	1	0-6
Pictish Saxon allies (List #100 Saxon, Anglo-Saxon, Frisian, Jutes)		
*Chariots with 2 horses ** Light chariot Upgrade to elite	7 +2	0-4
*Pictish horsemen ** Light cavalry javelin	6	2-8
*Pictish warriors ** Medium spearmen Add support	7 +1	8-24
Atecotti warriors Medium swordsmen impet. elite	9	0-4
Caledonian mercenaries Medium swordsmen impetuous	7	0-4
Light infantry bow	4	0-4
Light infantry javelin	4	0-4

Note

- Atecotti warriors were Pictish mercenaries feared for their ferocity.

100 - Saxon, Anglo-Saxon, Frisian, Jutes

250 – 804 AD
Plain, Forest
Command +2

These barbarian peoples of Germania occupied regions near the North Sea. They did not participate in the invasions of the Roman Empire and fought mainly on foot. A portion of them moved to Britain where they founded the Anglo-Saxon kingdoms that eventually became the English nation. Most of them however stayed on the continent where they were subjugated by the Carolingian Franks.

Troop type	Pts	Units
*Nobles ** Heavy swordsmen impetuous elite	10	2-4
Warriors Heavy swordsmen impetuous	8	6-24
Light infantry bow Light infantry javelin	4	0-4

101 - Romano-Britsh

407 – 945 AD
Plain, Mountain, Forest
Command +3

The Romano-British are romanised Britons in the former province of Britannia (like the Gallo-Romans in France). These people adopted some of the Roman habits without abandoning their own language and customs. The legendary figure of King Arthur is supposed to have lived at that time and have fought the Saxons. This list offers the possibility to use elite Arthurian cavalry from 475 to 539.

Troop type	Pts	Units
*Britons horsemen ** Medium cavalry Heavy cavalry	7 9	4-8
Scouts on pony Light cavalry javelin mediocre	4	0-2
Spearmen Medium spearmen Heavy spearmen Downgrade to mediocre	7 8 -2	8-24
Saxon mercenaries (before 442) Heavy swordsmen impetuous Upgrade to elite	8 +2	0-2
Irish mercenaries (before 580) Medium swordsmen	7	0-4
Bowmen Light infantry bow	7 4	0-2
Light infantry javelin	4	0-2
Christian martyrs (before 664) Levy mediocre expendable	1	0-1
Fortifications	1	0-8
Arthurian elite cavalry from 475 to 539		
*Replace some Briton horsemen ** Heavy cavalry impact elite	12	0-4

Note

- Western Roman allies (List #86 Late Imperial Roman or #87 Patrician Roman) before 470
- Saxon allies (List #100 Saxon, Anglo-Saxon, Frisian, Jutes) from 430 to 441

- Welsh allies (List #146 Welsh) before 580
- Viking allies (List #150 Viking and Leidang) after 790

EAST ROMAN

102 - Parthian

250 BC – 224 AD
Plain, Steppes
Command +3

The province of Parthia was located roughly in modern day Iran. It became independent from the Seleucid Empire for the first time around 250 BC. Parthia was reconquered by the Seleucid Antiochus III in 206 BC. From the second century the Parthians took advantage of the increasing weakness of the Seleucid Empire to control the territory east of Syria. From the 1st century BC the Parthians became the main enemy of Rome in the eastern Mediterranean. They destroyed the army of Crassus at the Battle of Carrhae in 53 BC. The Romans tried in vain to conquer them despite several campaigns under Trajan. The Parthians conquered territories in the east of the Greco-Indian kingdom and founded the Indo-Parthian kingdom. It was later overthrown by the Kushans. In 224 AD the Parthians were destroyed by the Sassanid Persians.

Troop type	Pts	Units
Cataphract horsemen * Cataphract Upgrade to elite (max 4)	11 +2	4-8
Replace some cataphracts Cataphract camelry	12	0-2
Horse archers Light cavalry bow Medium cavalry bow (max 8)	6 9	8-20
Greek militia Medium spearmen mediocre	5	0-4
Hill tribesmen Javelinmen Downgrade to mediocre	7 -2	0-2
Light infantry bow	4	0-2
Light infantry sling	4	0-2
Light infantry javelin	4	0-2
Only if Elymaien from 147 BC to 205 AD		
Bowmen Light infantry bow (max 6)	7 4	2-12
Only in 129 BC – No Saka or Armenian allies		
Captured Seleucid pikemen Pikemen mediocre	8	0-2
Suren Indo-Parthian Kingdom (95 BC – 75 AD) Saka allies (List #76 Scythian) only		
Elephant	13	0-1
Arachosian horsemen Light cavalry javelin	6	0-3
Indian levy Bowmen mediocre	5	2-4

Note

- Armenian allies (List #71 Armenian)
- Hatra allies (List #74 Aramaean)
- Arab nomad allies (List #75 Early Arab)
- Saka allies (List #76 Scythian)
- Sarmatian allies (List #77 Sarmatian)

103 - Judaean Jewish

168 BC – 6 AD
Plain, Mountain
Command +3

After the partition of Alexander's Empire, Judaea became a province of the kingdom of Syria. In 168 BC Antiochus IV, who wanted to restore the worship of the ancient Greek gods, sacked the temple of Jerusalem. This was the beginning of the Maccabees' revolt. In 141 BC the Jews gained independence and this was the beginning of the dynasty of the Hasmoneans. The Parthians occupied Judea in 40 BC before being expelled by the Romans. Herod, the last Hasmonean king, died in 4 BC after having enlarged the temple of Jerusalem. Judaea was annexed to the Roman Empire by Emperor Augustus.

Troop type	Pts	Units
Xystophoroi * Heavy cavalry impact Upgrade to elite	10 +2	0-2
Horse archers * Light cavalry bow Medium cavalry bow (max 4)	6 9	0-6
Bowmen Light infantry bow	7 4	2-6
Light infantry javelin	4	2-6
Light infantry sling	4	2-4
Fortified camp	6	0-1
From 168 to 141 BC - Maccabean		
Warriors * Medium swordsmen impact	8	4-12
Guerrillas, hillmen or bandits Javelinmen Downgrade to mediocre	7 -2	0-12

From 140 to 63 BC - Hasmonean Nabataean allies (List #74 Aramaean)		
*Thureophoroi (all of the same type)** Medium spearmen Heavy spearmen	 7 8	4-12
Replace some thureophoroi Pikemen mediocre	8	0-6
Guerrillas, hillmen or bandits Javelinmen Downgrade to mediocre	 7 -2	0-8
After 63 BC – Later period Roman allies (List #82 Triumvirate Roman or List #84 Early Imperial Roman) Parthian allies (List #102 Parthian)		
Germans or Celts Medium cavalry Upgrade to elite	 7 +2	0-2
Replace all horse archers by Thracian cavalry Light cavalry javelin Medium cavalry	 6 7	0-4
Arab nomads or Syrian Light cavalry javelin Ligt cavalry bow	6	0-4
*Thureophoroi (all of the same type) ** Medium spearmen Heavy spearmen	 7 8	4-12
Replace some thureophoroi by imitation legionaries Heavy swordsmen impact	9	0-6
Thracian and other mercenaries Javelinmen Medium swordsmen Medium swordsmen 2HW	 7 7 8	0-3
Hillmen or bandits Javelinmen mediocre	5	0-4
Religious zealots Levy impetuous	4	0-2

104 - Commagene

162 BC – 72 AD
Plain, Mountain
Command +4

Commagene was a small Hellenistic kingdom located south of Asia Minor. It was established in 162 BC by the governor Ptolemy, at the time of the disintegration of the Seleucid Empire. Commagene helped Pompey in his fight against the Parthians and was involved in the civil war between Marcus Antonius and Octavius. Commagene became a client of Rome until the Emperor Vespasian put an end to the dynasty in 72 AD.

Troop type	Pts	Units
*Xystophoroi ** Cataphract Upgrade to elite	 11 +2	1-3
Horse archers Light cavalry bow Medium cavalry bow (max 4)	 6 9	4-8
Tarentine cavalry Light cavalry javelin	6	0-2
*Phalangites ** Pikemen Downgrade to mediocre	 11 -3	0-4
Thureophoroi Medium spearmen	7	0-2
Thracian foot Javelinmen Medium swordsmen Medium swordsmen 2HW	 7 7 8	0-3
Galatian foot Heavy swordsmen impetuous Upgrade to elite	 8 +2	
Bowmen Downgrade to mediocre	7 -2	4-12
Light infantry bow	4	0-3
Light infantry sling	4	0-3
Light infantry javelin	4	0-2

105 - Mithridatic

110 – 47 BC
Plain, Mountain
Command +4

Mithridates VI was King of Pontus, a small kingdom located on the Black Sea in the north east of modern Turkey. Through an aggressive policy he seized the kingdom of Bosporus, drove off the king of Cappadocia and annexed Bithynia. After the massacre of the Romans in Asia Minor and the invasion of Greece, Mithridates came into conflict with the Romans in 88 BC. A treaty was concluded which left Mithridates free in Asia Minor. In 74 BC Nicomedes of Bithynia bequeathed his kingdom to Rome that opens a new conflict with the Romans. Mithridate was defeated by Lucullus and by Pompey in 66 BC and his son, Pharnaces, was defeated by Julius Caesar in 47 BC. On this occasion Caesar declared the famous maxim: "Veni, Vidi, Vici."

Troop type	Pts	Units
*Pontic horsemen ** Heavy cavalry Upgrade to elite	 9 +2	1-3
Light cavalry javelin	6	2-4

Sarmatians Heavy cavalry impetuous Medium cavalry bow	9	0-2
Scythians Light cavalry bow	6	0-2
Thureophoroi (all of the same type) Medium spearmen Heavy spearmen	 7 8	2-4
Thracians or Bastarnae Medium swordsmen Medium swordsmen 2HW	 7 8	0-2
Galatians Heavy swordsmen impetuous Upgrade to elite	 8 +2	0-2
Javelinmen Light infantry javelin	7 4	2-8
Bowmen Light infantry bow	7 4	0-4
Light infantry sling	4	0-2
Scythed chariot	3	0-2
Fortifications	1	0-6
Fortified camp	6	0-1
Before 84 BC		
Pikemen Downgrade to mediocre	11 -3	0-3
Imitation legionaries Heavy swordsmen impact Downgrade to mediocre	 9 -2	0-3
From 84 BC		
Imitation legionaries Heavy swordsmen impact Downgrade to mediocre	 9 -2	2-6
Chalybes Medium spearmen	7	0-2

Note

- Armenian allies (List #71 Armenian)

106 - Palmyran

260 - 273 AD
Plain, Desert, Steppes
Command +4

Palmyra was an oasis and a city in Syria. It came under Roman influence in the first century and afterwards became a Roman colony. In 260 AD Odaenathus, the Prince of Palmyra, became commander in chief of all the Roman armies in the East. He successfully fought the Sassanids but was assassinated in 267 AD. His wife Zenobia broke off all relations with Rome and conquered Egypt and Asia Minor for her own gain. She proclaimed her son Emperor but the army of Palmyra was finally defeated by Aurelian's Roman troops in 272 AD.

Troop type	Pts	Units
*Heavy cavalry ** Cataphract Upgrade to elite (max 4)	 11 +2	4-8
*Regular cavalry ** Medium cavalry bow	9	0-3
Equites Sagittarii Light cavalry bow	6	2-8
Equites Illyricani Light cavalry javelin	6	0-2
Guard caravan Light camelry bow Medium camelry bow	 7 10	0-2
Warriors with sword Heavy swordsmen Downgrade to mediocre	 8 -2	0-4
Regular archers Bowmen	7	2-6
Other archers Bowmen mediocre Light infantry bow	 5 4	0-6
Before 272 AD		
Roman cavalry Heavy cavalry	9	0-2
Roman legionaries Heavy swordsmen impact Add armour *(all or none)* Add support	 9 +2 +1	2-6
Roman auxiliaries Medium swordsmen impact Add support	 8 +1	2-4

Note

- Armenian allies (List #71 Armenian)
- Arab nomad allies (List #75 Early Arab)

Cataphracts

STEPPES

107 - Kushan

135 BC - 477 AD
Plain, Mountain, Forest, Steppes
Command +3

The Kushan Empire extended across Pakistan, Afghanistan and northern India. The Kushans originated from the Tarim Basin (modern Xinjiang in China) and were pushed west by the Hsiung-Nu. They expelled the Greco-Bactrians of Sogdiana around 135 BC. During the first century AD they established a vast Empire in northern India and over most of Central Asia. They were subjugated by the Sassanids around 240 AD and then lost their territories in the Gange valley in 270 AD. The Empire declined gradually before being conquered by the Hephthalite Huns in the fifth century AD.

Troop type	Pts	Units
Nobles * Cataphract Upgrade to elite (max 4)	 11 +2	 3-8
Horse archers Light cavalry bow Medium cavalry bow (max 8)	 6 9	 6-16
Elephant *	13	0-2
Light cavalry javelin	6	0-2
Light infantry bow	4	0-4
Only before 25 AD		
Graeco Bactrian remnants Pikemen mediocre	8	0-2
Indian troops from 50 BC to 410 AD		
Indian horsemen Medium cavalry mediocre	5	1-3
Indian archers Bowmen Downgrade to mediocre	 7 -2	2-4
Indian archers in mixed units ½ Medium swordsmen ½ Bowmen	9	
Indian warriors Medium swordsmen Javelinmen	7	0-3
Fortified camp	6	0-1

Note

- Scythian allies (List #76 Scythian)
- Hyrcanian allies (List #102 Parthian) before 100 AD
- Chionite allies (List #110 Huns) from 300 AD

108 - Alan

50 - 1500 AD
Steppes, Plain only after 650 AD
Command +3

The Alans were nomadic horsemen of Scythian origin and were related to the Sarmatians. They occupied the region between the Black and Caspian Seas but migrated around the Mediterranean. They appeared near the Persian territories and participated in the fall of the Parthian Empire before being pushed back by the Sassanids. Repelled by the Huns, they entered into Germania and Gaul where they were employed by the Romans. In the fifth century some Alans followed the Vandals into Spain and North Africa. In the east they were present within the Byzantine Empire and served as mercenaries in Hungary and Moldavia.

Troop type	Pts	Units
Horsemen * Heavy cavalry impetuous Upgrade to elite (max 6)	 9 +2	 0-12
Horse archers * Light cavalry bow Medium cavalry bow (max 8)	 6 9	 8-24
Warriors with axe Heavy swordsmen	8	0-4
Light infantry bow	4	0-3
Fortified camp	6	0-1
Later period (after 650 AD)		
Replace some horsemen * Heavy cavalry bow Upgrade to elite (max 6 in total)	 11 +2	 0-12

109 - Sassanid Persian

224 - 651 AD
Plain, Mountain
Command +4
Strategist: Khosrau I (531 to 579 AD)

After the fall of the Parthians, the Sassanids occupied a territory corresponding to modern Iran and Iraq. In the east their neighbours were the Hephthalites Huns and the Kushans. In the west there were many conflicts with the Romans until the conclusion of a peace treaty between Theodosius and Shapur III in 384 AD. The fifth century was a period of decline in which the Sassanids became dependent on the Huns. In the reign of Khosrau I (531-579 AD) the Sassanid Empire was reborn and was at its apogee. Khosrau fought many wars against the Byzantines in Armenia, Mesopotamia, Syria and Cappadocia. To the east he was allied with the Turks and defeated the Hephthalites Huns. The Empire eventually fell under Arab domination and collapsed in 651 AD.

Troop type	Pts	Units
Asavaran * Heavy cavalry bow Upgrade to elite (max 8, cf. Note)	 11 +2	 6-16
Horse archers Light cavalry bow	6	0-4
Arab auxiliaries Light cavalry javelin Light camelry bow mediocre	 6 5	 0-2
Only before 628 AD Elephant	13	0-3
Sassanid levy Medium spearmen mediocre Levy	 5 3	 2-4
Hill tribesmen Javelinmen Light infantry javelin	 7 4	 0-2
Light infantry bow	4	0-2
Light infantry sling	4	0-2
Fortified camp	6	0-1
Before 430 AD Armenian allies (List #71 Armenian) Kushan allies (List #107 Kushan) before 371		
Replace all horse archers Light cavalry bow	6	0-12
Replace some Asavaran * Cataphract Upgrade to elite (max 4)	 11 +2	 2-8
From 430 AD to 627 AD Alan allies (List #108 Alan) in 550		
Replace some Asavaran * Cataphract Upgrade to elite (max 4)	 11 +2	 0-4
Khosrau II from 591 to 627 AD Turkish allies (List #141 Central Asian Turkish)		
Dailami guardsmen Medium swordsmen impact elite Add support	 10 +1	 0-2
From 628 AD		
Replace all elephants Elephant elite	16	0-1

Note

- A maximum of 8 Asavaran can be upgraded to elite, whether they are Cavalry or Cataphracts.
- Arab nomad allies (List #75 Early Arab)
- Hunnic allies (List #110 Huns (Sabir option) or List #111 Hephthalite Huns) from 356 to 533

110 - Huns

374 – 466 AD
Plain, Steppes, Forest only for Sabir
Command +3
Strategist: Attila (Western Huns 433-453 AD)

The Huns came from Central Asia and were probably the descendants of the Hsiung-Nu. They appeared in Europe in 374 AD when they crossed the Volga. They subdued the Alans and Ostrogoths and pushed other barbarian peoples before them, which triggered the great barbarian invasions of the Roman Empire. Attila, leader of the Huns, fought across most of Europe from Hungary to Gaul but was defeated in 451AD by Aetius at the battle of Catalaunian Fields. He then ravaged Italy but died in 453 AD and his Empire disintegrated rapidly. Sabir Huns occupied the north of the Caspian Sea after the fall of the Western Huns. They provided mercenaries for the Byzantines and Sassanids. Later they were subjugated by the Avars.

Troop type	Pts	Units
Nobles * Heavy cavalry bow elite	13	0-2
Horsemen * Medium cavalry bow Upgrade to elite	 9 +2	8-24
Light cavalry bow Upgrade to elite	6 +1	
Light infantry bow	4	0-4
Western Huns		
Alans Light cavalry bow Medium cavalry bow	 6 9	 0-2
Heruls Medium cavalry impetuous Heavy cavalry impetuous	 7 9	 0-4
Franks, Burgundians or Goths Heavy swordsmen impetuous Upgrade to elite (max 4)	 8 +2	 0-8
Fortified camp	6	0-1
Sabir Huns from 463 to 570 AD		
Replace some horsemen by warriors Medium swordsmen impetuous	7	4-12

Note

- Gepid, Herul or Taifali allies (List #95 Gepid, Herul and Taifali) for western huns
- Ostrogoth allies (List #94 Ostrogoth) with Attila

Hunnic horse archers

111 - Hephthalite Huns

450 - 570 AD
Plain, Forest, Steppes
Command +2

The Hephthalite Huns (or White Huns) played an important role in the history of India and Persia. Around 450 AD they invaded northern Persia (Transoxiana, Bactria and Khurasan) and fought the Sassanids who had to pay tribute. In 563 AD they were defeated by the Sassanids and their Turkish allies and their Empire was dismantled. The Huns returned to India in the late fifth century, invaded the Punjab and made many raids in the Gangean plain. They were defeated by an alliance of Hindu Rajas and were assimilated into the population of northern India.

Troop type	Pts	Units
*Nobles ** Heavy cavalry bow elite	13	0-2
*Horsemen ** Medium cavalry bow Upgrade to elite	9 +2	8-24
Light cavalry bow Upgrade to elite	6 +1	
Light infantry bow	4	0-4
Fortified camp	6	0-1
Indian troops from 475 to 570 AD		
Elephant elite	16	1-3
Medium cavalry mediocre	5	1-2
Warriors with sword and halberd Medium swordsmen 2HW	8	0-2
Indian levy archers Bowmen mediocre	5	2-6
Indians Light infantry bow Light infantry javelin	4	0-2

ANCIENT AFRICA

112 - Blemmyes and Nobatae

30 BC - 650 AD
Plain, Desert
Command +2

The Blemmyes (or Beja) were a nomadic tribe that lived south of Nubian Egypt. They were subjects of the Kushites of Meroe. They conducted raids into Roman Egypt from the third century AD. The Nobatae settled in the region and were Christianized by the Emperor Diocletian. They helped him to push back the Blemmyes in the deserts of the east. Later the Empress Theodora of Byzantium sent a Coptic monk to convert the Nobatae to Monophysite Christianity. In 650 AD Egypt was invaded by the Arabs and Nubia was cut off from the rest of Christendom.

Troop type	Pts	Units
*Horsemen ** Medium cavalry Heavy cavalry (max 6) Upgrade to elite (max 2)	7 9 +2	2-12
Medium camelry impetuous	8	0-6
Light camelry bow	7	0-2
Light cavalry javelin	6	0-4
Kushite spearmen Medium spearmen mediocre Heavy spearmen mediocre	5 6	4-10
Bowmen mediocre Upgrade to ordinary (max 4)	5 +2	4-20
Light infantry bow (max 8)	4	
Blemmye warriors Javelinmen Medium swordsmen Downgrade to mediocre	7 7 -2	0-6

113 - Moors

25 - 696 AD
Plain, Mountain, Desert, Steppes
Command +2

The term "Moor" refers to the Berber people of North Africa and Mauretania (in the north of Morocco and north east of Algeria). The region became a Roman province between 37 and 42 AD. The Moors revolted again in 372 AD. They became independent after the Vandal invasion of North Africa in 429 AD. During the Byzantine re-conquest, the Moors were defeated in 533 AD but still revolted several times. The Arab conquest occurred in the seventh century and the region was annexed by the Umayyad Caliphates.

Troop type	Pts	Units
Moorish horsemen * Light cavalry javelin	6	6-16
Moorish javelinmen * Javelinmen Light infantry javelin (max 6)	7 4	6-18
Javelinmen behind camels Medium camelry mediocre	6	0-6
Light infantry bow Light infantry sling	4	0-4
Women and children Levy mediocre	2	0-2
Roman deserters (373 to 374) Heavy swordsmen impact Add armour *(all or none)*	9 +2	0-2
Vandal fugitives (533 to 548) Heavy cavalry impetuous	9	
Byzantine betrayers (546 to 548) Medium cavalry bow	9	

Note

- The trick of putting camels in front of javelinmen in order to frighten horses worked well against Romans and Vandals but failed against Byzantines.
- Byzantine allies (List #125 Justinian Byzantine) from 546 to 548 AD

114 - Kingdom of Axum

100 - 1200 AD
Plain, Mountain
Command +3

The kingdom of Axum was founded in Ethiopia in the first century in a town of the same name. It grew rapidly by annexing the smaller kingdoms around it and extended to the plateau of Tigray and the Nile Valley. It peaked in the fifth century, when it became a major trading power that issued its own currency. The kingdom became Christian in 340 AD when King Ezana was converted by Saint Frumentius. The Axumites launched an expedition against Mecca in 571 AD. Eventually the kingdom disappeared in the twelfth century and its land came under Muslim influence.

Troop type	Pts	Units
Horsemen * Light cavalry javelin	6	2-4
Warriors on camels Light camelry bow Medium camelry bow	7 10	0-2
Guardsmen with swords Medium swordsmen impact Upgrade to elite	8 +2	0-4
Warriors with mace and axe Medium swordsmen impetuous	7	8-16
Bowmen Downgrade to mediocre	7 -2	2-8
Light infantry javelin	4	0-4
Light infantry bow	4	0-4
Fortified camp	6	0-1
Before 970 AD		
Elephant mediocre *	10	0-1
From 970 AD No ally		
Replace all horsemen * Light cavalry javelin Medium cavalry	6 7	4-10

Note

- Kushite allies (List #59 Meroitic Kushite)
- Yemenite allies (List #75 Early Arab)
- Blemmye allies (List #112 Blemmyes and Nobatae)

115 - African Vandal

428 - 533 AD
Plain
Command +3
Strategist: Genseric (428-477 AD)

In 428 AD Genseric became king of the Vandals and Alans. Under pressure from the Visigoths, he decided to cross the Strait of Gibraltar with his people and to settle in North Africa. The Vandals established a kingdom (the kingdom of Carthage) on the Algerian and Tunisian coasts, which officially recognized by the Romans. In 53? Byzantine army led by Belisarius twice

Gelimer, the king of the Vandals, and entered into Carthage. The last Vandal king surrendered and the survivors were deported to Byzantium. Subsequently, Byzantium dominated North Africa for a brief period.

Troop type	Pts	Units
*Nobles ** Medium cavalry impetuous Heavy cavalry impetuous Upgrade to elite (max 8)	 7 9 +2	8-24
Alans before 500 AD Light cavalry bow Medium cavalry bow	 6 9	0-4
Warriors on foot Heavy swordsmen impetuous	8	0-6
Moors Light cavalry javelin	6	0-4
Moors Light infantry javelin	4	0-4
Moors Light infantry bow	4	0-2
Fortified camp	6	0-1

Note

- Moorish allies (List #113 Moors) before 500 AD

ANCIENT ASIA

116 - Hsiung-Nu

250 BC - 555 AD
Steppes, add Plain only for southern Hsiung-Nu
Command +3

In the third century BC the tribe of the Hsiung-Nu (or Xiongnu) imposed its rule over all the other nomadic tribes of Mongolia. The Hsiung-Nu fought against the Chinese who built the Great Wall of China to protect themselves. The Han Empire managed to significantly reduce their power and as a result of a civil war in 50 AD they were divided. The northern tribe was repelled and possibly formed the ancestors of the Huns. The southern tribe continued to form kingdoms on Chinese territory. They associated with the Juan-Juan before being conquered by the Gokturks.

Troop type	Pts	Units
*Nobles ** Medium cavalry bow Heavy cavalry bow Upgrade to elite	 9 11 +2	0-6
Horse archers Light cavalry bow Medium cavalry bow (max 8)	 6 9	8-24
Bowmen Light infantry bow	7 4	0-4
Tribal auxiliaries Javelinmen Medium swordsmen impetuous	7	0-4
Levy	3	0-2
Fortified camp	6	0-1
Southern Hsiung-Nu (304 - 439 AD) No allies		
*Replace all nobles ** Heavy cavalry impetuous Upgrade to elite	 9 +2	All
Cataphract Upgrade to elite	11 +2	All
Ch'iang or Ti infantry Medium swordsmen 2HW Add armour (max 4)	 8 +2	4-8
Ch'iang or Ti archers Bowmen Light infantry bow	 7 4	2-4

Note

- Han rebels allies (List #117 Han Chinese) from 220 to 100 BC
- Gokturk allies (List #141 Central Asian Turkish)

117 - Han Chinese

202 BC - 220 AD
Plain, Mountain, Forest
Command +5
Strategist: Ban-Chao (73-100 AD)

The Han Dynasty was founded in 202 BC after a revolt against the Qin. It had twenty eight emperors and was the longest dynasty in China. The Han frequently fought against the Hsiung-Nu but also went to war against Korea. General Ban Chao extended Chinese influence in the Tarim basin and controlled the Silk Route by pushing out the Hsiung-Nu. He even managed to reach the Caspian Sea and was in contact with the Parthian Empire.

Troop type	Pts	Units
*Chariots with 4 horses ** Heavy chariot impact elite	13	0-2
*Mounted guardsmen ** Heavy cavalry bow elite Heavy cavalry crossbow elite	13	0-2

*Horsemen **		
Medium cavalry	7	2-8
Heavy cavalry	9	
Medium cavalry crossbow	9	
Heavy cavalry crossbow	11	
Horse archers Light cavalry bow	6	2-6
Chinese horsemen Light cavalry impact	6	0-4
Steppes horsemen Light cavalry bow elite Medium cavalry bow	7 9	0-4
Guardsmen on foot Medium swordsmen 2HW elite Heavy swordsmen 2HW elite	10 11	0-2
Chinese halberdiers Medium swordsmen 2HW Heavy swordsmen 2HW Downgrade to mediocre	8 9 -2	2-6
Chinese crossbowmen Crossbowmen Downgrade to mediocre	7 -2	2-6
Replace some halberdiers and / or crossbowmen by mixed units ½ Medium swordsmen ½ Crossbowmen	9	0-8
Upgrade to heavy mixed units ½ Heavy swordsmen ½ Crossbowmen	10	
Tribal auxiliaries Javelinmen Medium swordsmen impetuous	7	0-2
War prisoners Levy expendable	2	0-4
Revolted peasants Levy impetuous	4	
Light infantry crossbow Light infantry bow	4	0-4
Light artillery	6	0-2
Fortifications	1	0-8
Fortified camp	6	0-1

Note

- Southern Hsiung-Nu allies (List #116 Hsiung-Nu)
- Hsien-Pi allies (List #118 Hsien-Pi)

118 - Hsien-Pi

90 – 1000 AD
Steppes, Plain if Mu-jung
Command +2

The Hsien-Pi (or Xianbei) was a nomadic tribe established in Mongolia in the second century AD. They were united by their leader Tan Shi-huai who defeated the Hsiung-Nu. They dominated Mongolia for a short time. Some tribes settled in China, including the Mu-jung until 431 AD. The Hsien-Pi were the ancestors of the Kithan.

Troop type	Pts	Units
*Nobles (all of the same type) ** Medium cavalry impetuous Heavy cavalry impetuous Upgrade to elite (max 4)	7 9 +2	2-8
Horse archers Light cavalry bow Medium cavalry bow (max 6)	6 9	6-20
Light infantry bow	4	0-4
Mu-jung kingdom from 300 to 431 AD Ch'in allies (List #81 Chiang and Ti)		
*Replace all nobles ** Cataphract Upgrade to elite (max 4)	11 +2	All
Chinese troops Heavy swordsmen 2HW mediocre	7	0-4
Chinese troops Crossbowmen mediocre	5	0-4
Levy	3	0-2

119 - Three Kingdoms Chinese

180 – 316 AD
Plain, Mountain, Forest
Command +4
Strategist: Cao Cao (184 – 220 AD) et Zhou Yu (208 AD)

At the end of the second century the Han dynasty lost power and China plunged into a period of instability. General Cao Cao took advantage of this disorder to lead a brilliant military campaign to unify China under his authority. He was beaten at the battle of the Red Cliffs in 208 AD by General Zhou Yu and that put an end to his conquests. The period between 220 and 265 is known as the Three Kingdoms period, in which the kingdoms of Wei, Shu Han and Wu competed for domination of China. This period ended in 265 AD with the foundation of the Jin Dynasty which was divided between Western Jin (265-316 AD) and Eastern Jin (317-420 AD).

Troop type	Pts	Units
*Nobles with spear ** Medium cavalry impact Heavy cavalry impact Upgrade to elite (max 2)	8 10 +2	2-6

Nobles with bow * Medium cavalry bow Heavy cavalry bow Upgrade to elite	9 11 +2	0-2
Horse archers Light cavalry bow	6	2-6
Horsemen with halberds Light cavalry impact	6	0-2
Spearmen and halberdiers Heavy spearmen Heavy swordsmen 2HW Add support Downgrade to mediocre	8 9 +1 -2	2-8
Bowmen Crossbowmen Downgrade to mediocre	7 7 -2	2-4
Fanatical warriors Medium swordsmen impetuous elite	9	0-2
Tribal auxiliaries Javelinmen Medium swordsmen Medium swordsmen impetuous	7	0-4
Light infantry bow Light infantry crossbow	4	0-4
Light artillery	6	0-1
Heavy artillery	10	0-1
Fortifications	1	0-8
Fortified camp	6	0-1
Only nort western armies in 211 No allies		
Replace all spearmen and halberdiers by militia with long spears Pikemen mediocre	8	All

Note

- Chi'ang allies (List #81 Ch'iang and Ti)
- Hsiung-Nu allies (List #116 Hsiung-Nu)
- Wu-huan allies (List #118 Hsien-Pi)

Chinese Commander

120 - Chinese Northern and Southern Dynasties

317 – 589 AD
Plain, Mountain, Forest
Command +4
Strategist: Daowu (386-409 AD) Northern Dynasties

From 317 AD the Eastern Jin dynasty reigned over Southern China until the establishment of dynasties in the north and south in 420 AD. China was suffering a troubled period named the Sixteen Kingdoms period. Small states of very short duration shared China. From 420 AD until the reunification of China by the Sui in 589 AD, there were nine successive dynasties (five in the north and four in the south).

Troop type	Pts	Units
Northern dynasties Chi'ang allies (List #81 Ch'iang and Ti) Juan-Juan allies (List #116 Hsiung-Nu or List #141 Central Asian Turkish) from 500		
Horsemen * Heavy cavalry impact Cataphract Upgrade to elite (max 4)	10 11 +2	4-12
Horse archers Light cavalry bow	6	0-8
Steppes nomads Heavy cavalry bow Upgrade to elite	11 +2	0-4
Steppes nomads Light cavalry bow elite Medium cavalry bow	7 9	
Levy spearmen and halberdiers Heavy spearmen mediocre Heavy swordsmen 2HW mediocre Add support	6 7 +1	4-8
Levy archers and crossbowmen Bowmen mediocre Crossbowmen mediocre	5	0-4
"Pug-nosed" archers Bowmen	7	0-2
Fanatical warriors Medium swordsmen impetuous elite	9	0-2
Tribal auxiliaries Medium swordsmen	7	0-3
Light infantry bow	4	0-4
Light artillery Heavy artillery	6 10	0-2
Fortified camp	6	0-1

Southern dynasties		
*Horsemen ** Heavy cavalry impact Upgrade to elite	10 +2	2-4
*Horsemen ** Cataphract Upgrade to elite	11 +2	
Horse archers Light cavalry bow Medium cavalry bow (max 4)	6 9	0-8
Spearmen Heavy spearmen Heavy swordsmen 2HW Add support Downgrade to mediocre	8 9 +1 -2	4-12
Elephant	13	0-1
Archers Bowmen Crossbowmen Downgrade to mediocre	7 7 -2	2-6
Fanatical warriors Medium swordsmen impetuous elite	9	0-2
Tribal auxiliaries Javelinmen Medium swordsmen impetuous	7	0-3
Light infantry bow	4	0-4
War wagon crossbow	10	0-2
Light artillery Heavy artillery	6 10	0-2
Fortifications	1	0-8
Fortified camp	6	0-1

121 - Tamil Indian

175 BC - 1370 AD
Plain, Forest
Command +2 or +3 if Chola

This list covers the armies of the kingdoms of southern India and Ceylon, more particularly the Chola, Pandya, Satiyaputra and Kerelaputra dynasties before their conquest by Vijayanagar in 1370 AD. The Chola kingdom extended its domination over Sumatra, the Maldives and Ceylon.

Troop type	Pts	Units
Elephant *	13	2-6
Chariots with 2 horses (before 900) Light chariot bow	9	0-2
Indian horsemen Medium cavalry mediocre	5	0-3
Guardsmen Medium swordsmen impact Upgrade to elite	8 +2	0-2
Warriors Medium swordsmen impetuous	7	2-8
Bowmen Downgrade to mediocre	7 -2	4-16
Light infantry bow	4	0-2
Tribal auxiliaries Javelinmen Light infantry javelin	7 4	0-4
Peasants and servants Levy	3	0-4
Only Chola from 979 to 1279		
Replace some impetuous warriors Medium swordsmen impact	8	0-4

Note

- Hoysala allies (List #164 Hindu Indian)

122 - Three Kingdoms Korean

300 - 935 AD
Plain, Mountain, Forest
Command +3

This list represents the armies of Korea until 935 AD. The kingdoms of Koguryo, Paekche and Silla developed during the Three Kingdoms period. Koguryo was the largest of the kingdoms and conquered vast territories in Manchuria. In the fourth century the Paekche kingdom enjoyed great prosperity and extended its influence even into China. In the early sixth century the Silla kingdom subjugated all cities state in its neighbourhood. In 660 AD it conquered Paekche and Koguryo with the help of the Tang Chinese. Thus began the period of the unified kingdom of Silla until 935 AD.

Troop type	Pts	Units
*Nobles ** Medium cavalry impact Heavy cavalry impact Upgrade to elite (max 4)	8 10 +2	2-6
*Nobles ** Cataphract Upgrade to elite (max 4)	11 +2	
Horse archers Light cavalry bow	6	0-4
Steppes auxiliaries Light cavalry bow elite Medium cavalry bow	7 9	0-2
Provincial troops Medium swordsmen 2HW Heavy swordsmen 2HW	8 9	2-4

Provincial troops Bowmen Crossbowmen	7	2-4
Replace some provincial troops by mixed units ½ Medium swordsmen ½ Bowmen or Crossbowmen	9	0-4
Militia Med. swordsmen 2HW mediocre Heavy swordsmen 2HW mediocre	6 7	2-8
Militia Bowmen mediocre	5	2-8
Red banner of Silla Pikemen	11	0-2
Light infantry bow	4	0-4
Fortifications	1	0-8

Note

- Hsiung-Nu allies (List #116 Hsiung-Nu)
- Hsien-Pi allies (List #118 Hsien-Pi)
- Kofun Nara allies (List #123 Japanese)
- Chinese allies (List #165 Sui and Tang Chinese or List #169 Tang and five dynasties Chinese)

123 - Japanese

250 – 1040 AD
Plain, Mountain
Command +3

This list covers the armies of pre-medieval Japan until 1040 AD. The Kofun period (250-538 AD) saw the emergence of the Yamato state that had a strong influence on the western part of Japan. The Yamato state was strengthened during the Asuka period (538-710 AD) helped by the introduction of the Buddhist religion in 538 AD. The capital moved to Nara in 710 AD before it was returned to Kyoto in 794 AD. The Heian period (794-1185) was the apogee of the classical period. The Japanese had close ties with China and carried out several raids in Korea.

Troop type	Pts	Units
Before 400 AD		
*Uji nobles ** Medium spearmen elite	9	2-8
Uji archers Bowmen pavise Downgrade to mediocre	8 -2	6-24
Uji spearmen Medium spearmen Downgrade to mediocre	7 -2	0-12
Scouts Light infantry bow	4	0-4
From 400 AD		
*Uji nobles ** Medium cavalry bow elite Heavy cavalry bow elite	11 13	2-4
*Uji nobles on foot ** Medium swordsmen 2HW elite	10	0-4
Uji archers Bowmen pavise Downgrade to mediocre	8 -2	6-24
Light infantry bow	4	0-4
From 700 AD		
Emishi cavalry Light cavalry bow Medium cavalry bow	6 9	0-6
Chinpei ½ Medium swordsmen ½ Bowmen	9	0-4
Oyumi Light artillery	6	0-2
From 900 AD		
*Replace all Uji nobles ** Heavy cavalry bow Upgrade to elite	11 +2	4-8

Note

- Korean allies (List #122 Three Kingdoms Korean)

124 - Emishi

400 – 1100 AD
Plain, Mountain
Command +3

The Emishi occupied the north of Honshu Island in the archipelago of Japan. Some tribes opposed the authority of the Emperor of Japan between the 7th and the 10th century. The Emishi were primarily foot archers and they did not become horse archers until the eighth century. During the Thirty-Eight Year's War between 774 and 812 AD the Emishi were finally subjugated. Thereafter they no longer represented a threat to the Emperor.

Troop type	Pts	Units
*Archers ** Bowmen Upgrade to elite (max 4 in total)	7 +2	8-24
Light infantry bow	4	0-8
After 700 AD		
*Replace some archers ** Medium cavalry bow Upgrade to elite (max 4 in total)	9 +2	8-24
Light cavalry bow	6	

DARK AGES

BYZANCE AND ARMENIA

125 - JUSTINIAN BYZANTINE

493 – 575 AD
Plain, Mountain
Command +6
Strategist: Belisarius (530-559), Narses (552-555)

This list represents the armies of the Eastern Roman Empire. The most interesting period is the reign of the Emperor Justinian (527-565) which marks the last attempt to restore the old Roman Empire. After having made peace with the Sassanids Justinian sent Belisarius, his best general, to attack the North African Vandal Empire and then the Ostrogoths in Italy. With Belisarius having fallen into disgrace, Narses completed the conquest of Italy. Justinian also managed to impose his authority on the Visigoths in Spain. Shortly after his death the Lombards reconquered Italy.

Troop type	Pts	Units
Boukellarioi * Heavy cavalry impact and bow Upgrade to elite	 12 +2	0-4
Kavallarioi Medium cavalry bow Heavy cavalry bow	 9 11	4-12
Gepids, Heruls or Goths Heavy cavalry impetuous	9	0-4
Dismounted Gepids, Heruls or Goths Heavy spearmen	8	
Scouts Light cavalry bow	6	0-2
Huns Light cavalry bow Upgrade to elite	 6 +1	0-3
Moors Light cavalry javelin	6	0-3
Skoutatoi Heavy swordsmen Add support Downgrade to mediocre	 8 +1 -2	2-8
Bowmen Light infantry bow	7 4	0-4
Isaurians Javelinmen Light infantry javelin	 7 4	0-4
Armenians or Slav Medium swordsmen	7	
Light infantry sling	4	0-2
Levy	3	0-2
Heavy artillery	10	0-1
Fortifications	1	0-8
Fortified camp	6	0-1

Note
- Ghassanid allies (List #75 Early Arab)
- Herul allies (List #95 Heruls, Gepids and Taifali)
- Sabir Huns allies (List #110 Huns)
- Lombard allies (List #142 Lombard)

126 - MAURIKIAN BYZANTINE

575 – 650 AD
Plain, Mountain
Command +6
Strategists: Maurice (582-602), Heraclius (609-628)

After the death of Justinian, the Empire was under determined attack: the Lombards conquered Italy and the Slavs invaded Greece and Illyria. Emperor Maurice was able to save what he could and founded the exarchates of Ravenna and Carthage. From 603 the Persians captured Egypt, Palestine and Syria. Heraclius waged a long war against the Persians to reconquer lost territories. From 634 the Arabs took over from the repulsed Persians as they conquered the Middle East, North Africa, Cyprus and Sicily. The reign of Heraclius marks a transition. The Empire evolves from the remnant of the Roman Empire into a Byzantine Empire of Greek instead of Latin Roman.

Troop type	Pts	Units
Boukellarioi * Heavy cavalry impact and bow Upgrade to elite	 12 +2	2-4

Defensores Medium cavalry impact and bow Heavy cavalry impact and bow	 10 12	4-12
Optimates Heavy cavalry impact Heavy cavalry impetuous Upgrade to elite	 10 9 +2	0-2
Cursores Light cavalry bow Medium cavalry bow	 6 9	0-4
Skoutatoi Heavy spearmen Add support Downgrade to mediocre	 8 +1 -2	0-6
Bowmen Light infantry bow	7 4	0-2
Lazoi or Tzanoi Javelinmen Light infantry javelin	 7 4	0-3
Heavy artillery Medium artillery	10	0-1
Fortified camp	6	0-1

Note

- Ghassanid allies (List #75 Early Arab)
- Sassanid allies (List #109 Sassanid Persian)
- Moorish allies (List #113 Moors)
- Khazar allies (List #156 Khazar)

127 - Thematic Byzantine

650 – 963 AD
Plain, Mountain
Command +5

Threatened by many external enemies, the Byzantine Empire went on the defensive. The thematic system allowed each province (or theme) to raise and maintain troops. From 743 a standing army was created, the Tagmatic army which could support the threatened themes as ncecessary. The Arabs besieged Constantinople in 672 and 717, but were defeated. They occupied Crete in 824 and ravaged Thessalonica in 904. The Russians also grew in power and attacked Constantinople in 860 and 941.

Troop type	Pts	Units
Thematic cavalry * Medium cavalry impact and bow Heavy cavalry impact and bow Downgrade to mediocre (max 6)	 10 12 -2	6-16
Tagmatic cavalry (after 743) * Heavy cavalry impact and bow Upgrade to elite	 12 +2	0-4
Cursores Light cavalry bow Medium cavalry bow	 6 9	0-4
Georgians Heavy cavalry impetuous Upgrade to elite	 9 +2	0-2
Bulgars and Alans Light cavalry bow Upgrade to elite	 6 +1	0-2
Skoutatoi Heavy spearmen Add support Downgrade to mediocre	 8 +1 -2	0-4
Bowmen Light infantry bow	7 4	0-2
Light infantry sling	4	0-2
Light infantry javelin	4	0-2
Heavy artillery Medium artillery	10	0-1
Fortified camp	6	0-1
From 834 and 839		
Caliphate deserters Medium cavalry impact Heavy cavalry impact	 8 10	0-4
Only after 903		
Kataphraktoi Cataphract elite	13	0-1
Menavlatoi Heavy swordsmen 2HW	9	0-1

Note

- Moorish allies (List #113 Moors) in 681 only. No Georgian, Bulgarian or Alan troops.
- Slav allies (List #153 Slav)

Byzantine Kataphraktoi

128 - NIKEPHORIAN BYZANTINE

963 – 1071 AD
Plain, Mountain
Command +6
Strategists: Nikephoros II Phokas (963-969), John Tzimiskes (969-976 AD) and Basil II (976 – 1025)

The Byzantine Empire reached the peak of its power with the warrior emperors Nikephoros Phokas, John Tzimiskes and Basil II ("the Bulgar-Slayer"). Syria, Crete and Cyprus were recaptured from the Arabs. Basil II led a war without mercy against the Bulgarians who were destroyed in the battle of Kleidion in 1014. Bulgaria was then integrated into the Empire. By the end of the reign of Basil the Byzantine Empire had become the major power in the Mediterranean world. From 1040 however the power of the Empire began to deteriorate. The Normans ravaged Italy and expelled the Byzantines. At the battle of Manzikert in 1071 the Seljuk Turks dealt a fatal blow to the Empire by depriving it of most of Anatolia.

Troop type	Pts	Units
Prokoursatores Light cavalry bow Medium cavalry bow	 6 9	0-4
Kataphraktoi Cataphract elite	13	0-2
Skoutatoi in mixed units ½ Heavy spearmen ½ Bowmen	10	3-9
Menavlatoi Heavy swordsmen 2HW	9	0-1
Light infantry javelin	4	1-3
Light infantry bow	4	1-3
Light infantry sling	4	0-2
Heavy artillery Medium artillery	10	0-2
Fortified camp	6	0-1
Before 1042		
Tagmatic Kavallarioi * Heavy cavalry impact and bow Upgrade to elite	 12 +2	2-8
Russian or Varangian mercenaries from 988 Heavy spearmen Heavy swordsmen 2HW	 8 9	0-4
From 1042		
Thematic Kavallarioi Medium cavalry impact Heavy cavalry impact	 8 10	2-6
Tagmatic Kavallarioi * Heavy cavalry impact and bow Upgrade to elite	 12 +2	0-2
Varangian guardsmen Heavy spearmen elite Heavy swordsmen 2HW elite Add armour	 10 11 +2	0-2
Norman knights Medium knight impetuous Upgrade to elite	 10 +2	0-2
Cumans or Pechenegs Light cavalry bow	6	2-4
Turk mercenaries Light cavalry bow elite	7	0-2

Note

- Armenian allies (List #130 Bagratid Armenian) from 974 to 976
- Hamdanid allies (List #139 Dynastic Bedouin) from 974 to 976
- Russian allies (List #160 Russian)
- Georgian allies (List #205 Georgian)

129 - ARMENIAN PRINCIPALITY

639 – 717 AD
Plain, Mountain
Command +2

During the Arabian conquest of the Sassanid Empire Armenia emerged as an independent Principality from the Arab Empire. It was recognized both by the Caliph and the Basileus of Byzantium. Caught between two powerful neighbours Armenia cunningly exploited the situation, while remaining mostly allied with the Arabs. However it ultimately lost its independence and completely fell under Arab domination at the beginning of the 8th century.

Troop type	Pts	Units
Heavy cavalry * Medium cavalry impact and bow Heavy cavalry impact and bow Upgrade to elite (max 4)	 10 12 +2	4-12
Horse archers Light cavalry bow Medium cavalry bow	 6 9	2-6
Medium spearmen Add support	7 +1	0-16
Light infantry bow	4	0-4
Light infantry sling	4	0-2

Note

- Arab allies (List #131 Arab conquest or List #132 Umayyad Arab)
- Byzantine allies (List #127 Thematic Byzantine)

130 - Bagratid Armenian

885 – 1045 AD
Plain, Mountain
Command +3

Armenia regained its independence from the Arabs in 885 AD. The new Kingdom was recognized both by the Arabs and the Byzantines. The Bagratid Armenian dynasty founded by Ashot I reigned over Armenia up to 1045 when the Kingdom was conquered by the Byzantines. They were driven out in turn by the Seljuk Turks following the battle of Manzikert in 1071.

Troop type	Pts	Units
Nobles * Heavy cavalry impetuous Upgrade to elite	 9 +2	 2-4
Followers * Medium cavalry Medium cavalry bow (max 4)	 7 9	 2-6
Scouts Light cavalry bow Light cavalry javelin	 6	 0-6
Turks and Alans Light cavalry bow elite	7	0-2
Georgian vassals Heavy cavalry impetuous	9	0-2
Muslim vassals Medium cavalry impact	8	
Peasant militia Heavy spearmen mediocre Add support	 6 +1	 4-12
Bowmen	7	0-4
Russian mercenaries (before 969) Heavy spearmen	8	0-2
Light infantry bow	4	0-4
Light infantry javelin	4	0-2
Levy	3	0-2
Fortified camp	6	0-1

Note

- Georgian allies (List #205 Georgian)
- Byzantine allies (List #127 Thematic Byzantine or List #128 Nikephorian Byzantine)

ARAB EMPIRE

131 - Arab Conquest

622 – 661 AD
Desert before 638, Plain from 638
Command +4
Strategist: Khalid ibn al Walid (632-642 AD)

The Prophet Muhammad was expelled from Mecca in 622 and fled to Medina. It was the beginning of the Arab conquest and when he died in 632, Muhammad had conquered the whole of Arabia. His successors were the first four Caliphs that expanded the Arab Empire and conquered Egypt, Palestine, and Syria from the Byzantines. The Sassanid Empire was dismantled and the Arabs gained control of Mesopotamia and Persia. The main architect of these victories was the General Khalid ibn al Walid, who, in more than one hundred battles, lost none!

Troop type	Pts	Units
City cavalry * Medium cavalry impetuous Upgrade to elite (all or none)	 7 +2	 0-4
Nomads and Bedouins Light cavalry impact Light cavalry javelin	 6	 0-6
Bedouins Light camelry bow Medium camelry bow	 7 10	 0-2
Disguised camlery (only in 636) Medium camelry mediocre	6	0-2
Fanatic warriors * Medium swordsmen impetuous Heavy swordsmen impetuous Upgrade to elite (all or none)	 7 8 +2	 8-16
Bowmen Light infantry bow	7 4	0-4
Javelinmen Light infantry javelin	7 4	0-2
Light infantry sling	4	0-2
Fortified camp	6	0-1
Only from 638		
Replace all city cavalry by Jund cavalry * Medium cavalry impact Upgrade to elite (all or none)	 8 +2	 4-12
Replace all fanatic warriors * Medium spearmen Heavy spearmen Upgrade to elite (all or none) Add support	 7 8 +2 +1	 4-12

Asawira (ex Sassanids) Heavy cavalry bow	11	0-2
Dailami infantry Medium swordsmen impact elite Add support	 10 +1	0-2

Note

- From 636, all fanatic warriors must be replaced by spearmen.

132 - Umayyad Arab

661 - 750 AD
Plain, Desert, Mountain, Steppes in Central Asia
Command +4

The Umayyad dynasty established its capital at Damascus in Syria. Between 696 and 708 the Arabs conquered North Africa from the Byzantines and then invaded Spain. After defeating the Visigoth army of King Roderic at the battle of Jerez de la Frontera in 711 they took control of almost the entire Spanish peninsula. Their momentum was broken by the victory of Charles Martel near Poitiers in 732. In the East they had conquered Afghanistan, Turkestan and part of India, but they failed to take Constantinople in 717. At the time when the Umayyads were dispossessed of the Caliphate in 750 the Arabian Empire extended without interruption from the south of Gaul to the northwest of India.

Troop type	Pts	Units
*Jund cavalry ** Medium cavalry impact Heavy cavalry impact Upgrade to elite (max 4) Downgrade to mediocre	 8 10 +2 -2	4-12
Arabs and Bedouins Light cavalry impact Light cavalry javelin	6	0-4
Arab spearmen Heavy spearmen Add support Downgrade to mediocre	 8 +1 -2	6-16
Bowmen Downgrade to mediocre	7 -2	0-4
Light infantry bow	4	0-6
Heavy artillery	10	0-1
Fortified camp	6	0-1
Central Asia, Iraq and Iran Sogdian or other Asian city state allies (List #140 Sogdian and Central Asia City States) Turkish allies (List #141 Central Asian Turkish) Tibetan allies (List #166 Tibetan) in 715		
Asawira (ex Sassanids) Heavy cavalry bow	11	1-4
Turks Light cavalry bow Upgrade to elite	 6 +1	0-3
Dailami infantry Medium swordsmen impact elite Add support	 10 +1	0-2
North Africa, Arabia, Syria and Egypt Berber allies (List #113 Moors)		
Bedouins Light camelry bow Medium camelry bow	 7 10	0-2
Berber horsemen Light cavalry javelin	6	0-3
Berbers and Maronites Javelinmen Light infantry javelin	 7 4	0-4

Arab cavalry

133 - North African Arab

696 - 1160 AD
Plain, Mountain, Steppes
Command +3

After the conquest of Egypt the Arabs invaded North Africa in 696. They fought against the Byzantines and the Berber tribes that occupied the region. They took Carthage in 698 and entered Spain in 711. After 740 several states were formed in the Maghreb. The Idrisids in Morocco rejected the authority of the Abbasids in 789 and founded their own Caliphate. They were defeated by the Fatimids in Tunisia in 926. The Aghlabids invaded Sicily in 827 and their Emirate lasted until 1091 when it was conquered by the Normans. Berber dynasties took control of the Maghreb From the middle of the 11th century.

Troop type	Pts	Units
Arab horsemen * Medium cavalry impact Heavy cavalry impact Upgrade to elite (max 4) Downgrade to mediocre	 8 10 +2 -2	4-12
Abbasiya Heavy cavalry bow	11	0-2
Berber horsemen * Light cavalry javelin	6	2-12
Guardsmen Heavy spearmen elite Add support	 10 +1	0-2
African and Arab spearmen Medium spearmen Heavy spearmen Add support Downgrade to mediocre	 7 8 +1 -2	4-10
Arab archers Bowmen Downgrade to mediocre	 7 -2	0-4
Berbers Javelinmen Light infantry javelin	 7 4	0-8
Berbers and Arabs Light infantry bow Light infantry sling	4	0-4
Fortified camp	6	0-1

Note

- Andalusian allies (List #134 Andalusian Arab) in 817 in Sicily
- Byzantine allies (List #128 Nikephorian Byzantine) in 1035 in Sicily
- Tuareg allies (List # 202 Tuareg) after 1000 AD outside Sicily

134 - Andalusian Arab

711 - 1172 AD
Plain, Mountain
Command +4
Strategist: El Cid (1079-1092 AD)

The Arabs invaded Spain in 711 with an army including many Berbers. This new country was given the name al-Andalus. In 720 a civil war broke out between the Arabs and Berbers. An Emirate was created in Cordoba after the overthrow of the Umayyads by the Abbasids. In 929 the Emir of Cordoba proclaimed himself Caliph and became the rival of the Caliph of Baghdad. Following a new civil war Cordoba was burned down in 1031 and the Muslim possessions were divided into a score of small states which then facilitated the Christian Reconquista. The Almoravids from Morocco conquered the peninsula and took control from 1086 to 1142. They were conquered in turn by the Almohads. The period ends in 1212 by the defeat of the Almohad dynasty against the Christians at the battle of Las Navas de Tolosa.

Troop type	Pts	Units
Arab and Andalusian horsemen * Medium cavalry impact Heavy cavalry impact Upgrade to elite (max 2)	 8 10 +2	0-4
Berber horsemen * Light cavalry javelin	6	4-12
Andalusian horse archers Light cavalry bow	6	0-2
Berber and Andalusian spearmen Heavy spearmen Downgrade to mediocre Add support	 8 -2 +1	4-8
African spearmen (before 1000) Medium spearmen Add support	 7 +1	0-2
Berbers Javelinmen Light infantry javelin	 7 4	0-8
Andalusian archers Bowmen Light infantry bow	 7 4	0-6
Andalusians and Africans Light infantry sling	4	0-4
Fortified camp	6	0-1
Christian mercenary troops from 1000 AD		
Christian knights * Heavy cavalry impetuous Medium knight impetuous Upgrade to elite	 9 10 +2	2-4

Christian spearmen Heavy spearmen	8	2-6
Christian crossbowmen Crossbowmen	7	0-2

Note

- Almoravid allies (List #196 Berber) from 1039

135 - Abbasid Arab

747 – 945 AD
Plain, Mountain, Steppes
Command +4

The Abbasids were a dynasty of Sunni Caliphs who overthrew the Umayyads in 750 and established their capital in Baghdad. Following the revolution the Empire fragmented mainly in its Western part where Spain and the kingdoms of Maghreb declared themselves independent. In the 9th century the Empire suffered from unrest: the Tahirids, Saffarids and Samanids in Iran formed independent dynasties. The Tulunids and the Ikhshidids did the same in Egypt and Syria. The central Shiites of Iran formed a dynasty and took Baghdad in 945. From this date Caliphs only retained a theoretical power. The last Abbasid Caliph was murdered by the Mongols in 1258.

Troop type	Pts	Units
*Ahl Khurasan ** Medium cavalry impact Heavy cavalry impact Downgrade to mediocre	 8 10 -2	4-12
Arabs and Berbers Light cavalry javelin	6	0-6
Khurasanian horse archers Light cavalry bow	6	0-3
Maghariba guardsmen Light cavalry impact elite	7	0-2
*Replace some Ahl Khurasan by Ghulams or Khurasanians ** Heavy cavalry bow Upgrade to elite	 11 +2	0-10
Spearmen Heavy spearmen Add support Downgrade to mediocre	 8 +1 -2	2-6
Archers Bowmen Light infantry bow	 7 4	0-6
Abna Medium spearmen elite Heavy spearmen elite	 9 10	0-2
Replace some spearmen and archers by Sudanese abid ½ Medium spearmen ½ Bowmen	9	0-6
Dailami infantry Medium swordsmen impact elite Add support	 10 +1	0-2
Ghazis Medium swordsmen impetuous	7	0-2
Light infantry javelin	4	0-4
Naffatun Light infantry firearm	4	0-1
Levy	3	0-2
Fortified camp	6	0-1

Note

- Hamdanid allies (List #139 Dynastic Bedouin) after 890 AD

136 - Arab Indian

751 – 1206 AD
Plain, Forest, Desert
Command +3

At the beginning of the 8th century the Arabs entered India and conquered territories in the North West. In 725 an army pushed towards the centre of India but was defeated by Hindus. A new attempt in 833 suffered another defeat. Islam still remained present in India in the form of partly Hindu kingdoms. From 872 these kingdoms were under the influence of the Saffarids and then of the Samanids before they were eradicated by the Sultanate of Delhi in 1206.

Troop type	Pts	Units
*Arab horsemen ** Medium cavalry impact Heavy cavalry impact Downgrade to mediocre	 8 10 -2	4-8
Hindu horsemen Medium cavalry Downgrade to mediocre	 7 -2	0-8
Light cavalry javelin (max 4)	6	
Hindu Elephant Elephant	13	0-1
Arab infantry Heavy spearmen Add support Downgrade to mediocre	 8 +1 -2	0-6
Hindu avec bow Bowmen Downgrade to mediocre	 7 -2	4-12

Hindu with sword Medium swordsmen impetuous	7	0-6
Hindu with javelin Javelinmen Light infantry javelin	 7 4	0-4
Ligth infantry bow	4	0-4
Levy	3	0-2
Fortified camp	6	0-1
After 872		
*Replace some Arab horsemen by Khurasanians or Ghulams ** Heavy cavalry bow Upgrade to elite	 11 +2	0-4

137 - Khurasanian

821 - 1003 AD
Plain, Mountain, Steppes
Command +4

Khurasan was the region in the northeast of Iran, which also encompassed Transoxiana (currently Uzbekistan) and Afghanistan. Several Iranian dynasties took power in this region during the Abbasid Caliphate. In the 9th century a conflict arose between the Arabs and the Iranians in the Abbasid Empire. The Tahirids established an independent State in Khurasan between 821 and 872. Following revolts, the Tahirids were overthrown by the Saffarids (861-1003). They conquered the north of India and almost reached Baghdad. The Caliph then appointed the Samanids to fight them and in 900 they occupied the majority of Khurasan. The dynasty of the Samanids was eliminated by the Turkish Qarakhanids in 1003.

Troop type	Pts	Units
*Khurasanian nobles ** Heavy cavalry bow Upgrade to elite	 11 +2	2-6
Khurasanian horsemen Light cavalry bow	6	0-6
Bedouins Light cavalry impact Medium cavalry impact	 6 8	0-6
Turkish mercenaries Light cavalry bow elite	7	0-3
Spearmen Heavy spearmen Add support Downgrade to mediocre	 8 +1 -2	2-6
Bowmen (max 2) Light infantry bow	7 4	0-4
Dailami infantry Medium swordsmen impact elite Add support	 10 +1	0-2
Kumijis Medium swordsmen Javelinmen	7	0-2
Ghazis Medium swordsmen impetuous	7	0-2
Levy	3	0-2
Fortified camp	6	0-1
Tahirids Abbasid allies (List #135 Abbasid Arab)		
*Turkish ghulams ** Heavy cavalry bow Upgrade to elite	 11 +2	0-4
Auxiliary horsemen Light cavalry bow Light cavalry javelin	6	0-2
Saffarids Indian allies (List #136 Arab Indian)		
*Turkish ghulams ** Heavy cavalry bow Upgrade to elite	 11 +2	2-6
Khawarij Medium cavalry	7	0-2
Auxiliary horsemen Light cavalry bow Light cavalry javelin	6	0-4
Indian warriors Medium swordsmen impetuous	7	0-2
Indian archers Bowmen Downgrade to mediocre	 7 -2	0-4
Samanids Indian allies (List #136 Arab Indian) Turkish allies (List #141 Central Asian Turkish) Ziyarid allies (List #191 Buyid) Ghaznavid allies (List #193 Ghaznavid)		
*Turkish ghulams ** Heavy cavalry bow Upgrade to elite	 11 +2	2-6
Elephant	13	0-1

Arab archers

138 - Tulunid and Iqshidid Egyptian

868 – 905 and 935 - 969 AD
Plain, Desert
Command +4

While the power of the Abbasids was declining, a Turkish officer by the name of Ahmad Ibn Tulu, sent to Egypt as Governor, acted as a true monarch. He ended all tax payments sent to Baghdad. In 878 he occupied Palestine and Syria to guard against an Abbasid attack. However his son proved less capable and after his assassination, the country fell under the Abbasid authority in 905. In 935, another prince defending Egypt against the Fatimids declared independence, founded the Ikhshidid dynasty and annexed Syria. However, his successors were not as able and Egypt fell under Fatimid control.

Troop type	Pts	Units
Turkish ghulams * Heavy cavalry bow Upgrade to elite	11 +2	4-10
Armenians Heavy cavalry impetuous	9	0-2
Berbers Light cavalry javelin	6	0-3
Bedouins Light cavalry impact Medium cavalry impact	6 8	0-4
Scouts on camels Light camelry bow	7	0-1
Sudanese guardsmen Medium swordsmen impact Upgrade to elite	8 +2	0-2
Sudanese abid ½ Medium spearmen ½ Bowmen	9	2-8
Ghazis Medium swordsmen impetuous	7	0-2
Berbers Javelinmen Light infantry javelin	7 4	0-4
Light infantry bow Light infantry sling	4	0-4
Ahdath militia Levy	3	0-2
Fortified camp	6	0-1
Only Tulunid from 885 to 905		
Bedouin guards Light cavalry impact elite	7	0-2

139 - Dynastic Bedouin

890 – 1150 AD
Plain, Steppes, Desert
Command +4

The collapse of Abbasid power permitted the emergence of several Bedouin dynasties in Syria and Iraq. These dynasties alternatively controlled the cities of Aleppo and Mosul. The Hamdanids controlled Mosul between 890 and 991 and Aleppo between 945 and 1008. The Uqaylids replaced the Hamdanids in Mosul from 996 to 1096 after the brief reign of the Buyids. The Mirdasids followed the Hamdanids in Aleppo from 1008 to 1079. The Mazyadids controlled the southern part of Iraq from 997 to 1150.

Troop type	Pts	Units
Bedouin and Kurd nobles * Heavy cavalry impact Upgrade to elite	10 +2	0-4
Others Bedouins Light cavalry impact Medium cavalry impact	6 8	8-24
*Ghulams * (except for Hamdanids)* Heavy cavalry bow Upgrade to elite	11 +2	0-4
Bedouins on camels Light camelry bow Medium camelry bow	7 10	0-3
Dailami infantry Medium swordsmen impact elite Add support	10 +1	0-4
Bedouin warriors Medium swordsmen Downgrade to mediocre	7 -2	0-4
Bedouin archers Bowmen Downgrade to mediocre	7 -2	0-4
Others Bedouins Light infantry sling Light infantry bow	4	0-4
Ahdath militia Levy	3	0-2
Fortified camp	6	0-1
Only Hamdanids of Aleppo (945 to 1008)		
Replace all Ghulams by Khurasanians Heavy cavalry bow Upgrade to elite	11 +2	0-6
Khurasanian horse archers Light cavalry bow	6	
Sudanese abid ½ Medium spearmen ½ Bowmen	9	0-3

Ghazis		
Medium swordsmen impetuous	7	0-3

Note

- Kurdish allies (List #192 Dynastic Kurdish) for Uqaylids

CENTRAL ASIA

140 - Sogdian and Central Asia City States

500 – 1000 AD
Plain, Steppes
Command +3

This list covers the armies of Central Asia and the Tarim basin civilizations prior to subjugation by the Arabs and Turks. The Sogdians originated in Iran. They controlled what is now Uzbekistan and the cities of Samarkand and Bukhara. From 630 the Tarim basin was under Chinese rule. The Umayyad Arabs defeated the Chinese at Talas in 751 and took control of the region. In the 9th century the region was under the influence of the Samanids who founded the state of Khurasan.

Troop type	Pts	Units
*Noble horsemen **		
Heavy cavalry bow	11	6-16
Upgrade to elite (max 6)	+2	
Horse archers		
Medium cavalry bow	9	2-8
Light cavalry bow	6	
Bowmen	7	0-8
Downgrade to mediocre	-2	
Light infantry bow	4	
Militia		
Heavy spearmen mediocre	6	0-4
Levy	3	
Only Sogdian		
Arab allies (List #132 Umayyad Arab)		
*Replace all horsemen **		
Heavy cavalry impetuous	9	All
Upgrade to elite (max 6)	+2	
Exiled Sassanid Persians		
Heavy cavalry bow	11	0-4
Only city of Khotan		
Elephant	13	0-1

Note

- Turkish allies (List #141 Central Asian Turkish)

141 - Central Asian Turkish

550 – 1330 AD
Steppes, add Plain if Uyghur or Qarakhanid
Command +3 or +4 if Qarakhanid Turks

The first Turkish people were the Gokturks who appeared around 6th century and probably originated from Mongolia. Afterwards different peoples of Turkish origin settled in Central Asia such as the Karluks, Uyghurs, Kyrgyz, Oghuz and Turkmen. The Qarakhanids overthrew the dynasty of the Samanids and ruled a powerful Empire up to 1212 when they were overthrown in turn by the Khwarazmians.

Troop type	Pts	Units
*Nobles **		
Heavy cavalry bow	11	2-8
Upgrade to elite (max 4)	+2	
Horse archers (unless Uyghur)		
Medium cavalry bow	9	6-24
Light cavalry bow	6	
Dismounted archers		
Bowmen	7	0-4
Downgrade to mediocre	-2	
Light infantry bow	4	
Levy	3	0-2
Uyghur Turks from 856 to 1330		
Tibetan allies (List #166 Tibetan)		
Replace all horse archers		
Light cavalry bow	6	All
Militia Spearmen		
Heavy spearmen mediocre	6	4-12
Add support	+1	
Militia archers		
Bowmen mediocre	5	0-6
Qarakhanid Turks from 999 to 1211		
Khitan allies (List #211 Khitan Liao)		
Turkish ghulams		
Heavy cavalry bow	11	0-2
Upgrade to elite	+2	
Kumijis		
Medium swordsmen	7	0-2

Note

- Arab allies (List #132 Umayyad Arab) in 717 and 737
- Sogdian allies (List #140 Sogdian and Central Asia City States) before 741
- Bulgar allies (List #155 Bulgar) in 576

WESTERN EUROPE

142 - Lombard

489 – 888 AD
Plain, add Mountain after 584
Command +3

The Lombards were a Germanic people originating from the Baltic area. At the end of the 5th century they settled in Pannonia. Many served as mercenaries in Byzantine armies in the fight against the Ostrogoths in Italy. In 568 the Lombards invaded Italy and, after a period of anarchy, founded a Kingdom in the north of the peninsula in 584. In 774 the Kingdom was conquered by the Carolingian Franks and from 888 it became an integral part of the Holy Empire.

Troop type	Pts	Units
*Nobles ** Heavy cavalry impetuous Upgrade to elite (max 6)	9 +2	2-12
Followers (only before 775) Medium cavalry impetuous	7	2-12
Bowmen Downgrade to mediocre	7 -2	2-6
Light infantry bow	4	0-4
Early Lombard (489 to 567) Suevi allies (List # 96 Franks, Alemanni, Burgundi, Suevi) Avar allies (List #154 Avar)		
Remplace some Followers Fantassin moyen impétueux	7	0-6
Fortified camp	6	0-1
Conquest of Italy (568 to 584) Bulgar allies (List #155 Bulgar)		
Saxon or Suevi warriors Heavy swordsmen impetuous	8	2-8
Slav warriors Medium swordsmen	7	2-6
Kingdom of Italy (585 to 774) Slav allies (List #153 Slav) in 603 Avar allies (List #154 Avar) from 590 to 601		
Bulgars or Magyars after 650 Medium cavalry bow Light cavalry bow	9 6	0-2
City militia after 650 Heavy spearmen mediocre	6	0-4
Carolingian Italy (775 to 888) Aghlabid allies (List #133 North African Arab)		
City or rural militia Heavy spearmen mediocre Levy (max 2)	6 3	4-12

143 - Italian Ostrogoth

493 – 561 AD
Plain, Mountain
Command +2
Strategist: Theodoric (493-526)

At the fall of the Roman Empire the Ostrogoths were sole masters of Italy and founded a Kingdom under King Theodoric. In 536 the Byzantine Emperor Justinian tasked his best general Belisarius with Italy's reconquest. He performed well and succeeded. Jealous of his successes, the Emperor sent Belisarius to fight the Persians. The new King of the Ostrogoths, Totila, regained the lost territories. Belisarius was recalled but, deprived of reinforcements and supplies by the ever jealous Emperor, he was reduced to the defensive. It was ultimately the eunuch Narses, replacing Belisarius, that beat Totila at the battle of Taginae in 552. After a last revolt, the Ostrogoths were subjugated once and for all in 561.

Troop type	Pts	Units
*Nobles ** Medium cavalry impetuous Heavy cavalry impetuous Upgrade to elite (max 6)	7 9 +2	6-16
Huns Light cavalry bow elite	7	0-2
Byzantine deserters (544-552) Medium cavalry bow	9	0-2
Spearmen Heavy spearmen Add support	8 +1	0-4
Bowmen mediocre Upgrade to ordinary (max 2)	5 +2	4-8
Light infantry bow (max 4)	4	
Levy	3	0-2
Fortified camp	6	0-1

Note

- Burgundi allies (List #96 Franks, Alemanni, Burgundi, Suevi)
- Frankish allies (List #144 Merovingian Frankish)

144 - Merovingian Frankish

512 – 751 AD
Plain, Forest
Command +3

After the death of King Clovis in 511 the kingdom of the Franks was divided between his sons, resulting in years of fratricidal strife. Chlothar II reunited the Kingdom in 613. At that time it included Austrasia (northeast France, Belgium, and the Lower Rhine), Neustria (northwest France excluding Brittany) and Burgundy (Burgundy and the centre of France). The end of Dagobert I's reign in 639 mrked the decline of the Merovingians, known as the era of the lazy Kings. The last Merovingian King Childeric III was overthrown by Pepin the Short in 751.

Troop type	Pts	Units
Nobles * Heavy cavalry impetuous Upgrade to elite (max 4)	9 +2	4-8
Gallo-Roman cavalry * Medium cavalry Heavy cavalry	7 9	0-4
Bretons or Basques Light cavalry javelin	6	0-2
Tribal warriors (before 600) Heavy swordsmen impetuous	8	6-24
Gallo-Roman spearmen Heavy spearmen Downgrade to mediocre	8 -2	
Light infantry bow	4	0-4
Light infantry javelin	4	0-2
Fortifications	1	0-6

Note

- Visigoth allies (List #97 Visigoths in Spain)
- Breton allies (Liste #145 Armourican Breton)

145 - Armourican Breton

580 – 1072 AD
Plain, Forest
Command +2

Following several invasions in Britain, some Britons migrated to the continent in Brittany and Normandy. During the 6th and 7th century, these Bretons fought the Franks to keep their independence. In 799 Charlemagne conquered Brittany but the region remained rebellious and uprisings were frequent. Brittany gained independence in 845 after the Battle of Ballon. The Normans took control of Brittany during the 11th century.

Troop type	Pts	Units
Nobles * Heavy cavalry Upgrade to elite	9 +2	0-4
Breton horsemen Medium cavalry Light cavalry javelin	7 6	6-24
Saxon Mercenaries (before 600) Heavy swordsmen impetuous	8	0-4
Breton militia Javelinmen	7	0-12
Light infantry javelin	4	0-4
Light infantry sling	4	0-2
Light infantry bow	4	0-2
Levy	3	0-2
After 1000 No allies		
Replace all Breton militia Medium spearmen	7	All
Light infantry crossbow	4	0-2

Note

- Saxon allies (List #100 Saxon, Anglo-Saxon, Frisian and Jutes) in 587
- Frankish allies (List #149 Carolingian Frankish)
- Viking allies (List #150 Viking and Leidang)

146 - Welsh

580 – 1282 AD
Mountain, Forest
Command +2

This list represents the armies of the kings and princes of Wales. Mountainous terrain and the fierce nature of Welsh prevented Saxon domination. The 11th century Normans invading England occupied the eastern part of Wales, but its conquest proved difficult. The Welsh resisted occupation. King Edward I of England only managed to impose his rule in 1282. Allegedly to appease the Welsh he created his son "Prince of Wales" and the Principality of Wales became an appanage of the English crown.

Troop type	Pts	Units
Nobles and followers * Medium cavalry Heavy cavalry (max 2) Upgrade to elite (max 4)	7 9 +2	2-6
Welsh warriors Medium swordsmen	7	8-24
Light infantry javelin	4	2-6
Before 1100 Saxon allies (List #147 Anglo-Saxon or List #173 Anglo-Danish) Viking allies (List #150 Viking and Leidang)		
Atecotti Warriors Medium swordsmen impetuous elite	9	0-3

From 1100 Irish allies (List #151 Feudal Irish) English allies (List #176 Feudal English)		
Light cavalry javelin	6	0-4
Replace all Welsh warriors Medium spearmen	7	4-16
Welsh archers Bowmen Longbowmen	 7 9	4-16
Light infantry bow	4	0-4

147 - Anglo-Saxon

617 - 1014 AD
Plain, Forest
Command +3
Strategists: Penda (626-655 AD) and Alfred the Great (871-894 AD)

Following the Romans' withdrawal from Britannia the province suffered a series of invasions. The two most important invaders were the Angles and the Saxons. Small kingdoms emerged in the 7th century. The fiercely pagan Anglian King Penda slowed Christianisation, but was defeated in 655 at the Battle of Winwaed. At the end of the 8th century the Vikings ravaged England and then began to settle. The Danes and Norwegians subjugated the northern kingdoms at the end of the 9th century. The Saxon King Alfred the Great fought against the invaders, whom he finally repulsed in 897. Athelstan, his grandson, completed the unification and the dynasty survived until the Norman Conquest.

Troop type	Pts	Units
*Hirdsmen ** Heavy cavalry Upgrade to elite	 9 +2	2-4
Heavy spearmen elite Add armour	10 +2	
British vassal Medium cavalry	7	0-2
Select Fyrd Heavy spearmen	8	6-12
Great Fyrd Heavy spearmen mediocre Levy (max 4)	 6 3	0-16
Light infantry bow Light infantry sling	4	0-2
Light infantry javelin	4	0-2

Note

- Welsh allies (List #146 Welsh)
- Viking allies (List #150 Viking and Leidang)

148 - Feudal Spanish

718 - 1340 AD
Plain, Mountain
Command +3
Strategist: El Cid (1068-1081 and 1094-1099 AD)

Coordinated Christian resistance began shortly after the fall of Spain to Muslim armies. The Kingdom of Asturias was created in 722 in the northwest of the peninsula. Later the kingdoms of Navarre, Aragon, Castile and Portugal were also created and they began the Reconquista. It was a long struggle, but it benefited from periods of disorder among the Arabs. Rodrigo Diaz de Vivar, also known as the Cid, was a hero of the Reconquista. He was initially in the service of the King of Castile before being exiled in 1081. He then took mercenary service with the Emir of Zaragoza. After conquering Valencia he fought against the Almoravids and governed Valencia until his death in 1099. Deemed to be undefeated, his name is legend.

Troop type	Pts	Units
*Hidalgos ** Heavy cavalry impetuous Upgrade to elite (max 4)	 9 +2	4-10
Caballeros villanos Heavy cavalry impetuous Medium cavalry impetuous	 9 7	0-4
Basques or Berbers Light cavalry javelin	6	0-3
Spanish spearmen Heavy spearmen Add support Downgrade to mediocre	 8 +1 -2	2-8
Javelinmen Javelinmen Light infantry javelin	 7 4	0-4
Bowmen Downgrade to mediocre	7 -2	0-3
Light infantry bow	4	
Light infantry sling	4	0-3
Fortified camp	6	0-1
After 1050		
*Replace all Hidalgos ** Medium knight impetuous Upgrade to elite (max 4)	 10 +2	All
Mounted Crossbowmen Light cavalry crossbow	6	0-2
Foot crossbowmen Crossbowmen mediocre Light infantry crossbow	 5 4	0-2

After 1150		
Almughavars Medium swordsmen impact elite Medium spearmen elite	 10 9	0-6
After 1200		
Jinetes Light cavalry javelin Upgrade to elite	 6 +1	2-6
*Knights of military orders ** Medium knight impact elite	13	0-2
Sergeants of military orders Heavy spearmen Add armour	 8 +2	0-2
Replace all foot crossbowmen Crossbowmen Add pavise	 7 +1	2-6

Note

- Andalusian allies (List #134 Andalusian Arab) from 1030 to 1110
- Marinid allies (List #196 Berber) after 1269
- Arab allies (List #219 Granadine) after 1238

149 - Carolingian Frankish

751 – 888 AD
Plain, Forest
Command +3 or +4 if Charlemagne
Strategist: Charlemagne (768-814)

Pepin the Short was the first King of the Carolingian dynasty, but it was his son Charlemagne who was the most illustrious. During his reign the Empire was extended to the whole of France (except Brittany), most of Germany, Italy and Spain. His son Louis the Pious succeeded in maintaining unity, but at his death the Empire was divided by the Treaty of Verdun in 843. At the end of the 8th century Viking invasions deeply affected the Empire and Frankish Kings seemed powerless. From 888 the Empire split in two parts, which are covered by other army lists.

Troop type	Pts	Units
*Caballarii ** Medium cavalry impetuous Heavy cavalry impetuous Upgrade to elite (max 6)	 7 9 +2	6-16
Bretons Medium cavalry	7	0-2
Basques or Gascons Light cavalry javelin	6	0-2
Heavy spearmen Add support	8 +1	4-12
Bowmen mediocre Light infantry bow	5 4	0-3
Basques or Gascons Light infantry javelin	4	0-2
Light infantry crossbow Light infantry sling	4	0-2
Peasants Levy	3	0-3
Fortified camp	6	0-1
Only if Charlemagne (768 – 814)		
Replace some Caballarii by Heavy cavalry impact Upgrade to elite (max 8)	 10 +2	0-8
Mounted archers with lance Medium cavalry impact Bowmen *(if dismounted)*	 8 7	0-2

Note

- Saxon allies (List #100 Saxon, Anglo-Saxon …)
- Lombard allies (List #142 Lombard)
- Breton allies (List #145 Armourican Breton)
- Slav allies (List #153 Slav)
- Croat allies (List #157 Serbo-Croatian)
- Viking allies (List #150 Viking and Leidang) after 857

Charlemagne Emperor

150 - Viking and Leidang

790 – 1280
Plain, Forest, add Mountain if Leidang
Command +3

"Viking" refers to all Scandinavian (Danish, Norwegian, Swedish and Icelandic) warriors conducting coastal raids on Europe from the end of the 8th century onwards. In their drakkars they plundered England, Scotland, Ireland, France and Spain. From the 9th century the Vikings began to found long term settlements, notably in part of northern France which was ceded to them in 911. The descendants of the Vikings in this region became known as Normans. Other Vikings moved eastward and founded colonies in Russia and attacked Constantinople several times. "Leidang" refers to the army of the Scandinavian countries on their own soil. It mostly consisted of farmers called Bondi armed with spears.

Troop type	Pts	Units
Vikings Irish or Scots allies (List #99 Caledonian, Irish, Scots and Pictish) Breton allies (List #145 Armourican Breton) English allies (List #173 Anglo-Danish)		
Huscarls * Heavy swordsmen 2HW elite Add armour	11 +2	2-6
Viking warriors (all of the same type) Medium swordsmen impetuous Heavy swordsmen	7 8	6-18
Berserkers Medium swordsmen impet. elite	9	0-2
Irish mercenaries Medium swordsmen Add 2HW	7 +1	0-4
Bowmen Light infantry bow	7 4	0-2
Light infantry javelin	4	0-2
Leidang Wend allies (List #153 Slav) Germanic allies (List #183 Feudal German)		
Huscarls * Heavy swordsmen 2HW elite Add armour	11 +2	2-6
Replace some huscarls * Heavy cavalry elite	11	0-4
Bondi (all of the same type) Medium spearmen Heavy spearmen Add support	7 8 +1	6-18
Bowmen Light infantry bow	7 4	2-6
German colonists Crossbowmen mediocre Light infantry crossbow	5 4	0-2
Light infantry javelin	4	0-2
Slaves Levy	3	0-2
Fortified camp	6	0-1

151 - Feudal Irish

795 - 1300 AD
Mountain, Forest
Command +3

During the 8th century Christian Ireland experienced an intellectual and religious golden age but was politically divided. The first Vikings raids occurred in 795. For 40 years they conducted increasingly extensive incursions. In 840 they began to set up bases on the island, founding the city of Dublin in 841. The Vikings were ultimately defeated by the victorious King Brian Boru at the battle of Clontarf in 1014. Ireland then enjoyed a brief period of respite until the Anglo-Norman invasion in 12th century.

Troop type	Pts	Units
Nobles * Medium swordsmen 2HW Heavy swordsmen 2HW Upgrade to elite	8 9 +2	0-4
Mounted nobles (from 1130) * Medium cavalry Upgrade to elite	7 +2	
Irish warriors Medium swordsmen Add 2HW	7 +1	8-24
Kerns Javelinmen Light infantry javelin	7 4	2-6
Light infantry bow Light infantry sling	4	0-2
Levy	3	0-2
Fortifications	1	0-6
Fortified camp	6	0-1
After 1260		
Galloglaich Heavy swordsmen 2HW Upgrade to elite	9 +2	0-2

Ostmen allies		
Viking warriors * Heavy swordsmen	8	2-6

Note

- Ostmen allies (see list above)
- Ostmen are Viking colonists installed in Ireland.
- Viking allies (List #150 Viking and Leidang)
- Norman allies (List #172 Norman and Frankish) from 1169 to 1205

152 - Pre-Feudal Scots

846 – 1124 AD
Mountain, Forest
Command +3

In 846 Kenneth McAlpine became the first King of the Scots and Picts. The country endured Norse invasions for almost 50 years. During the 10th and 11th centuries the Kingdom of Scotland was called Alba. It did not include the Viking controlled Orkneys, Caithness and Hebrides, nor independent Strathclyde. Little by little the Kingdom was extended and the Gaelic culture flourished.

Troop type	Pts	Units
Scot horsemen Light cavalry javelin	6	2-6
*Replace some horsemen by Scot Nobles ** Medium cavalry Heavy cavalry (max 2)	 7 9	0-4
*Thegns (all of the same type) ** Heavy swordsmen impetuous Add armour Upgrade to elite	 8 +2 +2	2-4
*Thegns (all of the same type) ** Heavy spearmen Add armour Upgrade to elite	 8 +2 +2	
Warriors Medium spearmen	7	8-20
Light infantry bow	4	0-4
Light infantry javelin	4	0-4
After 1052 Highlander allies (List #179 Scots isles and Highlanders)		
*Norman knights ** Medium knight impetuous Upgrade to elite	 10 +2	0-2

Galwegian allies		
*Galwegian warriors ** Medium swordsmen impetuous	7	4-8

Note

- Galwegian allies (see list above)
- Viking allies (List #150 Viking and Leidang)
- Strathclyde allies (List #101 Romano-British) before 945

EASTERN EUROPE

153 - Slav

476 – 1218 AD
Mountain, Forest
Command +2

The Slavs originated from an area between the Vistula and the Dniester. Following the migration of Germans into the Roman Empire at the end of the 5th century, they expanded to the Baltic, the Danube and into the Balkans. They reached the Adriatic coast and some even settled in Greece. The first Slav States emerged between the 7th and 11th centuries. The Slavs were gradually dominated by the peoples of the steppes (Avars, Bulgars, Magyars and Khazars) in the south and by the Franks in the west. In the north they were absorbed by the Rus'. The Wends along the Baltic coast were the only ones managing, until 1218 AD, to retain independence.

Troop type	Pts	Units
*Nobles ** Medium cavalry Heavy cavalry (max 3) Upgrade to elite (max 3)	 7 9 +2	2-6
*Slav warriors ** Medium swordsmen Downgrade to mediocre (max 6)	 7 -2	6-24
Slavic warriors with javelin Javelinmen	7	0-8
Bowmen Light infantry bow	7 4	2-6
Light infantry javelin	4	0-4
Fortified camp	6	0-1
Baltic Slavs (Wend) Batavian allies (List #100 Saxon, Anglo-Saxon, Frisian and Jutes)		
Viking mercenaries (before 1057) Heavy swordsmen	8	0-4
Danish or Saxons (from 1057) Heavy cavalry impetuous Medium knight impetuous	 9 10	0-2
Western Slavs (after 830) Magyar allies (List #158 Magyar) Pecheneg Allies (List #159 Pecheneg)		
Replace all Slav warriors Medium spearmen Downgrade to mediocre	 7 -2	All
Swabians or Franks Heavy cavalry impetuous	9	0-2
Pechenegs Light cavalry bow	6	0-2

Slav warriors

154 - Avar

553 - 822 AD
Steppes, Plain (only from 558 to 631)
Command +4

The Avars were a nomadic people related to the Juan Juan who migrated west after been driven out by the Chinese. In the 6th century they reached the Volga and the Danube. Allies and then enemies of the Byzantines, they also fought the Slavs and the Bulgars and controlled the steppes north of the Danube, from the Black Sea to the river Elbe. From 610 they attacked Italy and Bavaria. In 626 they unsuccessfully besieged Constantinople with the help of the Persians. During the 7th century they were pushed back and withdrew to Hungary. From 791 the Franks fought them without mercy and they disappear from the records after 822.

Troop type	Pts	Units
Nobles * Heavy cavalry bow Upgrade to elite (max 4)	 11 +2	 4-16
Horse archers Light cavalry bow Medium cavalry bow	 6 9	 0-6
Gepids Heavy cavalry impetuous	9	0-4
Fortified camp	6	0-1
Only from 558 to 631 Sassanid allies (List #109 Sassanid Persian) in 626		
Bulgar horsemen Light cavalry bow Medium cavalry bow	 6 9	 4-12
Slavic warriors Medium swordsmen Downgrade to mediocre	 7 -2	 2-8
Light infantry bow	4	0-4

Note

- Bulgarian allies (List #155 Bulgar) from 675

155 - Bulgar

559 - 1018 AD
Before 680: Steppes
From 680: Plain, Mountain, Forest
Command +3

The Bulgars came from the north of the Caucasus and the Sea of Azov. In the 6th century they fought the Avars and created a Kingdom south of the Danube, combining with the more numerous Slavs. They converted to Christianity in the 9th century and became the ancestors of current Bulgarians. Their Kingdom was conquered in 1008 by the Byzantine Emperor Basil II, nicknamed the Bulgar-slayer. Other Bulgars settled on the Volga and converted to Islam in 922 after contact with the Abbasid Caliphate. In 969 they were attacked by the Kievan Rus' and their capital was ransacked. The last survivors were integrated into the Golden Horde in the 13th century.

Troop type	Pts	Units
Nobles (only before 803) * Medium cavalry bow Heavy cavalry bow Upgrade to elite (max 4)	 9 11 +2	2-12
Nobles (any period) * Medium cavalry impetuous Heavy cavalry impetuous Upgrade to elite (max 4)	 7 9 +2	
Horse archers Light cavalry bow Medium cavalry bow	 6 9	 4-24
Only before 680 Fortifications	1	0-6
Only from 680 Fortified camp	6	0-1
Only from 680 to 851 Byzantine allies (List #127 Thematic Byzantine) from 803 to 851 Avar allies (List #154 Avar) in 812		
Slav horsemen Medium cavalry Heavy cavalry	 7 9	 0-2
Slav warriors (all of the same type) Medium swordsmen Medium spearmen Downgrade to mediocre	 7 7 -2	 4-12
Light infantry javelin	4	0-2
Light infantry bow	4	0-4
From 852		
Slav and Bulgar spearmen Heavy spearmen Downgrade to mediocre	 8 -2	 4-12

Bulgar archers Bowmen Light infantry bow	7 4	0-6

Note

- Pecheneg allies (List #159 Pecheneg) in 896

156 - Khazar

568 – 1083 AD
Plain, Steppes
Command +4

The Khazars came from Central Asia near the shores of the Caspian Sea. At its height the Khazar Empire stretched from the west of Kazakhstan, through Georgia and the Crimea, and into the east of the Ukraine. The Khazars allied with the Byzantines for protection against the Umayyad Caliphate and the Rus'. To keep their independence they embraced the Jewish religion. Following the Orthodox conversion of the Kievan Rus', the Byzantines supported the combined Rus'/Pecheneg war against the Khazars. The Empire was finally absorbed by the Kievan Rus' in the 11th century.

Troop type	Pts	Units
*Nobles ** Heavy cavalry bow Heavy cavalry impact (max 6) Upgrade to elite (max 4)	11 10 +2	4-12
Horse archers Light cavalry bow Medium cavalry bow	6 9	4-24
Guard Spearmen Heavy spearmen	8	0-4
Slav warriors (all of the same type) Medium swordsmen Medium spearmen Downgrade to mediocre	7 7 -2	0-6
Slav skirmishers Light infantry javelin Light infantry bow	4	0-2
Archer levy Bowmen mediocre Light infantry bow	5 4	0-2
Levy	3	0-2
Heavy artillery	10	0-1
Fortified camp	6	0-1

Note

- Turkish allies (List #141 Central Asian Turkish)

Khazar nobles

157 - Serbo-Croatian

627 – 1180 AD
Mountain, Forest
Command +2

The Serbs and Croats were Sarmatian tribes used by the Byzantine Emperor Heraclius to fight against the Avars. In return, and on condition of converting to Christianity, they were allowed to settle in the Balkans. There they mixed with Slavs and rapidly gained independence. The Croats were subjugated by Charlemagne at the end of the 8th century. Soon afterwards they regained their independence, until they were absorbed by the Hungarians in 1089. Tensions between the Serbs and the Byzantine Empire continued until the Serbian Empire's creation in 1180.

Troop type	Pts	Units
*Nobles ** Medium cavalry impetuous Heavy cavalry impetuous Upgrade to elite (max 4)	7 9 +2	4-12
Warriors before 850 Medium swordsmen	7	6-16
Warriors from 850 Medium spearmen	7	
Only Croats Javelinmen	7	0-8
Only Serbs Bowmen	7	0-8
Light infantry bow	4	0-4
Light infantry javelin	4	0-4

158 - Magyar

650 - 1000 AD
Steppes, Plain (only in later period)
Command +3

The Magyars were native to the Urals and are the ancestors of the present-day Hungarians. In the 7th century, driven by the Pechenegs, they migrated to the Volga. In the 8th century they settled between the Don and the Carpathian mountains in what is now the Ukraine. They then began to launch raids against Bulgaria and the Frankish Empire. In 895 they crossed the Carpathians and settled in Hungary, assimilating the local Slav populations.

Troop type	Pts	Units
Early period		
*Nobles **		
Heavy cavalry bow	11	0-6
Upgrade to elite (max 4)	+2	
Horse archers		
Light cavalry bow	6	8-24
Medium cavalry bow	9	
Later period (from 896)		
*Nobles **		
Heavy cavalry bow	11	2-8
Upgrade to elite (max 4)	+2	
*Guardsmen **		
Heavy cavalry impact elite	12	0-2
Horse archers		
Light cavalry bow	6	6-16
Medium cavalry bow	9	
Slav warriors		
Medium spearmen	7	0-6
Downgrade to mediocre	-2	
Bowmen mediocre	5	0-2
Light infantry bow	4	
Fortified camp	6	0-1

159 - Pecheneg

850 - 1122 AD
Steppes
Command +3

The Pechenegs were a nomadic Turkic people living in the north west of Kazakhstan. They formed an important part of the army of the Khazars from the 9th century onwards. At the end of the 9th century they migrated to the west, crossing the Volga and the Dnieper, pushing the Magyars into Hungary. Arriving in the Ukraine on the shores of the Black Sea, they encountered the Rus' who attempted to turn them against the Byzantines. In the 11th century they crossed the Danube, entered in the Byzantine Empire and captured Thrace. In 1090 they sided with the Seljuks and besieged Constantinople. The Byzantines used the Cumans to crush the Pechenegs. In 1122 the Pechenegs were permanently destroyed by the Emperor John II Komnenos.

Troop type	Pts	Units
*Nobles **		
Heavy cavalry bow	11	0-4
Upgrade to elite	+2	
Horse archers		
Light cavalry bow	6	6-24
Medium cavalry bow	9	
Infantry		
Bowmen	7	0-4
Levy	3	
Fortified camp	6	0-1
Replace all infantry and fortified camp		
War wagon bow	10	0-4

Note

- If the war wagon option is chosen then the army cannot include either infantry or the fortified camp.

160 - Rus

862 - 1054 AD
Plain, Forest
Command +3

The Varangians (Vikings, Swedes and Danes) founded the first Rus' State at Novgorod in 862 and afterwards at Kiev in 882. This state was called "Kievan Rus'". It comprised a Varangian elite ruling a Slav population. The Rus' were very aggressive and in 911 and 943 they besieged Constantinople without success. They also fought the Khazars, Bulgars, Poles, Croats and Cumans. Between the 10th and the 11th century they faced attacks by the Pechenegs from the southern Ukraine. The power of the State of Kiev began to decline from the 11th century onwards.

Troop type	Pts	Units
*Druzhina **		
Heavy spearmen armour	10	0-4
Upgrade to elite	+2	
Heavy cavalry	9	
Magyars, Pecheneg or Turks		
Light cavalry bow	6	0-6
Medium cavalry bow	9	

Rus' spearmen * Heavy spearmen Add support	8 +1	8-24
Bowmen Light infantry bow	7 4	0-6
Light infantry javelin	4	0-2
Fortified camp	6	0-1

Note

- Viking allies (List #150 Viking and Leidang) before 1036
- Bulgar allies (List #155 Bulgar)
- Pecheneg allies (List #159 Pecheneg)
- Polish allies (List #203 Feudal Polish)

SUDAN

161 - Christian Nubian

550 – 1517 AD
Plain, Desert
Command +2

In 550 Nubia, which corresponds to what is now Sudan, was composed of three kingdoms: Nobatia, Makuria and Alodia. Nobatia converted to Christianity at the end of the 3rd century; Makuria and Alodia at the end of the 6th century. The region was cut off from the rest of Christendom by the Arabs, who were however repulsed in 671. A peace treaty remained in force until the 13th century. In 1272 the Mamluk Sultan Baybars invaded Nubia marking the start of the Egyptian intervention and the beginning of the conversion to Islam. In 1517 Nubia was annexed to Egypt by the Ottoman Turks.

Troop type	Pts	Units
Nubian noblesmen * Heavy cavalry elite	11	0-3
Nubian horsemen Medium cavalry Light cavalry javelin	7 6	2-8
Warriors on camels * Medium camelry impetuous	8	0-8
Scouts on camels Light camelry bow	7	0-2
Bowmen Downgrade to mediocre	7 -2	4-16
Light infantry bow (max 8)	4	
Nubian (all of the same type) Medium swordsmen impetuous Medium spearmen mediocre	7 5	2-8
Light infantry javelin	4	0-2

From 1174		
Bedouin horsemen Light cavalry impact Medium cavalry impact	6 8	0-6
Bedouin warriors Medium swordsmen	7	0-4

Note

- Beja allies (List #162 Beja)
- Mamluk allies (List #253 Mamluk) from 1276

Warriors on camels

162 - Beja

831 – 1500 AD
Desert
Command +2

The Beja were a nomadic people of the Sudan already known at the time of the Romans under the name of "Blemmyes". They converted to Christianity in the 6th century. In 831 they were subjugated by the Abbasids. Then they were under the influence of Arab Bedouins that had migrated from the south of Egypt. During the 10th and 11th century they controlled trade between the Fatimids and the Christian Nubians and also the pilgrims trail to Mecca (blocked by the Crusades).

Troop type	Pts	Units
Arab horsemen * Medium cavalry impact Heavy cavalry impact Upgrade to elite	8 10 +2	0-4
Arabs and Bedouins * Light cavalry impact Medium cavalry impact	6 8	2-12
Warriors on camels Medium camelry impetuous	8	6-12

Scouts on camels Light camelry bow	7	0-2
Arab warriors Medium swordsmen impetuous	7	0-4
Javelinmen Javelinmen Downgrade to mediocre	7 -2	0-8
Bowmen Downgrade to mediocre	7 -2	0-12
Light infantry bow	4	0-6

Note

- Nubian allies (List #161 Christian Nubian)

FAR EAST

163 - Burmese

500 – 1526 AD
Plain, Mountain, Forest
Command +3

This list represents the armies of the kingdoms that controlled Burma. From about 500 to 900 AD the Pyu from Tibet settled in Burma and founded several city-states including Sri Ksetra. In 849 the Kingdom of Pagan emerged and grew in power until the reign of Anawrahta (1044-1077), who unified Burma. Until the 13th century Southeast Asia was dominated by the Kingdom of Pagan and the Khmer Empire. In 1277 the Kingdom of Pagan was invaded by the Mongols. After a period of instability the kingdoms of Ava in the north and Pegu in the south restored Burmese prosperity.

Troop type	Pts	Units
*Elephant and escorts (from 1043) ** Elephant elite	16	2-6
*Horsemen ** Medium cavalry	7	0-4
Militia horsemen Medium cavalry mediocre	5	0-2
Guardsmen Medium swordsmen 2HW Upgrade to elite	8 +2	0-2
Burmese warriors Medium spearmen	7	2-8
Burmese archers Bowmen	7	2-8
Burmese crossbowmen Crossbowmen	7	0-4
Militia spearmen Medium spearmen mediocre	5	0-6
Militia archers Bowmen mediocre	5	0-6
Light infantry bow Light infantry crossbow	4	0-4
Levy	3	0-4
Light artillery	6	0-1
Fortified camp	6	0-1
After 1400		
Handgunners Light infantry firearm Upgrade to elite	4 +1	0-2
Bombard Heavy artillery	10	0-1

Note

- Siamese allies (List #262 Siam) from 1240
- Chinese allies (List #263 Yuan Chinese) from 1240

164 - Hindu Indian

545 – 1510 AD
Plain, Mountain, Forest, Desert if Rajput
Command +3

After the fall of the Guptas several kingdoms emerged in the north and centre of India. The Rajputs were warrior clans known for their impetuosity. From the 8th century the Arabs came to India and spread the Muslim religion. However their influence remained tenuous until the 12th century when the Muslims established their authority with the Ghurid Dynasty and the Delhi Sultanate. Some Hindu kingdoms remained independent, like Vijayanagara, until the Mughal Conquest.

Troop type	Pts	Units
*Indian elephants ** Elephant elite	16	2-4
*Horsemen ** Medium cavalry Heavy cavalry (max 3) Upgrade to elite (max 3)	7 9 +2	3-9
Scouts Light cavalry javelin Light cavalry bow	6	0-2
Warriors Medium swordsmen Upgrade to impetuous (all or 0)	7	2-6
Bowmen Downgrade to mediocre	7 -2	4-12
Spearmen Medium spearmen	7	0-6
Javelinmen Light infantry javelin	7 4	0-6

Light infantry bow Light infantry sling	4	0-3
Levy	3	0-4
Rajput Kingdom Indian allies (List # 260 Delhi Sultanate) No other allies		
Replace all horsemen * Heavy cavalry impetuous Upgrade to elite (max 6)	9 +2	All
Replace all Scouts Light camelry impact	7	0-2
Vijayanagar Kingdom (after 1330) No allies		
Muslim mercenaries Heavy cavalry bow	11	0-2
Royal guards Bowmen elite	7	0-2
Rocket launchers Light artillery	6	0-4
Bombard Heavy artillery	10	0-1

Note

- Hun allies (Liste #111 Hephthalite Huns)
- Tamil Indian allies (List #121 Tamil Indian)
- Tibetan allies (List #166 Tibetan)
- Muslim allies (List #136 Arab Indian)
- Muslim Indian allies (List # 260 Delhi Sultanate)

165 - Sui and Tang Chinese

581 - 755 AD
Plain, Mountain, Forest
Command +5
Strategist: Li Shimin (617-649) Tang Dynasty

The Tang dynasty replaced the Sui (581-618) dynasty, both of which are included in this list. The period of the Tang dynasty was a golden age. The Empire had never been so powerful. Li Shimin ascended the throne in 626 and subjugated the Eastern Turks in 630. The King of Tibet accepted Chinese suzerainty in 641. Li Shimin's most important achievement was the restoration of the Silk Road by controlling the Turkic tribes of the Tarim Basin. When he died in 649 he left a strong China, feared and respected by its neighbours. For a century the Tang remained strong but in the 8th century a fierce civil war ravaged the country.

Troop type	Pts	Units
Spearmen and bowmen or crossbowmen in mixed units ½ Heavy spearmen ½ Bowmen or Crossbowmen	10	2-6
Crossbowmen Bowmen Downgrade to mediocre	7 7 -2	0-6
Halberdiers Medium swordsmen 2HW Heavy swordsmen 2HW	8 9	0-2
Tribal auxiliaries Javelinmen Medium swordsmen impetuous	7	0-3
Light infantry bow	4	0-4
Light artillery Heavy artillery	6 10	0-1
Fortified camp	6	0-1
Only Sui Dynasty (581 - 623) Turkish allies (List #141 Central Asian Turkish)		
Nobles (all of the same type) * Heavy cavalry impact Cataphract Upgrade to elite	10 11 +2	2-4
Other horsemen Medium cavalry impact Heavy cavalry impact	8 10	2-4
Horse archers Light cavalry bow	6	0-3
Disaffected conscript infantry Levy	3	0-4
Fortifications	1	0-6
Only Tang Dynasty (618 - 753) Hsien-Pi allies (List #118 Hsien-Pi) Korean allies (List #122 Three Kingdoms Korean) Khotan or other city states allies (List #140 Sogdian and Central Asian City States) Turkish allies (List #141 Central Asian Turkish)		
Nobles (all of the same type) * Heavy cavalry impact Cataphract Heavy cavalry bow Upgrade to elite	10 11 11 +2	0-2
Other horsemen * Medium cavalry bow Heavy cavalry bow Upgrade to elite (max 4)	9 11 +2	4-8
Mounted crossbowmen Medium cavalry crossbow	9	0-2
Horse archers Light cavalry bow	6	2-4
Turks and Mo-Ho nomads Light cavalry bow elite	7	0-4

166 - Tibetan

600 – 1246 AD
Plain, Mountain
Command +4

From the 7th century onwards Tibet was unified under the reign of Songtsän Gampo (609-650) and Buddhism became the state religion. During the 8th and 9th centuries the Tibetans tried to expand their territory by waging war against their neighbours. Allied with the Uighur Turks and the Abbasids, they won the battle of Talas in 751 against the Tang Chinese. Their influence spread into Central Asia. Tibetans were also at war with the Abbasids for the control of Samarkand and Kabul. Succession disputes eventually divided the country. In 1246 Tibet was conquered by the Mongols.

Troop type	Pts	Units
*Horsemen (all of the same type) ** Heavy cavalry impact Cataphract Upgrade to elite (max 4)	 10 11 +2	4-12
Nomads troops Light cavalry bow Medium cavalry bow (max 4)	 6 9	0-12
Garrison spearmen Heavy spearmen Add armour	 8 +2	0-4
Garrison archers Bowmen Add pavise	 7 +1	0-4
Hill tribesmen Medium spearmen	7	0-2
Light infantry bow Light infantry javelin (max 2)	4	0-4
Heavy artillery	10	0-1
Fortified camp	6	0-1
Abbasid troops from 795 to 801		
Medium cavalry bow Heavy cavalry bow	9 11	2-4
Heavy spearmen mediocre Add support	6 +1	0-2

Nepalese allies from 640 to 703		
Medium cavalry bow *	9	4-8
Medium swordsmen impact	8	0-2
Light infantry bow	4	0-2

Note

- Nepalese allies (cf. List above)
- Khotan or Sogdian allies (List #140 Sogdian and Central Asian City States) in 707
- Nan-Chao allies (List #168 Nan-Chao and Dali) from 754 to 793

167 - Khmer Empire and Champa

800 – 1400 AD
Plain, Forest
Command +3

The Khmer Empire was founded circa 800 by Jayavarman II. The capital was established at Angkor around 950. The Khmer Empire included regions which are currently parts of Cambodia, Laos, Vietnam and Thailand. Champa was a Kingdom that controlled the south of Vietnam. The Khmer Empire and the Kingdom of Champa engaged in a relentless struggle that ended with the victory of the Khmer Empire, but it in turn declined at the end of the 14th century.

Troop type	Pts	Units
*War elephant ** Elephant	13	2-6
Horsemen Medium cavalry mediocre Upgrade to ordinary (max 2)	 5 +2	0-4
Royal guardsmen Medium spearmen elite	9	2-4
Warrior Medium spearmen	7	2-6
Conscripts Medium spearmen mediocre	5	0-6
Bowmen Light infantry bow	7 4	0-4
Light infantry crossbow	4	0-2
Artillery on wheels (from 1100) Light artillery	6	0-2
Replace war elephant with artillery mounted on elephant (from 1100) Elephant with artillery	15	
Servants Levy	3	0-3
Khmer Empire Burmese allies (List #163 Burmese) Siamese allies (List #262 Siam) from 1300		
*Khmer chariot (before 1100) ** Light chariot bow	9	0-2
Warriors with two handed axe Medium swordsmen 2HW	8	0-2
Light infantry javelin	4	0-2

Champa Kingdom Vietnamese allies (List #213 Medieval Vietnamese) from 1284 to 1287		
Replace some horsemen (from 1170) Medium cavalry crossbow	9	0-2
Light cavalry bow	6	0-2
Trebuchet (after 1280) Heavy artillery	10	0-1

168 - Nan-Chao and Dali

737 – 1253 AD
Mountain, Forest
Command +3

The Kingdom of Nan Chao (or Nanzhao) was centred around present-day Yunnan in China. Originally several tribes shared the region. In 737 they were unified with the support of the Tang Chinese. In 750 the Kingdom of Nan Chao rebelled against the Tang but it was defeated in 751 and 754. Nan Chao was then subject to the Tibetans, but in 794 they sided with the Chinese against their Tibetan overlords. During the 9th century the Kingdom was prosperous and extended into Burma, Laos, Thailand and the North of Vietnam. The Nan Chao dynasty was overthrown in 902 and, after a troubled period, the Kingdom of Dali was founded in 937. It was conquered by the Mongols in 1253.

Troop type	Pts	Units
*Nobles ** Heavy cavalry bow Heavy cavalry crossbow Upgrade to elite	 11 11 +2	0-4
Horsemen Medium cavalry bow Medium cavalry crossbow	9	2-6
Scouts Light cavalry bow Light cavalry javelin	6	0-2
Tribal auxiliaries Light cavalry bow Medium cavalry bow	 6 9	0-2
Elephant	13	0-1
Guard spearmen Medium spearmen elite	9	2-4
Others spearmen Medium spearmen	7	4-12
Bowmen (max 4) Light infantry bow (max 4)	7 4	2-8
Crossbowmen (max 4) Add pavise	7 +1	
Tribal auxiliaries Javelinmen Medium swordsmen impetuous	7	0-4
Light infantry bow	4	0-2
Fortified camp	6	0-1

Note

- Burmese allies (List #163 Burmese)
- Tang allies (List #165 Sui and Tang Chinese)
- Tibetan allies (List #166 Tibetan)
- Siamese allies (List #262 Siam)

169 - Tang and Five Dynasties Chinese

755 – 960 AD
Plain, Mountain, Forest
Command +3

Around the middle of the 8th century a great civil war weakened the Tang Empire which lost a third of its population. The 9th century was marked by peasant revolts, the longest lasting 6 years. The dynasty finally collapsed in 907 and was followed by a troubled period known as "Five Dynasties and Ten Kingdoms". The Song Dynasty emerged in 960.

Troop type	Pts	Units
*Nobles ** Heavy cavalry bow Upgrade to elite (max 2)	 11 +2	2-6
Horse archers Light cavalry bow Medium cavalry bow	 6 9	0-4
Turkish horsemen Light cavalry bow elite	7	0-3
Guardsmen Heavy spearmen elite Heavy swordsmen 2HW elite	 10 11	0-2
Spearmen and Halberdiers Heavy spearmen Heavy swordsmen 2HW Downgrade to mediocre	 8 9 -2	4-8
Bowmen Downgrade to mediocre	7 -2	2-6
Light infantry bow	4	
Crossbowmen Add pavise	7 +1	0-2
Tribal auxiliaries Javelinmen Medium swordsmen Medium swordsmen impetuous	7	0-3

Revolted peasants Levy impetuous	4	0-4
Fortified camp	6	0-1
Five Dynasties and Ten Kingdoms period		
Only Southern Han Elephant	13	0-1
Only Northern Tang Heavy swordsmen 2HW	9	0-2

Note

- Hsien-Pi allies (List #118 Hsien-Pi)
- Uighur Turks allies (List #141 Central Asian Turkish)
- Tibetan allies (List #166 Tibetan)
- Nan-Chao allies (List #168 Nan-Chao and Dali)
- Turkish allies (List #170 Shatuo Turkish)
- Liao allies (List #211 Khitan Liao)

Tang horsemen

170 - Shatuo Turkish

808 – 951 AD
Steppes, Plain after 907
Command +3

The Shatuo were a Turkic tribe that significantly influenced the history of the Chinese Tang Dynasty. In the service of Tang during the 8th century they participated actively in the civil war that ravaged China. In 808 they supported the Tang against the Tibetans. When the Tang dynasty collapsed in 907 the Shatuo founded three of the five dynasties of the so-called period of "Five Dynasties and Ten Kingdoms". Their influence ended with the conquest of China by the Khitan.

Troop type	Pts	Units
Nobles * Heavy cavalry bow Upgrade to elite (max 4)	 11 +2	2-8
Horse archers Light cavalry bow Medium cavalry bow	 6 9	4-16
Bowmen Light infantry bow	7 4	0-4
Chinese troops after 907 Liao allies (List #211 Khitan Liao)		
Chinese horsemen Heavy cavalry impact Downgrade to mediocre	 10 -2	1-3
Chinese Spearmen and Halberdiers Heavy spearmen mediocre Heavy swordsmen 2HW mediocre Upgrade to ordinary (max 4)	 6 7 +2	4-8
Chinese militia Bowmen mediocre Crossbowmen mediocre Upgrade to ordinary (max 2)	 5 5 +2	2-6
Light infantry bow Light infantry crossbow	4	
Peasants Levy Upgrade to impetuous	 3 +1	0-2

Note

- Tatar allies (List #171 Tribal Mongol)

171 - Tribal Mongol

840 – 1218 AD
Steppes
Command +3

Mongolia was dominated by Turkic tribes until 840 when the Uighurs were beaten by the Kyrgyz. From this date Mongolia was occupied mainly by people from Manchuria: the Tatars, the Naimans, the Keraits and the Ongud. The Mongolian tribes were constantly at war with each other before being unified by Genghis Khan.

Troop type	Pts	Units
Shock cavalry * Heavy cavalry bow elite Add impact	 13 +1	0-4
Mongol horsemen * Medium cavalry bow Upgrade to elite	 9 +2	8-30
Light cavalry bow Upgrade to elite	6 +1	
Dismounted horsemen Bowmen Light infantry bow	 7 4	0-4
Fortified camp	6	0-1

FEUDAL AGES

FEUDAL EUROPE

172 - NORMAN OR FRANKISH

888 – 1072 AD
Plain, Forest
Command +3
Strategist: William the Conqueror (1066)

At the start of the second half of the 9th century the Vikings ravaged the north coast of France. Soon Vikings from Denmark and Norway began to settle in Normandy. This region was given to them by King Charles the Simple in 911. The colonisation spanned more than a century and it was only under the reign of William II that ducal power prevailed. Norman adventurers sought fortune in Spain, Sicily and southern Italy, becoming involved in the epic of the Crusades. In 1066 Duke William II invaded England and defeated King Harold at the Battle of Hastings, thus becoming known as "the Conqueror".

Troop type	Pts	Units
*Milites before 1041 ** Heavy cavalry impetuous Upgrade to elite (max 8)	9 +2	6-18
*Milites from 1041 ** Medium knight impetuous Upgrade to elite (max 8)	10 +2	
Gascon scouts Light cavalry javelin	6	0-2
Norman spearmen Heavy spearmen	8	0-6
Bowmen Light infantry bow	7 4	0-4
Crossbowmen Light infantry crossbow	7 4	0-2
Gascons Light infantry javelin	4	0-2
Levy	3	0-2
Normans in Italy or Sicily (after 1041) Frankish allies (List #182 Imperial Frankish) Aghlabid allies (List #133 North African Arab)		
Sicilian javelinmen Javelinmen Light infantry javelin	7 4	0-6
Conquest of England (1066) Breton allies (List #145 Armourican Breton)		
*Replace 1/3 to 2/3 Milites ** Heavy spearmen armour	10	1/3 to 2/3
Fortified camp	6	0-1

Note

- Viking allies (List #150 Viking and Leidang) before 923

173 - ANGLO-DANISH

1014 – 1075 AD
Plain, Forest
Command +3
Strategist: Harold (1053-1066 AD)

After being repulsed at the end of the 10th century, the Danes resumed their attacks on England. In 1016 the Danish King Cnut invaded England and added it to his Empire. Danish rule lasted until 1042 when the Saxons regained control. In 1066 King Harold raced north and defeated his rebellious brother Tostig and Harald Hardrada, King of Norway. When he learnt that the Normans had landed, he rushed south again to meet them but was defeated at the Battle of Hastings. It took the Normans several years to consolidate their rule.

Troop type	Pts	Units
*Huscarls ** Heavy swordsmen 2HW elite Add armour	11 +2	2-4
*Mounted Huscarls ** Heavy cavalry elite	11	
Anglo-Saxon warriors Heavy spearmen Add armour	8 +2	4-10
Poorly equipped warriors Heavy spearmen mediocre	6	0-16
Light infantry bow	4	0-4
Light infantry sling	4	0-2
Light infantry javelin	4	0-2
Levy	3	0-2

From 1042 to 1065 Scot allies (List #152 Pre Feudal Scots)		
Norman mercenaries * Medium knight impetuous Upgrade to elite	10 +2	0-2
Replace some Huscarls * Medium swordsmen 2HW elite	10	Any

Note

- One commander can be included in a Norman mercenaries unit.
- Welsh allies (List #146 Welsh)
- Viking allies (List #150 Viking and Leidang)

174 - Anglo-Norman

1072 - 1181 AD
Plain, Forest
Command +3

William the Conqueror was crowned King of England after defeating King Harold. He had previously been the vassal of the King of France, but was now his equal. His son, Henry I, reunited control of Normandy and England. After a period of anarchy between 1135 and 1154, Henry II re-established order. He was also the Duke of Aquitaine and of Normandy. The Angevin Empire was at its height.

Troop type	Pts	Units
Knights before 1085 * Heavy cavalry impetuous Upgrade to elite (max 6)	9 +2	4-12
Knights from 1085 * Medium knight impetuous Upgrade to elite (max 6)	10 +2	
Militia and mercenaries Heavy spearmen Add support Downgrade to mediocre	8 +1 -2	4-12
Flemish pikemen Pikemen mediocre	8	0-2
Saxon archers Bowmen Downgrade to mediocre	7 -2	2-6
Light infantry bow	4	
Only in England (no French allies)		
Welsh Medium cavalry impact	8	0-2
Welsh Medium spearmen	7	0-2

Only after 1150		
Brabançon and Mercenaries Heavy cavalry impact Medium knight impact	10 11	0-2
Genoese mercenaries Crossbowmen Add pavise Upgrade to elite	7 +1 +2	0-2

Note

- Welsh allies (List #146 Welsh)
- French allies (List # 75 Feudal French)

175 - Feudal French

1072 - 1330 AD
Plain, Forest
Command +3
Strategist: Philip II Augustus (1180 - 1223)

The Capetian dynasty was established by Hugh Capet in 987. Initially the King had less power than the great Lords but his authority steadily grew. At the accession of Philip Augustus in 1180, Henry II of England controlled about one-third of France. Between 1202 and 1205 Philip took several territories from Henry's son, King John. After his victory at Bouvines in 1214 he became the most powerful King in Europe. His grandson, Louis IX or Saint Louis, participated in the seventh crusade in Egypt where he was taken prisoner and subsequently ransomed. He died during the eighth Crusade at the siege of Tunis in 1270. Philip IV the Fair was the last of the great Capetian Kings and reigned from 1285 to 1314. All his direct heirs died in a short time. Philip VI was chosen to succeed, instead of Edward III of England. This was the origin of the Hundred Years war.

Troop type	Pts	Units
Knights from 1085 * Medium knight impetuous Upgrade to elite	10 +2	4-16
Feudal or communal militia Heavy spearmen mediocre Upgrade to ordinary (max 6) Add armour (max 2)	6 +2 +2	2-10
Foot with words and axes Medium swordsmen	7	0-2
Bowmen mediocre Light infantry bow	5 4	0-4
Crossbowmen Light infantry crossbow	4	0-2
Gascons or Breton javelinmen Light infantry javelin Upgrade to elite	4 +1	0-2

Ribauds and Peasants Levy	3	0-4
Brigans Medium swordsmen mediocre	5	
From 1150		
Mercenaries Medium knight impact	11	0-2
Mounted sergeants Heavy cavalry impact	10	0-2
Genoese mercenaries Crossbowmen Add pavise Upgrade to elite	7 +1 +2	0-2

Note

- Spanish allies (List #148 Feudal Spanish) with the army led by the King of Aragon in 1213.
- Crusader allies (List #187 Later Crusader) in 1250 during the crusade of Saint Louis
- Milanese allies (List #181 Communal Italian) with Charles of Anjou from 1266 to 1285.

French knights

176 - Feudal English

1181 - 1322 AD
Plain, Forest
Command +4
Strategist: Richard I the Lionheart (1194-1199), Edward I (1264-1307 AD)

When the Crusader King Richard the Lionheart died, his brother John succeeded him. He quickly lost all Angevin possessions in France, except for Guyenne, to the French King Philip Augustus. The English barons revolted against John in 1215 and against his son Henri III in 1258, challenging the royal authority. King Edward I restored royal authority and conquered Wales in 1284 and Scotland in 1291. He had to deal with several revolts in Scotland. The Scots regained their independence following the defeat of his son, Edward II, at the Battle of Bannockburn in 1314.

Troop type	Pts	Units
*Knights and sergeants ** Medium knight impetuous Upgrade to elite (max 6)	10 +2	4-12
Mercenaries Medium knight impact	11	0-2
Mounted sergeants Heavy cavalry impact	10	0-2
Welsh or hobilars Medium cavalry impact	8	0-2
Militia and mercenaries Heavy spearmen mediocre Upgrade to ordinary (max 4)	6 +2	2-8
English and Welsh archers Bowmen Upgrade to Longbowmen (max 4)	7 +2	2-12
Crossbowmen	7	0-2
Welsh spearmen Medium spearmen	7	0-4
Sherwood slingers Light infantry sling	4	0-1
Light infantry bow	4	0-2
Irish or Welsh kerns Javelinmen Light infantry javelin	7 4	0-2
Peasants Levy	3	0-2

Note

- Welsh allies (List #146 Welsh)
- Irish allies (List #151 Feudal Irish)
- French allies (List #175 Feudal French)

177 - Feudal Scots

1124 - 1286 AD
Plain, Mountain, Forest
Command +3

This list covers the armies of Scotland from the accession of King David I until the death of Alexander III. Gaelic culture had previously dominated Scotland, but David made many changes, including the introduction of feudalism, that shows the influence of his Anglo-Norman links.

Troop type	Pts	Units
Nobles * Medium knight impetuous Heavy swordsmen armour Upgrade to elite	 10 10 +2	0-3
Spearmen Heavy spearmen Downgrade to mediocre	 8 -2	8-24
Bowmen Downgrade to mediocre	7 -2	0-3
Light infantry bow	4	
Peasants Levy	3	0-2
Fortifications	1	0-6
Fortified camp	6	0-1

Galwegian allies (Before 1162)		
Galwegian warriors * Medium swordsmen impetuous	7	2-6

Highlanders allies		
Highlanders * Medium swordsmen bow	10	2-4
Island warriors Heavy swordsmen 2HW	9	0-4

Note

- Galwegian allies (see list above)
- Highlander allies (see list above)

178 - Anglo-Irish

1172 – 1494 AD
Plain, Mountain, Forest
Command +3

In 1171 Henry II of England used the tense situation between local Irish Lords and some Anglo-Norman adventurers as an excuse to invade. He established the "Lordship of Ireland", which office was restricted to important Anglo-Norman, and later Anglo-Irish, families. The Crown-appointed Lord had limited resources and mainly relied on the support of other Anglo-Irish Lords. In 1494 Irish Laws became subject to the approval of the English Parliament.

Troop type	Pts	Units
Irish lord troops		
English nobles * Medium knight impact Heavy swordsmen armour Upgrade to elite	 11 10 +2	0-2
Hobilars (only before 1400) Medium cavalry impact Medium spearmen	 8 7	0-2
English archers Longbowmen elite	11	0-2
Others lords troops		
Anglo-Irish cavalry * Heavy cavalry impetuous Heavy cavalry	9	2-6
Irish horsemen Light cavalry javelin	6	0-2
Anglo-Irish archers Longbowmen mediocre Upgrade to ordinary (max 6)	 7 +2	4-12
Scots Galloglaich Heavy swordsmen 2HW Upgrade to elite	 9 +2	0-6
Kerns Javelinmen Light infantry javelin	 7 4	4-8
Light infantry bow	4	0-2
Fortifications	1	0-6
Fortified camp	6	0-1
Only after 1330		
Replace all English nobles * Heavy knight impact Foot knight Upgrade to elite	 13 12 +2	All
Only from 1400		
Anglo-Irish billmen Heavy swordsmen 2HW Downgrade to mediocre	 9 -2	0-6
Replace all Anglo-Irish archers Longbowmen Downgrade to mediocre Add stakes (all or none)	 9 -2 +1	2-6
Heavy artillery	10	0-1

Note

- Irish allies (List #223 Medieval Irish)

179 - Scots Isles and Highlanders

1050 – 1493 AD
Mountain
Command +3

This list covers the armies of the Hebrides, the Orkneys, Caithness and the Highlands until the death of the last Lord of the Isles. The warriors of the Isles were the descendants of Viking settlers. Their favourite weapon was the two-handed axe but some less well equipped warriors had only a sword and a shield. The Highlanders were mainly bowmen but were also able to fight efficiently in melee and are classified as medium swordsmen with bow.

Troop type	Pts	Units
Island warriors * Heavy swordsmen 2HW Upgrade to elite (max 4)	9 +2	8-24
Others warriors Heavy swordsmen mediocre	6	0-6
Irish mercenaries Medium swordsmen Add 2HW	7 +1	0-4
Highlanders		
Highlanders archers * Medium swordsmen bow	10	2-8
Scouts Light infantry bow	4	0-4
Levy	3	0-2

Galwegian allies (before 1162)		
Galwegian warriors * Medium swordsmen impetuous	7	2-6

Note

- One commander can be included in a Highlander's unit.
- Viking allies (List #150 Viking and Leidang) after 1266

180 - Normans in Sicily

1072 – 1342 AD
Plain, Mountain
Command +3
Strategist: Frederick II (1215-1250 AD)

Starting in 1059 the Normans Robert and Roger Guiscard ousted the Byzantines from southern Italy and took Sicily from the Muslims. Sicily became a Kingdom under Roger's son in 1130 and was taken by Emperor Henry IV in 1194. His son Emperor Frederic II fought against the Pope and in 1266 the island was conquered by Charles of Anjou, the French King's brother. Many of Charles' French supporters were massacred in 1282 at the start of the War of the Sicilian Vespers, in which Peter III of Aragon, a descendant of Robert Guiscard and married to the daughter of the last Hohenstaufen King of Sicily, took the island.

Troop type	Pts	Units
Feudal knights * Medium knight impetuous Upgrade to elite	10 +2	4-8
Italian mercenaries Medium knight impact	11	0-4
Saracen nobles Heavy cavalry impact	10	0-2
Berber cavalry Light cavalry javelin	6	0-3
Sicilian spearmen Heavy spearmen mediocre Upgrade to ordinary (max 2)	6 +2	0-6
Sicilian crossbowmen Crossbowmen Light infantry crossbow	7 4	0-2
Saracens archers Bowmen mediocre Light infantry bow	5 4	2-8
Saracens close fighter (before 1267) Medium swordsmen	7	0-2
Peasants Levy	3	0-2
Only before 1200		
Grecs Medium swordsmen	7	0-4
Frederick II (1215 - 1250)		
German knights Medium knight impact	11	0-6
Replace all Sicilian crossbowmen by mixed units ½ Heavy spearmen ½ Crossbowmen	10	0-4
Saracens auxiliaries Light cavalry bow Light cavalry javelin	6	0-4
Peter III of Aragon (1282 - 1301)		
Aragonese lancers Light cavalry impact	6	1-3
Almughavars Medium swordsmen impact elite Medium spearmen elite	10 9	2-8
Aragonese crossbowmen Crossbowmen Light infantry crossbow	7 4	0-3

Note

- Crusader allies (List #187 Later Crusader) during the crusade from 1228 to 1232
- Italian allies (List #181 Communal Italian) before 1282
- Aragon allies (List #148 Feudal Spanish) after 1302

181 - Communal Italian

1029 – 1320 AD
Plain, Mountain
Command +4

During the 11th century, power in northern and centre of Italy rested on "great families" communal assemblies governing cities. Southern Italy was then under Norman domination. In 1162, Emperor Frederick I Barbarossa sought to expand his domination to both the Pope and the free city states which did not recognize his authority. He was beaten at Legano in 1176. Communal assemblies' independence was recognized in 1183. The 13th century was a period of great prosperity, trade development and enrichment of cities in northern Italy.

Troop type	Pts	Units
Italian knights before 1150 * Heavy cavalry impact Upgrade to elite	 10 +2	2-6
Italian knights from 1150 * Medium knight impact Upgrade to elite	 11 +2	
Feudal knights before 1150 Heavy cavalry impetuous	9	0-6
Feudal knights from 1150 Medium knight impetuous	10	
Communal militia Heavy spearmen mediocre Upgrade to ordinary (max 6) Add pavise (max 4)	 6 +2 +1	4-12
Communal crossbowmen Crossbowmen Add pavise	 7 +1	2-4
Light infantry crossbow	4	
Halberdiers Heavy swordsmen 2HW	9	0-2
Light infantry bow	4	0-2
Levy	3	0-2
Carroccio and guardsmen Fortified camp	6	0-1
Only from 1150 AD		
Plaustrella War wagon (no shooting)	8	0-3
Only from 1200 AD		
French mercenaries Medium knight impetuous elite	12	0-2
Mounted crossbowmen Light cavalry crossbow Medium cavalry crossbow	 6 9	0-2
Replace some crossbowmen by mixed units ½ Heavy spearmen ½ Crossbowmen	10	0-4
Replace some communal militia Medium spearmen	7	0-4
Only Papal Italian Byzantine allies (List #128 Nikephorian Byzantine) Norman allies (List #172 Norman or Frankish) Sicilian allies (List #180 Normans in Sicily)		
Papal guardsmen * Heavy spearmen armour elite	12	1

Note

- Germanic allies (List #182 Imperial Frankish or List #183 Feudal German)

182 - Imperial Frankish

888 – 1050 AD
Plain, Forest
Command +3

After the final division of Charlemagne's Empire, the eastern part, including Germany and Italy, kept the title of Roman Empire. The Empire began with the coronation of Otto II in 962 who took the title of *Imperator Romanorum*. This was the future "Holy Roman Empire". During the 10th century, the Magyars launched several raids and devastated Moravia and Italy.

Troop type	Pts	Units
Milites * Heavy cavalry impetuous Upgrade to elite (max 4)	 9 +2	4-16
Saxons and Thuringians Medium cavalry Heavy cavalry	 7 9	0-4
Spearmen Heavy spearmen Add armour (max 4)	 8 +2	4-16
Bowmen Downgrade to mediocre	7 -2	0-4
Light infantry bow	4	
Levy	3	0-2

Note

- Italian allies (List #181 Communal Italian)
- Western Slavs allies (List #153 Slav)
- Burgundian allies (List #172 Norman and Frankish)
- Polish allies (List #203 Feudal Polish)

183 - Feudal German

1051 – 1330 AD
Plain, Forest
Command +3
Strategist: Frederic II (1218-1250 AD)

The Holy Roman Empire was far from being unified. It was rather a confederation of principalities and city states more or less independent from central power. The Pope established the emperor's legitimacy at his coronation in Rome. All important decisions had to be approved by the imperial parliament (named the Diet). Emperor Frederick II affirmed imperial power over Italy and Sicily. He got in conflict with the Pope and excommunicated twice, despite participating to the crusade and delivering Jerusalem.

Troop type	Pts	Units
*Nobles, Mercenaries and knights from religious orders **		4-10
Medium knight	10	
Medium knight impetuous	10	
Medium knight impact	11	
Upgrade to elite (max 4)	+2	
Mounted sergeants		0-2
Heavy cavalry impact	10	
Mounted crossbowmen		0-2
Light cavalry crossbow	6	
Medium cavalry crossbow	9	
Hungarians		0-4
Light cavalry bow	6	
Spearmen or halberdiers		2-8
Heavy spearmen	8	
Heavy swordsmen 2HW	9	
Downgrade to mediocre	-2	
Mercenaries		0-2
Heavy spearmen armour	10	
Heavy swordsmen armour 2HW	11	
Low Country pikemen		0-2
Pikemen mediocre	8	
Crossbowmen	7	2-4
Downgrade to mediocre	-2	
Light infantry crossbow	4	
Bowmen	7	0-2
Downgrade to mediocre	-2	
Light infantry bow	4	
Free canton militia		0-6
Medium spearmen	7	
Downgrade to mediocre	-2	
Heerban		0-2
Levy	3	
Fortified camp	6	0-1

Note

- Leidang allies (List #150 Viking and Leidang)
- Italian allies (List #181 Communal Italian)
- Polish allies (List #203 Feudal Polish)
- Hungarian allies (List #204 Feudal Hungarian)

Mounted crossbowmen

CRUSADES

184 - Komnenan Byzantine

1071 – 1204 AD
Plain, Mountain
Command +6
Strategist: Alexis Comnène (1078-1116 AD)

After the disaster of Manzikert in 1071, the Byzantine Empire lost most of Anatolia, its main recruitment base. In 1081, Alexis Comnene acceded to the throne of an Empire threatened by the Turks, the Pechenegs and the Normans of Robert Guiscard who coveted the throne of Constantinople. He successfully controlled the arrival of the Crusaders in 1096 and took this opportunity to consolidate his position in Asia Minor. His successors, John II and Manuel I, carried on strengthening the Empire. However, the Venetians took advantage of the 4th crusade and captured Constantinople in 1204, laying the foundation of the Eastern Latin Empire.

Troop type	Pts	Units
Skythikon and Vardariotai		4-8
Light cavalry bow	6	
Medium cavalry bow	9	
Tourkopouloi, Alans and Bulgars		0-4
Light cavalry bow	6	
Upgrade to elite	+1	

Varagian guardsmen * Heavy swordsmen 2HW elite Add armour	11 +2	0-2
Kontaroi Heavy spearmen mediocre	6	0-4
Bowmen mediocre Upgrade to ordinary (max 2)	5 +2	2-6
Light infantry bow	4	
Light infantry javelin	4	0-2
Fortified camp	6	0-1
Only before 1150 Serbian allies (List #157 Serbo-Croatian) Cuman allies (List #207 Cuman)		
Kavallarioi * Heavy cavalry impact Downgrade to mediocre	10 -2	4-8
Latinikon Medium knight impact Upgrade to elite (max 2)	11 +2	0-4
Fanatic Slavs (Manichaeans) Medium swordsmen impetuous	7	0-2
Only from 1150 Norman allies (List #180 Normans in Sicily) Armenian allies (List #185 Cilician Armenian) Crusader allies (List #187 Later Crusader)		
Kavallarioi * Medium knight impact	11	2-4
Latinikon Medium knight impact Upgrade to elite (max 3)	11 +2	2-6

Note

- One commander can be included in a Varangian guardsmen unit.
- Seljuk Turk allies (List #195 Seljuk Turk)

185 - Cilician Armenian

1071 - 1375 AD
Plain, Mountain
Command +3

The Armenian Kingdom was conquered by the Byzantines in 1045. After the battle of Manzikert in 1071, the Seljuks took control of the region. Escaping servitude, prince Rupen led some of his compatriots into Cilicia in southern Asia Minor. Hosted by the Byzantines, he rebelled and established the Armenian Kingdom of Cilicia. The new Kingdom gained an important ally with the arrival of the Crusaders in the region. For two centuries, Armenians and Crusaders were to be sometimes allies or enemies. Mongols coming in the 13th century brought a new ally for the Armenians. When the Mongols were defeated by the Mamluks, the Armenians turned to the Franks of Cyprus. However, this did not prevent the fall of the Kingdom in 1375 after the capture of their capital by the Mamluks.

Troop type	Pts	Units
Armenian noblesmen before 1100 * Heavy cavalry impetuous Upgrade to elite (max 4)	9 +2	4-12
Armenian noblesmen from 1100 * Medium knight impetuous Upgrade to elite (max 4)	10 +2	
Armenian spearmen Medium spearmen Heavy spearmen Downgrade to mediocre	7 8 -2	4-12
Bowmen Downgrade to mediocre	7 -2	2-6
Light infantry bow	4	
Bedouin horsemen Light cavalry impact	6	0-3
Fortified camp	6	0-1
After 1150		
Templars and Hospitallers Medium knight impact elite	13	0-2
Frankish mercenaries Heavy spearmen armour Crossbowmen	10 7	0-2

Note

- Crusader allies (List #186 Crusader or List #187 Later Crusader) before 1264
- Lusignan allies (List #188 Frankish Cyprus) from 1300
- Seljuk Turk allies (List #195 Seljuk Turk) from 1128 to 1246
- Ilkhanid allies (List #255 Ilkhanid Mongol) from 1260

186 - Crusader

1096 – 1147 AD
Plain, Mountain, Desert
Command +2 or +3 from 1098 to 1099

At the end of the 11th century, the Byzantine Emperor Alexis Commene appealed to the West for assistance against the Seljuks. He gained the support of the Pope who launched the 1st crusade in 1095. The People's crusade led by Peter the hermit was exterminated shortly after its arrival in Asia. Thereafter, the French barons entered Anatolia with the help of the Byzantines. They took Antioch,

Edessa and finally sacked Jerusalem in 1099. As a result of the first crusade, the Franks settled permanently in Palestine and founded four fiefs: the County of Edessa, the Principality of Antioch, the County of Tripoli and the Kingdom of Jerusalem.

Troop type	Pts	Units
*Crusaders ** Medium knight impetuous Upgrade to elite (max 6)	 10 +2	4-12
Sergeants with spears Heavy spearmen Downgrade to mediocre	 8 -2	4-10
Sergeants with crossbow Crossbowmen Add pavise	 7 +1	2-6
Bowmen Downgrade to mediocre	7 -2	0-4
Light infantry bow	4	
Byzantine Turcopoles Light cavalry bow Medium cavalry bow	 6 9	0-3
Fanatical pilgrims Levy impetuous	4	0-6
Fortified camp	6	0-1
Entre 1098 et 1099 No allies and no Turcopoles		
*Replace some Crusaders ** Heavy spearmen armour Upgrade to elite (max 6)	 10 +2	0-8
After 1100		
Replace all Turcopoles Light cavalry bow Medium cavalry bow	 6 9	0-2
Maronites and Syrians Bowmen mediocre Light infantry bow	 5 4	0-2

Note

- A maximum of 6 mounted or dismounted crusaders can become Elite.
- Armenian allies (List #185 Cilician Armenian)
- Syrian allies (List #197 Syrian) after 1100

187 - Later Crusader

1147 - 1303 AD
Plain, Mountain, Desert
Command +3

The city of Edessa fell into the hands of the Turks in 1144 and the Crusaders situation became critical. A new crusade was launched in 1147 with the King of France Louis VII and the German Emperor Conrad III but it was a failure. In 1187, Saladin took over Jerusalem and the third crusade was launched with Richard the Lionheart, Philippe Auguste and Frederic Barbarossa Ist. It strengthened the position of the Crusaders but Richard, despite his victory at Arsuf in 1191, was unable to retake Jerusalem. In all there were to be nine crusades. Some of them had goals that were not the Holy Land (capture of Byzantium in 1204, attack on Egypt and on Tunisia). At the end of the 13th century, Muslims had captured Antioch (1268), Tripoli (1289) and Acre (1291).

Troop type	Pts	Units
*Crusader and Templars ** Medium knight impetuous Medium knight impact (max 4) Upgrade to elite (max 4)	 10 11 +2	4-10
Turcopoles Light cavalry bow Medium cavalry bow	 6 9	0-2
Bedouins Light cavalry impact	6	0-1
Sergeants with spears Heavy spearmen Downgrade to mediocre Add armour (max 4)	 8 -2 +2	4-10
Sergeants with crossbow Crossbowmen Add pavise	 7 +1	2-6
Maronites and Syrians Bowmen mediocre Light infantry bow	 5 4	0-2
Light infantry bow Light infantry crossbow	4	0-2
Fortified camp	6	0-1
Richard the Lionheart (1191 - 1192)		
Replace sergeants with crossbow by mixed units (all or none) ½ Heavy spearmen ½ Crossbowmen	10	All or none

Note

- Bedouin allies (List #139 Dynastic Bedouin)
- French allies (List #175 Feudal French) or German allies (List #183 Feudal German) for the second crusade in 1148
- Byzantine allies (List #184 Komnenan Byzantine) from 1163 to 1169
- Armenian allies (List #185 Cilician Armenian)
- Fatimid allies (List #194 Fatimid Egyptian) in 1167
- Syrian allies (List #197 Syrian)
- Mongol allies (List #218 Mongol Empire) after 1299

188 - FRANKISH CYPRUS

1192 - 1489 AD
Plain, Mountain
Command +3

Richard the Lionheart conquered Cyprus during the 3rd crusade in 1191. He hands over the island to Guy de Lusignan, former King of Jerusalem, landless following Saladin's conquest. In 1228, Emperor Frederick II reclaimed the Kingdom's suzerainty but was beaten by an alliance of the barons. In 1291, after the fall of Acre, the order of St. John settled in Cyprus before moving to Rhodes. At the end of the 14th century, Cyprus lost its independance and became a Genovese and then a Venetian protectorate in 1473. Venice annexed the island in 1489.

Troop type	Pts	Units
*Knights before 1330 **		
Medium knight impetuous	10	2-4
Upgrade to elite	+2	
*Knights from 1330 **		
Heavy knight impetuous	12	
Upgrade to elite	+2	
Mercenary before 1330		
Medium knight impact	11	0-2
Mercenary from 1330		
Heavy knight impact	13	
Turcopoles		
Light cavalry bow	6	0-2
Medium cavalry bow	9	
Spearmen		
Heavy spearmen	8	2-6
Add armour (max 2)	+2	
Crossbowmen	7	2-8
Add pavise	+1	
Bowmen mediocre	5	2-6
Upgrade to ordinary (max 2)	+2	
Light infantry bow	4	
Levy	3	0-2
Fortified camp	6	0-1
Onl y from 1330		
Bulgars, Tatars or Turkomans		
Light cavalry bow	6	0-6
Light cavalry bow elite	7	
Medium cavalry bow	9	
Almughavars mercenaries		
Medium swordsmen impact elite	10	0-2
Medium spearmen elite	9	
Only from 1291 to 1459		
Hospitallers		
Heavy knight impact elite	15	0-2
From 1474		
Italian stradiots		
Light cavalry javelin	6	0-2
Upgrade to elite	+1	
Italian halberdiers		
Heavy swordsmen 2HW	9	0-2
Add armour	+2	
Italian handgunners		
Light infantry firearm	4	0-2
Upgrade to elite	+1	

Note

- Mamluk allies (List #253 Mamluk) from 1460 to 1464

189 - EASTERN LATIN EMPIRE

1204 - 1261 AD
Plain, Mountain
Command +3

The Eastern Latin Empire was founded by Frankish lords of the 4th crusade after the capture of Constantinople. Baudouin of Flanders was elected Emperor and introduced feudal customs. He divided the Empire, which included Greece and part of Asia Minor, between several barons and his Venetian allies. The Empire was however attacked from all sides and the Franks were faced with the hostility of the Greek population. At the battle of Adrianople in 1205, the Franks were defeated by the Bulgarians of Tsar Kalojan. The Empire was reduced gradually and in 1261, the Byzantines took back the city by surprise and ousted the Franks from Constantinople.

Troop type	Pts	Units
Frankish knights		
Medium knight impetuous	10	4-10
Upgrade to elite (max 6)	+2	
Greek horsemen		
Medium cavalry impact	8	0-3
Heavy cavalry impact	10	
Downgrade to mediocre	-2	
Turks or Bulgars		
Light cavalry bow	6	0-2
Medium cavalry bow	9	
Frankish spearmen		
Heavy spearmen	8	0-6
Downgrade to mediocre	-2	
Frankish crossbowmen		
Crossbowmen	7	0-2
Add pavise	+1	
Greek archers		
Bowmen mediocre	5	2-12
Light infantry bow (max 6)	4	

Greek Javelinmen Javelinmen Light infantry javelin	7 4	0-4
Fortified camp	6	0-1

Note
- Seljuk Turk allies (List #195 Seljuk Turk)
- Cuman allies (List #207 Cuman)
- Byzantine allies (List #245 Later Byzantine)
- Catalan allies (List #248 Catalan Company)

190 - Order of St John

1291 - 1522 AD
Plain, Mountain
Command +4

The order of Saint John was an Hospitaller order created in the Holy Land during the 11th century. It settled successively in Jerusalem, Cyprus, Rhodes, Malta and Rome. During the Crusades, the hospitallers held strongholds such as the "Krak des chevaliers" in Syria. At the fall of Acre in 1291, they withdrew to Cyprus where Guy de Lusignan, the former King of Jerusalem, was already established. In 1310, they conquered Rhodes from the Byzantines and settled there until 1522.

Troop type	Pts	Units
Hospitaller knights * Medium knight impact elite Heavy swordsmen armour elite	13 12	2-4
Others knights Medium knight impetuous Heavy swordsmen armour	10	0-4
Turcopoles Light cavalry bow Medium cavalry bow	6 9	0-2
Colonists Heavy spearmen mediocre	6	0-6
Colonists Bowmen mediocre Crossbowmen mediocre	5	2-6
Mercenaries crossbowmen Crossbowmen Add pavise	7 +1	0-4
Light infantry bow Light infantry crossbow	4	0-6
From 1330		
Replace all Hospitaller knights * Heavy knight impact elite Foot knight elite	15 14	All
Replace all others knights Heavy knight impact Foot knight	13 12	All
From 1450		
Halberdiers Heavy swordsmen 2HW Add armour	9 +2	0-2
Handgunners Light infantry firearm Upgrade to elite	4 +1	0-2
Light artillery Heavy artillery	6 10	0-1

Note
- Armenian allies (List #185 Cilician Armenian) from 1300 to 1350.

Halberdiers

MUSLIMS

191 - Buyid

927 – 1063 AD
Plain, Mountain
Command +3

The Buyids were a Muslim Shi'ia dynasty which reigned, from Baghdad, over Persia during the 10th and 11th centuries. A branch of the Buyids reigned over Iraq from 932 to 1029 before being replaced by the Ghaznavids. The other branch reigned over Iran from 933 to 1063 and was replaced by the Seljuks. From Baghdad, the Buyid Emir supported the Abbasid Caliphate. He has no more than a theorecial power, but after all ensuring the Buyids' Emir legitimacy.

Troop type	Pts	Units
Dailami infantry * Medium swordsmen impact elite Add support	10 +1	6-18
Others Dailamis Bowmen Light infantry bow	7 4	0-4

Kurds Medium cavalry impact Heavy cavalry impact	8 10	0-2
Bedouins Medium cavalry impact Light cavalry impact	8 6	0-3
Fortified camp	6	0-1
Only Buyid from Baghdad Saffarid allies (List #137 Khurasanian) Bedouin allies (List #139 Dynastic Bedouin)		
Turkish ghulams * Heavy cavalry bow Upgrade to elite	11 +2	2-8
Elephant	13	0-1
Indian mercenary Medium swordsmen impetuous	7	0-2
Levy	3	0-2

Note

- Armenian allies (List #130 Bagratid Armenian)
- Kurdish allies (List #192 Dynastic Kurdish)

192 - Dynastic Kurdish

950 – 1085 AD
Plain, Mountain
Command +3

After the fall of the Abbasids, the Kurdish dynasties gained power in the regions of modern days Azerbaijan, east of Turkey and north of Iraq. These were the Shaddadids, the Rawadides, the Annazides, the Hasanuyides and the Marwanids. The Kurdish dynasties were deposed by the Seljuk Turks.

Troop type	Pts	Units
Nobles * Heavy cavalry impact Upgrade to elite	10 +2	0-4
Others horsemen Medium cavalry impact Heavy cavalry impact	8 10	8-24
Scouts Light cavalry impact Light cavalry javelin	6	0-4
Bowmen Light infantry bow	7 4	0-4
Levy	3	0-2
Only Marwanids		
Turkish ghulams * Heavy cavalry bow Upgrade to elite	11 +2	0-3
Only Annazids		
Bedouins Light cavalry impact Medium cavalry impact	6 8	0-8

Note

- Buyid allies (List #191 Buyid)

193 - Ghaznavid

962 – 1187 AD
Plain, Mountain, Steppes
Command +4
Strategist: Mahmoud (997-1030 AD)

The Ghaznavids issue from a dynasty of Turkish origin founded at the end of the 10th century by Samanids slave-guards. Following Samanids' power collapse, the Ghaznavids took control of Afghanistan and Punjab and established their capital at Ghazni in Afghanistan. Sultan Mahmoud extended his influence to Iran and led seventeen expeditions in northern India bringing back huge booty. This was the golden age of the Ghaznavids. In 1040, they were defeated by the Seljuk Turks in Dandanaqan and lost their western territories. Ghazni was taken by the Ghurids in 1149. They moved the capital to Lahore where they ruled until 1187.

Troop type	Pts	Units
Turkish ghulams * Heavy cavalry bow Upgrade to elite (max 6)	11 +2	4-10
Turks and Nomads Light cavalry bow Medium cavalry bow	6 9	2-6
Elephant * Upgrade to elite	13 +3	0-3
Arabs Light cavalry impact Light cavalry javelin	6	0-3
Kurds Medium cavalry impact Heavy cavalry impact	8 10	0-2
Ghaznavid infantry Bowmen	7	0-3
Ghaznavid infantry ½ Heavy spearmen ½ Bowmen	10	
Afghans Medium spearmen	7	0-2
Dailami infantry Medium swordsmen impact elite Add support	10 +1	0-2

Indian warriors Medium swordsmen impetuous	7	0-2
Indian or afghan archers Bowmen mediocre Light infantry bow	5 4	0-2
Indian skirmishers Light infantry javelin	4	0-2
Naffatun Light infantry firearm	4	0-1
Heavy artillery	10	0-1
Fortifications	1	0-6
Fortified camp	6	0-1

Note

- Qarakanid allies (List #141 Central Asian Turkish)
- Hindu allies (List # 164 Hindu Indian)

Fatimid infantry

194 - Fatimid Egyptian

969 - 1171 AD
Plain, Desert
Command +4

The Fatimids were Shia Arabs established in the Maghreb at the time of the Umayyad conquest (see Arabs in North Africa). In 969, they conquered Egypt and founded the city of Cairo as the new capital. They extended their conquests to Syria, Malta and part of Sicily. From 1060, the territory controlled by the Fatimids was reduced to Egypt but in 1098, they captured Jerusalem before being ousted by the Crusaders one year later. Thereafter, they briefly took Cairo in 1168. In 1171 Saladin put an end to the Fatimid dynasty and founds the Ayyubid dynasty.

Troop type	Pts	Units
*Arabian and Syrian lancers ** Heavy cavalry impact Upgrade to elite (max 6 in total)	10 +2	4-12
*Mamluks ** Heavy cavalry bow (max 6) Upgrade to elite (max 6 in total)	11 +2	
Abid Sudanese ½ Medium spearmen ½ Bowmen	9	2-6
Abid Guard Medium swordsmen elite	9	0-1
Others Abid archers Bowmen Light infantry bow	7 4	0-2
Crossbowmen	7	0-1
Warriors with two-handed mace Medium swordsmen 2HW	8	0-1
Sudanese warriors Medium swordsmen Medium swordsmen impetuous	7	0-4
Saririya phalanx Heavy spearmen Pikemen mediocre	8	0-2
Berber javelinmen Javelinmen Light infantry javelin	7 4	0-4
Ahdath militia Levy	3	0-2
Fortified camp	6	0-1
Before 1074		
Berber horsemen Light cavalry javelin	6	0-4
Berber spearmen Heavy spearmen mediocre support	7	0-4
Dailami infantry Medium swordsmen impact elite Add support	10 +1	0-2
From 1074 Crusader allies (List #187 Later Crusader) Syrian allies (List #197 Syrian)		
Turkomans Light cavalry bow elite	7	0-2
Bedouins Light cavalry impact Medium cavalry impact	6 8	0-4
Armenians Bowmen	7	2-4
Heavy artillery	10	0-1

Note

- A maximum of 6 Arabian / Syrian lancers or Mamluks can be upgraded to elite.

195 - SELJUK TURK

1038 – 1276 AD
Plain, Mountain, Steppes
Command +5
Strategist: Alp Arsan (1063-1072 AD)

The Seljuk Turks originated north of the Aral Sea. They migrated south and captured Khorasan in the 10th century. In 1038, Tugrul Bey proclaimed himself Sultan and conquered Baghdad. His nephew, Alp Arsan, extended the Seljuk Empire from its capital Tehran. He won a great victory over the Byzantines at the battle of Manzikert in 1071, and gave rise to the branch of the Seljuks of Anatolia (or Rum Sultanate). At its peak, the Seljuk Empire encompassed Iran, Iraq, Anatolia, Syria and most of Central Asia. Civil wars brought the Empire's downfall. The Rums of Anatolia stood up to the Crusaders until 1276.

Troop type	Pts	Units
*Nobles ** Heavy cavalry bow Upgrade to elite	 11 +2	2-8
*Turkomans ** Light cavalry bow elite Medium cavalry bow	 7 9	6-18
Bedouin (only before 1128) Light cavalry javelin	6	0-2
Bowmen Light infantry bow	7 4	0-3
Javelinmen Light infantry javelin	7 4	0-4
Fortified camp	6	0-1
Only in Syria and before 1128 Syrian allies (List #197 Syrian)		
Replace some Nobles by Kurdish and Syrian lancers Heavy cavalry impact Upgrade to elite	 10 +2	0-4
Ahdath militia Levy	3	0-2
Only Eastern Seljuks Dailami allies (List #191 Buyid) Ghaznavid allies (List #193 Ghaznavid) Khwarazmian allies (List #200 Khwarazmian)		
Elephant	13	0-1
Dailami infantry Medium swordsmen impact elite Add support	 10 +1	0-2
Only not in Syria and before 1128 Turkish allies (List #141 Central Asian Turkish) Saffarid allies (List #137 Khurasanian)		
From 1220 to 1276 (Rum Sultanate) Ilkhanid allies (List #255 Ilkhanid Mongol) Khwarazmian allies (List #200 Khwarazmian)		
Frankish knights Medium knight impetuous Upgrade to elite	 10 +2	0-2
Armenians and Georgians Heavy cavalry impetuous Upgrade to elite	 9 +2	
Byzantines Heavy cavalry impact	10	
Heavy spearmen Downgrade to mediocre	8 -2	0-2
Crossbowmen	7	0-2

Note

- One commander can be included in a Turkoman unit.
- Bedouin allies (List #139 Dynastic Bedouin) before 1092

196 - BERBER

1039 – 1574 AD
Plain, Mountain, Desert
Command +3 or +4 for Almoravids

Several Berber dynasties (ethnic groups originating from North Africa) emerged in the Maghreb during the Middle Ages. From 1039, the Almoravids dominated Morocco and then entered Spain and reunified the peninsula until 1142. Thereafter, the Almohads who took over between 1145 and 1269 expanded control to the entire coast of North Africa up to Egypt. The Marinids supplanted the Almohads in Morocco. The Hafsids, previously allies of the Almohad dynasty, took control of Tunisia and ousted the Marinids out of Morocco. The Berber territories were conquered by the Ottomans during the 16th century.

Troop type	Pts	Units
*Berber nobles ** Medium cavalry Upgrade to elite	 7 +2	0-2
*Berber horsemen ** Light cavalry javelin	6	6-16
Christian knights Medium knight impetuous Upgrade to elite	 10 +2	0-3
Turkish mercenaries Light cavalry bow elite	7	0-2

Christian crossbowmen		0-2
Crossbowmen	7	
Add pavise	+1	
Berber spearmen		2-12
Heavy spearmen	8	
Add support	+1	
Downgrade to mediocre	-2	
Berber archers		2-6
Bowmen	7	
Downgrade to mediocre	-2	
Light infantry bow	4	
Berber and African javelinmen		0-6
Javelinmen	7	
Light infantry javelin	4	
Light infantry sling Light infantry crossbow	4	0-2
Fortified camp	6	0-1
Almoravids (from 1042 to 1145)		
Lamtuna and Black Guard *		2-6
Heavy spearmen	8	
Upgrade to elite	+2	
Add support	+1	
African warriors		0-4
Medium swordsmen	7	
Add support	+1	
Tuaregs		0-4
Medium camelry impetuous	8	
Upgrade to elite	+2	
Only after 1145		
Tuaregs		0-2
Medium camelry impetuous	8	
Upgrade to elite	+2	
Bedouins		0-2
Light camelry bow	7	
Medium camelry bow	10	
Almohads (from 1145 to 1269)		
Arab spearmen		3-6
Medium cavalry impact	8	
Downgrade to mediocre	-2	
Black Guard *		0-2
Heavy spearmen elite	10	
Marinids (after 1269)		
Christian spearmen		0-2
Heavy spearmen	8	
Almughavars		0-2
Medium swordsmen impact elite	10	
Medium spearmen elite	9	

Note

- Christian knights cannot be used with Tuaregs or Bedouins
- Andalusian allies (List #134 Andalusian Arab) before 1269

197 - Syrian

1092 – 1286 AD
Plain, Mountain, Desert
Command +3

After the death of Seljuk Sultan Malik Shah in 1092, more or less independent States emerged in Syria. They were the sultanates of Aleppo, Antioch, Damascus and Jerusalem and smaller kingdoms in Haman, Homs, Shaizar and Tripoli. Division eased the implantation of the first Crusaders in 1096. Subsequently many conflicts opposed the Crusaders to the Syrians but it was not uncommon for them to be allies. From 1286, the Mamluks of Egypt took control of Syria.

Troop type	Pts	Units
Turkish ghulams *		2-4
Heavy cavalry bow	11	
Upgrade to elite	+2	
Syrians, Kurds and Armenians		4-8
Medium cavalry impact	8	
Heavy cavalry impact	10	
Upgrade to elite (max 4)	+2	
Turkomans		0-8
Light cavalry bow elite	7	
Medium cavalry bow	9	
Bedouins		0-6
Light cavalry impact	6	
Medium cavalry impact	8	
Militia		0-4
Heavy spearmen mediocre	6	
Add support	+1	
Mercenaries		0-2
Crossbowmen	7	
Heavy spearmen	8	
Bowmen	7	0-3
Downgrade to mediocre	-2	
Light infantry bow	4	
Ghazis		0-3
Medium swordsmen impetuous	7	
Javelinmen	7	0-2
Light infantry javelin	4	
Ahdath militia		0-2
Levy	3	
Fortified camp	6	0-1

Note

- Crusader allies (List #186 Crusader or List #187 Later Crusader)
- Khwarazmian allies (List #200 Khwarazmian) in 1246

FEUDAL EASTERN EUROPE

203 - Feudal Polish

966 – 1333 AD
Plain, Forest
Command +3

Poland was founded in 966 by King Mieszko I. During the Middle Ages, it became a very important state of Central Europe. In 1138, its power declined and Poland was dismantled into four Duchies until 1320. King Władysław I reunited the country. Located at the crossroads of the Christian, Orthodox, Pagan and Muslim worlds, the Kingdom of Poland suffered many foreign agressions, such as the Mongol invasion in the 13th century. However, their most important conflict occured against the order of Teutonic Knights. This army list ends with the death of Władysław I in 1333.

Troop type	Pts	Units
*Nobles **		
Heavy cavalry impetuous	9	4-10
Upgrade to elite (max 4)	+2	
Spearmen		
Heavy spearmen	8	2-10
Peasants with bow		
Bowmen	7	2-12
Light infantry bow (max 6)	4	
Peasants with sling		
Light infantry sling	4	0-4
Levy	3	0-2
After 1150		
*Replace all nobles **		
Medium knight impetuous	10	All
Upgrade to elite (max 4)	+2	
After 1242		
Russian mercenaries		
Heavy cavalry bow	11	0-2
Lithuanians		
Light cavalry javelin	6	0-3
Light infantry bow	4	
Hungarians or Cumans		
Light cavalry bow	6	0-2
Peasants with heavy axe		
Medium swordsmen 2HW	8	0-2

Note

- Viking allies (List #150 Viking and Leidang) before 1150
- Slav allies (List #153 Slav) before 1150
- Russian allies (List #160 Russian) before 1150
- Germanic allies (List #183 Feudal German)
- Hungarian allies (List #204 Feudal Hungarian)
- Teutonic allies (List #209 Teutonic Knights) after 1150

204 - Feudal Hungarian

1001 – 1245 AD
Plain, Steppes
Command +3

Upon the Magyars settling process in 1001, King Saint Stephen founded the Kingdom of Hungary. The Kingdom experienced a rapid development despite the terrible Mongolian invasion of 1241-1242. Hungary became a major European power and famed gelded horses were highly sought after. Croatia joined the Kingdom of Hungary in 1102.

Troop type	Pts	Units
*Hungarian nobles **		
Heavy cavalry impetuous	9	2-6
Upgrade to elite	+2	
Horse archers		
Light cavalry bow	6	4-12
Szekelers		
Light cavalry bow elite	7	0-6
Medium cavalry bow elite	11	
Slav and Croat spearmen		
Heavy spearmen	8	2-4
Downgrade to mediocre	-2	
Slav and Croat archers		
Bowmen	7	0-6
Downgrade to mediocre	-2	
Light infantry bow	4	
Croats or Vlachs		
Medium swordsmen	7	0-2
Javelinmen		
Before 1150		
Polish allies (List #203 Feudal Polish)		
Russian allies (List #206 Feudal Russian)		
Croat Nobles		
Heavy cavalry impetuous	9	0-2
Upgrade to elite	+2	
Hungarian horsemen		
Medium cavalry bow	9	0-4
From 1150		
Cuman allies (List #207 Cuman)		
Mongol allies (List #240 Golden Horde)		
*Replace all Hungarian nobles **		
Medium knight impetuous	10	All
Upgrade to elite	+2	
German or Italian mercenaries		
Medium knight impetuous	10	0-2

Hospitallers Medium knight impact elite	13	0-1
Replace Hungarian horsemen Heavy cavalry bow	11	0-2
Fortified camp	6	0-1

Hungarian horse archers

205 - Georgian

1008 - 1505 AD
Plain, Mountain
Command +3

The Christian Kingdom of Georgia was founded in 1008 by King Bagrat III. The Kingdom extended to almost all of the Caucasus and a large part of the north coast of modern day Turkey. Following the battle of Manzikert in 1071, Georgia was invaded by the Seljuk Turks until King David IV reconquered the country. When Byzantium was taken by the Franks in 1204, the Georgians occupied the provinces east of the Empire that become the Empire of Trebizond enfeoffed to the Georgians. During the 13th century, Georgia was invaded by the Mongols and had to pay tribute. It was then destroyed by the Timurids between 1386 and 1403. King Constantin II (1478-1505) was the last King of united Georgia. After him, the Kingdom was divided before being absorbed by Russia in the 19th century.

Troop type	Pts	Units
Nobles * Heavy cavalry impetuous Upgrade to elite (max 6)	9 +2	6-16
Horse archers Light cavalry bow	6	0-6
Heavy spearmen Downgrade to mediocre	8 -2	0-4
Russians from 1027 to 1213 Heavy spearmen Add support	8 +1	0-2
Bowmen Downgrade to mediocre	7 -2	0-4
Light infantry bow	4	
Light infantry javelin	4	0-2
From 1118		
Replace all nobles * Heavy cavalry bow Upgrade to elite (max 4)	11 +2	4-12
Cumans or Alans Light cavalry bow Medium cavalry bow (max 6)	6 9	4-18
Alan nobles from 1120 Heavy cavalry impetuous Heavy cavalry bow Upgrade to elite	9 11 +2	0-2
Crusaders from 1118 to 1144 Medium knight impetuous Upgrade to elite	11 +2	0-2

Note

- Seljuk Turk allies (List #195 Seljuk Turk) from 1124 to 1243

206 - Feudal Russian

1055 - 1246 AD
Plain, Forest
Command +3

During the 11th and 12th century, constant nomadic Pechenegs and Cumans invasions led to a massive migration of Slavic populations to the north. At the same time, the authority of Kiev was challenged, and in 1136 the Republic of Novgorod was created. During 13th century, Russia was invaded by the Mongols and the Tatars of the Golden Horde. Consequently, southern Russia fell under Mongol domination for several centuries.

Troop type	Pts	Units
Druzhina * Heavy cavalry Upgrade to elite (max 6)	9 +2	6-16
Pechenegs and Cumans Light cavalry bow Medium cavalry bow	6 9	0-12
German knights from 1150 Medium knight Medium knight impetuous Medium knight impact	10 10 11	0-2
Polish knights before 1150 Heavy cavalry impetuous	9	0-2
Polish knights from 1150 Medium knight impetuous	10	

Lithuanians from 1150 Light cavalry javelin Light infantry bow	6 4	0-4
City militia Heavy spearmen Add support Add armour (max 4) Downgrade to mediocre	8 +1 +2 -2	2-8
Light infantry bow	4	0-4
Light infantry javelin	4	0-2
Levy	3	0-2
Fortified camp	6	0-1

Mordvin allies		
Horsemen * Medium cavalry bow	9	1-2
Medium swordsmen	7	1-4
Bowmen (max 2) Light infantry bow	7 4	1-4

Note

- Mordvin allies (see list above)
- Polish allies (List #203 Feudal Polish)
- Hungarian allies (List #204 Feudal Hungarian)
- Cuman allies (List #207 Cuman)

207 - Cuman

1054 – 1394 AD
Steppes
Command +2

The Cumans (or Kipchak Turks) were nomadic tribes that appeared north of the Caspian Sea in the 11th century. They conducted raids against the Byzantines, Hungarians and Russians and were also used as mercenaries. During the 13th century, they were defeated by the Mongols and the survivors were integrated into the Golden Horde.

Troop type	Pts	Units
Nobles * Heavy cavalry bow Upgrade to elite	11 +2	0-6
Horse archers Light cavalry bow Medium cavalry bow	6 9	6-24
Vlachs from 1122 to 1269 Javelinmen Light infantry javelin	7 4	0-2
Vlachs from 1122 to 1269 Light infantry bow	4	0-2
Levy	3	0-2
Captured artillery from 1180 Medium artillery	10	0-1
Fortified camp	6	0-1

Note

- Alan allies (List #108 Alan – later period)

208 - Prussian and Estonian

1200 - 1283 AD
Forest
Command +2

This list presents the armies of Prussians and Estonians during the Baltic crusade led by the Teutonic order. Estonians were submitted by Teutonics in 1227 with the help of the German Princes. The Prussians resisted until 1283.

Troop type	Pts	Units
Horsemen * Medium cavalry Heavy cavalry (max 2) Upgrade to elite (max 2)	7 9 +2	0-6
Light cavalry javelin	6	0-3
Danish or Saxon mercenaries Medium knight impetuous	10	0-2
Noble warriors * Medium swordsmen impet. elite	9	0-4
Others warriors Medium swordsmen impetuous	7	8-24
Poorly equipped warriors Medium swordsmen mediocre	5	0-8
Bowmen Light infantry bow	7 4	2-6
Crossbowmen Light infantry crossbow	7 4	0-2
Fortifications	1	0-6

Note

- Polish allies (List #203 Feudal Polish)
- Novgorod allies (List #206 Feudal Russian)

209 - Teutonic Knights

1201 - 1522 AD
Plain, Forest
Command +4

The Teutonic order was founded in the Holy land at Saint John of Acre, but its main action took place in the Baltic countries. Their action began in 1226 with the call of Conrad, Prince of Masovia, to fight the pagans in Prussia and Estonia. Then they extend their influence over all the Baltic countries.

Alexandre Nevsky, a Russian prince, defeated them in 1242 but it did not slow their progress. In the 14th century, the order was at its peak of power. The union between Poland and Lithuania in 1386 threatened their supremacy. It triggered a war culmunating in the crushing defeat of Tannenberg in 1410. Thereafter, the order was on decline and lost another war against Poland in 1466. The order disappeared at the beginning of the 16th century.

Troop type	Pts	Units
Brother knights * Medium knight impact elite	13	2-6
Crusaders and Vassals Medium knight impetuous	10	2-8
Mounted crossbowmen Light cavalry crossbow Medium cavalry crossbow	 6 9	0-2
Prussians and Livonians Medium cavalry impetuous	7	0-2
Balts Light cavalry javelin	6	0-2
Livonians or Hungarians before 1230 Light cavalry bow	6	2-6
Turcopoles (from 1230) Light cavalry javelin Medium cavalry	 6 7	
Serving brothers or mercenaries Heavy spearmen Add armour	 8 +2	0-2
Serving brothers or mercenaries Crossbowmen Add pavise	 7 +1	0-2
Feudal troops Bowmen Crossbowmen Downgrade to mediocre	 7 7 -2	0-2
German town militia Heavy spearmen mediocre	6	0-4
Balt and Livonian subjects Medium spearmen mediocre	5	0-4
Balt and Livonian subjects Light infantry bow	4	0-2
Levy	3	0-3
From 1330		
Replace all Brother knights * Heavy knight impact elite	15	2-4
Replace all Crusaders and Vassals Heavy knight impetuous Heavy knight impact	 12 13	2-4
English archers (from 1352 to 1392) Longbowmen elite	11	0-1
Handgunners (from 1380) Light infantry firearm Upgrade to elite	 4 +1	0-1
Bombard (from 1380) Heavy artillery	10	0-1

Note

- Polish allies (List #203 Feudal Polish) before 1242
- Germanic allies (List #183 Feudal German) before 1330 or (List #227 Medieval German) from 1330

Samurais

Militia Medium spearmen mediocre	5	4-12
Militia Bowmen mediocre	5	4-12
Tribal infantry Javelinmen Light infantry javelin	 7 4	0-4
Light infantry bow	4	0-4
After 1350		
Culverin or bombard Medium artillery Heavy artillery	10	0-2

Tribal allies		
Tribal warriors * Medium swordsmen impetuous	7	2-6
Light infantry bow	4	1-4

Note

- Tribal allies (see list above)
- Cham allies (List #167 Khmer Empire and Champa) from 1280 to 1286

214 - Song Chinese

960 – 1279 AD
Plain, Mountain, Forest
Command +4
Strategist: Yueh Fei (Southern Song, 1130 - 1141)

The Song dynasty reigned over China between 960 and 1279. They reunified the country after the period of instability following the fall of the Tang dynasty. Until 1127, the Song dominated the whole country but then the north passed under the domination of the Jurchen. During the war against the Jurchen, General Yueh Fei resisted the invaders victoriously. He was betrayed, discredited and finally executed on the orders of the emperor. In 1234, the Mongols occupied northern China, destroyed the Song dynasty in 1279 and established the Yuan dynasty.

Troop type	Pts	Units
Horsemen * Medium cavalry bow Heavy cavalry bow Downgrade to mediocre	 9 11 -2	2-4
Standing troops Medium swordsmen 2HW Downgrade to mediocre	 8 -2	4-8
Standing troops Bowmen Crossbowmen Downgrade to mediocre	 7 7 -2	4-8
Replace some standing troops by mixed units ½ Medium swordsmen ½ Crossbowmen	9	0-8
Spearmen and halberdiers Heavy spearmen Heavy swordsmen 2HW	 8 9	0-3
Militia Medium swordsmen mediocre Bowmen mediocre Crossbowmen mediocre	5	0-8
Tribal auxiliaries Javelinmen Medium swordsmen Medium swordsmen impetuous	7	0-4
Light infantry bow Light infantry crossbow	4	0-4
Stampeding herd Scythed chariot	3	0-1
Fortifications	1	0-8
Fortified camp	6	0-1
Northern Song Hsien-Pi allies (List #118 Hsien-Pi) before 979		
Guardsmen * Heavy cavalry bow Upgrade to elite	 11 +2	2-6
Light artillery Heavy artillery (max 1)	6 10	0-3
Southern Song		
Guardsmen * Heavy cavalry bow Upgrade to elite	 11 +2	0-4
Mongol deserters after 1250 Light cavalry bow Upgrade to elite	 6 +1	0-4
Medium cavalry bow Upgrade to elite	9 +2	
Guard crossbowmen Crossbowmen pavise elite	10	0-2
Fire tube armed infantry after 1200 Light infantry firearm	4	0-2
Light artillery	6	0-4
Medium artillery Heavy artillery	10	0-2

215 - Xi-Xia

982 – 1227 AD
Plain, Mountain
Command +4

The Xi-Xia (or Hsi-Hsia) was a Kingdom founded by Tangut nobles from Tibet in the northwestern China. The Kingdom was founded in 982 by Li Deming. The

Junchen-Chin who reigned over northern China at the time considered it as a vassal state while it was, in fact, independent. The Kingdom was conquered by the Mongols of Genghis Khan in 1227.

Troop type	Pts	Units
*Tangut horsemen **		
Heavy cavalry impact	10	4-12
Upgrade to elite (max 4)	+2	
Nomads		
Light cavalry bow	6	0-6
Medium cavalry bow	9	
Spearmen and halberdiers		
Heavy spearmen	8	0-2
Heavy swordsmen 2HW	9	
Standing troops		
½ Medium swordsmen ½ Bowmen or Crossbowmen	9	2-6
Irregular troops		
Medium swordsmen	7	0-8
Downgrade to mediocre	-2	
Bowmen mediocre	5	0-4
Light infantry bow	4	
Fire tube armed infantry Light infantry firearm	4	0-2
Light artillery	6	0-2
Heavy artillery	10	0-1
Fortifications	1	0-6
Fortified camp	6	0-1

Note

- Uighur allies (List #141 Central Asian Turkish)
- Tibetan allies (List #166 Tibetan)
- Jurchen allies (List #216 Jurchen-Chin)

216 - Jurchen-Chin

1115 – 1234 AD
Plain, Mountain, Forest
Command +4

The Jurchen were a native people from Manchuria. They took the name of Manchu when they invaded China in the 17th century. They overthrew the Kithan Liao dynasty between 1115 and 1125. They founded the Chin (Jin) dynasty which reigned over northern China until the arrival of the Mongols in 1234.

Troop type	Pts	Units
*Jurchen horsemen **		
Medium cavalry impact bow	10	4-12
Heavy cavalry impact bow	12	
Upgrade to elite (max 6)	+2	
*Khitan horsemen **		
Heavy cavalry impact (½)	10	0-4
Heavy cavalry bow (½)	11	
Steppe scouts		
Light cavalry bow	6	0-4
Medium cavalry bow	9	
After 1126 : Jin Chinese		
Chinese spearmen or halberdiers		
Heavy spearmen	8	0-2
Heavy swordsmen 2HW	9	
Chinese infantry		
½ Medium swordsmen ½ Bowmen or Crossbowmen	9	2-6
Other Chinese troops		
Crossbowmen	7	0-6
Bowmen (max 2)	7	
Medium swordsmen 2HW (max 2)	8	
Downgrade to mediocre	-2	
Light artillery	6	0-1
After 1180		
*Replace all Jurchen horsemen **		
Heavy cavalry bow	11	All
Medium cavalry bow	9	
Downgrade to mediocre	-2	
Chinese mercenaries Medium swordsmen 2HW	8	2-4
Fire tube armed infantry Light infantry firearm	4	0-2

Note

- Jurchen horsemen initially fought in mixed units of spearmen and bowmen. After 1180, this mixed formation disappeared at the same time as the quality of the horsemen decreased.
- One commander can be included in a Khithan horsemen unit.
- Mongol allies (List #171 Tribal Mongol)

217 - Qara-Khitan

1122 – 1218 AD
Steppe, Desert
Command +4

The Kithan Liao were driven out of China by the Jurchen and the last Liao Emperor died in 1122. Part of the Kithans returned to nomadism in eastern China and occupied the Turfan and Koutcha regions. They reach the territory of the Qarakhanid Turks and they subjugated them in 1144. Thereafter they founded the State of Qara-Khitan in Eastern Turkestan. In 1218, the Mongols took possession of the Kingdom of Qara-Khitan.

Troop type	Pts	Units
Khitan horsemen *		
Heavy cavalry impact (½)	10	4-12
Heavy cavalry bow (½)	11	
Upgrade to elite (max 6)	+2	
Tribal nobles		
Heavy cavalry bow	11	0-2
Tribal horsemen		
Light cavalry bow	6	2-12
Medium cavalry bow	9	
Only in 1210		
Elephant	13	0-1
Tribal infantry		
Bowmen mediocre	5	0-3
Light infantry bow	4	
Militia		
Heavy spearmen mediocre	6	0-4
Levy	3	

Note

- It is mandatory to take as many Khitan horsemen with bow as with impact.
- Uighur or Qarakhanid Turks allies (List #141 Central Asian Turkish)
- Naiman allies (List #171 Tribal Mongol)
- Khwarazmian allies (List #200 Khwarazmian)

Khitan horsemen

218 - Mongol Empire

1206 - 1260 AD
Steppes
Command +6
Strategists: Genghis Khan (1206-1227 AD), Mukhali (1218-1223 AD) or Subedei (1220-1241 AD)

Genghis Khan had a tumultuous life before being successful as Khan. He imposed his domination on other Mongolian tribes (Tatar, Merkit and Naimans) and was proclaimed Great Khan of the Mongols in 1206. Genghis Khan began his conquests by submitting the Kingdom of Xi-Xia and then of the Jurchen-Chin with general Mukhali's help. In 1220, he defeated the Empire of the Khwarazmians and sent forces to India and Russia. Ogodei, son of Genghis Khan, pursued the conquests by launching a campaign in Europe between 1236 and 1242 under the direction of General Subedei. He crushed the Russian, Polish, and Hungarian armies and the Mongols wreaked devastation everywhere. The Empire expanded also to Tibet, Iran and Iraq. The Seljuk Caliphate was overthrown in 1253. The Empire reached its peak under Kubilaï Khan (see list 263 Yuan Chinese) who conquered southern China in 1276 but failed in its attempt to invade Japan.

Troop type	Pts	Units
Khan's guardsmen *		
Heavy cavalry bow elite	13	0-4
Add impact	+1	
Mongol horsemen *		
Medium cavalry bow	9	8-24
Upgrade to elite	+2	
Light cavalry bow	6	
Upgrade to elite	+1	
Khitan or Jurchen		
Heavy cavalry bow	11	0-4
Upgrade to elite	+2	
Georgians or Armenians		
Heavy cavalry impetuous	9	0-2
Upgrade to elite	+2	
Cumans, Alans or Turks		
Light cavalry bow	6	0-6
Upgrade to elite	+1	
Dismounted horsemen		
Bowmen	7	0-4
Light infantry bow	4	
Heavy artillery	10	0-2
Hostages and war prisoners		
Levy mediocre expendable	1	0-4
Fortified camp	6	0-1

Note

- Georgian and Armenian troops cannot be used if allies are used.
- Uighur Turks allies (List #141 Central Asian Turkish)
- Korean allies (List #212 Koryo Korean)
- Chinese allies (List #214 Song Chinese)
- Jurchen allies (List #216 Jurchen-Chin)

LATE MIDDLE AGES

MEDIEVAL EUROPE

219 - GRANADINE

1226 - 1492 AD
Plain, Mountain
Command +4

The fall of the Almohads in 1226 triggered a new period of troubles in Spain. In 1238 the Arabs of Nasrid dynasty founded an emirate in Granada. They swore allegiance to King Ferdinand of Castile and were the last Arabic bastion on the Iberian Peninsula. This kingdom corresponded to the region of Andalusia increased by Seville, Cordoba and Gibraltar. It lasted until 1492, when Granada was taken by armies of Castile and Aragon.

Troop type	Pts	Units
Granadine lancers * Heavy cavalry impact Upgrade to elite	10 +2	2-4
Berbers Light cavalry javelin	6	4-12
Muslim mercenaries Light cavalry crossbow Light cavalry bow	6	0-2
Christian mercenaries Heavy knight impetuous Upgrade to elite	12 +2	0-2
Peasants with crossbow Crossbowmen Downgrade to mediocre	7 -2	4-12
Light infantry crossbow (max 6)	4	
Militia or mercenaries Heavy spearmen Downgrade to mediocre	8 -2	0-4
Militia or mercenaries Crossbowmen Bowmen	7	0-2
Border guards Medium swordsmen mediocre	5	0-2
Handgunners after 1450 Light infantry firearm Upgrade to elite	4 +1	0-2
Light infantry sling	4	0-2
Fortified camp	6	0-1

Note
- Marinid allies (List #196 Berber) before 1340

220 - SWISS

1240 - 1515 AD
Mountain
Command +5

Switzerland was part of the Holy Roman Empire but the population cannot stand the domination of local lords. The first revolt of the Swiss cantons broke in 1240 but was strongly repressed. It was in 1291 that Switzerland was created by the pact of "Eternal Alliance". In 1315, following the Battle of Morgarten, the Swiss renewed their desire for independence. From the three original cantons, Switzerland grew to eight in the 14th century and then thirteen in the 15th century. The Swiss earned a reputation of invincibility against the troops of Holy Roman Empire and then against those of Charles the Bold, Duke of Burgundy who attacked them between 1476 and 1477. This invincibility ended in 1515 when the Swiss were defeated by the French at Marignan.

Troop type	Pts	Units
Mounted crossbowmen Light cavalry crossbow	6	0-2
Halberdiers * Medium swordsmen 2HW Upgrade to elite	8 +2	6-20
Pikemen Pikemen elite	13	0-4
Crossbowmen Light infantry crossbow	4	2-4
Organ gun Light artillery	6	0-1
Fortified camp	6	0-1
Seulement jusqu'à 1400		
Enfants perdus Light infantry javelin	4	0-2
Fortifications	1	0-6

After 1400		
Replace all halberdiers Medium swordsmen 2HW Upgrade to elite	8 +2	0-6
*Replace all Pikemen ** Pikemen elite	13	4-14
Replace some crossbowmen by handgunners Light infantry firearm Upgrade to elite	4 +1	2-4
Burgundian war 1476 to 1477		
*Lorrainer knights ** Heavy knight impact	13	1-3

Note

- One commander can be included in Lorrainer knights unit.

221 - Medieval Scandinavian

1250 - 1521 AD
Plain, Forest
Command +3
Strategist: Valdemar IV (Denmark in 1361)

Sweden was founded as a state in 1250. The Kingdom extended to Finland and was frequently at war with the principality of Novgorod until the signature of a treaty in 1323 which established the borders. In 1397 the states of Sweden, Norway and Denmark united in the Kalmar Union. Denmark dominated the Union and Norway was in fact no more than a Danish province. During the 15th century Denmark tried to take the control of Sweden which broke into rebellion several times. Sweeden eventually left the Union in 1521.

Troop type	Pts	Units
*Men-at-arms before 1330 ** Medium knight impetuous Upgrade to elite (max 3)	10 +2	2-6
*Men-at-arms from 1330 ** Heavy knight impetuous Upgrade to elite (max 3)	12 +2	
Valets and servants Medium cavalry Downgrade to mediocre	7 -2	0-2
Mounted crossbowmen/handgunners Heavy cavalry crossbow Heavy cavalry firearm	11	0-2
Crossbowmen Light infantry crossbow	7 4	0-4
Handgunners (from 1397) Light infantry firearm Upgrade to elite	4 +1	0-2
Canons (from 1397) Heavy artillery Light artillery	10 6	0-1
Fortified camp	6	0-1
Sweden before 1397 or Sweden in rebellion		
Militia in mixed units ½ Heavy swordsmen ½ Crossbowmen Add pavise	10 +1	4-16
Fortifications	1	0-8
Denmark-Norvegian or Kalmar Union Swedish allies (List #221 Médieval Scandinavian) German allies (List #227 Medieval German)		
German knights Heavy knight impact	13	0-2
Obudshaer in mixed units ½ Heavy swordsmen pavise ½ Crossbowmen	11	2-6
Obudshaer with halberds Heavy swordsmen 2HW Medium swordsmen 2HW Add armour	9 8 +2	
Landevaernet Heavy spearmen mediocre Add support	6 +1	0-12
German mercenaries (before 1488) Heavy swordsmen 2HW Add armour	9 +2	0-2
German landsknechts (from 1488) Pikemen	11	0-4

222 - Medieval Scots

1286 – 1512 AD
Plain, Forest, Mountain (unless in France)
Command +3
Strategist: Sir James Douglas (1308-1328 AD)

This list covers the armies of medieval Scotland. In 1286 the kingdom of Scotland moved closer to its English neighbour. England coveted the crown of Scotland which resulted into many conflicts between the 12th and the 14th century. Between 1419 and 1429 many Scots fought on the continent supporting the French and the Burgundians.

Troop type	Pts	Units
*Nobles ** Heavy knight impetuous Foot knight Upgrade to elite (max 1)	12 12 +2	1-3
Scots spearmen (all of the same type) Pikemen mediocre Heavy spearmen	8	6-18

Longbowmen Downgrade to mediocre	9 -2	0-4
Light infantry bow	4	
Levy	3	0-2
Fortifications	1	0-4
Fortified camp	6	0-1
Only after 1340		
Light artillery Heavy artillery	6 10	0-2
Only in 1385 in England or Scotland		
French knights * Heavy knight impetuous Foot knight Upgrade to elite	 12 12 +2	2-4
Crossbowmen	7	0-2
Only in France from 1419 to 1429 French allies mandatory (List #226 Hundred Years War French). No nobles, spearmen or Highlanders allies		
Men-at-arms * Heavy swordsmen armour 2HW Foot knight (max 4)	 11 12	2-8
Longbowmen Downgrade to mediocre	9 -2	4-16

Highlanders allies		
Highlanders * Medium swordsmen bow	10	2-4
Island warriors Heavy swordsmen 2HW	9	0-4

Note

- Highlanders allies (see list above)

223 - Medieval Irish

1300 – 1494
Mountain, Forest
Command +3

This list represents the armies of Ireland from the introduction of cavalry up to total English domination of Ireland. Galloglaich were professional soldiers, descendants of the Scots. They were grouped into clans (MacDonnell, MacDougall, Macrory ...) and had a solid reputation. Edward Bruce, brother of the King of Scotland, was crowned King of Ireland in 1316.

Troop type	Pts	Units
Irish nobles * Heavy cavalry Heavy cavalry impetuous Upgrade to elite	 9 9 +2	0-2
Irish horsemen * Light cavalry javelin	6	2-4
Galloglaich Heavy swordsmen 2HW Upgrade to elite	 9 +2	2-8
Kerns with javelin Javelinmen Light infantry javelin (max 8)	 7 4	8-24
Others kerns Light infantry bow Light infantry sling	4	0-3
Levy	3	0-2
Fortifications	1	0-4

Scots pikemen

Edward The Bruce from 1315 to 1318		
*Scots nobles ** Heavy knight impetuous Foot knight Upgrade to elite	 12 12 +2	1-2
Scots spearmen (all of the same type) Pikemen mediocre Heavy spearmen	8	1-3

Note

- The Galloglaich was Scots mercenaries equipped with heavy two-handed axes.

224 - Condottieri

1320 - 1495 AD
Plain, Mountain
Command +4
Strategist: Carmagnola (Venice in 1427 AD)

During the 14th century flourishing Italy plunged into recession. The expansion of the Ottomans disrupted trade, and plague and famine decimated the population. This situation caused many revolts and widespread disorder. Towns and cities relied heavily on mercenaries, whose leaders were called Condottieri, to protect their interests. At first they were mainly foreigners (German, Spanish and English) but in the 15th century they were mostly Italians. The list ends with the defeat of Italian forces by the French at the Battle of Fornovo.

Troop type	Pts	Units
*Men-at-arms and mercenaries ** Heavy knight impact Foot knight	 13 12	4-12
Mounted crossbowmen Light cavalry crossbow Medium cavalry crossbow	 6 9	1-3
Spearmen militia Heavy spearmen mediocre	6	0-2
Crossbowmen militia Crossbowmen mediocre Light infantry crossbow	 5 4	0-2
Halberdiers (from 1400) Medium swordsmen 2HW Heavy swordsmen 2HW	8 9	0-2
Mercenaries (from 1400) Pikemen	11	0-2
Mercenaries Crossbowmen Add pavise	 7 +1	0-2
Handgunners (from 1400) Light infantry firearm Upgrade to elite	 4 +1	0-1
Light artillery Heavy artillery	6 10	0-2
Levy	3	0-2
Fortifications	1	0-4
Fortified camp	6	0-1

Papal states Free Company allies (List #230 Free Company)		
Hungarians Light cavalry bow	6	0-3
Papal guardsmen Heavy spearmen elite	10	0-1
English archers (before 1400) Longbowmen elite	11	0-2

Venetian Swiss allies (List #220 Swiss)		
Dalmatian knights after 1440 Heavy knight impetuous Upgrade to elite	 12 +2	0-2
Stradiots Light cavalry javelin Upgrade to elite Medium cavalry impact Upgrade to elite	 6 +1 8 +2	2-8
Turks Light cavalry bow	6	0-3
Dalmatian militia Crossbowmen	7	0-2
English archers Longbowmen elite Add stakes (after 1415)	 11 +1	0-2
Handgunners after 1400 Light infantry firearm Upgrade to elite	 4 +1	0-2
Light infantry bow	4	0-2

Neapolitan Albanian allies (List #250 Albanian)		
Feudal knights Heavy knight impetuous Upgrade to elite	 12 +2	0-4
Hungarians or Turks Light cavalry bow	6	0-3
Guardsmen Heavy spearmen elite	10	0-1
Almughavars Medium swordsmen impact elite Medium spearmen elite	 10 9	0-2
Aragonese mercenaries Light infantry crossbow	4	0-3
Light infantry bow	4	0-2

Florentine Swiss allies (List #220 Swiss) Free Company allies (List #230 Free Company)		
Hungarians Light cavalry bow	6	0-3
Replace all crossbowmen militia by mixed units ½ Heavy spearmen ½ Crossbowmen Add pavise	10 +1	0-2
Replace all spearmen militia Pikemen mediocre	8	0-2
English archers Longbowmen elite Add stakes (after 1415)	11 +1	0-2

Milanese		
*Royal family guardsmen ** Heavy knight impact elite Foot knight elite	15 14	0-1
Handgunners (after 1400) Light infantry firearm Upgrade to elite	4 +1	0-2

Genoese in Cyprus		
Bulgars and Slavs Light cavalry bow Medium cavalry bow (max 4)	6 9	0-8

225 - Hundred Years War English

1322 - 1455 AD
Plain, Forest
Command +4
Strategist: Henry V (1403-1422) and Duke of Bedford (1423-1429 AD)

The Hundred Years War began in 1337 when King Edward III responded to the French confiscation of Aquitaine by claiming the French crown. After the victories of Crecy (1346) and Poitiers (1356) he held the entire south west of France and Calais. The Black Death ravaged England in 1348 and the country was shaken by several revolts. Meanwhile Bertrand du Guesclin retook English possessions in France. Henry V resumed the war against France and won the battle of Agincourt in 1415. He was recognised as the heir of the French throne and when he died his son, Henry VI, was crowned King of France in Paris. However Jeanne d'Arc and Charles VII successfully retook all the English possessions in France except Calais.

Troop type	Pts	Units
*Mounted English and Gascons ** Heavy knight Heavy knight impetuous	12	0-3
Hobilars Medium cavalry impact Medium spearmen	8 7	0-2
*English and Gascons on foot ** Foot knight Upgrade to elite (max 4)	12 +2	2-8
Halberdiers and men-at-arms Heavy spearmen Heavy swordsmen 2HW Add armour	8 9 +2	0-4
Longbowmen Longbowmen elite Add stakes (from 1415, none or all)	11 +1	4-12
Gascons Crossbowmen	7	0-2
Brigans and coutiliers Medium swordsmen mediocre	5	0-2
Welsh spearmen (before 1415) Medium spearmen Downgrade to mediocre	7 -2	0-2
Kerns, Bretons or Bidets Light infantry javelin Upgrade to elite	4 +1	0-2
Light artillery	6	0-1
Fortifications	1	0-8
Fortified camp	6	0-1
From 1415		
Irish horsemen Light cavalry javelin	6	0-1
Replace all light artillery Heavy artillery	10	All

Note

- Medieval German allies (List #227 Medieval German) between 1339 and 1340
- Flemish allies (List #232 Low Countries) in 1340

226 - Hundred Years War French

1330 - 1445 AD
Plain, Forest
Command +3
Strategists: Bertrand du Guesclin (1364-1380 AD), Dunois and Jeanne d'Arc (1429 AD)

Between 1337 and 1364 the English won several victories over the French including Crecy in 1346 and Poitiers in 1356. The Treaty of Brétigny in 1360 gave Edward III sovereignty of about a third of France. From 1364 to 1380 Charles V began a slow reconquest with the help of Bertrand du Guesclin, who avoided pitched battles. At the beginning of the 14th century a civil war broke out between the Armagnacs and the Burgundians. The English took the opportunity to regain territory and inflict a severe defeat to the French at Agincourt in 1415. The Treaty of Troyes in 1420 disinherited the Dauphin of France. Henry VI of England was crowned King of France when he was only a few months old. In 1429 the rise of Jeanne d'Arc enabled the coronation of Charles VII in Reims. A second reconquest was initiated by Dunois and Jeanne d'Arc and by 1453 only Calais remained in English hands.

Troop type	Pts	Units
*Nobles **		
Heavy knight impetuous	12	4-12
Foot knight	12	
Upgrade to elite	+2	
Mercenaries		
Heavy knight impact	13	0-2
Foot knight	12	
Valets and Sergeants (from 1400)		
Heavy cavalry impact	10	0-2
Heavy spearmen armour	10	
French and Spanish crossbowmen		
Crossbowmen mediocre	7	2-6
Downgrade to mediocre	-2	
Light infantry crossbow	4	
Genoese crossbowmen		
Crossbowmen	7	0-2
Add pavise	+1	
Upgrade to elite	+2	
Pavisiers (before 1400)		
Heavy spearmen	8	0-4
Add pavise	+1	
Voulgiers (from 1400)		
Heavy swordsmen 2HW	9	
Add armour	+2	
Bretons or Bidets (before 1400)		
Light infantry javelin	4	0-2
Upgrade to elite	+1	
Brigans		
Medium swordsmen mediocre	5	2-4
Ribauds and peasants		
Levy	3	
Upgrade to impetuous (Jacquerie)	+1	
Light artillery	6	0-1
Heavy artillery	10	
Fortified camp	6	0-1

Note

- Scots allies (List #222 Medieval Scots) after 1418.

227 - Medieval German

1330 - 1519 AD
Plain, Mountain, Forest
Command +3

In the mid-fourteenth century plague decimated Germany; some areas lost half their population. In the 15th century a Czech uprising culminated to the Hussite war (1415-1436) against the Germans. In the second half of the 15th century the Holy Empire was shaken by civil war. From 1493 the Emperor Maximilian attempted to reform the Empire but failed to impose his authority. This list stops at the beginning of the reign of Emperor Charles V in 1519.

Troop type	Pts	Units
*Men-at-arms and mercenaries **		
Heavy knight	12	2-8
Heavy knight impact	13	
Foot knight	12	
Mounted crossbowmen		
Medium cavalry crossbow	9	1-3
Heavy cavalry crossbow	11	
Halberdiers		
Heavy swordsmen 2HW	9	0-2
Add armour	+2	
Free canton militia		
Medium spearmen	7	0-6
Downgrade to mediocre	-2	
Militia (not mandatory after1450)		
Crossbowmen	7	2-6
Downgrade to mediocre	-2	
Add pavise	+1	
Light infantry crossbow	4	
Bowmen mediocre	5	0-2
Light infantry bow	4	
Heerban		
Levy	3	0-3
Fortified camp	6	0-1
Only from 1420 to 1457		
No Swiss allies with Hungarians		
Hungarians		
Light cavalry bow	6	0-4
After 1426		
War wagon crossbow	10	0-2
War wagon artillerie	12	0-1
Medium artillerie	10	
Heavy artillery	10	0-1
Handgunners		
Light infantry firearm	4	0-2
Upgrade to elite	+1	

Before 1450		
*Replace some men-at-arms and mercenaries by feudal knights ** Heavy knight impetuous Upgrade to elite	 12 +2	0-4
Spearmen Heavy spearmen Downgrade to mediocre Add armour (max 2)	 8 -2 +2	2-4
Low Country pikemen Pikemen mediocre	8	0-2
From 1450		
Replace some mounted crossbowmen Medium cavalry firearm Heavy cavalry firearm	 9 11	1-3
Light lancers Heavy cavalry impact	10	0-3
German landsknechts Pikemen Downgrade to mediocre	 11 -3	2-6

Note

- Swiss allies (List #220 Swiss). If used, Hungarian troops are excluded.
- Militia crossbowmen are no longer mandatory after 1450.

228 - Medieval Spanish

1340 – 1492 AD
Plain, Mountain
Command +3

In 1340 Granada was the only Muslim state remaining in Spain. The rest of the country was divided between the Kingdoms of Portugal, Aragon (including Catalonia) and Castile (including Leon). In 1469 Ferdinand of Aragon married Isabella of Castile thus uniting their two kingdoms. They determined to pursue the Reconquista and attacked the Emirate of Granada. The city was taken in 1492 and Spain became a powerful unified kingdom.

Troop type	Pts	Units
*Nobles and Men-at-arms ** Heavy knight impetuous Upgrade to elite (max 4)	 12 +2	4-8
*Military order men-at-arms ** Heavy knight impact elite Foot knight elite	 15 14	0-2
Mounted crossbowmen Light cavalry crossbow	6	0-2
Militia Heavy spearmen mediocre	6	2-6
Crossbowmen Crossbowmen Downgrade to mediocre	 7 -2	2-6
Light infantry crossbow	4	
Handgunners (after 1400) Light infantry firearm Upgrade to elite	 4 +1	0-2
Heavy artillery	10	0-1
Levy	3	0-2
Fortified camp	6	0-1
Aragonese French allies (See List below)		
*Replace some Nobles and men-at-armes by mercenaries ** Heavy knight impact	13	0-6
Jinetes Light cavalry javelin Upgrade to elite	 6 +1	0-4
Almughavars Medium swordsmen impact elite Medium spearmen elite	 10 9	2-4
Mercenary pikemen (after 1450) Pikemen	11	0-2
Muslim archers Bowmen mediocre Light infantry bow	 5 4	0-2
Light infantry javelin	4	0-2
Castilian French or Navarrese allies (See List below)		
Jinetes Light cavalry javelin Upgrade to elite	 6 +1	2-10
Replace some militia Heavy spearmen armour Pikemen (max 2 after 1476)	 10 11	0-4
Almughavars (after 1476) Medium swordsmen impact elite Medium spearmen elite	 10 9	0-2
Javelinmen Light infantry javelin	7 4	0-3
Muslim archers Bowmen mediocre Light infantry bow	 5 4	0-2
Light infantry sling	4	0-3
Portuguese English allies (See List below) before 1390		
*Replace some Nobles and men-at-armes by mercenaries ** Foot knight Upgrade to elite (max 4)	 12 +2	0-8
Jinetes Light cavalry javelin Upgrade to elite	 6 +1	0-3

Replace some Crossbowmen Bowmen Downgrade to mediocre	7 -2	0-6
Light infantry bow	4	
Javelinmen Light infantry javelin	7 4	0-6
Fortifications	1	0-6

Free company allies (English, French or Navarrese) only before 1476		
English, French or Navarrese * Foot knight Upgrade to elite	12 +2	0-3
Only French or Navarrese * Heavy knight impetuous Upgrade to elite	12 +2	
Only English Longbowmen elite	11	1-3
Only French or Navarrese Crossbowmen	5	0-2

Note

- One option Aragonese, Castilian or Portugal must be chosen.

229 - Navarrese

1349 - 1378 AD
Plain, Mountain
Command +3

This list presents the army of the Navarrese kingdom of Charles II the Bad. He was the great grandson of Philip IV the Fair and reigned from 1349 to 1387. In 1350 he claimed the throne of France and tried to destabilise the kingdom. He switched sides several times in the Hundred Years' War; either being allied to the Dauphin Charles or the English. He ended up being discredited and isolated. He lost his possessions in Normandy and Languedoc in 1378. Reduced to its Pyrenean core, his kingdom declined. His son Charles III the Noble remained faithful to the King of France.

Troop type	Pts	Units
Knights and men-at-arms * Heavy knight impetuous Foot knight Upgrade to elite (max 4)	12 12 +2	4-8
Almughavars Medium swordsmen impact elite Medium spearmen elite	10 9	2-6
Gascon crossbowmen Crossbowmen	7	0-3
Gascon Brigans Medium swordsmen mediocre	5	0-3
Gascon Bidets Light infantry javelin Upgrade to elite	4 +1	0-2
Light infantry sling	4	0-2
Heavy artillery	10	0-1
Fortified camp	6	0-1
Free Company mercenaries		
English men-at-arms * Foot knight Upgrade to elite	12 +2	0-2
English longbowmen Longbowmen elite	11	1-3

230 - Free Company

1357 - 1444 AD
Plain, Forest
Command +4
Strategist: John Hawkwood (1359-1394 AD)

Free companies were groups of adventurers and unemployed mercenaries that ravaged France, and fought elsewhere, during the Hundred Years' War. They were composed mostly of foreigners from many nations. Notorious free companies included the Tard-Venus, the Flayers, the White Company of John Hawkwood and the Catalan Company serving the King of Aragon (see separate list). In 1364 King Charles V resolved to rid himself of the free companies. He tasked Bertrand du Guesclin to lead them across the Pyrenees to fight in Spain.

Troop type	Pts	Units
Mounted Men-at-arms * Heavy knight Heavy knight impetuous Heavy knight impact Upgrade to elite (max 2)	12 12 13 +2	0-6
Lesser men-at-arms Medium cavalry impact Heavy cavalry impact	8 10	0-2
Foot men-at-arms * Foot knight Upgrade to elite (max 4)	12 +2	4-12
Foot men-at-arms * Heavy swordsmen 2HW Add armour	9 +2	
English archers Longbowmen elite Add stakes (from 1415)	11 +1	0-6
French or Gascons Crossbowmen	7	0-4

Troop type	Pts	Units
Brigans Medium swordsmen mediocre	5	0-4
Breton or Gascon Bidets Light infantry javelin Upgrade to elite	 4 +1	0-2
Light infantry crossbow	4	0-2
Handgunners (after 1400) Light infantry firearm Upgrade to elite	 4 +1	
Ribauds and peasants Levy	3	0-2
Only in 1444 Heavy artillery	10	0-1
Fortified camp	6	0-1

John Hawkwood

231 - Burgundian

1363 - 1471 AD
Plain, Forest
Command +3
Strategist: Philippe the Good (1421-1453 AD)

In 1363 Philip the Bold, the 4th son of the King of France, was given the Duchy of Burgundy. He gained Flanders by his marriage to Margaret of Dampierre and became the most powerful lord of the kingdom. The French King's death in 1380 resulted in a succession crisis between the Burgundians and the Armagnacs and led to a civil war in 1407. The Burgundians joined forces with the English between 1420 and 1435 and expanded their territory. In 1435 peace was restored between France and Burgundy. At the death of Philip III of Burgundy, called the Good, the Burgundian duchy was the most powerful in Christendom.

Troop type	Pts	Units
*Burgundian and French knights ** Heavy knight impetuous Heavy knight Foot knight Upgrade to elite (max 2)	 12 +2	4-6
Replace some Burgundian and French knights by valets d'armes Medium cavalry impact Heavy cavalry impact	 8 10	0-2
*French knights ** Heavy knight impetuous Foot knight Upgrade to elite	 12 12 +2	0-2
Italian knights Heavy knight impact Foot knight	 13 12	0-2
Italian or German Mercenaries Light cavalry crossbow Medium cavalry crossbow	 6 9	0-2
Picard archers Longbowmen	9	2-6
Low Country crossbowmen Crossbowmen Downgrade to mediocre	 7 -2	2-4
Low Country spearmen (before 1450) Heavy spearmen	8	0-3
Low Country pikemen (from 1450) Pikemen mediocre	8	
Swiss pikemen (after 1464) Pikemen elite	13	0-1
Handgunners (after 1430) Light infantry firearm Upgrade to elite	 4 +1	0-2
Ribauds and peasants Levy	3	0-2
Organ guns (after 1430) Light artillery	6	0-2
Heavy artillery	10	0-1
Fortified camp	6	0-1

English allies		
*English men-at-arms ** Foot knight Upgrade to elite	 12 +2	0-2
English longbowmen Longbowmen elite Add stakes (after 1415)	11	0-2

Note

- One commander can be included in a French knight unit.
- English allies (see List above).

232 - Low Countries

1384 - 1478 AD
Plain
Command +4

The Flemish people occupied the County of Flanders and the Duchy of Brabant (generally referred to as the Low Countries). Between the 14th and 15th century the Burgundians brought the seventeen provinces that made up the region under their authority. After the death of Charles the Bold in 1477 King Louis XI of France and the Holy Roman Emperor shared his possessions. The latter received the Netherlands while Louis XI regained Burgundy.

Troop type	Pts	Units
*Burgher men-at-arms **		
Heavy knight	12	1-3
Foot knight		
*Mercenaries and sergeants **		
Heavy knight impetuous	12	0-3
Heavy knight impact	13	
Foot knight	12	
Low Country spearmen (before 1450)		
Heavy spearmen	8	6-18
Low Country pikemen (from 1450)		
Pikemen mediocre	8	
Upgrade to ordinary	+3	
Halberdiers		
Heavy swordsmen 2HW	9	0-2
Crossbowmen	7	0-2
English archers (after 1336)		
Longbowmen elite	11	0-2
Add stakes (After 1415)	+1	
Bowmen mediocre	5	0-2
Light infantry bow	4	
Handgunners (after 1410)		
Light infantry firearm	4	0-2
Upgrade to elite	+1	
Organ guns (after 1410)		
Light artillery	6	0-3
Fortifications	1	0-6
Fortified camp	6	0-1

233 - Medieval Welsh

1400 – 1409 AD
Mountain, Forest
Command +3

This list presents the Welsh army during the rebellion against England between 1400 and 1409. The Welsh, with some English rebels, took and destroyed many of the English castles. They were victorious at Bryn Glas (1402), Shrewsbury (1403) and lastly at Worcester (1405) with French support.

Troop type	Pts	Units
*Welsh horsemen **		
Medium cavalry impetuous	7	2-6
Heavy cavalry impetuous	9	
Upgrade to elite (max 2)	+2	
*Welsh knights **		
Heavy knight impetuous	12	0-2
Foot knight	12	
Upgrade to elite	+3	
Light cavalry impact	6	0-2
Welsh spearmen		
Medium spearmen	7	6-18
Welsh archers		
Longbowmen	9	2-8
Militia billmen		
Heavy swordsmen 2HW mediocre	7	0-2
Light infantry javelin	4	0-4
Light infantry bow	4	0-4

Note

- French allies (List #226 Hundred Years War French) in 1405

234 - French Ordonnance

1445 - 1503 AD
Plain, Forest
Command +4

In 1445 King Charles VII created the ordonnance companies. Each company was divided into "lances", each comprising a knight with horse, a coutilier with a polearm, two archers, a page and a valet (these last two being non-combatants). The ordonnance companies helped push the English out of France and were used during the Italian wars.

Troop type	Pts	Units
*Ordonnance men-at-arms **		
Heavy knight impact elite	15	2-6
Foot knight elite *(before 1466)*	14	
Italian and Savoy men-at-arms		
Heavy knight impact	13	0-2
Foot knight	12	
Mounted crossbowmen		
Light cavalry crossbow	6	0-2
Ordonnance archers		
Longbowmen	9	2-6
Upgrade to elite	+2	
Add stakes	+1	

Partisans Heavy swordsmen 2HW Add armour Downgrade to mediocre	9 +2 -2	0-2
Gascons Crossbowmen Downgrade to mediocre Add pavise	7 -2 +1	0-4
Light infantry crossbow	4	
Bidets and Bretons Light infantry javelin Upgrade to elite	4 +1	0-2
Handgunners Light infantry firearm Upgrade to elite	4 +1	0-1
Culverin Light artillery Medium artillery	6 10	0-1
Bombard Heavy artillery	10	0-2
Fortifications	1	0-8
Fortified camp	6	0-1
Until 1465		
Feudal men-at-arms Heavy knight impetuous Upgrade to elite	12 +2	0-2
Francs archers Bowmen mediocre Longbowmen mediocre	5 7	2-8
Spearmen Heavy spearmen mediocre	6	0-2
From 1466 Italian allies (List #224 Condottieri)		
Replace some ordonnance archers by cavalry Medium cavalry impact	8	0-2
Replace all spearmen Pikemen mediocre	8	0-2
Francs archers (before 1480) Heavy swordsmen 2HW mediocre Longbowmen mediocre	6 7	0-4
From 1480 Swiss mercenaries		
*Swiss pikemen ** Pikemen elite	13	0-3
Swiss halberdiers Medium swordsmen 2HW elite	10	0-1
Swiss skirmishers Light infantry crossbow Light infantry firearm Upgrade to elite	4 4 +1	0-2
From 1494		
Genetaires Light cavalry impact elite	7	0-1

Note

- Ordonnance men-at-arms can dismount as foot knight only prior 1466.
- One commander can be included in a Swiss pikemen unit.
- Swiss allies (List #220 Swiss) before 1480

235 - Burgundian Ordonnance

1471 - 1477 AD
Plain, Forest
Command +3

Charles the Bold became Duke of Burgundy in 1471. He sought to consolidate his power by converting his duchy into a kingdom. To do this he reformed his army in order to make it more efficient. Unfortunately he suffered a series of defeats against the Swiss in 1476 and 1477 and he died at the siege of Nancy. Soon thereafter his kingdom was divided between France and the Holy Roman Empire.

Troop type	Pts	Units
*Household men-at-arms ** Heavy knight impact elite Foot knight elite	15 14	0-1
*Ordonnance men-at-arms ** Heavy knight impact Foot knight	13 12	4-8
Feudal men-at-arms Heavy knight Foot knight	12	0-2
Demi-lancers and coutiliers Heavy cavalry impact	10	0-2
Italian mercenaries Light cavalry crossbow Light infantry crossbow	6 4	0-2
Ordonnance archers Longbowmen Add stakes	9 +1	2-6
Ordonnance spearmen and pikemen Heavy spearmen Pikemen	8 11	0-3
Replace some ordonnance spearmen, archers and pikemen by mixed units ½ Heavy spearmen ½ Longbowmen	12	0-6
Italian Crossbowmen Crossbowmen Downgrade to mediocre Add pavise	7 -2 +1	0-2
Ordonnance handgunners Light infantry firearm Upgrade to elite	4 +1	0-2

Troop type	Pts	Units
Low Country pikemen Pikemen mediocre	8	0-3
Light artillery	6	0-3
Heavy artillery	10	0-2
Fortifications	1	0-8
Fortified camp	6	0-1

Note
- Each mixed unit replaces half-unit of spearmen and pikemen and one entire unit of bowmen.
- Yorkist allies (List #236 Wars of the Roses)

The Duke of Burgundy and his bodyguards

236 - Wars of the Roses

1455 - 1487 AD
Plain, Mountain, Forest
Command +4
Strategist: Edward IV (1461-1483 AD)

This list presents armies from the English civil war. The player must select an option between Yorkist (Y), Lancastrian (L), Richard III (R3), Tudor (T) and post 1485 Yorkist pretenders. The Yorkist Edward IV was crowned in 1461 after the Battle of Towton. He was an excellent military leader and was never defeated in battle. In 1470 his most powerful ally, Richard Neville, Earl of Warwick, turned against him and Edward was forced to seek refuge with the Duke of Burgundy. Returning in 1471 with a small army he regained power and reigned until 1483. The wars resumed at his death and ended with the coronation of Henry VII in 1485.

Troop type	Pts	Units
*Royal bodyguards (L, R3, T, YP) ** Heavy knight impact elite Foot knight elite	 15 14	0-1
*Mounted men-at-arms ** Heavy knight Foot knight	12	0-2
Currours Heavy cavalry impact	10	0-2
Knights and retinue billmen Heavy swordsmen armour 2HW Foot knight Foot knight elite (max 2)	 11 12 14	2-6
Retinue archers Longbowmen elite Add stakes (all or none)	 11 +1	2-8
Northern border / militia (L, Y, R3, T) Heavy swordsmen 2HW mediocre Heavy spearmen mediocre	 7 6	0-3
Northern border / militia (L, Y, R3, T) Longbowmen mediocre	7	0-4
Northern border horsemen (L, R3) Light cavalry impact Medium cavalry impact	 6 8	0-2
Welsh spearmen (L, Y, T) Medium spearmen	7	0-2
Welsh archers (L, T) Longbowmen	9	0-3
Irish kerns (L, YP) Javelinmen (max 2 if Lancastrian) Light infantry javelin	 7 4	0-6
French mercenary (L, T) Crossbowmen Add pavise	 7 +1	0-2
German Mercenary pikemen (Y, YP) Pikemen (max 2 if Yorkist) Downgrade to mediocre	 11 -3	0-3
Bretons (T) Light infantry javelin Upgrade to elite	 4 +1	0-3
Mercenary handgunners (Y, T, YP) Light infantry firearm Upgrade to elite	 4 +1	0-2
Light artillery	6	0-1
Heavy artillery	10	0-1
Fortifications	1	0-6
Fortified camp	6	0-1

Note
- Scots allies (List #222 Medieval Scots) only for Lancastrians (L) but the army cannot have any Welsh or Irish troops.

MEDIEVAL EASTERN EUROPE

237 - LITHUANIAN

1236 – 1435 AD
Plain, Forest
Command +3

The Grand Duchy of Lithuania was founded in 1236 by Mindaugas who converted to Christianity in 1253. At his death the kingdom returned to paganism. The Golden Horde ravaged the country in 1241, 1259 and 1275. In the 14th century, with the help of German settlers, Lithuanian territory was extended into the Ukraine and Belarus. The Grand Duke Jogaila also became King of Poland in 1386 by a royal wedding. This personal union of the two states lasted several centuries. In 1431 the Lithuanian nobles elected Švitrigaila as Grand Duke of Lithuania. The Poles and the Western Lithuanians were angered by this and it triggered a civil war. Švitrigaila and his Hussite and Teutonic allies were finally defeated at the Battle of Pabaiskas in 1435.

Troop type	Pts	Units
*Lithuanian nobles ** Heavy cavalry Upgrade to elite	9 +2	0-6
*Lithuanian horsemen ** Light cavalry javelin Medium cavalry	6 7	8-24
Replace some Lithuanian horsemen Bowmen Light infantry bow	7 4	0-24
Tatars Light cavalry bow elite Medium cavalry bow	7 9	0-3
Lithuanian spearmen Medium spearmen	7	0-4
Fortifications	1	0-4
Fortified camp	6	0-1
After 1386		
Teutonic knights Heavy knight impact elite	15	0-2
*Polish knights ** Heavy knight impetuous	12	0-4
Polish Followers Medium cavalry crossbow	9	0-2
Russian cavalry Heavy cavalry bow (max 2) Medium cavalry bow	11 9	0-6
Heavy artillery	10	0-1
Only in 1435 with Švitrigaila No Teutonic Order or Polish troops Teutonic allies (List #209 Teutonic Knights) mandatory		
Hussite chariots War wagon crossbow	10	0-3
Hussite foot Heavy swordsmen 2HW Add armour	9 +2	0-3

Note

- Lithuanian horsemen are equipped with a bow that is used only dismounted. Thus light cavalry can dismount as light infantry with bow and medium cavalry as bowmen.
- Teutonic allies (List #209 Teutonic Knights) from 1250 or 1253 or in 1435
- Tatar allies (List #240 Golden Horde) after 1419

238 - MEDIEVAL HUNGARIAN

1245 - 1526 AD
Plain, Steppes
Command +3 or +4 from 1442
Strategists: Janos Hunyadi (1442-1456 AD) or Pál Kinizsi (1456-1492 AD)

Following Mongol invasions in 1241 and 1242, Hungary became the rampart of Europe, first against the Mongols and then against the Turks. In 1442 Janos Hunyadi organised a crusade against the Turks with the help of the Poles, French knights and the Vlach prince Vlad II Dracul (known as Dracula). He failed but did not give up and began a new crusade in Serbia in 1448 which also failed. In 1456 he successfully defended Belgrade against the Turks and pushed them back into Bulgaria. His son, Matthias Corvinus, reigned from 1458 to 1490. He raised an army of mercenaries called the "Black Army" commanded by General Pál Kinizsi who defeated the Turks at the Battle of Breadfield.

Troop type	Pts	Units
*Hungarian nobles ** Medium knight impetuous Upgrade to elite (max 4)	10 +2	2-8
Hungarians and Cumans Light cavalry bow	6	3-12
*Szeklers or Tatars ** Light cavalry bow Upgrade to elite	6 +1	0-8
Medium cavalry bow Heavy cavalry bow (max 2) Upgrade to elite	9 11 +2	

Hungarian spearmen (before 1442) Heavy spearmen Downgrade to mediocre	8 -2	0-6
Hungarians, Croats or Bosnians Bowmen Downgrade to mediocre	7 -2	0-6
Light infantry bow	4	
Fortified camp	6	0-1
After 1330		
*Replace all Hungarian nobles ** Heavy knight impetuous Heavy knight impact (max 4) Upgrade to elite (max 4)	12 13 +2	All
Before 1442 German allies (List #227 Medieval German) Tatar allies (List #240 Golden Horde) Polish allies (List #241 Medieval Polish) Moldavian allies (List #249 Vlach and Moldavian) Crusader allies (see list below) in 1396		
From 1442 Polish allies (List #241 Medieval Polish) Serbian allies (List #243 Serbian Empire)		
Bohemian and German knights Heavy knight Heavy knight impact	12 13	0-4
Serbian hussars Light cavalry impact elite	7	0-4
Armati Heavy swordsmen 2HW armour Add support	11 +1	0-2
Replace all Hungarian spearmen by Clipeati Heavy spearmen armour Add support	10 +1	0-4
War wagon crossbow Upgrade to Light artillery (max 1)	10 +2	0-3
Handgunners Light infantry firearm Upgrade to elite	4 +1	1-3
Light infantry crossbow	4	0-2
Crusading peasants Levy impetuous	4	0-3
Light artillery Heavy artillery	6 10	0-1

Crusader allies at Nicopolis in 1396		
*Crusaders knights ** Heavy knight impetuous Passer élite (max 4)	12 +2	2-6

Note

- One commander can be included in a Szekler unit.

239 - Muscovite Russian

1246 - 1530 AD
Plain, Forest, Steppes
Command +3

After the Mongol invasion all of the southern Rus' states came under the control of the Golden Horde. In the north Novgorod and Vladimir retained some measure of independence and became tributaries. This period saw the rise of power of the Muscovites who collaborated with the Mongols. In 1380, at the Battle of Kulikovo, the Russians won a great victory that began the decline of Mongol power in Russia. After that date the Rus' started to employ Cossack mercenaries. In the 15th century the Muscovites took control of the city of Novgorod.

Troop type	Pts	Units
*Nobles ** Heavy cavalry bow Upgrade to elite	11 +2	2-4
Other horsemen Medium cavalry bow Heavy cavalry bow	9 11	6-16
Militia Heavy spearmen mediocre	6	0-4
Militia Bowmen mediocre Light infantry bow	5 4	0-4
Levy	3	0-2
Gulay-gorod Fortification	1	0-6
Fortified camp	6	0-1
After 1380 No allies after 1380		
Replace all Gulay-gorod and fortified camp by war wagons War wagon bow mediocre	8	0-2
Tatars and Cossacks Light cavalry bow elite	7	0-6
Foot Cossacks Light infantry bow	4	0-2
Cossack handgunners (after 1470) Light infantry firearm Upgrade to elite	4 +1	0-4
Light gun Light artillery	6	0-1

Note

- Fortifications and fortified camp can be entirely replaced by war wagons after 1380.
- Lithuanian allies (List #237 Lithuanian)
- Tatar allies (List #240 Golden Horde)

240 - Golden Horde

1251 - 1550 AD
Plain, Steppes
Command +4

After the invasion of Russia, the Mongols established a khanate which included Russia, the Ukraine, Moldavia, Kazakhstan and the Caucasus. The population was composed mostly of Kipchak, Kyrgyz, or Khwarazmian Turks, which are commonly called Tatars. The Golden Horde exacted tribute from the Central European and Balkan states. In the 14th century the emergence of Lithuania and the rise of the Muscovites weakened the khanate. A plague followed by a long civil war exacerbated the situation. At the end of the 14th century the Timurids crushed the army of the Golden Horde and plundered its capital. In the 15th century the khanate broke up into small kingdoms that often fought against each other and were absorbed by Russia. The Crimean Khanate persisted until 1783.

Troop type	Pts	Units
*Shock cavalry **		
Heavy cavalry bow elite	13	0-4
Add impact	+1	
*Mongol horsemen **		
Medium cavalry bow	9	6-18
Upgrade to elite	+2	
Light cavalry bow	6	
Upgrade to elite	+1	
Cumans or Alans		
Light cavalry bow	6	0-8
Upgrade to elite	+1	
Armenian or moslem		
Bowmen	7	0-4
Downgrade to mediocre	-2	
Light infantry bow	4	
Siberians		
Medium swordsmen impetuous	7	0-2
Naffatun (after 1340)		
Light infantry firearm	4	0-1
Levy	3	0-2
Fortified camp	6	0-1

Note

- Georgian allies (List #205 Georgian)
- Russian allies (List #239 Muscovite Russian)
- Ottoman allies (List #246 Turkoman or #251 Ottoman Empire)

241 - Medieval Polish

1333 - 1510 AD
Plain, Forest
Command +4
Strategist: Vytautas (1410 AD)

King Casimir III reigned over Poland from 1333 to 1370. He reformed the army and conquered lands from the Rus'. In 1343 he concluded the Treaty of Kalisz which ended the war between Poland and the Teutonic Order. In 1385 the Union of Krewo led to the personal union of the Kingdom of Poland and the Grand Duchy of Lithuania. In 1410 the Teutonic Knights were defeated at the Battle of Tannenberg (or Grunwald) by the combined forces of Poland and Lithuania led by Vytautas. Subsequently Poland was allied with Hungary. Both countries contributed to the Papal army that was defeated by the Ottomans at the Battle of Varna in 1444.

Troop type	Pts	Units
*Nobles **		
Heavy knight impetuous	12	4-8
Upgrade to elite (max 4)	+2	
Followers with crossbow		
Medium cavalry crossbow	9	4-8
Lithuanians		
Light cavalry javelin	6	0-6
Medium cavalry	7	
Vlachs, Moldavians or Tatars		
Light cavalry bow elite	7	0-3
Hungarians and Cumans		
Light cavalry bow	6	0-3
Militia in mixed units		
½ Heavy spearmen ½ Crossbowmen	10	0-3
Swordsmen with axe		
Medium swordsmen 2HW	8	0-2
Light infantry bow Light infantry crossbow	4	0-2
Fortifications	1	0-6
After 1400		
Replace some nobles and/or followers by lancers		
Heavy cavalry impact	10	0-6
Serbian hussars		
Light cavalry impact elite	7	0-3
Handgunners		
Light infantry firearm	4	0-2
Upgrade to elite	+1	
War wagon crossbow	10	0-2
Light artillery	6	0-1
Fortified camp	6	0-1

Note

- Lithuanian allies (List #237 Lithuanian)
- Hungarian allies (List #238 Medieval Hungarian)
- Bohemian allies (List #242 Hussite)

242 - Hussite

1419 - 1434 & 1464 - 1471 AD
Plain, Forest
Command +4
Strategist: Jan Žižka (1420 – 1424)

The assassination of the religious reformer Jan Hus led to unrest and eventually revolt in Bohemia. Jan Žižka was a leader of the Hussites and won many battles against the Germans and Hungarians. He used war wagons equipped with cannons and protected by halberdiers. Despite a civil war between two rival Hussite factions, Catholics forces were not able to win any battles. A peace treaty was finally concluded in 1434. Between 1464 and 1471 a new crusade was triggered against the Hussites by the Hungarians and the Silesians.

Troop type	Pts	Units
*Bohemian nobles ** Heavy knight Upgrade to elite	12 +2	0-4
*Hussite horsemen ** Heavy cavalry impact	10	0-4
*Hussite wagons ** War wagon crossbow Upgrade to Light artillery (max 2)	10 +2	4-12
Scouts Light cavalry crossbow	6	0-2
Halberdiers and heavy flails Heavy swordsmen 2HW Add armour (max 4)	9 +2	0-8
Peasants skirmishers Light infantry bow Light infantry sling	4	0-4
Fanatical peasants Levy impetuous	4	0-4
Separately deployed light guns Light artillery	6	0-2
Bombards and trebuchet Heavy artillery	10	0-2
Fortifications	1	0-12
Fortified camp	6	0-1

Note

- Light guns can be included in war wagon units or be deployed separately.
- Polish allies (List #241 Medieval Polish)

TURKS AND BALKANS

243 - Serbian Empire

1180 – 1459 AD
Plain, Mountain
Command +3

During the reign of Stefan Nemanja, called Saint Simeon (1166-1196), Serbia became an independent kingdom although keeping close ties with the Byzantines. In the 13th century Byzantium was occupied by the Crusaders while Hungary as well as Bulgaria was devastated by the Mongols. These events helped Serbia to become the dominant Slav state. Subsequently Serbia was at war against the Byzantines, Bulgarians and Hungarians. In 1389 the Ottoman Turks fought the Serbs at the Battle of Kosovo. The battle was hard won by the Ottoman Turks but it allowed them a strong foothold in the Balkans. From the 15th century Serbia was subject to the Ottoman Empire and was finally absorbed in 1459.

Troop type	Pts	Units
*Serbian nobles ** Heavy cavalry impetuous Upgrade to elite	9 +2	6-16
Mercenary knights Medium knight impact Heavy knight impact	11 13	0-2
Turkomans or Tatars Light cavalry bow elite Medium cavalry bow	7 9	0-6
Hungarians or Cumans Light cavalry bow	6	0-3
Voynuks Heavy spearmen Heavy swordsmen 2HW Add armour	8 9 +2	0-2
Serbians, Croats or Bosniacs Medium swordsmen	7	0-4
Serbians, Croats or Bosniacs Bowmen Downgrade to mediocre	7 -2	2-8
Light infantry bow	4	0-4
Levy	3	0-2
Only after 1340		
*Replace all Serbian nobles ** Medium knight impetuous Heavy knight impetuous Upgrade to elite	10 12 +2	All
Serbian hussars Light cavalry impact elite	7	2-6

Only after 1380 Albanian allies (List #250 Albanian) Ottoman allies (List #251 Ottoman Empire)		
Mercenaries Crossbowmen Add pavise	 7 +1	0-2
Handgunners Light infantry firearm Upgrade to elite	 4 +1	
Light artillery Heavy artillery	6 10	0-1

Note

- Byzantine allies (List #245 Later Byzantine) before 1380

244 - Later Bulgarian

1186 – 1395 AD
Plain, Mountain
Command +2

In 1186 the Bulgarians and Vlachs revolted against the Byzantines and founded the kingdom of Bulgaria-Wallachia which was ruled by Tsars Peter and Ivan Asen. During the reign of Tsar Kalojan (1197-1207) new territories were won from the Byzantines, including Macedonia and Thrace. Following the Mongol invasion of the 13th century Bulgaria was devastated and had to pay tribute to the Golden Horde. The kingdom lost provinces to the Hungarians and the Byzantines and was greatly reduced in size. Bulgaria was finally conquered by the Ottoman Turks in 1395.

Troop type	Pts	Units
Nobles * Heavy cavalry impetuous Upgrade to elite (max 4)	 9 +2	4-8
Bulgars, Cumans and Vlachs Light cavalry bow Light cavalry bow elite Medium cavalry bow (max 12)	 6 7 9	4-24
Greek horsemen Medium cavalry mediocre	5	0-2
Greeks, Vlachs and Bulgars Heavy spearmen mediocre	6	0-6
Greeks, Vlachs and Bulgars Bowmen Downgrade to mediocre	 7 -2	0-6
Light infantry bow	4	

Note

- Tatar allies (List #240 Golden Horde)
- Serbian allies (List #243 Serbian Empire)

245 - Later Byzantine

1204 - 1461 AD
Plain, Mountain
Command +4

After the fall of Constantinople the great Byzantine families founded several states in the territories remaining under their control. These were the Empire of Nicaea, the Despotates of Epirus and Morea and the Empire of Trebizond. In 1261 Michael Palaeologus retook Constantinople by surprise and was crowned Emperor Michael VIII. He reorganised the Byzantine state, but it remained weak and threatened from all sides. A civil war broke out in 1354 and the Empire lost most of its territories and was reduced to just Constantinople and Salonica. Constantinople falls to the Turks in 1453 but Empire of Trebizond remains independent until 1461.

Troop type	Pts	Units
Stratiotai * Medium cavalry impact Heavy cavalry impact Downgrade to mediocre	 8 10 -2	2-6
Pechenegs, Cumans, Vlachs, Bulgars or Turks (except Morea) Light cavalry bow Medium cavalry bow	 6 9	2-12
Greeks, Albanians or Vlachs Bowmen mediocre Upgrade to ordinary	 5 +2	2-12
Light infantry bow	4	
Kontaroi Heavy spearmen Downgrade to mediocre	 8 -2	0-2
Hillmen (except for Palaiologan) Javelinmen Downgrade to mediocre	 7 -2	0-4
Light infantry javelin	4	
Levy	3	0-1
Fortified camp	6	0-1
Empire of Nicaea (1204 – 1261) Seljuk Turk allies (List #195 Seljuk Turk) Cuman allies (List #207 Cuman) Bulgarian allies (List #244 Later Bulgarian) Despotat of Epirus allies (List #245 Later Byzantine)		
Frankish knights Medium knight impetuous Medium knight impact Upgrade to elite (max 2)	 10 11 +2	2-6
Vardariot guardsmen Light cavalry bow elite Medium cavalry bow elite	 7 11	0-2

Despotat of Epirus (1204 - 1340)		
Angevin allies (List #180 Normans in Sicily)		
Bulgarian allies (List #244 Later Bulgarian)		
Palaiologan allies (List #245 Later Byzantine)		
Albanians		
Light cavalry javelin elite	7	0-4
Medium cavalry impact	8	
Frankish knights		
Medium knight impetuous elite	12	0-2
Medium knight impact	11	
Despotat of Morea (1262 - 1460)		
Turk allies (List #247 Ottoman Turkish)		
*Albanians **		
Light cavalry javelin elite	7	0-8
Medium cavalry impact	8	
Frankish knights (after 1445)		
Medium knight impetuous elite	12	0-2
Heavy knight impetuous elite	14	
Empire of Trebizond (1204 - 1461)		
Georgian allies (List #205 Georgian)		
Turk allies (List #246 Turkoman)		
Replace Stratiotai (some after 1360 or all after 1400)		
Medium cavalry bow	9	2-6
Heavy cavalry bow	11	
Upgrade to elite	+2	
Palaiologan Byzantine (1261 - 1384)		
Tatar allies (List #240 Golden Horde)		
Serbian allies (List #243 Serbian Empire)		
Bulgarian allies (List #244 Later Bulgarian)		
Turk allies (List #246 Turkoman or List #247 Ottoman Turkish)		
Vardariot guardsmen		
Light cavalry bow elite	7	0-2
Medium cavalry bow elite	11	
Frankish knights		
Medium knight impact elite	13	0-2
Heavy knight impact elite	15	
Catalan or Tzakones guards		
Medium swordsmen impact elite	10	0-2
Medium spearmen elite	9	

246 - TURKOMAN

1260 - 1491 AD
Plain, Steppes
Command +3

The Turkomans (or Turkmens) were a people of Central Asian origin. Some tribes appeared in Anatolia after the weakening of the Seljuks. Most were subjugated by the Ottomans in the 14th century before being liberated by the arrival of Timurids. The Ottomans subjugated them again at the end of 15th century.

Troop type	Pts	Units
*Nobles **		
Heavy cavalry bow	11	0-6
Upgrade to elite	+2	
Turkoman horsemen		
Light cavalry bow elite	7	8-24
Medium cavalry bow	9	
Medium spearmen	7	0-4
Bowmen	7	0-4
Downgrade to mediocre	-2	
Light infantry bow	4	
Only after 1380		
Light artillery	6	0-3
Heavy artillery (max 1)	10	
Levy	3	0-2

Note

- Trebizond allies (List #245 Later Byzantine)
- Ottoman allies (List #247 Ottoman Turkish)
- Mamluk allies (List #253 Mamluk)

247 - OTTOMAN TURKISH

1299 - 1361 AD
Plain, Steppes
Command +3

The Ottomans were a Turkic tribe that had moved to Anatolia. After the breakup of the Seljuk Empire the tribe, commanded by Osman I, started its conquests. The Ottoman Empire was founded in 1299 after the capture of the Byzantine town of Thebasion (Söğüt in Turkish). The power of the Ottomans expanded rapidly in Asia Minor and they entered the Balkans in 1347. This list ends just before the creation of the Janissary corps in 1362.

Troop type	Pts	Units
*Sipahis **		
Medium cavalry bow	9	0-6
Heavy cavalry bow	11	
Upgrade to elite	+2	
*Ghazis **		
Light cavalry bow elite	7	8-24
Medium cavalry bow	9	
Medium cavalry bow elite	11	
Spearmen		
Medium spearmen	7	0-2
Heavy spearmen	8	
Downgrade to mediocre	-2	

Azabs Bowmen Downgrade to mediocre	7 -2	2-4
Light infantry bow	4	
Azabs Light infantry sling Light infantry javelin	4	0-2
Levy	3	0-2
Fortified camp	6	0-1

248 - Catalan Company

1302 - 1388 AD
Plain, Mountain
Command +4

The Catalan company was formed by Roger de Flor to fight against the Turks threatening the Byzantine Empire. It was made up of knights and Catalan infantry, called Almughavars, who were known for their ferocity in battle. The Catalans landed in Constantinople in 1303 and were sent to fight the Turks. They quickly chased them from Asia Minor and were then sent back to Europe to fight the Bulgarians. The indiscipline of the company and the ambitions of Roger de Flor led to his murder in 1307. In retaliation the Catalans massacred the inhabitants of Gallipoli, settled there and ravaged the region. The Emperor was powerless especially when the Catalans received reinforcements from Spain. Leaving Gallipoli the Catalans founded a kingdom in Greece which lasted nearly 80 years.

Troop type	Pts	Units
*Men-at-arms ** Medium knight impact Heavy knight impact Upgrade to elite	11 13 +2	0-2
*Aragonese horsemen ** Medium cavalry impact Heavy cavalry impact Upgrade to elite (max 4)	8 10 +2	2-4
*Almughavars ** Medium swordsmen impact elite Medium spearmen elite	10 9	6-16
Crossbowmen Light infantry crossbow	7 4	0-3
Greek prisoners Bowmen mediocre Light infantry bow	5 4	0-3
Almughavar scouts Light infantry javelin Upgrade to elite	4	0-4
Fortified camp	6	0-1

Only after 1305		
Turks (after 1305) Light cavalry bow Medium cavalry bow (max 4)	6 9	4-8
Albanians (after 1380) Light cavalry javelin elite Medium cavalry impact	7 8	

Note

- Palaiologan Byzantine allies (List #245 Later Byzantine) only before 1305
- Alan allies (List #108 Alan) only before 1305

249 - Vlach and Moldavian

1330 - 1504 AD
Plain, Mountain, Forest
Command +4
Strategists: Vlad III the Impaler (1456-1462 and 1476 AD), Stephen III the Great (1457-1504)

The Vlachs occupied the province of Wallachia in what is now Romania. They became independent from Hungary in 1330. They resisted the Ottomans until forced to accept their suzerainty in 1415. However several rulers rebelled against the Turks. This was the case with Vlad III the Impaler (known as Dracula) who rebelled against the Ottomans with support of the Hungarian King. He was assassinated in 1476. In the early Middle Ages Moldavia was a powerful and prosperous state. King Stephen III the Great won numerous victories over his neighbours: the Hungarians, Tatars, Turks and Poles.

Troop type	Pts	Units
*Vlach or Moldavian nobles ** Heavy cavalry bow Upgrade to elite	11 +2	2-4
Other horsemen Light cavalry bow Medium cavalry bow	6 9	4-12
Voynuks Heavy swordsmen 2HW Add armour	9 +2	0-2
Curteni archers Bowmen Add Pavise	7 +1	0-4
Bowmen mediocre Light infantry bow	5 4	4-12
Peasant levy Medium spearmen mediocre Levy	5 3	0-4
Light infantry firearm Upgrade to elite	4 +1	0-2

Light infantry crossbow	4	0-2
Heavy artillery	10	0-1
Fortified camp	6	0-1
Only Vlach		
Mercenaries Heavy knight impact	13	0-2
Fortifications	1	0-6
Only Moldavian Crimean Tatars allies (List #240 Golden Horde) Polish allies (List #241 Medieval Polish)		
*Replace some nobles after 1400 ** Medium knight impetuous Upgrade to elite	10 +2	0-4
Fortifications	1	0-12

Note

- Hungarian allies (List #238 Medieval Hungarian)
- Ottoman allies (List #251 Ottoman Empire)

250 - Albanian

1345 - 1430 and 1443 - 1479 AD
Mountain
Command +3
Strategist: George Kastrioti Skanderbeg (1443-1468)

Albania was controlled successively by the Byzantines, the Normans and the Serbs. In 1345 the Albanians rebelled against Serbian authority and became independent until 1430. They fought victoriously against the Franks of Sicily and then the Venetians. In 1430 Albania was conquered by the Ottomans. In 1443 Skanderbeg led a revolt and inflicted severe defeats to the Turks without being able to drive them out. Shortly after his death the Ottomans regained control of Albania.

Troop type	Pts	Units
*Albanian veterans ** Light cavalry javelin elite Medium cavalry impact elite	7 10	2-6
Albanian horsemen Light cavalry javelin Medium cavalry impact	6 8	6-24
Mounted crossbowmen Light cavalry crossbow	6	0-4
Bowmen Downgrade to mediocre	7 -2	4-12
Light infantry bow	4	
Crossbowmen Downgrade to mediocre	7 -2	0-4
Light infantry crossbow	4	
Heavy swordsmen 2HW Add armour	9 +2	0-2
Javelinmen Light infantry javelin	7 4	0-4
Levy	3	0-2
Light artillery Heavy artillery	6 10	0-1
From 1450		
Mercenaries Heavy knight impact	13	0-2
Light infantry firearm Upgrade to elite	4 +1	0-2

Venetian or Neapolitan allies		
*Men-at-arm ** Heavy knight impact	13	0-2
Crossbowmen Add pavise	7 +1	0-2
Light infantry crossbow	4	
Light infantry firearm Light infantry bow	4	0-2

Note

- Venetian or Neapolitan allies (see List above)

251 - Ottoman Empire

1362 – 1512 AD
Plain, Mountain
Command +6
Strategist: Bayezid I Yldirim (1389-1402 AD)

The Janissary corps was created in 1362. It was formed from prisoners and Christian boys forced to convert to Islam. The Ottoman Empire won the decisive battle of Kosovo in 1389 which ended the independence of Serbia and Albania and gave the Turks control of the Balkans. In 1453 Sultan Mehmet II captured Constantinople and put an end to the Byzantine Empire. Thereafter the Ottoman Empire extended its rule over Egypt and the Maghreb. In Europe the Ottomans were faced by a coalition of nations, led by Hungarians, who opposed their further advance. The Ottoman Empire reached its apogee during the reign of Suleiman the Magnificent

Troop type	Pts	Units
*Qapukulu ** Heavy cavalry bow elite Add impact	13 +1	0-2
*Sipahis ** Medium cavalry bow Heavy cavalry bow Upgrade to elite (max 6)	9 11 +2	4-10

Akinji horse archers Light cavalry bow	6	4-12
Turkomans Light cavalry bow elite	7	0-3
Bedouins or Delis Light cavalry impact Upgrade to elite (*Delis*)	6 +1	0-3
Syrians and Kurds Medium cavalry impact Heavy cavalry impact	8 10	0-2
Janissaries Medium swordsmen bow elite	12	0-4
Voynuks Heavy swordsmen 2HW Add armour	9 +2	0-2
Spearmen Medium spearmen Heavy spearmen Downgrade to mediocre	7 8 -2	0-2
Azabs Bowmen Downgrade to mediocre	7 -2	2-4
Light infantry bow	4	
Azabs Light infantry sling Light infantry javelin	4	0-2
Azab handgunners (after 1430) Light infantry firearm Upgrade to elite	4 +1	
Only after 1441 War wagon firearm	10	0-2
Levy	3	0-2
Light artillery Heavy artillery	6 10	0-2
Fortifications	1	0-8
Fortified camp	6	0-1

Note

- Tatar allies (List #240 Golden Horde)
- Serbian allies (List #243 Serbian Empire)
- Turkoman allies (List #246 Turkoman)
- Vlach allies (List #249 Vlach and Moldavian)
- Albanian allies (List #250 Albanian)

252 - Besieged Byzantine

1384 - 1453 AD
Plain, Mountain
Command +3

In the second half of the 14th century the Ottoman Turks extended their influence in Anatolia and crushed the crusaders at Nicopolis in 1396. Sultan Bayezid I was preparing to besiege Constantinople when he was attacked and defeated by the armies of Tamerlane. This was only a brief respite for Byzantines. In 1422 the Sultan Murad II besieged the city but was repulsed. The Byzantines lost their last territories including Salonika in 1430. They begged military aid from western nations but the Crusaders were again beaten. In 1453 Sultan Mehmet II determined to succeed and assembled a large army. Constantinople fell in May 28, 1453 and the last Emperor Constantine XII died with weapon in hand.

Troop type	Pts	Units
*Stratiotai ** Medium cavalry impact Heavy cavalry impact Downgrade to mediocre	8 10 -2	2-4
Kataphraktoi or mercenaries Heavy knight impact Downgrade to mediocre	13 -2	0-2
Burgundian knights Heavy knight impetuous Foot knight	12	0-2
Albanian veterans Light cavalry javelin elite	7	0-6
Medium cavalry impact Upgrade to elite (max 2)	8 +2	
Garrison and peasants Bowmen mediocre Light infantry bow	5 4	6-10
Urban militia Medium spearmen mediocre	5	0-6
Gianitzaroi guardsmen Medium swordsmen elite	9	0-2
Kontaroi Heavy spearmen Downgrade to mediocre	8 -2	0-2
Peasants and hillmen Medium swordsmen Downgrade to mediocre	7 -2	0-4
*Genoese mercenaries ** Crossbowmen Upgrade to elite Add pavise	7 +2 +1	0-4
*Genoese mercenaries ** Heavy swordsmen 2HW (max 2)	9	
Light artillery Heavy artillery	6 10	0-1
Fortification	1	0-12

Note

- For the final siege, one commander can be included in a Genoese mercenary unit.
- Albanian allies (List #250 Albanian)
- Ottoman allies (List #251 Ottoman Empire)

MEDIEVAL EGYPT

253 - Mamluk

1250 - 1517 AD
Plain, Desert
Command +5
Strategist: Baybars (1260-1277 AD)

The Mamluks were originally slave soldiers. In Egypt their power grew and in 1250 they overthrew their Ayyubid masters. The Mamluk Sultan Qutuz defeated the Mongols at Ain Jalut in 1260, but on the way back to Cairo he was assassinated by Baybars. Baybars and his successors ruled over Egypt, the Levant and part of Arabia. In 1291 they ended the Frankish presence in Syria by taking Acre, the last vestige of the Crusader Kingdom of Jerusalem. The Ottoman Turks were intent on the destruction of the Mamluks and took Cairo in 1517.

Troop type	Pts	Units
Royal Mamluks * Heavy cavalry bow elite Add impact	 13 +1	 0-2
Amir's Mamluks Heavy cavalry bow Upgrade to elite	 11 +2	 4-12
Turkomans Light cavalry bow elite Medium cavalry bow	 7 9	 2-6
Halqa Medium cavalry bow Bowmen	 9 7	 0-6
Syrians and Kurds Medium cavalry impact Heavy cavalry impact	 8 10	 0-2
Bedouins Light cavalry impact	6	0-4
Crossbowmen	7	0-1
Bowmen Light infantry bow	7 4	0-2
Javelinmen	7	0-2
Naffatun or handgunners Light infantry firearm	4	0-1
Levy	3	0-2
Light artillery Heavy artillery	6 10	0-1
Fortified camp	6	0-1

Note

- Syrian allies (List #197 Syrian) before 1286

CENTRAL ASIA

254 - Islamic Persian

1245 - 1393 AD
Plain, Steppes
Command +4

When Persia was invaded by the Ilkhanid Mongols the Persian dynasties swore allegiance to their new overlords. At the death of the last Ilkhan in 1336 the Muzaffarids took the opportunity to extend their control to include southern Persia. The list ends with the Timurid conquest in 1393.

Troop type	Pts	Units
Persian horsemen * Medium cavalry bow Heavy cavalry bow Upgrade to elite (max 8)	 9 11 +2	 8-20
Turkomans Light cavalry bow elite Medium cavalry bow	 7 9	 0-4
Persian archers Bowmen mediocre Light infantry bow	 5 4	 0-4
Afghans Medium spearmen (max 3) Bowmen (max 3)	 7	 0-6
Levy	3	0-2

255 - Ilkhanid Mongol

1251 - 1355 AD
Plain, Mountain, Steppes
Command +5

Hulagu Khan, the grandson of Genghis Khan, founded the Ilkhanid Mongol dynasty, which reigned over the Middle East from Transoxiana to Syria. He overthrew the Seljuk Turks and established his control over the Armenians of Cilicia and the Sultanate of Rum. The Ilkhanids were opposed by the Mamluks of Egypt, who were victorious at Ain Jalut (1258) and Homs (1260). Attempts to make an alliance with the Crusaders against the Mamluks failed. Starting from 1335 the Khanate disintegrated quickly to the benefit firstly of the Jalayirids and then the Timurids.

Troop type	Pts	Units
Khan's guardsmen * Heavy cavalry bow elite Add impact	 13 +1	 1-4

*Mongol horsemen **		
Medium cavalry bow	9	
Upgrade to elite	+2	6-24
Light cavalry bow	6	
Upgrade to elite	+1	
Turkomans		
Light cavalry bow elite	7	0-6
Medium cavalry bow	9	
Kurds		
Medium cavalry impact	8	0-2
Heavy cavalry impact	10	
Franks or Hospitallers		
Medium knight impetuous elite	12	0-2
Medium knight impact elite	13	
Franks		
Crossbowmen	7	0-2
Dismounted horsemen		
Bowmen	7	0-4
Light infantry bow	4	
Heavy artillery	10	0-2
Fortified camp	6	0-1

Note

- Armenian allies (List #185 Cilician Armenian)
- Seljuk Turk allies (List #195 Seljuk Turk)
- Syrian allies (List #197 Syrian)
- Georgian allies (List #205 Georgian)
- Tatar allies (List #240 Golden Horde)
- Persian allies (List #254 Islamic Persian)

256 - Steppes Mongol

1266 – 1508 AD
Steppes
Command +4

This list covers all the Mongol tribes and khanates after the disintegration of the Empire, excluding the Golden Horde and the Ilkhanids. This includes the Chagatai Khanate in Central Asia before the Timurids seized power there. It also includes the descendants of the Yuan that were chased from Mongolia and who conducted raids on the Chinese border during Ming period.

Troop type	Pts	Units
*Shock cavalry **		
Heavy cavalry bow elite	13	0-4
Add impact	+1	
*Mongol horsemen **		
Medium cavalry bow	9	
Upgrade to elite	+2	8-30
Light cavalry bow	6	
Upgrade to elite	+1	

Dismounted horsemen		
Bowmen	7	0-4
Light infantry bow	4	
Levy	3	0-2
Fortified camp	6	0-1

Note

- Persian allies (List #254 Islamic Persian)
- Ilkhanid allies (List #255 Ilkhanid Mongol)

257 - Jalayirid

1336 - 1432 AD
Plain, Steppes
Command +4

The Jalayirids were a Muslim Mongol dynasty originated from the Ilkhanids. When the last Ilkhan died in 1336 the founder of the dynasty, Hasan Buzurg, took control of Baghdad. His successors expanded their territory to encompass much of Iraq and western Iran. The Timurids of Tamerlane subjugated the Jalayirids but they retained control of the Basra region until 1432, before being overthrown by the Turkomans of the *Black Sheep* tribe.

Troop type	Pts	Units
*Ghulams and Mongol nobles **		
Heavy cavalry bow	11	2-6
Upgrade to elite	+2	
Horse archers		
Light cavalry bow	6	4-16
Medium cavalry bow (max 8)	9	
Bedouins		
Light cavalry impact	6	2-6
Medium cavalry impact	8	
Turkomans		
Light cavalry bow elite	7	0-4
Medium cavalry bow	9	
Levy	3	0-2

Note

- Georgian allies (List #205 Georgian)
- Turkoman allies (List #259 Black Sheep and White Sheep Turkoman)

258 - Timurid

1360 - 1506 AD
Plain, Steppes
Command +5
Strategist: Tamerlane (1360-1405 AD)

Tamerlane was born in the region of Samarkand in 1336. He was the son of a minor noble of the Barlas tribe and built a huge Empire by spreading terror and destruction. In 1369 he seized power in the Western Chagatai Khanate. In the next decade he took the rest of Central Asia and by 1385 he held Afghanistan and Persia too. Continuing his expansion westwards he added Iraq, Azerbaijan, Armenia, and Georgia. In 1398 he turned to India and destroyed the Delhi Sultanate, committing great atrocities (making pyramids of skulls, etc). In 1400 he fought in the west against the Ottomans and the Mamluks. He took Baghdad in 1401, defeated the Ottoman Sultan Bayezid in 1402 and captured Ephesus and Smyrna. He died in 1405 while preparing a campaign against China. During the reign of his successors the Empire was gradually eroded before being destroyed by the attacks of the descendants of the Golden Horde.

Troop type	Pts	Units
*Timurid nobles **		
Heavy cavalry bow	11	6-14
Upgrade to elite (max 8)	+2	
Add impact (max 4)	+1	
Persians, Georgians or Turkomans		
Medium cavalry bow	9	0-6
Heavy cavalry bow	11	
Turkomans		
Light cavalry bow elite	7	0-6
Elephant	13	0-2
Timurid archers		
Bowmen	7	0-3
Persian archers		
Bowmen mediocre	5	0-4
Light infantry bow	4	
Afghan spearmen or hillmen		
Medium spearmen	7	0-2
Javelinmen		
Stampeding herd		
Scythed chariot	3	0-2
Handgunners (after 1470)		
Light infantry firearm	4	0-2
Upgrade to elite	+1	
Heavy artillery	10	0-1
Hostages and war prisoners		
Levy mediocre expendable	1	0-2
Fortified camp	6	0-1

Note

- Mongol allies (List #256 Steppes Mongol)
- Turkoman allies (List #259 Black Sheep and White Sheep Turkoman)

259 - Black Sheep and White Sheep Turkoman

1378 - 1466 and 1387 - 1508 AD
Plain, Steppes
Command +4

The Black Sheep Turkoman tribe (Qara Qoyunlu) brought down the Jalayirids and took control of eastern Anatolia, northern Iraq and Azerbaijan. During the war against the Timurids in the early 15th century, they first lost and then regained territory. In 1466 they suffered a serious defeat against the tribe of the White Sheep (Aq Qoyunlu) that caused their collapse. The White Sheep tribe had to face the pressure of the Ottomans and then a war against the Persian Safavids that caused their fall in 1508.

Troop type	Pts	Units
*Turkoman nobles **		
Heavy cavalry bow	11	2-4
Upgrade to elite	+2	
Turkomans		
Light cavalry bow elite	7	6-20
Medium cavalry bow	9	
Kurds		
Medium cavalry impact	8	0-4
Heavy cavalry impact	10	
Bowmen	7	2-6
Light infantry bow	4	
Levy	3	0-2
Fortified camp	6	0-1
Only White Sheep from 1472		
Heavy artillery	10	0-1
Handgunners		
Light infantry firearm	4	0-2
Upgrade to elite	+1	
Fortifications	1	0-4

Note

- Georgian allies (List #205 Georgian)
- Turkoman allies (List #246 Turkoman)
- Turkoman allies (List #259 Black Sheep and White Sheep Turkoman)

MEDIEVAL ASIA

260 - Delhi Sultanate

1206 - 1526 AD
Plain, Forest
Command +3

This list represents the armies of the various Indian Muslim dynasties. The Delhi Sultanate was founded by a slave general who rebelled against the Ghurids in 1206. The Muslims then extended their influence southward. Only the Hindu kingdom of Vijayanagar resisted until 1565. The Sultanate repulsed Mongol invasions in 1398. It was also invaded by the armies of Tamerlane who sacked Delhi without destroying the power of the Sultanate. Babur incorporated the Sultanate into the Mughal Empire in 1526.

Troop type	Pts	Units
Royal guardsmen * Heavy cavalry bow elite Add impact	13 +1	0-2
Mamluks and Jagirs Heavy cavalry bow Upgrade to elite	11 +2	4-8
Tribal cavalry and Ghazis Heavy cavalry bow Medium cavalry bow	11 9	0-8
Elephants with handgunners Elephant elite	16	0-3
Horse archers Light cavalry bow	6	0-2
Afghans Light cavalry javelin	6	0-2
Afghans Medium spearmen	7	0-2
Afghans Bowmen	7	0-2
Hindu archers Bowmen Downgrade to mediocre	7 -2	2-8
Hindu swordsmen Medium swordsmen Upgrade to impetuous	7	1-4
Hindu skirmishers Light infantry bow Light infantry javelin	4	0-3
Hindu levy Levy	3	0-2
After 1340		
Abyssinian bodyguards Medium swordsmen impact elite	10	0-1
Handgunners Light infantry firearm Upgrade to elite	4 +1	0-2
Rocketeers Light artillery	6	0-4
Bombards Heavy artillery	10	0-1

Rajput allies from 1316 to 1388		
Rajput horsemen * Heavy cavalry impetuous Upgrade to elite	9 +2	2-4

Note

- Rajput allies (see list above)

Elephants with handgunners

261 - Indonesian and Malay

1222 - 1511 AD
Plain, Mountain, Forest
Command +3

This list represents the armies of the different kingdoms that dominated Indonesia and Malaysia during the Middle Ages. The kingdom of Singhasari was founded in 1222 in eastern Java. Between 1254 and 1292 the kingdom extended its influence throughout the region and controlled the trade of pepper and nutmeg. In the 14th century Singhasari fell under the influence of the Majapahit kingdom. Around 1400 the city of Malacca in Malaysia became the largest port in the region. It was capture by the Portuguese in 1511.

Troop type	Pts	Units
Nobles * Medium cavalry Upgrade to elite	 7 +2	0-2
Light cavalry javelin	6	0-2
Elephant *	13	0-4
Warriors * Medium swordsmen impetuous	7	6-24
Archers Bowmen Downgrade to mediocre	 7 -2	2-8
Light infantry bow	4	
Light infantry javelin	4	0-6
Levy	3	0-2
After 1400		
Light infantry firearm Upgrade to elite	4 +1	0-2
Light artillery Heavy artillery	6 10	0-1

Note

- Khmer allies (List #167 Khmer Empire and Champa)
- Yuan Chinese allies (List #263 Yuan Chinese)
- Ming Chinese allies (List #265 Ming Chinese)

262 - Siam

1238 - 1518 AD
Plain, Mountain, Forest
Command +3

Siam is the former name for Thailand. In the 13th century the Thais freed themselves from Khmer control. They founded the Sukhothai kingdom in 1238. The kingdom declined slowly during the 14th century and in 1378 fell under the domination of the Ayutthaya kingdom. For centuries Siam suffered invasions from the Burmese who eventually plundered the city of Ayutthaya in 1559.

Troop type	Pts	Units
War elephant * Elephant	13	1-3
Medium cavalry Downgrade to mediocre	7 -2	0-4
Royal guardsmen Medium swordsmen impact elite Add support	 10 +1	0-2
Warriors (all of the same type) Medium swordsmen Medium swordsmen impetuous	7	6-24
Archers Bowmen Downgrade to mediocre	 7 -2	2-8
Light infantry bow	4	
Porters and servants Levy mediocre expendable	1	0-3
Fortified camp	6	0-1
After 1400		
Light infantry firearm Upgrade to elite	4 +1	0-2
Light guns Light artillery	6	0-1

Note

- Burmese allies (List #163 Burmese)
- Malay allies (List #261 Indonesian and Malay)

263 - Yuan Chinese

1260 - 1368 AD
Plain, Mountain, Steppes
Command +4

The Mongols completed the conquest of southern China in 1276 and founded the Yuan dynasty that reigned over the whole of the country. Kublai Khan claimed authority over the other Mongol khanates, but his control was largely nominal. This was the case with Chagatai in Central Asia, the Ilkhanids in Iran and Afghanistan and the Golden Horde in Russia. After the death of Kublai Khan in 1294 the power of the Yuan weakened and the Mongols were expelled from China by the Ming in 1368.

Troop type	Pts	Units
Khan's guardsmen * Heavy cavalry bow elite Add impact	 13 +1	1-4

Mongol horsemen Medium cavalry bow Upgrade to elite *(before 1275)*	9 +2	2-12
Light cavalry bow Upgrade to elite *(before 1275)*	6 +1	
Chinese guardsmen Heavy swordsmen 2HW Add armour	9 +2	0-2
Chinese halberdiers and swordsmen Medium swordsmen 2HW Medium swordsmen impact Downgrade to mediocre	8 8 -2	2-6
Chinese archers and crossbowmen Bowmen Crossbowmen Downgrade to mediocre	7 7 -2	2-6
Light infantry bow Light infantry javelin (max 2)	4	0-4
Heavy artillery	10	0-1
Before 1275 Chinese allies (List #216 Jurchen-Chin) Mongol allies (List #218 Mongol Empire)		
Chinese horsemen Medium cavalry bow Heavy cavalry bow Downgrade to mediocre	9 11 -2	0-2
Chinese Kan-T'ao-Lu militia Medium swordsmen mediocre	5	0-6
From 1275		
Replace all mongol horsemen Medium cavalry bow Light cavalry bow	9 6	All
Only from 1279 to 1294 Elephant *	13	0-1
Tribal auxiliaries Medium cavalry	7	0-4
Tribal auxiliaries Javelinmen Medium swordsmen Medium swordsmen impetuous	7	0-2
Replace some Chinese archers and crossbowmen by mixed units ½ Medium spearmen ½ Bowmen or Crossbowmen	9	0-4
Fire tube Light infantry firearm	4	0-2
Light guns and rocketeers Light artillery	6	0-3

Note

- Uighur allies (List #141 Central Asian Turkish)
- Korean allies (List #212 Koryo Korean)
- Javanese allies (List #261 Indonesian and Malay) in 1293 and with no Tribal auxiliary troops.

264 - Later Samurai

1350 - 1550 AD
Plain, Mountain
Command +4

This list corresponds to the Muromachi period. During this period Japan was controlled from Kyoto by the Shoguns of the Ashikaga family. This was a troubled period with numerous wars. By 1573 Oda Nobunaga had extended his control to the whole of Japan.

Troop type	Pts	Units
Mounted samurai * Heavy cavalry impact Heavy cavalry bow Upgrade to elite	10 11 +2	0-4
Foot samurai Heavy swordsmen 2HW Add armour Upgrade to elite	9 +2 +2	4-12
Ronin Medium swordsmen 2HW Upgrade to elite Downgrade to mediocre	8 +2 -2	0-2
Ashigaru with yari before 1465 Medium spearmen mediocre	5	4-12
Ashigaru with yari or naginata from 1465 Medium spearmen Medium swordsmen 2HW	7 8	
Followers with bow Bowmen mediocre Upgrade to ordinary Add pavise	5 +2 +1	0-4
Fortifications	1	0-6
From 1465		
Ikkō-ikki fanatics Levy impetuous	4	0-6

Warrior monk allies		
Mounted warrior monks * Medium cavalry bow	9	0-1
Foot warrior monks * Medium swordsmen 2HW	8	0-4
Poorly armed monks Medium swordsmen mediocre Levy	5 3	0-2

Note

- Warrior monk allies (see list above)
- Ikkō-ikki fanatics cannot be used if Warrior monk allies are used.

265 - Ming Chinese

1356 – 1540 AD
Plain, Mountain, Forest
Command +4

In the mid-14th century several Chinese factions rebelled against the Mongol-led Yuan dynasty. Having overcome their rivals, the Ming dynasty was established in 1368 and lasted until 1644. It was a period of cultural revival in China with the expansion of trade to the Indian Ocean and even Africa. The Ming maintained an army of over one million men and rebuilt the Great Wall to protect against further Mongol invasions. From the 15th century China turned inward and entered a period of stagnation.

Troop type	Pts	Units
*Guardsmen (before 1420) ** Heavy cavalry bow elite	13	0-3
*Chinese horsemen (before 1420)** Heavy cavalry bow	11	3-9
Mongols or Jurchens Light cavalry bow Medium cavalry bow	 6 9	2-6
Halberdiers and swordsmen Medium swordsmen 2HW Heavy swordsmen 2HW Downgrade to mediocre	 8 9 -2	0-6
Chinese archers and crossbowmen Bowmen Crossbowmen Downgrade to mediocre	 7 7 -2	2-8
½ Medium spearmen ½ Bowmen or Crossbowmen	9	
Handgunners Light infantry firearm Upgrade to elite	 4 +1	0-2
Light infantry bow Light infantry crossbow	4	0-4
Stampeding herd Scythed chariot	3	0-2
Light guns and rocketeers Light artillery	6	0-5
Fortifications	1	0-8
After 1420		
*Replace all guardsmen and chinese horsemen ** Heavy cavalry bow Medium cavalry bow Downgrade to mediocre	 11 9 -2	2-6
*Chinese mercenaries ** Heavy cavalry bow mediocre Medium cavalry bow mediocre	 9 7	0-4
Tribal auxiliaries Javelinmen Medium swordsmen Medium swordsmen impetuous	7	0-3
War wagon firearm	10	0-2
Replace some guns and rocketeers Medium artillery Heavy artillery	10	0-2
Levy	3	0-4

Note

- Burmese allies (List #163 Burmese) after 1420
- Mongol allies (List #256 Steppes Mongol)

266 - Yi Korean

1392 - 1525 AD
Plain, Mountain, Forest
Command +4

The Yi or Choson Dynasty was founded by Yi Song-gye in 1392. It began with a period of prosperity for the kingdom, during which Confucianism was adopted. The Jurchens were repelled and a wall was built in the north to protect Korea from invasions.

Troop type	Pts	Units
*Korean horsemen ** Heavy cavalry impact Upgrade to elite (max 4)	 10 +2	4-8
Steppes horsemen Light cavalry bow Medium cavalry bow (max 6) Heavy cavlry bow (max 2)	 6 9 11	0-8
Guardsmen Heavy swordsmen 2HW elite Crossbowmen pavise elite	 11 10	0-2
Lancier lourd Pikemen mediocre	8	2-6
Bowmen Crossbowmen	7	2-6
Levy	3	0-4
Light infantry bow Light infantry javelin (max 2)	4	0-6
Light infantry firearm Upgrade to elite	4 +1	0-2
Light artillery Heavy artillery (max 2)	6 10	0-4
Fortifications	1	0-8

Note

- Ming Chinese allies (List #265 Ming Chinese)

AMERICA

These lists represent the armies of the pre-Columbian peoples of America up until the arrival of Spanish conquistadors in the sixteenth century. Most lists correspond to the Medieval or Early Renaissance periods but the armament of the troops is much closer to that of the Ancient period. We have therefore set these lists apart and leave it to the players to include them in the most appropriate period.

Horses were unknown before their introduction by the Europeans and armies were composed entirely of infantry. Metalworking was mainly for ornamentation and, apart from the Incas who used bronze to make tools, the weapons were mostly made of wood, stone or bone. The swords were usually made of wood with a cutting edge composed of obsidian flakes. Heavy maces used with both hands are classified as 2HW.

Some pre-Columbian peoples made extensive use of spear-throwers like the atlatl, which allowed flexible spears or darts to be thrown further. Troops armed with the atlatl use it as a ranged weapon, but it does not give them the javelin ability as flexible javelins are of no use in close combat.

Armour, when used, was light and covered only the head and torso. It was usually made of several layers of cloth and sometimes pieces of wood. Shields were widely used.

Maya Commander

CENTRAL AMERICA

267 - MAYA

600 BC - 1542 AD
Plain, Forest
Command +3

The Maya was a Mesoamerican civilisation, whose territory encompassed southern Mexico, the Yucatan Peninsula and northern Central America (Guatemala, Belize, El Salvador and Honduras). During the Classical period the Maya established many cities; the best known were Tikal, Palenque, Copan and Calakmul. In the 9th century, for unknown reasons, many cities were abandoned. Some important centres in the Yucatan still flourished when the Spanish arrived in 1517. The conquistadors failed to subjugate the Yucatan with two expeditions launched between 1527 and 1535. They finally succeeded in 1542, but the Mayan kingdom of Petén in modern Guatemala was not conquered until 1697.

Troop type	Pts	Units
Classical period until 900 AD		
*Nobles and warriors **		
Medium swordsmen	7	12-30
Upgrade to elite (max 6)	+2	
Others warriors		
Medium swordsmen mediocre	5	0-4
Atlatl bearers		
Light infantry javelin	4	0-4
Slingers		
Light infantry sling	4	0-4
Fortifications	1	0-6
Post Classical period after 900 AD		
*Nobles and warriors * (before 1300)*		2-8
Medium swordsmen atlatl	8	
Medium swordsmen bow (max 4)	10	
Upgrade to elite (max 4)	+2	
*Nobles and warriors * (after 1300)*		
Medium swordsmen impact	8	
Medium swordsmen 2HW (max 4)	8	
Upgrade to elite (max 4)	+2	

Toltec mercenaries (before 1300) Medium swordsmen atlatl elite	10	0-4
Toltec mercenaries (after 1300) Medium swordsmen 2HW elite Medium swordsmen impact elite	10	
Warriors with bow Bowmen Downgrade to mediocre	7 -2	4-16
Others warriors Medium swordsmen mediocre	5	2-6
Zabinob Javelinmen elite Light infantry javelin elite	9 5	0-2
Atlatl bearers and slingers Light infantry javelin Light infantry sling	4	0-4
Light archers Light infantry bow	4	0-4

268 - Zapotec and Mixtec

300 – 1520 AD
Plain, Mountain
Command +3

The Zapotec civilisation developed in the fertile Oaxaca valley in central Mexico. From their capital, Monte Alban, they dominated the region before their power declined around 700 AD. In the early 10th century, the Mixtecs, coming from the west of Mexico, pushed back the Zapotecs and founded a brief Empire in the region. Around 1420 the Aztecs took the region under their control. The last vestiges of Zapotec civilisation disappeared with the Spanish invasion in 1520.

Troop type	Pts	Units
Nobles and warriors * Medium swordsmen atlatl elite Medium swordsmen 2HW elite	10	2-6
Other warriors Medium swordsmen Add atlatl	7 +1	8-30
Skirmishers with atlatl Light infantry javelin	4	2-4
Skirmishers with sling Light infantry sling	4	2-6
From 1200		
Warriors with bow Bowmen Light infantry bow	7 4	2-6

Note

- Tarascan allies (List #271 Tarascan) after 1458.

269 - Toltec

900 – 1200 AD
Plain, Mountain
Command +3

The Toltecs occupied the centre of Mexico near Teotihuacan. They practiced human sacrifice and erected mountains of skulls at the base of their temples. They were the source of the legend of the feathered serpent Quetzalcoatl later adopted by the Aztecs. Their capital Tula (or Tollan) was conquered by the Chichimecs from northern Mexico in 1168 AD.

Troop type	Pts	Units
Nobles and warriors * Medium swordsmen atlatl elite Medium swordsmen 2HW elite	10	2-4
Other warriors Medium swordsmen Add atlatl	7 +1	8-30
Atlatl bearers and slingers Light infantry javelin Light infantry sling	4	2-6
Chichimec troops Light infantry bow	4	0-4

270 - Chinantec

1200 – 1500 AD
Plain, Mountain
Command +3

The Chinantecs occupied the mountainous region north of Oaxaca. They were conquered by the Aztecs in the 15th century but survived until the Spanish arrived. The Spanish made a detailed description of their method of fighting, which they compared with that of European pikemen. The Chinantecs used long spears with an obsidian blade.

Troop type	Pts	Units
Nobles * Medium swordsmen atlatl elite Medium swordsmen 2HW elite	10	2-4
Spearmen (all of the same type) Medium spearmen Pikemen mediocre	7 8	8-24
Warriors with bow Bowmen Downgrade to mediocre	7 -2	4-8
Skirmishers with bow or sling Light infantry bow Light infantry sling	4	0-6

271 - Tarascan

1300 – 1530 AD
Plain, Mountain
Command +4

The Tarascans (or Purépechas) occupied lands in northwestern Mexico in the state of Michoacán. The Tarascan Empire was contemporary with the Aztecs against whom they were regularly at war from 1470. At the time of Spanish conquest the Tarascan were the second most powerful Empire after the Aztecs. They lost their independence and were conquered by the Spanish around 1530.

Troop type	Pts	Units
*Nobles ** Medium swordsmen impact elite Medium swordsmen 2HW elite	10	2-6
Otomi mercenaries Medium swordsmen impetuous Bowmen Upgrade to elite	7 7 +2	0-4
Warriors with bow Bowmen Downgrade to mediocre Add pavise (max 6)	7 -2 +1	8-30
Replace some warriors with bow by spearmen Medium spearmen	7	0-12
Skirmishers with bow or sling Light infantry bow Light infantry sling	4	0-6

272 - Aztec

1325 – 1521 AD
Plain, Mountain
Command +5
Strategist: Ahuizotl (1486 – 1502 AD)

Originally, the Aztecs (or the Mexicas to use their real name) were a Chichimec tribe who migrated from northern Mexico. They absorbed Toltec culture and in 1325 founded the city of Tenochtitlan at the present site of Mexico City. Within a century the Aztecs extended their power over the whole region and formed a triple alliance with the neighbouring cities of Texcoco and Tacuba. This was the birth of the Aztec Empire with the king Montezuma I. In 1519 the conquistador Cortes landed in Mexico. He joined forces with the Tlaxcalans, enemies of the Aztecs, and besieged and destroyed Tenochtitlan. The Aztec Empire collapsed quickly and then disappeared.

Troop type	Pts	Units
*Jaguar and Eagle warriors ** Medium swordsmen impact elite Medium swordsmen 2HW elite	10	1-3
*Warrior priests ** Medium swordsmen impact Medium swordsmen 2HW Upgrade to elite (max 3)	8 8 +2	2-6
Cuachic shock troops Medium swordsmen impact elite	10	0-2
Telpochcalli warriors Medium swordsmen Add atlatl Downgrade to mediocre (max 8)	7 +1 -2	8-24
Otomi mercenaries Medium swordsmen impetuous Bowmen (max 2) Upgrade to elite	7 7 +2	0-4
Tarascan mercenaries Bowmen Downgrade to mediocre	7 -2	0-2
Skirmishers with bow or sling Light infantry bow Light infantry sling	4	2-8
Fortifications	1	0-4

Note

- Cholula allies (List #273 Texcala) from 1428 to 1518 AD.

Elite troops in front of the Temple

Mayan warriors

273 - Texcala

1168 – 1521
Plain, Mountain
Command +4

To the east of Aztec territory there were several city-states comprising the descendants of the Toltecs and their Chichimec invaders. The largest cities were those of Huexotzingo, Cholula and Tlaxcala. They were most often allied against the Aztecs, though Cholula was sometimes allied with the Aztecs. The Texcalas (or Tlaxcalans) were constantly at war with the Aztecs for decades and opposed their extension to the east. The Texcalas saw the arrival of Cortez in 1519 as an opportunity to reduce the power of the Aztecs and offered him a military alliance.

Troop type	Pts	Units
Military orders * Medium swordsmen impact elite Medium swordsmen 2HW elite	10	1-3
Telpochcalli warriors Medium swordsmen Add atlatl	7 +1	4-12
Warriors with long spears Medium spearmen	7	0-4
Archers Bowmen Downgrade to mediocre Add pavise (max 6)	7 -2 +1	4-12
Replace some archers and/or warriors by mixed units ½ Medium swordsmen ½ Bowmen	9	0-6
Skirmishers with bow or sling Light infantry bow Light infantry sling	4	2-8
Fortifications	1	0-4
Spanish Conquistadors from 1519		
Mounted Conquistadors * Heavy cavalry impact elite Medium knight impact elite	12 13	1
Conquistador infantry Heavy swordsmen armour elite Add 2HW or impact	12 +1	1-2
Conquistador crossbowmen Crossbowmen elite Light infantry crossbow elite	9 5	0-2
Totonac levies Medium swordsmen Downgrade to mediocre	7 -2	2-4
Conquistador handgunners Light infantry firearm elite	5	0-2
Light guns Light artillery Medium artillery	6 10	0-1

Note

- All Spanish conquistadors' troops must be in the same army corps and cannot be mixed with other troops.
- The Spanish commander cannot be unreliable.

SOUTH AMERICA

274 - Inca

1438 – 1534
Plain, Mountain, Forest
Command +5
Strategists: Pachacutec (1438 – 1463 AD) and Túpac (1463 – 1493 AD)

The Inca Empire was created in less than a century and extended its dominion over the western part of South America including Peru, Ecuador, Chile and parts of Bolivia, Colombia and Argentina. The capital was Cuzco in modern Peru. This was a gigantic city from which the Empire was administered through a very extensive network of paved roads. The expansion began in 1438 with the Inca Pachacutec, who conquered southern Peru and subjugated the Chancas. His son, Túpac, was appointed head of the army in 1463. He seized the kingdom of Chimor and pushed the boundaries of the Empire to the heart of Chile. The maximum extent of the Empire was reached during the reign of Huayana Capac (1493-1527). The Spanish reached the Incas in 1526 and Pizarro began his conquest in 1532. Disease and civil war had already weakened the Incas and the last independent Inca Emperor Atahualpa was soon captured and executed.

Troop type	Pts	Units
*Guardsmen ** Medium swordsmen 2HW elite	10	0-3
*Cañares guardsmen (after 1490) ** Medium spearmen elite	9	
Warriors Medium swordsmen Upgrade to elite (max 4)	7 +2	8-24
Militia Medium swordsmen mediocre	5	0-6
Skirmishers Light infantry sling	4	2-12
Chanca subjects Medium spearmen	7	0-4
Chimu subjects Medium swordsmen 2HW	8	
Amazonian archers Bowmen mediocre Light infantry bow	5 4	0-4
Bracamoro Indians Javelinmen elite Light infantry javelin elite	9 5	0-2
Quechuas and Aymara militia Medium swordsmen mediocre	5	0-4
Quechuas and Aymaras Light infantry javelin	4	0-2
Stone parapets and ditches Fortification	1	0-8

Note

- Chanca allies (List #275 Chanca) in 1440 to 1462
- Chimu allies (List #276 Chimu) in 1468 to 1475
- No Chanca or Chimu subjects can be selected if the corresponding allies are used.

275 - Chanca

1200 – 1440 AD
Mountain, Plain
Command +2

The Chancas were a people living in the Peruvian region of Ayacucho. At the beginning of the fifteenth century they came into conflict with the Incas and launched a surprise attack against their capital in 1438. They were repelled and then subjugated by the Incas who integrated them into their Empire.

Troop type	Pts	Units
*Warriors with spear ** Medium spearmen Upgrade to elite (max 4)	7 +2	8-24
Quechuas warriors Medium swordsmen	7	0-6
Light infantry sling	4	2-8

276 - Chimu

1300 – 1464 AD
Plain, Desert
Command +3

The Chimor kingdom was extended along the coast of Peru between the ocean and the Andes cordillera. The capital, Chan Chan, was located in the Moche valley near the present city of Trujillo. Living in an arid region, Chimu developed an ingenious irrigation system with underground tanks. They were conquered by the Incas in a series of campaign between 1461 and 1464.

Troop type	Pts	Units
*Warriors with maces and axes ** Medium swordsmen 2HW Upgrade to elite (max 4)	8 +2	12-36
Conchoco mercenaries Medium swordsmen impetuous	7	0-6
Light infantry sling Light infantry javelin	4	0-8

277 - Tupi

1400 – 1500 AD
Forest
Command +2

The Tupi were an ethnic group that inhabited the coast of Brazil and practised cannibalism. They were fierce warriors with the various tribes being constantly at war against each other. The Tupi used bows and had large wooden clubs for close combat. They fought naked, their bodies covered with tattoos, paintings and various ornaments (necklaces, feathers, bones, etc).

Troop type	Pts	Units
Warriors with bow * Bowmen	7	8-24
Warriors with heavy stick * Medium swordsmen 2HW	8	2-12
Replace all warriors with bow and sticks by mixed units * ½ Medium swordsmen ½ Bowmen	9	All or none
Scouts Light infantry bow	4	0-6

Note

- Tupi warriors were equipped both with bow and heavy stick. It is thus possible to replace all warriors by mixed units.

278 - Mapuche

1400 – 1500 AD
Plain, Forest
Command +3

The Mapuche, also known as the Araucanians, were a group of peoples that occupied northern and central Chile and part of Argentina. They successfully resisted the expansion of the Inca Túpac. The Spanish conquistadors also failed to subjugate them during the Arauco War in the sixteenth century.

Troop type	Pts	Units
Warriors with bow * Bowmen	7	4-12
Warriors with maces or spears Medium swordsmen Medium spearmen Medium swordsmen 2HW (max 4)	 7 7 8	4-16
Skirmishers Light infantry bow	4	0-6

NORTH AMERICA

279 - Chichimec

800 – 1500 AD
Plain, Desert
Command +2

This list includes the various nomadic peoples of northern Mexico and southwestern United States, as well as more recent migrants such as the Apaches and Navajos. They ranged over arid land where agriculture was barely possible. They were often in conflict with more settled tribes who saw them as barbarians and called them "Dog People" or Chichimec. In the twelfth century some migrated south causing the fall of the Toltec Empire. Subsequently they formed small kingdoms by integrating survivors of the Toltec civilisation.

Troop type	Pts	Units
Warriors * Medium swordsmen impetuous Add atlatl Upgrade to elite (max 4)	 7 +1 +2	0-8
Archers Bowmen Light infantry bow (max 12)	 7 4	12-36
Light infantry sling Light infantry javelin	4	0-4
Only before 900 AD		
Replace all archers Medium swordsmen atlatl Light infantry javelin (max 12)	 8 4	All

Note

- Pueblo allies (List #280 Pueblos)

280 - Pueblos

900 – 1500 AD
Plain, Desert
Command +2

The Pueblos lived in northern Mexico, Arizona and New Mexico. They were a sedentary people occupying fortified villages (names *pueblos*) and cultivating corn. Two of the main Pueblo tribes were the Hopi and Zuni.

Troop type	Pts	Units
Warriors * Medium swordsmen Upgrade to elite (max 4)	 7 +2	4-12

Troop type	Pts	Units
Archers Bowmen Downgrade to mediocre	7 -2	4-16
Skirmishers with bow Light infantry bow	4	2-6
Skirmishers with sling or javelin Light infantry sling Light infantry javelin	4	0-4
Women and children Levy mediocre	2	0-2

Note

- Chichimec allies (List #279 Chichimec)

281 - Forest Indian

900 – 1620 AD
Forest
Command +2

This list covers the Indian tribes living in the forests of North America. Two of the most notable were the Algonquins and the Iroquois. The bow was the main weapon, but they also used stone-headed clubs, spears and sometimes shields or wooden armour. The list ends with the introduction of firearms brought by French and English settlers.

Troop type	Pts	Units
*Brave warriors ** Medium swordsmen impetuous Upgrade to elite	7 +2	2-6
Warriors with bow Bowmen	7	4-24
Warriors with tomahawk Medium swordsmen impetuous	7	0-16
Woodsmen Light infantry javelin Light infantry bow	4	2-6
Women and children Levy mediocre	2	0-2

282 - Mississippi Indian

900 – 1720 AD
Plain, Forest
Command +2

The Mississippi basin was the home of the Mound Builder culture. These peoples raised large earthen mounds of conical or pyramidal shape whose use is still debated today: tombs, temples or observatories. From the 14th century the activity of the Mound Builders ceased but their traditions were inherited by tribes such as the Creeks and the Natchez.
Their society was very hierarchical with Nobles, Men of Honour and common people. As with other Indians, the bow was the predominant weapon.

Troop type	Pts	Units
*Nobles ** Bowmen elite Medium swordsmen elite	9	2-6
Men of Honour Bowmen Medium swordsmen	7	4-16
Common people Bowmen mediocre Medium swordsmen mediocre	5	2-12
Scouts Light infantry javelin (max 2) Light infantry bow	4	0-6
Women and children Levy mediocre	2	0-2

Note

- At least half of the units must be bowmen.

283 - Plains Indian

900 – 1500 AD
Steppes
Command +2

These Indian tribes, such as the Sioux, Comanches and Cheyenne, occupied the large plains at the centre of the United States. Some tribes were sedentary but most were nomadic and travelled with their tipis to hunt bison. In pre-Columbian times the horse was unknown; it was introduced by the Europeans.

Troop type	Pts	Units
*Warriors ** Medium swordsmen impetuous Upgrade to elite (max 6)	7 +2	6-24
Warriors with bow Bowmen	7	4-12
Scouts Light infantry bow	4	0-6
Women and children Levy mediocre	2	0-2

DESIGNER'S NOTES

What is of primary importance in war is to be as quick as lightning; One cannot afford to miss an opportunity. Sun Tzu

This chapter describes some of the principles and concepts that are used in *l'Art de la Guerre* and how they tie in with each other.

Size of the game

The basic idea behind the development of this set of rules is to offer a format that is different from the existing ones. Why should we have to spend four hours and have a huge amount of figures to play a game? *L'Art de la Guerre* allows you to play smaller games than other rules in terms of number of figures and playing area. This approach results in shorter games, lasting from only two to two and a half hours. Of course, those who have more time to play can easily play bigger games with more figures if they wish.

Cohesion points

One of the central concepts in *L'Art de la Guerre* is that of cohesion points. Each unit starts with a level of durability that progressively decreases during the battle. It takes into account both the physical losses of the unit and its level of disorganisation. When a unit has lost some cohesion it is in disorder and it has a penalty in combat. It may be possible to rally with the help of the general or if the unit is far enough away from any enemy. When the unit has lost all its cohesion points it becomes ineffective as a fighting force and it is simply eliminated: the soldiers have fled the battlefield.

The gradual loss of cohesion points is essential to simulate the results of shooting. The main effect is to reduce the resistance of the enemy before the melee. A combat result that is limited to either complete elimination or just a retreat is not subtle enough. A unit under fire did not just recoil; it suffered losses and disorganisation. Moreover heavy infantry units were rarely eliminated by missile fire alone.

To record the loss of cohesion points it is necessary to use markers. This can affect the aesthetics of the battlefield but we think it is not a major drawback. These markers can be made with appropriate figures on a small base or coloured tokens can be used instead.

Troop types

Troops are classified in a clear and simple way, avoiding acronyms that can put off newcomers to historical gaming. Troops are classed as "Bowmen", "Heavy spearmen", "Knights", etc; descriptions that are more meaningful for everyone. Only *troop categories* use abbreviations for simplicity and they are very easy to remember such as HI for Heavy Infantry.

Command

Troops are allocated to army corps because it is historically accurate. Each general can only control units from his own corps. There were very few exceptions to this rule in historical battles. If the general commanding the infantry was killed, the one who controlled the cavalry would not come to give orders to the infantry.

Armies are not all identical in terms of command and control. Only some can have a general classed as a Strategist. The budget takes this situation into account, as each point of command must be paid for. Thus armies with a good command value have to be more flexible and must manoeuvre in order to defeat another army more numerous but not so well commanded.

Movement

Movement often causes problems in tabletop wargames. This has therefore been simplified in order to avoid problematic situations, for example where a unit cannot charge the enemy because a tiny part of another unit blocks its path. Numerous diagrams in the rules help to resolve most of the cases that may arise.

There is no recoil in combat. This avoids many problems and absurd situations. Moreover to avoid dubious tactics it is not always necessary to strictly conform units corner-to-corner in melee.

Sliding to one side during movement simplifies manoeuvres to avoid obstacles. For example a group cannot be stopped or slowed because a small part of the base of one unit is facing a wood: a shift of a few millimetres enables the group to advance straight towards the enemy.

Shooting

In *l'Art de la Guerre* all units that historically had missile weapons can use them on the battlefield. Horse archers assume their historical role as tactics such as evade and feigned flight can be reproduced. Light infantry units are confined to their harassing role and are not able to engage in melee with heavy troops.

Melee

Particular attention has been paid to the interaction of the different types of troops in combat. The table on page 20 summarises bonuses and penalties for all units and will reward close study by players. Each troop type has advantages and disadvantages compared to others and it is important to know them in order to employ units in the best circumstances.

The simplicity of the combat system allows players to estimate quickly their chance of success:

1D6	Win	Draw	Loss
0	42%	16%	42%
+1	58%	14%	28%
+2	72%	11%	17%
+3	84%	8%	8%

The *impact* ability, combined with the -1 penalty for a unit that is disordered, makes the first round of combat extremely important. The unit that wins the first round in a melee has an important advantage. It is also important to disrupt the enemy by shooting before engaging a melee.

Notes on the 3rd Edition

This third edition incorporates various things from the FAQ and clarifications. The army lists have also been revised to make them more playable and more consistent with the historical data. Here are the major changes from previous edition:

- Bowmen now have a +1 factor for the first phase of a melee against mounted units.
- Medium infantry has a basic factor of +1 against all ennemies except **Kn.**
- Cavalry has a +1 bonus for the first phase of melee against medium infantry.
- Cavalry has a basic factor of +1 against heavy infantry if attacking from flank or rear.
- Elephants have a basic factor of + 2 against mounted and +1 against foot troops.
- Cv and Kn have a basic facor of +1 against elephants.
- Spearmen and pikemen no more cancel *impact* of elephants.
- Rules for artillery have been revised to be more consistent and make artillery more playable.
- *2HW* ability has been modified.
- *Impact* ability has been modified.
- *Missile Support* ability has been improved.
- Heavy chariots now have the *armour* ability.
- It is now possible to dismount if the opponent deploys elephants.
- Initiative value for army has been modified and reflects the number of LH in the army.
- It is now possible to make a wheel with a contraction manoeuvre.
- The charging corner against corner issue has been resolved.
- Impetuous units performing an uncontrolled charge must respect ZoC rules. If contacting enemy is not possible, the unit do not make an uncontrolled charge.
- Mounted units cannot pass through other mounted that cause panic to them.
- Javelinmen can disengage in melee againt heavy infantry or elephants.
- If two or more shooters have the same target, the player can choose the main shooter.
- A LH can now support the shooting of another LH if it is aligned directly behind it.
- The fortified camp counts now as one unit for the calculation of army demoralization.
- The attacking player always starts to play first.
- Rules for terrain and deployment have been modified.
- A new optional rule to allow rerolls has been added.
- Some budget values have been modified.

ALPHABETICAL INDEX OF ARMY LISTS

Abbasid Arab 154
Achaemenid Persian 115
African Vandal 142
Akkad (Sumer and Akkad) 83
Alemanni 133
Alan 139
Albanian 218
Alexander the Great 100
Alexandrian Macedonian 99
Almohad (Berber) 186
Almoravid (Berber) 186
Amorite Highlanders 84
Ancient Bedouin 91
Ancient British 134
Ancient Hebrew 93
Ancient Spanish 130
Andalusian Arab 153
Anglo-Danish 173
Anglo-Irish 176
Anglo-Norman 174
Anglo-Saxon 135
Annazid (Kurdish Dynasties) 184
Apulian 107
Arab (Abbasid) 154
Arab (Andalusian) 153
Arab (North African) 153
Arab (Umayyad) 152
Arab Conquest 151
Arab Early 121
Arab Indian 154
Aragonese (Medieval Spanish) 205
Aramaean 120
Aramean and Neo-Hittite 94
Armenian Principality 150
Armenian Bagratid 151
Armenian Cilician 180
Armenian 118
Armourican Breton 159
Assyrian Empire and Sargonid 87
Assyrian 86
Avar 164
Axum Kingdom of 142
Ayyubid Egyptian 188
Aztec 229
Babylonian (Kassite) 85
Babylonian (Old Assyrian) 85
Bagratid Armenian 151
Bedouin (Ancient) 91
Bedouin Dynastic 156
Beja 167
Berber 186
Bithynian 116
Black Sheep Turkoman 222
Blemmyes and Nobatae 141
Bosporan Kingdom 118
Breton (Armourican) 159
British (Ancient) 134
British (Romano-British) 135
Bruttian 107
Bulgar 164
Bulgarian (Later) 215
Burgundi 133
Burgundian 207
Burgundian Ordonnance 209
Burmese 168
Buyid 183
Byzantine (Besieged) 219
Byzantine Justinian 148
Byzantine Komnenan 179
Byzantine Later 215
Byzantine Maurikian 148
Byzantine Nikephorian 150
Byzantine Thematic 149
Caledonian, Irish, Scots and Pictish 134
Camillan Roman 107
Campanian, Lucanian, Apulian, Bruttian 107
Canaan (Syria, Canaan and Ugarit) 93
Cappadocian 117
Carolingian Frankish 161
Carpi (Dacian and Carpi) 130
Carthaginian Early 109
Carthaginian 109
Castilian (Medieval Spanish) 205
Catalan Company 217
Celtiberian (Ancient Spanish) 130
Celts 97
Central Asia City States 157
Central Asian Turkish 157
Ch'iang and Ti 124
Ch'in (Ch'iang and Ti) 124
Champa 170
Chanca 231
Chichimec 232
Chimu 231
Chin (Jurchen-Chin) 197
Chinantec 228
Chinese Five Dynasties 171
Chinese Han 143
Chinese Ming 226
Chinese Northern & Southern Dynasties 145
Chinese Shang 98
Chinese Song 196
Chinese Spring and Autumn 98
Chinese Sui and Tang 169
Chinese Tang 171
Chinese Three Kingdoms 144
Chinese Yuan 224
Chola (Tamil Indian) 146
Christian Nubian 167
Cilician Armenian 180
City States (Syrian) 91
Classical Greek 112
Classical Indian 123
Commagene 137
Communal Italian 178
Company (Catalan) 217
Condottieri 202
Conquest (Arab) 151
Croatian 165
Crusader (Later) 181
Crusader 180
Cuman 192

Cyprus (Phoenicians of Cyprus) 97
Cyprus (Frankish) 182
Cyrenian Greek 111
Dacian and Carpi 130
Dali 171
Danish (Anglo-Danish) 173
Danish (Medieval Scandinavian) 200
Delhi Sultanate 222
Dynastic Bedouin 156
Dynastic Kurdish 184
Early Arab 121
Early Carthaginian 109
Early Imperial Roman 126
Early Macedonian 99
Early Successors 100
Eastern Latin Empire 182
Egyptian (Ayyubid) 188
Egyptian (Fatimid) 185
Egyptian (Kushite) 90
Egyptian (Libyan) 90
Egyptian (New Kingdom) 89
Egyptian (Old and Middle Kingdom) 88
Egyptian Saitic 111
Egyptian (Tulunid and Iqshidid) 156
Elamite 84
Elymaian (Parthian) 136
Emesa (Aramaean) 120
Emishi 147
English (Feudal) 175
English (Hundred Years War) 203
Epirus (Later Byzantine) 215
Estonian 192
Etruscan 105
Fatimid Egyptian 185
Feudal English 175
Feudal French 174
Feudal German 179
Feudal Hungarian 190
Feudal Irish 162
Feudal Polish 190
Feudal Russian 191
Feudal Scots 175
Feudal Spanish 160
Florentine (Condottierri) 202
Forest Indian 233
Frankish (Carolingian) 161
Frankish Cyprus 182
Frankish (Imperial) 178
Frankish (Merovingian) 158
Franks (Franks and Norman) 173
Franks, Alemanni, Burgundi, Suevi 133
Free Company 206
French (Feudal) 174
French (Hundred Years War) 203
French Ordonnance 208
Frisian 135
Galatian 119
Gallic 129
Garamantes (Lybian) 88
Gasgans(Amorite Highlanders) 84
Genoese (Condottieri) 202
Geometric Greek 96
Georgian 191
Gepid, Herul and Taifali 132
German (Feudal) 179
German (Medieval) 204
German 130
Ghaznavid 184
Ghurid 188
Golden Horde 213
Graeco-Bactrian and Graeco-Indian 104
Graeco-Indian (Graeco-Bactrian) 104
Granadine 199
Greek (Geometric) 96
Greek Classical 112
Greek Hellenistic 113
Greek Cyrenian 111
Gulf States (Oman) 91
Guptas (Classical Indian) 123
Gutis (Amorite Highlanders) 84
Hamdanid (Dynastic Bedouin) 156
Han Chinese 143
Hasmonean (Judaean Jewish) 136
Hatra (Aramaean) 120
Hebrew (Ancient) 93
Hellenistic Greek 113
Hephthalite Huns 141
Heruli 132
Highlanders (Amorite) 84
Highlanders (Scots Isles) 176
Hindu Indian 168
Hittite 92
Horde (Golden) 213
Hsien-Pi 144
Hsiung-Nu 143
Hundred Years War English 203
Hundred Years War French 203
Hungarian (Feudal) 190
Hungarian (Medieval) 211
Huns 140
Hurri-Mitanni 92
Hussite 214
Hyksos 89
Iberian (Ancient Spanish) 130
Ilkhanid Mongol 220
Illyrian 114
Imperial Frankish 178
Inca 231
Indian (Arab) 154
Indian (Forest) 233
Indian (Hindu) 168
Indian (Mississippi) 233
Indian (Plains) 233
Indian (Tamil) 146
Indian (Vedic) 98
Indian (Classical) 123
Indonesian and Malay 224
Indo-Parthian (Parthian) 136
Indus Valley 97
Iqshidid Egyptian 156
Irish (Anglo-Irish) 176
Irish (Feudal) 162
Irish (Medieval) 201
Irish 134
Islamic Persian 220
Italian (Communal) 178
Italian (Condottieri) 202
Italian Ostrogoth 158
Italian Tribes 105
Jalayirid 221

Japanese 147
Jewish Judaean 136
Judaean (Jewish) 136
Jurchen-Chin 197
Justinian Byzantine 148
Jutes 135
Kassite Babylonian 85
Khazar 165
Khitan (Qara-Khitan) 197
Khitan-Liao 194
Khmer Empire and Champa 170
Khurasanian 155
Khwarazmian 188
Komnenan Byzantine 179
Korean Koryo 195
Korean Three Kingdoms 146
Korean Yi 226
Koryo Korean 195
Kurdish Dynasties 184
Kushan 139
Kushite Egyptian 90
Kushite Meroitic 112
Late Imperial Roman 127
Later Achaemenid Persian 117
Later Bulgarian 215
Later Byzantine 215
Later Crusader 181
Later Macedonian 104
Later Samurai 225
Latin Empire 182
Leidang (Viking and Leidang) 161
Liao (Khitan-Liao) 194
Libyan Egyptian 90
Libyan 88
Lithuanian 211
Lombard 158
Low Countries 208
Lucanian 107
Lusitanian (Ancient Spanish) 130
Lydian 115
Lycian 116
Maccabean (Judaean Jewish) 136
Macedonian Alexandrian 99
Macedonian Early 99
Macedonian Later 104
Magyar 166
Malay 224
Mamluk 219
Mapuche 232
Marinid (Berber) 186
Marwanid (Dynastic Kurdish) 184
Maurikian Byzantine 148
Mauryas (Classical Indian) 123
Maya 227
Medes 95
Medieval German 204
Medieval Hungarian 211
Medieval Irish 201
Medieval Polish 213
Medieval Scandinavian 200
Medieval Scots 200
Medieval Spanish 205
Medieval Vietnamese 195
Medieval Welsh 208
Meroitic Kushite 112
Merovingian Frankish 158
Middle Imperial Roman 126
Milanese (Condottieri) 202
Ming Chinese 226
Mississippi Indian 233
Mitanni (Hurri Mitanni) 92
Mithridatic 137
Mixtec 228
Moldavian 217
Mongol (Tribal) 172
Mongol Empire 198
Mongol Ilkhanid 220
Mongol Steppes 221
Moors 142
Mu-Jung (Hsien-Pi) 144
Muscovite Russian 212
Mycenaean 96
Nabataea (Aramaean) 120
Nan-Chao and Dali 171
Navarrese 206
Neapolitan (Condottieri) 202
Neo-Babylonian 86
Neo-Hittite (Aramean and Neo-Hittite) 94
New Kingdom Egyptian 89
Nicaea (Later Byzantine) 215
Nikephorian Byzantine 150
Nobatae (Blemmyes and Nobatae) 141
Norman (Anglo-norman) 174
Norman or Frankish 173
Normans in Sicily 177
North African Arab 153
Northern Dynasties Chinese 145
Norwegian (Medieval Scandinavian) 200
Nubian (Christian) 167
Nubian 88
Numidian 110
Old and Middle Kingdom Egyptian 88
Old Assyrian and Babylonian 85
Oman and Gulf States 91
Order of St John 183
Ordonnance (Burgundian) 209
Ordonnance (French) 208
Ostrogoth 132
Ostrogoth (Italian) 158
Ottoman Empire 218
Ottoman Turkish 216
Palaiologan (Later Byzantine) 215
Palmyran 138
Parthian 136
Patrician Roman 128
Pecheneg 166
Pergamon 120
Persian Achaemenid 115
Persian Islamic 220
Persian Achaemenid Later 117
Persian Sassanid 139
Philistine 94
Phoenicians of Cyprus 97
Phrygian 95
Pictish 134
Plains Indian 233
Polish (Feudal) 190
Polish (Medieval) 213
Portuguese (Medieval Spanish) 205
Pre-Feudal Scots 163

Principality of Armenia 150
Prussian and Estonian 192
Ptolemaic 103
Pueblos 232
Pyrrhic 103
Qarakhanid (Central Asian Turkish) 157
Qara-Khitan 197
Rajput (Hindu Indian) 168
Republican Roman 108
Roman Camillan 107
Roman Early Imperial 126
Roman Late Imperial 127
Roman Middle Imperial 126
Roman Patrician 128
Roman Republican 108
Roman Triumvirate 125
Roman Tullian 106
Romano-Britsh 135
Roxolani (Sarmatian) 122
Rum (Seljuk Turk) 186
Rus 166
Russian (Feudal) 191
Russian (Muscovite) 212
Sabir (Huns) 140
Saffarid (Khurasanian) 155
Sahelian Empire 189
Saitic Egyptian 111
Saka (Scythian) 121
Samanid (Khurasanian) 155
Samnites (Italian Tribes) 105
Samurai (Later) 225
Samurai 194
Sargonid 87
Sarmatian 122
Sassanid Persian 139
Saxon, Anglo-Saxon, Frisian, Jutes 135
Scandinavian (Medieval) 200
Scots (Feudal) 175
Scots (Medieval) 200
Scots (Pre-Feudal) 163
Scots Isles and Highlanders 176
Scots 134
Scythian 121
Sea Peoples 93
Seleucid 102
Seljuk Turk 186
Serbian Empire 214
Serbo-Croatian 165
Shang Chinese 98
Shatuo Turkish 172
Siam 224
Sicily (Normans) 177
Slav 163
Sogdian and Central Asia City States 157
Song Chinese 196
Southern Dynasties Chinese 145
Spain (Visigoths) 133
Spanish (Feudal) 160
Spanish (Medieval) 205
Spanish Ancient 130
Spartacus 125
Spring and Autumn Chinese 98
St John Order 183
Steppes Mongol 221
Successor (Sumerian) 83
Successors (Early) 100
Suevi 133
Sui and Tang Chinese 169
Sultanate (Delhi) 222
Sumer and Akkad 83
Sumerian Successor 83
Swedish (Medieval Scandinavian) 200
Swiss 199
Syracusan 106
Syria, Canaan and Ugarit 93
Syrian City States 91
Syrian 187
Tahirid (Khurasanian) 155
Taifali 132
Tamil Indian 146
Tang and Five Dynasties Chinese 171
Tarascan 229
Teutonic Knights 192
Texcala 230
Thematic Byzantine 149
Thracian 114
Three Kingdoms Chinese 144
Three Kingdoms Korean 146
Tibetan 170
Timurid 221
Toltec 228
Trebizond (Later Byzantine) 215
Tribal Mongol 172
Tribes Italian 105
Triumvirate Roman 125
Trojan (Mycenaean) 96
Tuareg 189
Tullian Roman 106
Tulunid Egyptian 156
Tupi 232
Turk Seljuk 186
Turkish (Central Asian) 157
Turkish Ottoman 216
Turkish (Shatuo) 172
Turkoman 216
Turkoman (Black Sheep and White sheep) 222
Ugarit (Syria, Canaan and Ugarit) 93
Uighur (Central Asian Turkish) 157
Umayyad Arab 152
Urartu 95
Valley of Indus 97
Vandal (African) 142
Vandal 131
Vedic Indian 98
Venetian (Condottieri) 202
Vietnamese (Medieval) 195
Vietnamese 122
Viking and Leidang 161
Visigoth 131
Visigoths in Spain 133
Vlach and Moldavian 217
Wars of the Roses 210
Warring States 124
Welsh (Medieval) 208
Welsh 159
White sheep Turkoman 222
Xi-Xia 196
Yi Korean 226
Yuan Chinese .... [illegible]
Zapotec and Mixtec .... [illegible]